**NOT
QUITE
WHITE**

The Welsh are blessed in the smallest of ways
– by being not quite white.

Osi Rhys Osmond

NOT QUITE WHITE

SIMON THIRSK

Gomer

To

Teleri and Owain

Published in 2010 by
Gomer Press, Llandysul, Ceredigion, SA44 4JL

Reprinted 2010

ISBN 978 1 84851 199 6
A CIP record for this title is available from the British Library.

This book is published with the financial support of the
Welsh Books Council.

Printed and bound in Wales at
Gomer Press, Llandysul, Ceredigion

Acknowledgements

My grateful thanks to Lord Dafydd Elis-Thomas for providing an interesting and illuminating foreword and heartfelt thanks to many friends for their kind support and often irrational encouragement and understanding: Susanna Jones and Courttia Newland for superb tutoring at the wonderful Arvon Foundation centre at Clun and to Julia Buckley for being an inspiring classmate and friend; to Anne Oosthuizen, Hilary and Osi Rhys Osmond for unflagging patience and encouragement; to Mike Hunt, Marc Lee, Angharad Elias, Adrian Johnson, Katy Tong, Olwen Foreman, Alison Fox and Nansi Thirsk for seeing chinks of light through the drudge of the many dreary drafts, and to Gwynedd Jones for his painstaking critique; Dr Iwan Bryn and Dylan Jones for helping with my Welsh; and especially to Angharad Price, Helen Dunmore, Will Mackie, Neil Astley and Annette Charpentier for their literary advice and friendship and invaluable comments and suggestions. Also to Ceri Wyn Jones for his support and patience and John Barnie for his diligence. And most of all to Wales and the Welsh language for welcoming me in.

To all of you, a toast: *Iechyd da*!

Simon Thirsk 2010

Foreword

By Lord Elis-Thomas

Nearly forty years ago when I was selected parliamentary candidate for Meirionnydd, I was given a serious piece of advice by a very senior member of the party in the constituency which I have followed until this moment. It was the local equivalent of 'don't mention the war': never raise the issue of Celyn. At the time I did not quite understand why.

As a pale schoolboy I had attended the dissolution service at the chapel with my father, who had preached there many times, and later I joined other students from Bangor University to disrupt the official opening ceremony. My attitude towards the acts of violence on the construction site had been ambivalent. But neither could I sign up to 'Remembering Tryweryn'. The advice I was given was that Celyn had been seriously divisive within the local community, turning neighbour against neighbour and family against family.

After 1974 I decided I had been right to take the advice. Within less than ten years of the opening of the enforced lake an elected representative of the party that had most strongly opposed the project now represented that site in the UK Parliament. This, and the subsequent creation of a Welsh National Water Development Authority, with the devolution of legislative power some twenty years later, meant that such an environmental, social and cultural act of submersion could never happen again.

I actively supported the gradual repatriation of the site, most publicly at the exciting white water canoeing centre, Canolfan Tryweryn, where developing local and Welsh athletes began to challenge other international teams in a new sport. More privately I would stop to think and even pray at the site of the memorial chapel designed by R L Gapper in the shape of a boat. 'Cwch ein diwylliant yn dod i'r lan' I heard him say. A boat symbolising our culture makes the shore.

This is also what reading Simon's at once witty and satirical, but also socially and culturally deadly serious, narrative has done for me. In a metaphor which I'm sure will not appeal to everyone I want to say that out of the total immersion of Celyn a new people were born. As huge characters they populate this novel, alongside those who quite justifiably do not wish to forget the tragedy. But here, in a new landscape, in fiction and in faith, we may together make another shore.

Welsh Landscape

To live in Wales is to be conscious
At dusk of the spilled blood
That went into the making of the wild sky,
Dyeing the immaculate rivers
In all their courses.
It is to be aware,
Above the noisy tractor
And hum of the machine
Of strife in the strung woods,
Vibrant with sped arrows.
You cannot live in the present,
At least not in Wales.
There is the language for instance,
The soft consonants
Strange to the ear.
There are cries in the dark at night
As owls answer the moon,
And thick ambush of shadows,
Hushed at the fields' corners
There is no present in Wales,
And no future;
There is only the past,
Brittle with relics,
Wind-bitten towers and castles
With sham ghosts;
Mouldering quarries and mines;
And an impotent people,
Sick with inbreeding,
Worrying the carcase of an old song.

RS Thomas, *Selected Poems 1946-1968*
(Bloodaxe Books, 1986)

Etifeddiaeth

Cawsom wlad i'w chadw,
darn o dir yn dyst
ein bod wedi mynnu byw.

Cawsom genedl o genhedlaeth
i genhedlaeth ac anadlu
ein hanes ein hunain.

A chawsom iaith, er na cheisiem hi,
oherwydd ei hias oedd yn y pridd eisoes
a'i grym anniddig ar y mynyddoedd.

Troesom ein tir yn simneiau tân
a phlannu coed a pheilonau cadarn
lle nad oedd llyn.
Troesom ein cenedl i genhedlu
estroniaid heb ystyr i'w hanes,
gwymon o ddynion heb ddal
tro'r trai.
A throesom iaith yr oesau
yn iaith ein cywilydd ni.

Ystyriwch; a oes dihareb
a ddwed y gwirionedd hwn:
Gwerth cynnydd yw gwarth cenedl
a'i hedd yw ei hangau hi.

Gerallt Lloyd Owen,
from *Cerddi'r Cywilydd*.
(Gwasg Gwynedd)

The town of Llanchwaraetegdanygelyn and all its inhabitants are fictitious. If it existed, it would lie somewhere between Cwmtirmynach and Ysbyty Ifan, on the Migneint, an infamous bog area, but in this novel, it is a fictitious County Council, a few miles to the north of Llyn Celyn.

I imagine Llanchwaraetegdanygelyn as being like the village of West Burton in Wensleydale, which has exactly the right kind of green and waterfall, but is, unfortunately not in Wales, though the Dales and Wales have more than their rhyme in common.

Gwrêngham is also fictitious as is the Leyburn Institute and all the characters associated with it. All characters are fictional and any resemblance to living people is purely accidental.

The stairway up Cadair Idris and The Grenadier pub, in Knightsbridge, however, are both true and well worth finding, as is the London Welsh Centre.

MY NAME IS Gwalia. I am an Island. Head of Brân. Soul of
Llywelyn.

Gwalia – what possessed my Mam to call me that?

This was my mantra in those darkest days. My notes here,
in my diary, are very confused. These words are written many
times, sometimes gouged and sometimes scrawled: *My name
is Gwalia. I am an Island.*

As you learned, Jon, all names have meaning here. Names
of people. And of places. All our history is here. This is our
language and culture. Ancient and living still.

Ramblings, dangerous with significance. Gwalia was the
invader's name for Wales, long before the Normans came and
it mutated. Gwalia meaning foreigners. What dull trait of
character led us to let our conquerors name us strangers in
our own fine land? And then accept that name! We, the Celts,
we came here first. Before the Romans, even (wasn't it they
who lumped us all together and named us Britons?) And
wasn't Gwales the island where they took the still-living head
of Brân the giant, last Celtic ruler of the whole of Britain, and
feasted with him for eighty years, until they broke the spell by
looking back towards the mainland? And wasn't he, the last
great Celt, then taken to be buried on White Hill in London?
Is that where the bones of our history lie?

In our own language *we* don't call it *Wales*, we call it
Cymru, land of the compatriots. You can call us Wales, Jon, if
you must, but only for now. We are Cymry, the people of
Cymru. Understand that! We are Cymry.

I don't know what possessed my Mam to call me Gwalia.

I am stranger to neb – to nobody.

I explained this to the doctors many times: but it was
foreign to them. So they could not have been expected to
understand.

So where to start? My notes here, in my diary, are *so* confused.
Snatches of my agonisings over who I was and what my
history had made me. Things that Mam and Anti Gwenlais

11

said. Silly things. Jumbled up, scrawled down, crossed out. And sometimes missing where I'd ripped out pages in despair.

Keep a therapeutic journal, they said. 'Can I keep it in Welsh?' I asked them. 'Yes,' they told me, 'It doesn't matter. It's only for you to read.'

Doesn't matter indeed!

'Try to imagine how you are from the point of view of others,' they said. 'A daily diary. It'll be a way of measuring your progress.'

Progress!

As if such an entity as I was worth the measuring of!

Me, the broken-faced Gwalia.

It is really my Anti Gwenlais who starts my story – our story, Jon – so far as I can ever remember, my Anti Gwenlais was the fount of all my stories.

The smell of cigarette smoke always preceded her. She arrived in a cloud and stayed in fug. Her skin was older than her years, and her voice had that smoker's croak. Sometimes she laughed and coughed and cackled. And I loved her. And her gossip.

'Your Yncl Penhaearn says Boudiccea has written to ask them to send a man from Westminster. And I have it on good authority that they've agreed.' She winked. 'From a think tank, whatever that might be. Your Yncl Penhaearn has had a warning. The spirits have told him. A think tank, mark you. Did you know that there are think tanks now? – Imagine that – a tank of people thinking about us. Did you know that, Gwênfer?'

My mother, Gwênfer, just smiled.

I said nothing. And carried on with my golchi dillad – washing the clothes – waiting for Mam to remonstrate with me: 'If I've told you once, I've told you a thousand times: you have to wash the whites and coloureds separately.'

Mainly, it was Dad's and Awena's clothes that were coloured. I rather liked to boil our things up all together, it brought us closer. My contribution. But I kept my peace when Mam and Anti Gwenlais were talking. Everything that could ever possibly be said had all been said many times before, in one form or another, in our cosy kitchen, for whatever good it did, which was less than keeping clothes white.

'What have we, in our little town, done to deserve a woman like Boudiccea?' demanded Mam. 'And why on earth would she get the idea into her head that we would want the attentions of a man from Westminster?'

As it happens, I did know what a think tank was. Like Dad, I read the English papers. And I admit it did cross my mind to wonder what he would be like, this man from Westminster.

'We have done nothing to deserve it, Gwênfer? Only that we have kept ourselves to ourselves.'

'And what reward do we get? I'll tell you now. Strangers in our midst. Preventing us from speaking our own language, in our own valley. And we have done nothing to them.'

'And we have nothing for them either. Nothing at all that they would want. But still they come. And then when they get here, they complain there is nothing here for them.'

'It's the colonial instincts, you see. They have to colonise, don't they? They cannot bear to see other people happy and leave them be. They cannot stand that. We're like an itchy sore they must keep on scratching.'

So far, Jon (as you would soon discover), we had succeeded in keeping our town to itself and virtually a hundred per cent Welsh-speaking. English people had started to move in. Each year more came creeping in up the valley, into the old farm houses vacated as the old farmers died and more of our young people moved away to fill their lungs with the air of prosperity and opportunities of elsewhere. Those who came – retired couples mainly – who could sell their now-expensive houses in the Midlands to buy cheap houses here and live off investment income from the difference. We all knew it was only a matter of time before they started buying houses in the town – and that that would mark the end of our Welshness. It takes only one English person in a room for a whole community to feel awkward and defensive talking Welsh. That is how the English speakers over generations had taught us to feel about ourselves, our culture.

'They complain they are being pushed out of their own land by the hoards of immigrants and different coloured faces and strange clothes. Then they come and settle here. With no thought that they are doing the same to us.'

'Quite right, Gwênfer! They complain about the curry smells where they used to live. And then complain when they get here that we have no Chinese or Indian takeaways. They are never happy, the English. They can never settle.'

'And what do you think a man from a think tank is going to do about it?'

'Nothing I shouldn't have thought, though Boudiccea has it in her head to change everything. She wants us to have mains electricity. Running water. All to be paid for through tourism. With Curry Shops on every corner, I shouldn't wonder.'

'Paned arall?'

'Os gwelwch yn dda.'

'A man from a think tank is sure to look like a frog, I should think,' said Mam. And they both sniggered.

'With big glasses and a green pin-striped suit.'

'You must mobilise your forces, Gwalia,' Anti Gwenlais winked at me.

She meant that it was time for Dewi and I to go out felling the signposts again, cutting out English names and posting our warning slogans, as occupied nations have always done. Why lead the enemy to your door? Always deter them in subtle ways.

'Does she have to, Gwenlais? I'd be so much happier if you didn't encourage her in such activities.' Mam always worried about me.

'It does her very much good, Gwênfer. You know that. It's good for her to go out with Dewi, I'm sure.'

They didn't ask for my opinion.

So I continued washing clothes and Mam and my Anti Gwenlais leaned across the kitchen table sipping their tea and twt-twt-twting their tongues endlessly about Saeson – almost spitting out the word. We knew that you would be a Sais, Jon. A typical Englishman. We were sure of that. They thought they knew exactly what you would be like.

'They come here wanting to improve us and modernise us. When will they learn? And now here they are, sending another. Well, if they do, we shall send him packing, too, like all the others.'

'All the Saeson have ever done is deface our landscape, plunder our coal and slate and cover our hillsides with their ugly tree plantations. We need independence. That's what we really need. We need to go in the same direction as Ireland and Scotland.'

'It's colonialism,' Mam nodded, always anxious to prove to her elder sister that she was completely up to date with her understanding of international matters.

'It's in their genes, you know, Gwenlais. Capitalists is what they are. And look where it's got us all.'

'You're not wrong there, Gwênfer. Not wrong at all. They plundered our country for their fleeting pomp and self-aggrandisement, stole all our coal and slate.'

'And burned the coal all far too quickly for a quick profit and greed. To build big houses for themselves in London.'

'And now all that heat has warmed the planet and melted the ice caps.'

Mam had a way of thinking about things.

'And you know what? If you went to look at those big houses today you'd find them all looking very shabby. Rented out to immigrants the lot of them. And practically falling down.'

'Oh yes, I have heard they are over-run by immigrants. Lorry drivers are bringing them in by the container-load through the Channel tunnel, you know. And they have camps for them in France, I heard.'

'The Saeson will soon be finding themselves foreigners in their own country, if they don't look out.'

I took the clothes to ring out through the mangle in the scullery, hung them out on the line, and fetched, and took, and changed the water in the big old kettle on the Aga, ready to put the next load in to boil.

And still they drank their endless cups of tea. And talked out cigarette smoke. And twt-twt-twted.

'The English have colonialism in their genes, Gwênfer. They're unable to help themselves.'

'Quite right, Gwenlais. They think they have all the answers in the world, they do. But they have none. Would the Irish have been so successful without their independence?' She glanced at me: 'I hope you're remembering to keep the coloureds separate from the whites.'

'Of course, Mam.'

'Well, that just goes to show then, doesn't it now?'

'Exactly. The English take control of other people's lives, countries, whole continents. All in the name of God. Their arrogant Protestant God, of course, invented by Henry VIII, in his exact own image. Then take whatever they want. Neglect us for generations. And then behave as if we were a part of them and should be grateful for it! Wales – their first great conquest and colony – the most neglected colony of all. They don't think twice about us. And still they call us foreigners. And they don't even know it.'

'But, in some ways, Gwenlais, that is to the good because we want them to leave us alone, we do. They bring us only harm.'

'They should hang their heads in shame. And we will make them. One day we will make them hang their heads in shame. You mark my words.'

They twt-twt-twted in chorus.

'As if we don't know for ourselves what's best for us.'

And they half-giggled, half-cackled, and twt-twted in that way that Welsh women who are no longer girls have cackled and twt-twted since before the days when they wore black hats and dresses and white lace – if they ever did – and certainly before they ever started going to chapels.

I had chores enough, without troubling myself with Mam's useless gossip politics. Chores would be the key to my personal salvation. That had been agreed by everyone. 'Work hard, Gwalia, and put your nightmares behind you.'

'Another fat, middle-aged Englishman, coming here thinking he knows everything that's good for us?' Mam said. 'Think of that now, Gwalia.'

'What if he isn't fat?' I piped up, suddenly, surprising myself with my own voice. 'What if he is young?'

Anti Gwenlais turned to me, 'Oooh. Now there's a thought. Isn't that a thought, now, Gwênfer? You could befriend him, Gwalia.'

Mam tensed on my behalf. I sensed her maternal hackles rising. She was very maternal was my Mam. I saw her glancing to see if I had slipped Gethin's black socks or Awena's red bib into the boil.

'Gwalia should have nothing to do with him, Gwenlais. He will only corrupt her. Corrupt us. Only by keeping ourselves to ourselves and having nothing to do with them can we survive.'

'There'd be no harm in befriending him, though, just for a few days. To know what he is planning. And – if he were to be young – then Gwalia would be ideally placed, wouldn't she? Surely, you wouldn't mind her keeping a little eye on him while he was here? To see what he was up to? That would do no harm, now, would it?'

'I suppose,' Mam agreed begrudgingly.

'There's more than enough in this town who would do us down, you know, Gwênfer. Some of them our own.' She looked at Mam with the stern, controlling eye of the older sister.

'I know that very nicely.'

Mam reached out from where she was sitting and slipped

17

her arm around me as I wriggled behind her chair to reach the cord for the pulley to let the airing frame down from the ceiling, ready to haul the clothes up to dry above the Aga.

'Look what the English have done in South Wales. The hwntws are virtually clones of the English themselves. Vast areas of our country where the Welshness has been all but bred out of them. We don't want that happening here in the North, now, do we?'

'Mind you, the hwntws practically invite enemies in. Romans, Vikings, Normans, Irish, English, it matters not a jot to them. Even the Italians with their ice cream. They don't have the sense of nation that we Welsh in the Gogledd have.'

My Anti Gwenlais had a lovely way of talking.

As a child it was always Anti Gwenlais who would sit me down by the fireside in the evenings and recite the old Welsh stories. How all animals all over the world would always understand if you spoke to them in Welsh. Even a charging lion. How Welsh was the language of heaven, just as the Welsh harp was the chosen instrument of angels and cupids and fairies.

Perhaps because she had never married herself, it was Anti Gwenlais who was always first to suggest summer picnics to secret waterfalls and lakes in hidden valleys, and who always knew where the best caves were and what mythical creatures and legends lived there. She knew about dragons and unicorns and the tylwyth teg – the Welsh fairies.

And she had a great stock of ghost stories she could tell us. Because she went ghost hunting with my Yncl Penhaearn. And one day, she had told us, they were going to meet the ghost of Wales's last prince and learn his secrets.

She never tired of telling us (and we never tired of listening) how Wales had once been a great and magical kingdom, full of princes and heroes and real dragons. And how – even now – it had the greatest poets and the finest singers.

And how King Arthur – Wales's greatest hero (except for

Llywelyn and Owain Glyndŵr, and, possibly, Lloyd George) – was not really dead but only sleeping with his knights in caves around these mountains, waiting to rise up again against the English when the moment was right. And how the armies of Glyndŵr and Llywelyn had melted into the landscape and were still, even now, lying in wait.

'And you know, Gwalia,' she would lean forward and say it in a whisper, 'we here in Llanchwaraetegdanygelyn are here for a reason.'

Even when I grew up and read the stories for myself, and realised how fanciful Anti Gwenlais's versions had been, the romance stayed with me, beguiling me as it beguiles all true Cymry, especially in the Gogledd.

I delighted in reading the Mabinogion for myself, with its poetic codifying of all-but-forgotten struggles between the Welsh and Irish warrior kings and ancient rivalries and betrayals. The tragic history of the ancient Welsh Princes. Stories of Llywelyn and Owain Glyndŵr only deepened my sense of tragedy as it must for all true Welshmen, leaving a deep vexation in our very souls for the anguish of our country and her people – and our own lost selves – to be called Welsh, foreigners in our own land.

Mam (as Dad would delight in saying) typically decided to be decisive and asserted herself by changing her mind.

'No, I'm sorry Gwenlais, you cannot ask Gwalia to spy on the man from Westminster.'

'I'm only suggesting she keep her eyes open, Gwênfer. And if she happened to find out a thing or two about him . . .' She winked at me.

'We don't know definitely that he'll be coming yet. Boudiccea has only written to ask them to send someone, unless I've misunderstood.'

'No, no, that's right, Gwênfer. But he is coming. I can tell you that.'

'And if all the signs are taken down, he might get lost and never find us. Like so many over the centuries, so *they* say.'

They were the great authority in Mam's world, though she had never explained who *they* were. Or what authority *they* had.

I wondered if Mam had any idea about satellite navigation or internet route finders. Like most in the town, she had never used a computer and never read anything which wasn't in Welsh. There were no daily Welsh-language newspapers, and we saw only our own, very local, paper, written by whoever submitted a story or took a picture, and without a reporter or any real news. Nor were there any women's magazines in Welsh – or men's magazines or computer magazines, though there was a weekly national paper, but very few took it.

There was no television reception in our valley either. What with the absence of mains electricity and the cost of generators, we didn't want it. Only the English agitated for such things. We had our families and our gossiping and more than enough committees and choirs and events to keep us more than busy. Who wanted to see moving pictures of other people's lives, anyway; were their own lives not sufficient for them?

Anti Gwenlais wagged her finger. 'Penhaearn thinks that they will send a strategist from the think tank. And your Yncl Penhaearn usually isn't wrong about such things.'

Mam glanced between us. She sensed that Anti Gwenlais and I were up to something she couldn't quite understand.

Sometimes I wanted to scream at Mam. I wasn't stupid! I didn't need protecting all my life! I was fed up with everyone always worrying about me, making me think inwards at myself, instead of outwards to the world.

As I later came to understand, it was Mam who had slowed the pace of my recovery: underrated me; mis-understood the damage my awful trauma had done to my self-confidence and taken my damaged self at its face value. Her sister, my Anti Gwenlais, understood how Mam had over-protected me, allowed me to exaggerate my misshapen nose, and my own self-loathing, my hand always going up to cover it whenever anyone looked at me. She somehow sensed, with that great wisdom some old spinsters in traditional communities have, that Mam had taken what the doctors called my post-traumatic stress and kept it as a fact, static and frozen for a whole seven summers, and she knew that the time had come for my soul to be thawed.

Perhaps we all sensed in that moment, that this might be the catalyst I needed to turn my thinking outward again – and to my future.

'I *could* spy on him.' I ventured. And I was thinking: he might be young and handsome.

Mam read my thoughts. And panicked.

'He won't be young, you know. Planners and town developers are never young. And they are always bald.'

But Anti Gwenlais was warming to the idea.

'He'd be bound to take you into his confidence if he was young, Gwalia. A man away from home. A pretty girl like you.'

Twt-twt-twt-twt-twt. Mam jumped up, clicking her tongue and shaking her head in a most disapproving manner and scrutinised the washing for the faintest smudge of grey or pink.

'What are you suggesting! It is unthinkable after all that she has been through. Heaven forbid that such a thing should even cross your mind, Gwenlais.'

'Oh no. Of course not, Gwênfer. But you wouldn't mind being civil to him, would you, Gwalia? Picking his brains a little. Especially if it did turn out he was handsome? You'd be ideally placed for that, working at Y Ddwy Ddraig.'

Y Ddwy Ddraig – The Two Dragons – was our hotel, handed down from riches to rags through five generations. Little more than a public bar now, it seemed to have fallen to me to pull the pints, wipe the tables and change the sheets for the occasional misguided visitor. And they dignified those chores with the title rheolwraig – manageress.

Mam shook her head emphatically.

'I will not hear of it.'

'It might do her good.'

Good old Anti Gwenlais. Always trying to 'do me good'. As if the great trauma that had ruined everything might magically vanish from my mind if only something magical could happen. The kiss of a prince perhaps.

Only three months before she had put my name forward to take the minutes at Council meetings, not in any official position, you understand, but to assist the Clerk. 'For your own good,' she assured me. 'To help you get better.' But I knew quite nicely that she wanted to avoid the job herself and use me as her understudy to sniff out gossip. Especially about the English. Or disloyal Welsh people.

She reached out her hand to mine, winked at Mam and said: 'She could bring him here for supper. Then you could get the information out of him yourself. You could be the Mata Hari then, Gwênfer. It wouldn't matter, then.'

She cackled at her own joke. Her smoker's laugh.

Mam relented and joined in. And I laughed, too, wondering if there was a hint of a cackle already in my laugh too.

'What is it that you will be wanting to know so badly, then?' I asked her.

'His plans, of course. They want to change the town. Beyond all recognition, so your Yncl Penhaearn says. Change our way of life forever.'

I didn't yet have the courage to say it out loud, but as young people always do, I knew that there were many things in Llanchwaraetegdanygelyn that needed modernising. Urgently.

It was just that Yncl Penhaearn was so powerful. And so opposed to any change at all, unless his spirits, as he called them, approved. Which they never did.

He couldn't see that ghosts are from long past ages, and therefore, by definition, extremely old-fashioned and outdated in their ideas, or that the rest of the world had developed more sophisticated methods of making decisions.

Which is one reason most young people left. And nothing changed.

'I think you quite fancy the idea of spying on him, Gwalia. Don't you now?'

'Maybe.'

They cackled again.

'You could be the Mata Hari of Gwrthsafiad.'

I doubted if Anti Gwenlais knew anything about the hapless Mata Hari except the name. And I wasn't sure she knew much about Gwrthsafiad – the Welsh Resistance – either. But, at that moment, I suppose, the seeds of my mission were sewn.

'I expect I could try if my country required it of me,' I smiled.

They looked at each other, and I knew what they were thinking. Perhaps she is starting to snap out of it, coming back to being the Gwalia she ought to be.

'Your Yncl Penhaearn would be more than grateful, I'm sure.'

'You'll see, one of these days, it will all come right.'

How could things come right for me? You can't go back and change what has happened to you? Change your culture. The rich know very well what has to be done to pick up stinking excrement and dispose of it, but they cannot bring themselves to do it, can they? Some people can't touch spiders and they scream at the thought of mice or rats. And no amount of logic will persuade them. Dad, for instance, cannot pick up and kill a wounded animal, something at which I am particularly adept, wounded or not. But none of us are perfect. In my case, my unmentionable horror was not some minor, incidental phobia, it was central to my life, a part of me. Something deep inside of me was frozen.

So I was an island, severed from myself like the head of Brân in the old Welsh myth, surrounded, trapped and constantly dismayed, not by stinking excrement or mice or spiders or wounded rats (they would be easy for me), but my own revolting history and self.

'You need to behave as if you are normal,' the doctor said. 'You can do that, can't you? Behave normally and before you know it, you will have forgotten your trauma.'

So that is what I had been trying to do. And my notes of that time are not entirely pessimistic: 'Being busy is better than those long, long months of sitting in my room, thinking only that none of it was *my* doing, none of it *my* fault.'

'Time doesn't wait for you to catch up; lives flow on.'

'The problem is that people have learned to make allowances for me, and my aberrations have become normal to them, their expectations of me are so low.'

'I am Gwalia – stranger to myself. Sum of all the stories told by Gwenlais. Head of Brân, severed from my body, kept alive until his followers turn to England, land of the conquering Angles. And then they took it to be buried in London. On the White Hill. Gwales. Looking for her lost causeway.'

Was I waiting, Jon, for you, without even knowing it?

'ERRM . . . YES. Okay. Right.'

They are looking at me expectantly.

'Hello.' I nod.

There is an awful silence.

So I blunder into it with my mind shut.

'The main point is, you see, that this ripple effect – well, really successive waves – of immigrants moving outwards from the poorer areas, to more affluent areas, as they establish themselves, creates a number of tensions right across the spectrum of the different communities.'

It had sounded so much better last night, in the early hours, when I was tapping it into my laptop in my room, at home. It isn't easy trying to spin a tangle of complicated issues into a coherent strand of argument. My grandfather calls all talking 'spinning yarns' and does it well. Obviously that gene eluded me.

Now they are looking at me blankly.

I smile and nod.

Smiling and nodding gets listeners on your side. (Communication theory says so.)

'I mean the communities they impact upon.'

'I think we are aware of the principles, old boy.' The man in a loud bow-tie and chalk-striped suit is getting impatient. 'What we really want to know is whether this will be replicated with the East Europeans?'

(Communications theory is not infallible.)

He is Freddy Morgan, senior adviser on immigration to the Home Office, and chairman of the Board of Trustees of the Leyburn Institute, my employers. His body gives off ambition like a pheromone.

I glance at my boss, Professor Angela Lain, who has been standing to the side of the platform area. She smiles encouragingly. I am also aware of my friend Nisha, sitting at the control desk above the video wall behind me, waiting for me to cue her to start running the graphs and statistics sequence she has helped me prepare. Nisha is a goddess, from India, come to protect me.

I can feel my mouth opening and closing. Whatever programme is running in my brain has crashed. The yarn has snapped. This is a dream come true turned nightmare. You know – a living one.

Ten months ago I was a possibly slightly nerdy PhD student gently fermenting in academia, fantasising about opportunities like this. Until Professor Lain appeared in the department as my external assessor, read my thesis on Post Industrial Community Regeneration, based on County Durham former pit villages (we are neat with titles in the Social Sciences) and plucked me from university to work at the Leyburn. Now I am a slightly-less-nerdy researcher. It is the most thrilling thing I have ever done in my life. (Except possibly for Maria.) And also the second most intimidating. (After Maria.)

'Errr,' I begin again.

Now Freddy Morgan is smiling at me. Laughing at me under his breath. How is it that you can know all the things that are wrong with you, know exactly what you would like to be like and yet not be able to be it?

I am aware that I am grinning. First social defence mechanism of the vulnerable. Grinning. (Note to self: Communication Theory doesn't mention that. Must be a Biology thing.)

Of the dozen people sitting around the Hub, two are MPs, the others are fellow researchers, like myself. Freddy Morgan sits prominently to the side. This man has direct access to the Prime Minister. When I took the job I had no idea I would be intimidated by that. But the pheromones of power these people exude are truly terrifying. (Another area of knowledge where Biology needs to help Communications out.)

Professor Angela Lain moves smoothly across the floor to touch me on the arm.

'Let me just step in here, for a moment, Jon,' she says sweetly.

I glance towards Nisha. She and her boyfriend Andrew

(who is currently working on road transport strategies) are my guardian angels at the Leyburn. Nisha has raised her eyebrows slightly but is sitting serenely in her sari, her gold rings and glass rubies sparkling on her fingers

I am still grinning stupidly, my mind slowly starting to reboot. The reboot process is ponderous. Much worse than on Windows XP. I get random thoughts like this one: 'Remember they don't know what's going on in your head.' Andrew, who everyone thinks is like a young version of Woody Allen is always telling me that. Just now, this seems doubtful. The thoughts in my own head are so loud, everyone in the world must be able to hear them.

Fortunately, everyone in the world is looking at Professor Angela Lain, who is prettier than me.

'We understand your urgent political concerns, Freddy. Taking into account the recent spate of terrorist bombings, growing social unrest in our inner cities and the unfortunate tendency of the media to lay the blame for all this at the doors of your department.'

She gets a titter of laughter for that.

Freddy is about to interrupt but she holds up her hand and switches to serious mode.

'Society senses – we think rightly – that the ramifications of social change involved in mass migration are huge. Morally and politically, I think, we are all puzzled because we don't know which elements of this change represent progress and which elements represent a dangerous threat to our cultural identity. We don't know what to do for the best, or what to do to be right.'

There are murmurs of agreement around the audience. She glances at me. I nod. I have recovered. I am ready now.

'What Jon here has done is to research one element of this. We aren't trying to give you the whole picture this morning. And we haven't got a crystal ball. But Jon's research does suggest very strongly that when people's cultural identity is under threat – especially when a rural village culture from, say Pakistan, is transplanted into the plethora of Western cultural values – that is precisely the moment when their panic at our society can so easily be turned to violence, terrorism and radicalism – if certain catalysts are present. We think it's important that you know what we know.'

She smiles at her audience, looks at me, and then back at Freddy Morgan.

'So, perhaps if we can just stick with Jon's ten minute presentation and *then* open it for discussion? All right, Freddy?'

Freddy nods. It is part of Angela's skill that her relative youth and pretty smile belie her intelligence. Freddy hardly realises he has been rebuked and brought to heel.

She smiles at me and glides off to the side. I start again, deciding to skip my homily on the repercussions of empire, echoes of past wrongs, Islam, slavery.

'Errm. What outrages Middle England is the . . . er . . . thought that . . . why would the children of immigrants, born and brought up in England – with all the . . . umm . . . education and welfare and hospitality our great country offers – why would they want to blow up innocent people? And destroy the nation that has taken them into its . . . uh . . . bosom?'

I glance at Nisha to make sure she knows where I am in the script, and nod to her. The first pie chart comes up on the screen behind me, showing immigration figures with different colours for different countries of origin (I spent a long time choosing the colours). We move on to the map of Britain, showing concentrations of immigrants, in the same colours. Then focus on Birmingham, tracing the successive waves of migration over the last sixty years at ten year intervals, and tracking the dispersal of first and second generations through the community.

'We must be careful to . . . um . . . distinguish between integration and assimilation,' I am saying. The hesitation has almost disappeared now. I am on familiar territory. It is as if my audience is looking over my shoulder and seeing the same thing I'm seeing. I'm back on script.

This is good. I am standing in the famous Hub at the Leyburn Institute, delivering a strategy paper I have written. Influencing Government social strategy. Perhaps.

As students we all aspired to work in a place like this. Professor Angela Lain was the doyen of political philosophers, the Leyburn – her brainchild – was the best of think-tanks, the crucible of liberal policy. We never missed her appearances on *Tonight* or *Question Time* if we could help it. According to undergraduate mythology, the Leyburn Institute was a vast open-plan office, on a top floor, right opposite the Houses of Parliament, all green carpet and sustainable-wood furniture with glass room dividers and potted plants. And at the heart of it, we knew, was The Hub, the seminal seminar area, said to have been designed as a facetious reference to John le Carré's George Smiley trilogy: a ring of red, leather-covered benches, arranged like a circus ring, with a sawdust coloured carpet and a bank of TV screens at one point and a control desk above it. It wasn't quite like that, but close enough. And the metaphors of Ringmaster, high wire acrobats and clowns were apposite enough. (Though you quickly tire of all those puns and jokes when you work there.)

'So . . . er . . . If a hundred thousand Eastern European immigrants are coming in each year, and the economy needs them to do the jobs that English people won't do, then where are we going to put them? Rhetorical question, obviously. There isn't actually a policy for *putting* them anywhere. They are impelled into the cheapest housing and worst conditions, in the most deprived areas and least attractive conurbations in Britain.'

At least they are all now watching me and listening.

'So this is the start of this ripple effect with the current residents moving out and then displacing those already in the suburbs . . . and so on . . . ending with English people in outlying areas moving abroad and out to France or Spain, or out to the countryside. From Birmingham, a significant proportion moves to Wales. We call this the White Wave.'

Angela flashes me a smile.

'The White Wave is particularly conspicuous amongst parents. As we know, white parents are very quick to move to areas with what they see as better schooling. Nowhere is this more true than in strongly ethnic areas. Many otherwise liberal white parents exhibit a real dread of their children being in a minority in schools where black and Asian children dominate.'

I decide I may be doing all right. (At my first appraisal six months ago, Angela told me I was a 'nervous boy, brilliant enough in your thinking, but full of personal self-doubt – you need to work on that.')

It was after sharing that with Andrew and Nisha that they adopted me as their project.

'What kind of friends and social strategists would we be, if we failed to take care of one of our own?' Or, as Andrew put it: 'No girlfriend. Still living at home with your parents and seriously nerdy. Rapid integration into adult society needed.' Their project is still in its SWOT analysis stages. My Strengths and Opportunities needed more work.)

'It isn't only the resistance to change and the resentment of each community to the incomers, it is also the anger and jealousy of the incomers as they experience the discrimination, exploitation and maltreatment from the stratas of society above them. And, naturally, ladies and gentlemen, that pressure is at its greatest at the bottom.

'As we all know, six months ago, three airports were targeted by Al Qaeda terrorist cells. What shocked us was that these were people born and brought up in this country, under our own educational system.

'The kind of vulnerable young men recruited by Al Qaeda extremists had their origins here in our inner cities. And the psychological poison here in these immigrant communities is mirrored in the white communities, as shown by these figures showing the increase in demonstrations by white nationalists – especially in our Northern cities – protesting against what they see as uncontrolled immigration.'

I nod to Nisha and a fresh display comes up on the screens.

'To sum up, taking mass migration as a fait accompli, beyond any desirable political solution, our focus has to move to better management of its effects. Our primary challenge, I would suggest, is to remedy the alienation suffered, not only by young men and women in minority cultures but also in our own indigenous people.'

I glance at Nisha. Unlike many Indian girls, she has successfully avoided an arranged marriage and gone to university, though her parents still don't accept or approve of Andrew. But, then again, his Jewish family are not entirely delighted in his choice of true love either. They are both working on it. Cheerfully and with great love for their families and each other. Society, like all relationships, is evolving – work in progress.

'It is the job of other agencies to tell you how many bombers have already been recruited and trained; what this model tells us is where those vulnerable groups are likely to be, why they are there. And – more importantly – ways of developing possible strategies to counteract the mechanisms which motivate and drive social disintegration.'

I stop and wait.

Freddy Morgan is inevitably first to speak. He ignores me and speaks across me to Professor Angela Lain.

'This is all just speculation, Angela. Isn't it? Where's the evidence for what he's saying? Does this get any closer to how we begin to integrate – sorry, assimilate – these people? How do we measure any of this?'

These people! These people!

I am bubbling with indignation. I look to Professor Lain. Her eyes meet mine. With an almost imperceptible nod, she gives me permission to answer.

'Technically, our key indicator to lack of assimilation – i.e. potential antagonism – is language. Do the immigrants speak to each other in their original language or in the language of the host country? In this case, English.'

'So all you're saying is that we should teach them to speak English and the threat of terrorism will go away?'

I want to tell him he is being simplistic. I cannot tell if he is being facetious.

'I'm not . . . errrm . . . saying that at all. Language is only the indicator. Lack of language may cause isolation and obviously lessens British and Western influences.'

I look around then shut my eyes and carry on.

'Ethnic groups from poorly-educated rural communities who have been actively discouraged from mixing with English people and learning the English language perpetuate their own set of values, often distorting them.'

Someone is nodding. This is good.

'The more isolated people are, the more acute the distortion. They are panicked and confused by our permissiveness. Our liberal values. They don't have the same ability that the English middle classes have to distance themselves from crime and the sex industry. They live in the poor areas; they are surrounded by it. In the case of many immigrants, lured or trafficked here, they are part of it. It is unsurprising that they are driven towards the secure simplicity of religious fundamentalism.'

'I'm sorry. I just don't buy it, I'm afraid. These are just bad people.'

I start to splutter again but Angela moves forward, smiling, taking back control.

'Thank you all for coming this morning.'

The meeting breaks up quickly. The audience is relieved to be standing up after the low benches. I see Freddy Morgan talking to Angela Lain. They glance across at me.

Nisha appears with print-outs of the presentation and hands them around.

'Was I all right?' I ask her. 'I mean, did I get my points across properly?'

'You were fine.'

I get waylaid answering a few more questions, but everyone has other, more urgent business to move on to. They melt away quite suddenly. On to their next priority. Angela comes over.

'Jon, before you disappear, I need a word.'

I wait.

'Freddy has a Welsh problem he needs help with. He's asked for you.'

'Me! Welsh problem! Why would I know anything about Wales? That man's impossible. There's no logic to him. Yet he's supposed to be . . .'

Angela holds her hand up.

'You mentioned Wales when you talked about people moving out of Birmingham. In his eyes that makes you an expert. He said he was impressed with your notion of The White Wave. Besides, he's our chairman, I need you to do this. Do you want me to tell you about it?'

Nisha is looking at me warningly. I swallow the words that are grouping on my tongue and in my throat for suicide attack.

'A small town in Wales has come up on their radar as a potential political embarrassment. No electricity or running water, even after nine years of a Labour Government . . . English moving in. Local opposition. You see the problem? Freddy thinks it needs your innocent approach. He's sending the papers over this afternoon.'

'Innocent approach!'

'Precisely.'

'But I know nothing about Wales.'

I want to scream.

'Don't be so spiky, Jon,' She is starting to move away. 'It's an opportunity for you. A step nearer a job at the Downing Street Policy Unit perhaps.'

She is gone. On to the next thing.

I look at Nisha.

'How does she know my secret ambitions?'

'A little Eastern word of wisdoms for you, Jon.'

'Yes.'

'Don't ever be joining with the secret service.'

'Why not'

'Your secrets are written all over your face.'

She goes back up the little staircase to the head-height desk above the screens, closes down the system and turns the main screen over to BBC NEWS 24. I hang around.

'So was I really all right?'

'You were fine, Jon.'

'But they're sending me to Wales.'

'It's not exile.'

'What will Andrew think?'

'He'll think you should get yourself a girlfriend. As soon as possible.'

ANTI GWENLAIS arrived with fresh gossip.

In my town, sooner, rather than later, everyone gets to know *everything*. But Anti Gwenlais has the advantage in that it is usually she who makes it up. It is as if she sniffs the air, smells rumours on the wind, and manufactures them. Often they turn out to be true. Or perhaps it is that her stories are so good, they become the truth. 'I could not possibly imagine lies,' she tells anyone who accuses her of carrying clecs.

'I have important news,' she announced, bustling in with her cloud of nicotine as we were finishing breakfast, trying to clear up and get Awena and Gethin off to school, while Dad sat reading the paper which had just been pushed through our door.

As soon as she arrived Dad pulled up the paper and pretended not to be there. He always tried to avoid talking to Anti Gwenlais. And since Mam was busy getting the children ready for school, I had to play the hostess, not that Anti Gwenlais was ever other than totally at home in our house – or that it would ever have occurred to her that her presence might be at all inconvenient.

'Bore da, Gwalia, sut wyt ti bore 'ma?' She sniffed my air to see if I had any fresh gossip on my person.

I replied that I was fine, thank you and asked how she was. Dach chi eisiau paned?'

'If you're having one, I'll join you.'

She plonked herself down.

As you will remember only too well, Jon, my Anti Gwenlais was always perfectly placed to know every coming and going in the town: her house overlooked the Maes from the bottom of the town, and her shop – Y Fferyllfa – overlooked it from the side. And since the Maes is the centre of everything in our town, she saw every coming and going and knew everybody's business, often better than they did – certainly in terms of what they *ought* to have done.

Thanks to her cousin, my Yncl Penhaearn, she was also on

both the Town and Parish Councils. And she was party to his inner circle and, through his spirit séances, and ghost-hunts, privy to the wisdom of our great Welsh leaders, long departed.

Anti Gwenlais, at least in her own view, was therefore ideally placed to give vent to an encyclopaedic kind of wisdom that only elderly spinsters who have devoted their love and lives to the whole community, have it in their gift to give. As she often said: 'Think what I would have been like if I had frittered my life away on one undeserving man.'

Unfortunately, as a girl, she had been advised to leave school too young to qualify as a pharmacist like my maternal grandfather, so these days Y Fferyllfa sold only proprietary drugs, shampoos and herbal medicines, but this was enough to satisfy all her medical instincts.

'Well. Come on, then. Tell us the gossip,' Mam begged impatiently.

'Well, since you ask, Gwênfer, I must confess to having had a very interesting day already, this morning. I was talking to Jack Post, not half an hour ago, and he happened to mention that he had delivered a very official-looking registered package to Mrs Leakin, just now. Isn't that interesting, Gwalia?'

She gave me a look as if to say 'my plan for you is going rather well, my girl'.

Yesterday she had wanted me to become a spy. What did she want of me today?

I never turned down the chance of things to occupy me. Running Y Ddwy Ddraig and doing my best to help Mam look after Awena, even helping the Clerk to the Council with the minutes – none of it really seemed somehow difficult enough. Being busy was good; it stopped me thinking about myself, and, perhaps, if I worked hard enough, one day I might do enough to forget myself and obliterate all my guilt and self-disgust.

I smiled at Anti Gwenlais. She really was helping me build my self-confidence. Without her *meddling,* as Mam called it, I would not have discovered that compared with other people, I was really not as stupid or incompetent as I had thought.

At my very first Council Meeting, I was shocked to discover that the official Town Clerk, Islwyn, was actually illiterate, though not devoid of wisdom or local knowledge.

Like many Welsh speakers of his generation, Islwyn had suffered at school from a regime that refused to teach him Welsh as it took up valuable brain space that could be devoted to 'more useful pursuits'. In those days everyone believed the Welsh language would die – should die. His difficulty with formal written Welsh – which is different from spoken Welsh in many respects (as you found out, Jon) made him seem much less clever than he really was. Throughout his sixty-five years in this town, he had never succeeded in finding a single one of those 'more useful pursuits', though it would have been more than handy to have been able to write the convoluted, old-fashioned grammar in his own written language. I think my Anti Gwenlais had once had a rather soft spot for Islwyn.

'I don't know what some package has to do with me, o gwbl,' I said.

'Well now, that's where you are entirely wrong you see. Because this package, I can assure you, has something to do with all of us. A letter addressed to Boudiccea Leakin. From Westminster. Fancy! Westminster calling Mrs Leakin by her nickname of Boudiccea, if you please.'

Everyone knew that Victoria Leakin liked her nickname Boudiccea. My Taid had thought it up for her (of course, grandparents have the time for that kind of thing), and everyone had found it so entirely apposite that it stuck.

'She thinks the nickname brings her luck,' I said.

'The least she needs, I should say. Any woman who has to advertise for a husband in a newspaper dating column needs far more than luck,' Mam said.

'I think it was quite a respectable paper,' Dad said, emerging momentarily.

'Rubbish,' said Anti Gwenlais. 'It's English.'

'Wasn't it him who advertised, not her?' I queried
Anti Gwenlais twted.

'I saw the advertisement myself. And very disappointed in
him I was, too. A Welshman advertising in an English
newspaper.' Twt-twt. 'And Penhaearn's business partner, too.
As if he hasn't enough embarrassments to bear. I went straight
away to their office and told your Yncl Penhaearn
immediately. Completely inappropriate behaviour for an
undertaker. I said so at the time, isn't it?'

Now that the Chapel had only a part-time minister, shared
with other towns, Penhaearn's position as undertaker had
given him an almost religious status in many people's eyes,
particularly those nearest to requiring his services. Besides,
most of the young ministers they sent couldn't hold a candle
to Penhaearn's solemnity and gravitas.

'You don't much like your Yncl Penhaearn, do you,
Gwalia?' said Anti Gwenlais, sniffing at me. It was true that
I didn't. He always seemed very cold, to my way of seeing
him, one of those old men who was always trying to be jolly
to people because he wanted to be liked. He made me
shudder. And that wasn't just because I couldn't look at him
without thinking of all those cold stiff bodies he and his
partner Lawns had to manhandle into coffins in upstairs
rooms to make them presentable for families crying
downstairs.

'He never speaks to me,' I said. 'And I don't like Lawns
either. The thought of all those bodies they handle.' What was
even more shocking was that Lawns was married to
Boudiccea. He never spoke English, and she barely spoke
Welsh. Though she was struggling painfully to learn it.

'You didn't know him in the old days. Such a comical
character when he was young. I remember the time poor old
Rockaway died. The wake it was. Coffin in the front room,
Penhaearn and Lawns waited until everyone had gone to the
Dragons to drown their sorrows – there was no drink in the

houses in those days – then off-ed with the lid, lifted the body out and Penhaearn lay down in the coffin himself.

'When the mourners returned, they heard this knocking from the coffin. And their blood froze to their bones. And they watched in terror as the lid gently lifted. And a hand came out. And a voice that sounded very much like poor old Rockaway's said: "Forsake the drink. Forsake the drink." And then the lid fell back again.

'There were a few stopped drinking that night, I can tell you.' And she and Mam cackled while Dad scowled and shook his head behind his paper.

I had heard the story before many times. It didn't raise my opinion of any of them.

'And then there was the time Iwan Rags lay dying in his upstairs bedroom, in Celyn Street, behind the Post Office. And he wanted to see his old, trusty horse that had pulled his cart, just one last time. It was young Penhaearn who went and fetched the horse and took it upstairs, you know. He couldn't do enough for people.'

'But then the snag was, they couldn't get it back downstairs,' Mam butted in.

'I'm coming to that, Gwênfer. Yes, Gwalia. They had to take the window out, erect a hoist and lower the old horse down in a sling. They say that Iwan Rags died laughing. And no one ever had a better end.'

'Quite right,' Mam said, nodding and straightening Gethin's tie. 'No one did. But I hope when my time comes, *they'll* leave me be.'

I tried to help Awena with her hair but she pulled away.

'No. I want Mam to do it.' I felt a shifting of the awful coldness inside me. What was it about me that made her be like that?

'Personally, I hope Boudiccea and Lawns are very happy,' I said. 'Perhaps one day, then, *I* should put an advert in *The Guardian*.'

'A woman who has to advertise for men, must be

exceptionally desperate, that's all I have to say,' Anti Gwenlais snapped. And then she felt guilty in case her words might have stung me.

'Poor Gwalia.' She moved and put her arm around my shoulder and tried to pull my face to her bristly chin. But I ducked away.

'I should have thought that Lawns, being Penhaearn's business partner, would have found it particularly off-putting to be married to a woman posing as the ancient Warrior Queen of the Britons,' she said.

'Taid gave her that name,' I protested. 'I think it suits her very nicely. Boudiccea was a Celtic queen, feared by the Roman conquerors. I think she wants to rescue us from our English conquerors.'

Anti Gwenlais bristled.

'She can't possibly do that. She's English herself.'

'I think the nickname is only meant as a bit of fun, Anti Gwenlais.'

'Fun! You do realise she's come here to destroy our way of life, don't you, Gwalia?'

'Well I think she's a very nice lady. She's fallen in love with Lawns and with us. She's trying to learn Welsh, to start a new life and put her past behind her. And she is making a great effort to help this town.'

Anti Gwenlais didn't like that at all.

'And why do you think we should want to be organised by an English woman?' She demanded. 'Haven't we got our own women organisers?'

'You don't happen to know what was in this package, do you,' I asked, to change the subject.

'Of course I do,' she said. And then she smiled. 'And since you ask me, I shall tell you.'

She leaned forward, looked around, and spoke in a whisper.

'It's the blueprint Boudiccea will use to ruin our town.'

Mam sighed. 'Oh dear me. That is terrible news. Terrible.'

'What is?' Gethin asked.

'Yes. We must be firm. And resilient. That is what Penhaearn says. And I agree with him.'

Mam shook her head. 'It has come to this at last. I knew it, I knew it.' And then shook it again. And twted some more.

'Be sy'n bod, Mam?' Awena asked.

'Don't you think we're getting this out of proportion, Gwênfer?' Dad asked cautiously, emerging from behind the headlines, which attracted the children's attention across to him.

'No, I do not,' said Mam. 'I think you are stupid not to see the dangers, Artwr. The English are going to have us under siege!'

'Are the English going to attack us? With tanks and stuff?' asked Gethin, ducking behind a chair and pointing his fingers at me and making shooting noises. Dad shook his head. Gethin looked disappointed.

'You don't think, then, that the town might benefit from some improvements?' Dad suggested gently.

'Not from the English, no.' She turned to her elder sister. 'You must forgive him, Gwenlais. This is what reading English papers has done to his mind.'

My Anti Gwenlais touched her younger sister's arm sympathetically.

'Don't be so mean to Dad!' I exclaimed. And they all looked at me in surprise. 'He's only being open-minded,' I said. 'There's nothing wrong with that.'

Dad smiled and raised his eyebrows a touch and said under his breath: 'Being open-minded isn't the wisest policy in the company of bigots.'

'Open-minded,' said Mam. 'I've never heard of such a thing.'

'You can't go round believing everything you hear, my girl,' Anti Gwenlais told me, wagging her nicotine-stained finger. 'My heart trembles to think about it. We must all be strong and resist the temptation to be seduced by open-minded ideas. Progress they call it. Being progressive. But what they really want is to take over our town. To bring in English people to live here, in their droves. To buy our houses for holiday homes and build caravan sites and flood us with thousands of visitors all summer. Mark my words. It'll be the death of our town as we know it.'

'My Dad is a very clever man,' I said. 'Maybe we should listen to what he says.'

'God protect us from clever men,' Anti Gwenlais sighed. 'I knew a clever man once. Mark my words: you don't hear clever men agreeing any more than stupid ones. They disagree about what is best for us as much as stupid men do. And if you think about it that means half of them are always wrong, doesn't it not? And a girl doesn't always know that when she falls in love.'

Anti Gwenlais started twt-twting furiously.

And Mam twt-twted, too.

'Coming here with their water mains and electricity. Wanting to improve the place. Well, we won't let them.'

Dad looked at me and rolled his eyes. I went over to him and kissed him on his bald head, and sat down on the arm of his chair.

'I feel sick inside just at the thought of all those English people moving in here, destroying our language. We've seen it all around us. The Town Council over in Talyffrydd had one English woman join the Council and they all had to stop speaking Welsh from then on. And the same in their Golf Club. And their Summer Fair Committee. They only dare speak Welsh at home behind closed doors now. It could happen here, too. Mark my words.'

'She's right, you know, Gwalia. One English person in a room is all it takes and we are all supposed to speak *their* tongue.'

'I admire your Uncle Penhaearn for resisting that. We are the last pure town in Wales now, it is said. We must take pride in that and all of us must play our part,' said Anti Gwenlais.

Like most of her political sayings, I recognised them as Penhaearn's words. 'You see, Gwalia, how important it is for you to get inside this man's briefcase.'

'It's fine,' I said. 'I'm going to do it. I'm going to be the Welsh Mata Hari.'

'Do you know the story of Mata Hari?' Dad asked me quietly.

'Of course I do,' I said.

'Then you'll know that she was shot by a firing squad in the end,' he said. 'For being a traitor.'

'I don't care,' I said. 'At least she lived.'

Mam looked so serious it made me want to giggle. 'Don't talk silly. You're not going to do any such thing. We must all stop talking so much nonsense this instant.'

But for the first time since my trauma, my digwyddiad, I felt something stir. Excitement, perhaps. Anticipation.

I gave Dad another kiss and jumped up. I had a lot to do. There was no time to waste. I would go straight across to Y Ddwy Ddraig, to sort out your room for you, Jon, though, of course, I only knew you then as the man from Westminster. And it was by no means certain that you would come. But somehow I knew you would.

I didn't know when you would arrive but I knew I had to be prepared.

You'd come to the Hotel, and I would greet you. And then you would go to the Council Meeting, and since I'd be taking the notes, I'd have a ringside seat.

Unless you got lost and couldn't find us, of course, for lack of signposts.

Whatever you do for the best, as Mam liked to say, there is always a snag, isn't there not?

MERELY GOING TO the Leyburn canteen with Nisha was an education. She greets everyone in their own tongue.

'Guten morgen' to the German cook, 'Marhaban' to the Arab women serving, 'Namaste' to the Hindus, and 'Dzień dobry' to the Poles.

'How many languages do you know, Nisha?' I ask her. I have asked her this before. Always I get a different answer.

She shrugs. 'How do you count?'

'OK then. How many are you fluent in?'

'Ahh, fluency. That is being another thing altogether. The difficulty isn't in the speaking, it is in the listening.'

I choose cottage pie and chips, she chooses fruit.

She tells me that there are an estimated six thousand and five hundred languages in the world, though probably a third of them have never been written down.

I get a coffee, she takes yoghurt.

'In Nigeria alone, there are an estimated 450 languages.'

'The language of statistics – of language!' I say. 'That confusion, at least, is international.'

'Don't mock, Jon. Every fortnight one language somewhere in the world is dying. In the East Indies a thousand languages have been shrinking to about two hundred.'

'So why preserve them? Wouldn't it be better if we all understood each other?'

She waits while I get my cutlery and sachets of tomato sauce. I know what the Leyburn Institute chips are like. They will need three sachets.

'Diversity of language and ideas is important. When everyone speaks the same tongue, you get only inbreeding. Ideas turn in on themselves. The world needs linguistic diversity. Now more than ever, diversity of language means diversity of ideas; a way of seeing yourself as others see you.'

We find a free table next to the huge glass windows overlooking Parliament and Big Ben. I glimpse Andrew arriving at the self-service, he will make fun of me for eating junk.

'Languages dying is as bad as species becoming extinct, Jon. But not as trendy, not as easy to capture on film or understand. Think of it: every month languages are being killed by globalisation, colonisation, communities being scattered and assimilated into others, sometimes politicians want to eradicate them.'

The chips are dry and like cotton wool. The mince in the cottage pie is mostly soya. But I am starving and it would be good to finish before Andrew arrived.

'Why?' I ask. I need to keep her talking so as to stuff as many chips into my mouth as quickly as possible.

'Language is where a people's culture resides. It preserves identity. Language is often the rallying point for independence – Bangladesh, Catalonia, Brittany. Politicians and conquerors want to drive that out. It's what kept the countries of the Soviet Bloc feeling independent, even at the height of Russian power: however much they were forced to learn Russian at school, they spoke their own languages at home. My language is what makes me feel that I'm a Gujarati and an Indian. Even though I'm English now as well. My multiple identities are the languages I speak. And the cultural jewels they hold within them.'

'So you've caught Freddy's eye,' Andrew says, arriving and sitting down. 'Impressive.'

I push my plate aside, half finished.

'Only for exiling to Wales.'

Nisha changes the subject.

'I think he is needing a girlfriend.'

'I had a girlfriend.'

'Five years ago,' Andrew exclaimed.

'Ahh! Yes. Maria, I think was her name.'

I am not in the mood to discuss Maria. The one disastrous relationship in my life. The worst. But also the best.

Andrew knows my story off by heart. He doesn't need to recite it yet again. But he does.

'Ah, yes. The project. Let's consider Wales in that context.

45

Strength. Weakness Opportunity. Or Threat? Let's recap: Jon's sex life: The story so far.'

Andrew picks up his packet of sandwiches opens it and takes a mouthful. I should have had a sandwich.

'Maria,' he says. 'The tragic story of . . .'

I interrupt.

'Beginning: Maria. End: Maria. That's it. The whole story. A story without plot or theme, merely tone: tragic. And more a soliloquy than a duet. It wouldn't even make a light opera.'

I make a joke of it. Of course I do. Maria. A beautiful Spanish archaeology student with long dark curls, a Catholic pedigree and a battered old Skoda. Most of the story composed in my head.

But Andrew will not relent.

'Months of teasing and frustration. And going on walks and digs. Am I right, Jon?'

'Don't be mean,' Nisha tells him. But we are all laughing, even me.

'I'm not being mean. This is therapy. Social therapy. The way men are together. What friends are for. You don't mind, Jon, do you?'

'Well, let's say . . . it no longer pains me to tell you – a testament to the success of your therapy, I'm sure – she cuckolded me. After telling me she was a true Catholic and would never sleep with anyone outside marriage. Ever. She persuaded me – against my better judgement, I should add, – to go on a summer dig in the West Country – camping, of all things – but separate sleeping bags. Obviously.'

'You don't have to tell us,' Nisha says.

But I know that Andrew wants to hear it yet again so carry on anyway.

'Then. In the early hours. I woke up one night in the tent alone.'

Andrew is nodding. And chewing.

'"Maria," I called. But she was in the sleeping bag of her blond-bearded professor. And, the following morning, she looked happier than I had ever made her feel, in ways she had never allowed me to attempt. I left the dig the following morning, my interest in archaeology extinguished forever.'

Andrew swallows and takes up the story. This is his favourite bit, his analysis.

'See! Subconsciously, at that moment, you vowed to forsake your own sexual happiness forever and devote yourself to the betterment of humanity as a social researcher and scientist. And that has clearly left you with a permanent phobia of archaeology and women.'

We all laugh.

'That is rubbish!' Nisha is saying.

'Tell you what,' Andrew continues. 'Let's put Wales down as an Opportunity, shall we? It may even turn out a Strength. We'll work out a full strategy later.'

'I should never have told you about Maria.'

'You had no choice, my boy. It was turning to neurosis. Basic Freudian psychology.'

Andrew thinks that being Jewish means he has a genetic predisposition to psychoanalysis – and everything else that any Jewish person has ever excelled at, from Moses to Einstein. His ambition is to lead people to their promised lands.

'I'm over it, OK. It's no big deal. And I do not have phobias about archaeology and women.'

'You're sure?'

'Yes.'

'But you have never unearthed anyone else.'

Nisha giggled.

'So? Look. Drop it. Where shall we go tonight?'

They look at each other.

'Andrew wants us to go to a poetry reading at the South Bank. I want to do the opening at the Serpentine Gallery.'

'Shall we cut the baby in half, Solomon?' Nisha asks, neatly mocking both Andrew and modernism.

'Let's do bowff, then,' I say in my best mock-cockney. 'Seeing as 'ow yer actual wisdom is not just a Jewish Solomon fing. Art and a glass of wine first, then grab a taxi to go to be read to.'

We agree.

'Your skin is too thin, Jon.'

Andrew is trying to analyse me again and, as always, adopt a superior position.

'No. It isn't,' I say. 'I like being a sensitive, caring person. If everyone were a bit less hard-nosed, we might start solving a few more problems of the world, instead of just sitting here letting it all happen around us.'

'What problems, Jon?'

This time I fail to spot that Andrew's setting me up and walk straight into it.

'Global warming. War. Poverty. Massacre. Terrorism – do I need to go on? If we expended a tenth as much energy on making the world a better place – or even if we just stopped trying to do everyone else down – we could solve most of these problems in a generation.'

Nisha and Andrew glance at each other. Nisha laughs and touches me on the arm.

'You are so innocent, Jon. In India we have solved these problems a thousand times. Every religion has its blueprint for the perfect life. They just don't work.'

'Why don't they?'

'Human nature. We just can't bear to live the way we ought to. But you, Jon, I think, are going to solve that problem for us any minute.'

Nisha is looking at me over the top of her water glass, displaying the many rings on her fingers regally, trying to hide her giggle.

I finally realise they are winding me up.

'Oh you!' I turn and slap Andrew's arm playfully with the back of my hand. And we all laugh.

We are silent for a moment.

'So what's this about Wales?'

'Dunno,' I said. 'I suppose I'll find out on Monday.'

THE NIGHT BEFORE you were supposed to come Dewi and I had gone out in the clapped-out van that is Gwrthsafiad's only military transport. We had driven up to the crossroads, then the turning, and taken down all the road signs. We knew that the County Council would, as usual, replace them, as they were obliged to do. But all of us – as I then believed – have our roles, our chores, our destinies.

Then we had gone up to the main road.

Dewi had made me hold his hand, in case I was nervous, he said. I think that he was much more nervous than I. And then he made me hold the metal pole while he took his hacksaw to it.

We had almost finished when the police car came, catching us in its headlights like frightened rabbits.

'Godrapia!' Dewi cursed. And threw the hacksaw down.

It was only Myrfyn.

'Evening all,' he said mockingly in English, winding down the window and grinning, his eyes going up and down my body. 'Putting the road signs straight for our English visitors, are we?'

His torch went to my face. I felt him looking at my nose. And felt my hand go up to cover it. Then the beam moved up and down and settled on my breasts.

'Do you want a hand from your friendly neighbourhood policeman, then?' he asked, getting out of the patrol car and putting on his cap.

'No thanks,' said Dewi, motioning me to take hold the steel pole again and picking up the hacksaw and resuming work.

Myrfyn carried on smiling at me. And ran his eyes down my body, his gaze lingering blatantly at my crotch. He nodded towards me. 'So you have joined the Welsh Resistance, Gwalia, I don't remember that you did any metalwork at school.'

'I was a bit too much of a swot in those days to be bothered with practical things,' I told him, a shade defiantly.

He knew I was not with Dewi. Not really.

'Aye. You were a clever one, Gwalia. That's for sure. But not so clever in other ways, eh?'

I stiffened. Dewi looked up sharply. And then stood up and placed himself in front of Myrfyn, resplendent in his uniform and festooned with paraphernalia and pockets – steel handcuffs, radio, riot stick and notebook.

Myrfyn grinned. He'd done well for a boy who'd stayed, not gone away. Better than either of us, you might say. He liked to rub that in.

'Haven't seen you at rugby practice lately, Dewi,' Myrfyn said.

Dewi's eyes dropped.

'No. I'm usually working.'

'Be careful then, the two of you,' he said, getting back into the car. 'Let me know if you see any vandals about, defacing Council property.'

And then he was gone.

'Do you think he'll report us?' Dewi asked.

'I shouldn't think so. He's not on the side of the English.'

'He's a funny one, though. He'll arrest you one day then expect to have a drink with you the next.'

'He's just doing his job, isn't he?'

'That's what he says.'

Good old Dewi.

How you must hate to see that name, Jon.

Dewi, the farmer's boy, big and strong. Handsome in that rugged sort of way that you distrust. I know you always saw him as a hard and ignorant lout. But I saw another side of him: behind that hard-set jaw and serious mouth, those dark eyes held a strength. A promise.

Some days, I could play him like a puppet.

Other days, it was hopeless.

I arrived in the kitchen to find Mam trying to persuade Awena to eat more.

Gethin had bolted his breakfast and pushed past me back upstairs.

'Don't forget your homework,' Dad called to him from behind his paper.

'I'm going to do it now, Dad. Duh!'

And Awena ran off after him.

Dad winked conspiratorially and I knew that he and Mam were squabbling and would now have to rehearse their ritual morning debate which (I now think) was purely for my benefit.

'I wish you wouldn't read that paper at the table, Artwr. You know I don't like you reading an English paper,' she complained. 'You should only read Welsh in front of the children.'

Dad sighed, and put *The Guardian* down: 'It's a shame that there is no comparable Welsh-language paper to read.'

'It skews your sympathies towards the English.'

'I have a duty to read it, Gwênfer. It's the accepted paper for teachers.'

'There! You see. That just goes to prove my point. Running Wales down as usual. Artwr, you're already subverted.'

He sighed and winked at me yet again. So I winked back, impatient to read the paper after him, but knowing there wasn't now time for even a quick flick through.

'You must have lots to do today,' Mam said to me, as I got out my cereal bowl. 'What with the man from Westminster coming and everything.' She spat the words *San Steffan* meaning Westminster.

'I have,' I answered brightly. 'First I'll open up Y Ddraig, then I'll air his room – the bed is made and it's all tidy.'

I counted off on my fingers the chores I had listed in my head.

'And then I'll wash the dragons.' (No one was quite sure which had come first, the hotel's name – Y Ddwy Ddraig – or the two concrete dragons, one painted red and the other white, which sat chest-high, wings back and tails curled, at either side of the entrance. What was important was to keep them clean so they could look English visitors in the eye when they arrived.)

'Then I have to organise Dewi to collect wood for the fire. Maybe I'll pick fresh flowers, too. I could pick them while Dewi gets the wood. Besides he'll take hours if I don't go with him.'

'You need to buy something for lunch and supper and breakfast.'

'I thought you wanted me to bring him here for supper – for you to spy on him.'

Mam laughed.

'I don't think Gwenlais was serious. But I suppose you could, if you wanted to. See what you think of him. You'll still need provisions for breakfast and snacks, though.'

The hotel had so very few people to stay, it made no sense to keep a larder, besides there was no electricity for refrigerators and it was only worth running the generators for those few hours a day when we knew the bar was going to be used.

Y Ddwy Ddraig was Dad's hotel (Mam tried to avoid it totally), passed on to him by his father, my Taid, himself a reluctant inheritor from his dad. Taid had long since retired and turned philosopher *dros dro*.

We had to keep Y Ddwy Ddraig open because the drinkers in the town had nowhere else. Not that everyone approved. Mam and Anti Gwenlais were not the only ones who had been brought up as teetotal Methodists. When they were young, the County of Migneint had been a 'dry area' with no pubs allowed to open on Sunday. Except that, as a hotel, Y Ddwy Ddraig was exempted – which infuriated people like Mam's family. Lemon suckers Taid calls them – *sugnwyr lemwn* – he says you can spot them by the way they hold their mouths.

By those days the place didn't bring in enough to even cover its costs. Certainly not to include redecoration or repairs. Dad himself had to earn our real living from being headmaster of the school. Fortunately for the town and all of us, teaching was his true vocation.

'I don't suppose your man from Westminster will stay, once he sees the place,' mother chirped, anticipating snags as usual. Visitors who booked enthusiastically by phone, delighted by its cheapness, quite often made excuses and left when they smelled the damp and saw the cold reality.

'Didn't the last couple leave complaining at being woken at dawn by birdsong?' she pointed out, gleefully, finding another snag. 'People these days are too soft. Always complaining about something. And sending busybodies in to sort things out. How long do you think he'll last, Gwalia, this man from Westminster?'

' Gwênfer! Leave her be, poor girl,' Dad said.

Mam looked at him and sniffed.

'He'll be gone in two days just like all the others,' she said. 'You mark my words now.'

'Doesn't matter,' I pointed out. 'He's pre-paid his room for the whole week.'

'Your Yncl Penhaearn'll soon see him off. He'll just refuse to speak English to him, I expect,' Mam said. 'And quite right, too.'

'How will we ever get things to improve?' I asked. 'If we refuse to let people help us?'

'We don't want their help. Not if they can't speak our language or respect our country.'

'I understand all that,' I said. 'And I do believe in it, I do. But the town is so run down. Couldn't we just take his help and then get rid of him?'

'That would be quite immoral,' Mam said.

'And hypocritical,' added Dad, without moving his *Guardian*.

'Quite right, Artwr. We cannot accept charity at the expense of our nationality!'

Some things they agreed on.

'So Penhaearn will refuse to speak anything but Welsh and

the visitor will speak none. And he will be sent away like all the others,' I recited.

'They should have learned by now to send only people who can speak our language then, shouldn't they?' Mam said brusquely.

I opened my mouth to argue but she looked at me sharply.

'If everyone in Wales believed in the importance of speaking Cymraeg as firmly as we do here, we would not be so much under the heel of the English as we are.'

'But . . .'

'Don't weaken now, Gwalia. I don't want you selling out like all those collaborators who do all the harm they do to our sense of nation.'

Mam smiled, confident she had won the argument. Proud to be the daughter of a great Welsh Nationalist.

'How do we know he doesn't speak Welsh?' Dad asked, just to prompt her to have the last word.

'Because they never do,' she said in a voice that made me shiver.

Gethin came back in.

'What don't they do?' he asked. 'Why are you arguing?'

'I was just saying that Wales needs a lot more men like your Yncl Penhaearn, if Cymru is ever to become an independent nation again with all of us speaking Cymraeg. You want that, don't you Gethin?'

He nodded. Dutifully mustering all the gravitas a fourteen-year-old can.

'Is it true, Mam, that Yncl Penhaearn is descended from Llywelyn the Great, the last real Prince of Wales?'

'Yes, Gethin, it is.'

'And am I related to the Welsh princes, too?'

'Of course you are,' she said, as she always did whenever he asked this question.

'Complete nonsense,' muttered Dad from behind the paper. 'You shouldn't be filling his head with such nonsense. All this stupid chasing after ghosts.

'We must rid this land of its demons, just as we must reconcile Cymru to the destiny which haunts us.'

'You don't really believe in ghosts, Mam, do you?' Gethin asked.

'We all have our demons, Gethin.' She looked at me. 'Your sister Gwalia, of all people, appreciates that.'

Dewi believed he had been in love with me for as long as either of us could remember. He believed we were destined for each other. 'Hand-picked we are, like a perfect breeding pair,' was how he put it. Most days I hoped we weren't, but we had known each other since forever, and we got along. He was waiting for me outside the front door of Y Ddwy Ddraig, overlooking the Maes, when I arrived to unlock.

And in his mind, the time for fulfilling our destiny was long overdue.

If it hadn't been for what had happened to me seven years before, I would probably have gone off to university like everyone else from school. All my classmates who weren't stupid (and many who were) had gone to Cardiff or Bangor or Aberystwyth, as every generation did, coming back only at Christmas and holidays, like previous years, first alone, then with boyfriends and girlfriends, and then, later, with children and tales of successful jobs in cities far away. There was no one eligible left for me but Dewi.

I might have convinced myself I was in love with him, but I had been stripped of my naivety. No one could love me now. Not with my mutilated nose and frozen emotions. Even Awena pulled away from me. She always pulled away from me. However much I tried to help her and to please her.

I needed somebody. Don't we all! So if Dewi believed he was in love with me, that was fine. It was handy to have someone prepared to do almost everything I asked. (Was that horrid of me, Jon?) And he accepted me the way I was, though I don't think he had any idea of how destroyed I felt.

Dewi could be jealous, sometimes, though, especially

when he thought other men were showing an interest, but he had a soft, gentle side. It was he who encouraged me to start playing the harp again. He used to take my hand and lead me into the cold, damp meetings room and pull the cover off the one that stood by the raised dais. I tried to tell him it was warped and out of tune, but I don't think he cared or noticed. He insisted that I play. I think he saw it as a kind of therapy. I still couldn't play for anyone else but I played for him. I think he took it as a sign of love.

Oh Bachgen! Poor Dewi. That was as far as I allowed our intimacy to go. For five years I had forbidden him from mentioning what he called 'our love' out loud. Even after he had the harp tuned for me for Diwrnod Santes Dwynwen. And I wouldn't even let him kiss me. I couldn't bear the idea. So instead, he wrote me poems. For someone who had been hopeless at school, he wrote very good poems. He had an ear for the strict Welsh patterns, cynghanedd and englyn.

I see now that I shouldn't have encouraged him. Letting him write me poems, and me playing him music and never letting him touch me, had turned what might have been a fleeting schoolboy crush into an obsession. Something that, for Dewi, was hugely romantic. Poetic. Tragic. Vast.

'Have you seen the Supermart today?'

'No.'

'Don't you think the Supermart manager is completely intolerable?'

'I haven't seen.'

I wasn't really interested in the Supermart. I was impatient for the drama to begin. The drama in which I was now determined I would have a part. Something that would wake me up and lift me out of myself once and for all.

'An enormous new set of posters and not one word of Welsh.'

I sighed.

'Sometimes, Dewi, you choke my brain with your questions.'

He thrust an envelope into my hand and waited for me to open it. It would be another of his poems about the wrinkles at the corners of my mouth, or the way I kept pushing my light-brown curls back behind my right ear. He had run out of things to say about my dark-blue eyes. The things you boys find interesting! Recently, he'd written very daringly, about the different ways that T-shirts hung on the curves of my breasts. And these last few weeks he had been staring so much at my bottom in my new black jeans that I had stopped wearing them. He never wrote poems about my mutilated nose.

I knew that he was wanting me to open it, hungry for me to be glowing with pleasure at his clever flattery. Instead I was impatient.

'Oh not another of your stupid poems, Dewi,' I said, and put it aside.

He grimaced, bit his lip, then picked it up and put it back in his pocket for later.

Dewi was not insensitive; on the contrary, he had an irritating habit of sometimes guessing my mood with disconcerting accuracy and then tactlessly commenting on it.

He composed himself and turned back to me, imperceptibly sadder. Why was I so mean to him? He took a deep breath.

'I expect it's a mood swing,' I told him curtly, quoting my doctor. 'Don't worry. I'm fine.'

And I turned my bright cheerful self back on, almost without thinking, by way of apology.

'Well, you don't seem to be taking much interest in this outrage against our language. Or anything else. You don't want to see English advertisements plastered all over the place, do you?'

'O Dewi, not now,' I scolded him. 'There's always some fuss or other about English notices or posters going up and disrespecting and undermining Welsh. I just want to use my language, not go looking for things to take offence at all the time.'

'I see.'

I sensed him flinch again as my impatience stung his eagerness for a second time. He was lucky, I told myself. He had those little hurts to tell him he was still alive. I envied him that. And the way he seemed to relish his own, exquisite, emotional martyrdom. I had had one big hurt that had deadened everything.

I knew he viewed the love between us as a kind of credit system. Every hurt I made him suffer, and every sacrifice he made, counted as another emotional credit to be repaid in the future with even more of my inevitable love. He believed he would be deluged with my love one day. I had this sense that he felt I owed him an enormous debt for every rejection, hurt and denial of our love.

What nonsense. If that was true, then what did the world owe me! People have some silly ideas, don't they, Jon? Especially boys.

'You know I have to be at the meeting this morning,' I told him brightly. 'And that we have this man from Westminster coming. So I want you to direct him if he comes when I'm not here.'

'Bastard. Coming here to destroy our town, our language.'

'He's not coming to destroy the language. He's coming to help us get mains electricity and water. If you had to do the washing and the cooking, you might think differently about it.'

'On their side now, are you?'

'I'm not on anybody's *side,* as you put it. There's no reason for a little modern technology to destroy us, that's all.'

'You're just quoting what your Dad says. It's your Mam you should be listening to.'

'I wish I'd never told you about my parents' little quarrels. I knew you couldn't understand the subtlety of Dad's arguments. If the English want to help us, why shouldn't we use that to make ourselves stronger?'

'What's so subtle to understand about that? You know,

Gwalia, one of these days you are going to need to make some real decisions.'

Real decisions! What *real* decisions did I *need* to make? I didn't *need* to do anything. I didn't *need* to tell him I'd assigned myself to spy on the man from Westminster. I certainly didn't *need* to make him jealous. *Start* making some *real* decisions indeed!

'You didn't used to care a jot about the importance of our threatened language, till you came to work here and I told you about it,' I reminded him.

'Well I do now. And about the importance of the language for Wales as a nation; for preserving its history, culture and identity.'

'That's just quoting Gwrthsafiad,' I taunted. 'Why don't you come up with your own ideas?'

'There's nothing wrong with Gwrthsafiad – Wales needs a resistance movement against the English occupation. Anyway, you're a member. Or had you forgotten last night?'

'Yes, but I don't swallow every syllable they utter without even thinking about it.' I recognised Dad's words coming out of my mouth.

It had been me that had introduced Dewi to Gwrth-safiad. They were harmless enough: pulling down English signs, graffiti-ing Welsh slogans around the place – 'Keep Wales Welsh', 'English out', 'Hold on to your land' and 'Remember Y Gelyn' – to remind people of their loyalties and the need for vigilance. But a new lad had taken control recently and he was rather too bossy and militaristic for my gentle tastes.

It was inevitable, I suppose, that Dewi would want to be a Gwrthsafiad hero.

After organising Dewi and giving him strict instructions about what to do if the man from Westminster came, I collected my spiral-bound notebook and walked across the Maes to the Town Hall. I had plenty of time. It was nice to dawdle and gossip.

My grandfather – Dai Call – was sitting with his two friends, Elwyn and Irfon, outside Caffi Cyfoes, sipping tea from their usual mugs. After lifetimes of sheep-farming, they preferred to be outside unless the rain and cold made it unfit even for farmers. The new wooden bench, left to the town the previous year by their late friend Jac, had been a splendid innovation.

'I see Jac's bench is coming in handy, Taid,' I said.

'No thanks to *your* Council,' said Taid mischievously. His wrinkled face and wry smile always lifted my spirits. 'Until we got Jac's bench we had to perch on those painful concrete barriers.' And Elwyn pantomime-pointed at the ugly concrete bollards outside the Town Hall.

I had heard this story so many times I knew the script by heart. But always it enspirited me (you remember that word, Jon, ysbrydoli?).

'Erected by *your* Town Council. And do you know why? To stop *your* councillors parking on the grass when they attend your meetings.'

'Not my Town Council,' I said. 'My role is purely administrative. I merely take notes for Islwyn. Out of the kindness of my heart.'

'Bollards. 'Rected at scandalous expense,' Irfon complained. 'Monuments to the vanity of councillors. Jac would have told you.'

They all nodded respectfully at the mention of Jac's name. And waited for Taid's comment. Taid – my father's father – was famous for his epithets.

'No one stupid enough to be a councillor could possibly be expected to have the intelligence to park properly,' he proclaimed. And they all chortled in an amused and knowing way, as only very old men – who have already learned much more than enough – can.

These old men stirred warmth into that great space where my love should have been.

This morning, there were two cars parked there already,

skewed inconsiderately sideways across the bays, taking up enough room for six parked properly.

'You're not late, are you?' Irfon asked, suddenly concerned and checking his pocket watch. But I knew the real reason he was checking the time.

I shook my head.

'Having a pre-meeting meeting, I expect. Some of them like to be early to get a good seat,' Elwyn said.

'Waiting for Boudiccea, are you?' I asked as innocently as I could.

They shifted uncomfortably, worried I might have glimpsed their old men's fantasies, which indeed I had.

'You can set your watch by Boudiccea's daily invasion,' Taid said. 'Almost to the second.'

And Irfon and Elwyn sniggered because they knew that no one for miles around cared a jot about good time keeping. Except for Boudiccea.

The three sipped from their mugs of tea and waited patiently – at their age, they were in no hurry for time to pass any more quickly than it already had.

'I hear there is to be an important meeting this morning,' Elwyn said.

'There is,' I assured them.

More councillors were already arriving.

I watched Councillor Penhaearn 'Tegid Foel' Jones, squeeze his empty hearse up past the concrete barrier and behind the designated parking bays. He wasn't actually wearing his undertaker's suit, but that didn't matter: whatever he wore, people somehow always pictured him in his mourning suit. And, today, despite the green trousers, and loud sports jacket, it was no different. He still looked like an undertaker.

Though he only washed and polished the hearse for funerals (washing it was part of the ritual of respect for the dear departed, and it was deemed to be tempting providence to wash and polish it when no corpse lay unburied in the llan), nevertheless, the hearse was always a slightly chilling sight in a town where we always drew our curtains when the cortège went by. Or perhaps I was just so conditioned to feeling a chill run down my spine when I saw him, it didn't matter whether there was a funeral or not.

'He wants all the advantages of wealth but none of the envy,' said Taid. 'Or he'd buy an ordinary car as well. He could certainly afford it.'

Elwyn nodded. 'That's how power and wealth corrupts you. In little vanities.'

My uncle, County Councillor Penhaearn Tegid Foel, got out of the corpseless hearse and smiled his terrible false-teeth smile (some said he had taken the teeth from Neli the opera singer when she died, but Mam and Anti Gwenlais denied this vehemently). The affable manner he adopted in his councillor mode always seemed ill-suited to his mournful face and cold, bleak eyes. He wrinkled his nose in distaste at having to negotiate a little honest mud, and then straightened his jumper, and turned his smile on us holding out his hand and reciting his litany of greetings.

'Sut dach chi?' He had a particular mannerism of rubbing his hands together when he was pleased with himself. And the more pleased he was, the harder he rubbed and the more long-faced he looked.

'Iawn, diolch,' they answered him suspiciously. I knew he would completely ignore me.

If you didn't know him as well as we all did, you might have thought that Yncl Penhaearn actually cared about more than himself and the ghosts that he believed haunted him.

The trio of old men watched suspiciously as he strode off and disappeared into the shabby Town Hall.

'He has better things to do than talk to joskins, wouldn't you say?' Elwyn remarked. And they giggled like naughty boys. Joskins was a rather disrespectful, old-fashioned term for farmers, putting one in mind of peasants, so offensive, in fact, that only joskins could use it.

'How does he maintain that air of superiority even while grovelling to us for our votes?' asked Elwyn. 'That is the question.'

'If we knew the answer to that, we would all have the same power he has,' said Taid, profoundly.

The door of the Caffi Cyfoes opened and Branwen, the waitress – who had been at school with me, and had been there on the night that caused me to be how I am – brought them out fresh mugs of tea. She gave me a smile and a nod and I acknowledged her with a wave. She always made me think of those horrible things, even though I had no one to blame for what had happened but myself.

'Paned arall, Dai Call?' she, asked brightly, enunciating the 'll' very clearly like a 'th' but through her side teeth, in that way the English find so hard to master.

My Taid and his friends gratefully exchanged their empty mugs for new ones. And then stood waiting.

Taid and Elwyn turned and stared at Irfon until he fished in his pocket for change.

You could see a lot from Jac's bench. It was an excellent vantage point, being half way up the long side of the triangular Maes. An excellent place for spying, an excellent vantage point, I noted, for an aspiring Mata Hari.

At the top of the Maes by Y Ddwy Ddraig, Dafydd Y Drol's two big shire horses grazed as usual. On the other side, you could see all the comings and goings in the shops – especially the Supermart which everyone complained about because it wasn't owned and run by Welsh people but which everybody used.

They especially complained about the garish English slogans. BUY! *This.* SAVE! *that.* SPECIAL OFFERS NOW ON!

But they always snapped these bargains up immediately, and then complained about the quality. If they did occasionally patronise the Welsh shops – the butcher's and the greengrocer's, the rather sad clothes shop where the window display always looked two generations out of date, or the shoe shop where you had to choose the style from a catalogue and wait for mail order – they then complained about the prices. That was the sugnwyr lemwn's way, you see.

This is my town, Jon. And then, as now, I know every face and every name and every story.

As usual on market day, the town was full of old Land Rovers – with sheep-trailers cluttering the road outside the Supermart. No one bothered to park properly. They just stopped and went in, and never mind what traffic jam they caused or who was waiting. And they didn't mind if they had a chat with someone else on the way out either.

The Mayor, Hiraethog Jones, arrived on foot, flustered, sweaty and confused as usual, his Mayoral Chain clanking awkwardly around his neck, one brass badge for each previous incumbent, most now dead and carted off in Penhaearn's hearse.

He waved awkwardly at us and then vanished into the Town Hall, looking very worried. Worried about what Penhaearn wanted him to say. Worried about whether he could do it. And worried about whether Penhaearn would lay him out nicely, when his time came, if he didn't.

I had no immediate desire to go and sit up there in the gloom of the Council Chamber listening to the small talk that was so familiar that I knew each person's interests and way of speaking off by heart. Besides, they usually said the same things in the same words about almost everything. So I dawdled.

Irfon reminded us all that Hiraethog was Penhaearn's trusty brother-in-law, married to Penhaearn's stepsister, Dwynwen. Did that make him some kind of yncl-in-law to me? Actually I think he was some kind of third cousin of my mother's anyway.

'I would not want to be Penhaearn's brother-in-law,' said Elwyn. 'Or married to Dwynwen. It would have been the death of me long ago.'

The trio paused for a moment, and raised and lowered their mugs in unison, silently imagining themselves married to Hiraethog's dear wife, Dwynwen.

'A formidable woman indeed,' said Irfon.

'I'll have you know that Dwynwen is a very important woman,' I said, in mock disgust, '*the* local reporter for the Welsh language radio and television stations – Radio Cymru and S4C.'

They were slopping their tea, in merriment now.

'You wait until we get electricity,' I said. 'You'll be able to see her every night on the television, then.'

'I'm not a one for television myself,' said Elwyn.

'Nor the radio,' said Irfon.

They kept glancing up across the wet slate rooftops and chimneys towards the long road that dropped down the side of the mountains into town. They were getting impatient for their first glimpse of Boudiccea whose appearance would tell us it was exactly four minutes to ten. I kept glancing in that direction too, but for a different reason.

All that was to be seen at the moment was a line of Land Rovers slowly wending their way down the hill.

If you watched a particular vehicle disappear behind the roofs and counted together – ten-and-twenty seconds... ten-and-two-and-twenty... ten-and-three-and-twenty... in the traditional Welsh way – you could bet on when it would reappear, and see who was right when it turned up into the town at the bottom of the Maes, where the road came out through a narrow gap between two stone built cottages, cottages so old their walls had started to lean together like old Welsh married couples.

This was a town built for slower, closer-together days. Not cars.

Taid and his old friends had played that counting game as pupils together in the red-bricked first school at the bottom of the Maes where Dad was now headmaster. And where I too had been a pupil once upon a time.

'How many seconds did you count when people drove sheep into town on foot?'

'We counted seven times twenty,' Elwyn said.

'Never!' said Irfon. 'One and a half hundred.'

Less speedy times.

I suppose I was thinking of old photographs and what seemed in many ways like better times: farmers with pipes and hats and flannel trousers, their clever sheep dogs – then as now – keeping track of every sheep in each flock and keeping the flocks separate but the sheep together.

DESPITE WHAT I'D BEEN TOLD about Freddy Morgan having chosen me for this project because – incomprehensibly – he had been impressed by my knowledge of Wales, I had a strong suspicion that I was being comprehensively banished to the provinces as punishment for my incompetence.

Professor Angela Lain expected her researchers not only to be smart but also completely professional. My little problem with nerves and forgetting my lines at the briefing meeting were a sign that I was still too green.

But how on earth could they expect me to be an expert on a country I'd never researched, and never even been to before?

Even in a think tank, not everything is logical.

Perhaps it is not surprising, then, how Wales turned out to be such an elusive place for me. And no part of it more so than your almost-secret, hidden-away town.

I found Llangollen, no problem, and even Cerrigydrudion, but then I found myself somewhere between Glasfryn and Cwm Penmachno, with a chorus of useless advice ringing in my head. And my objectives slipping through my fingers like sand through the waist of an hour glass.

Even with the entire wisdom and resources of the Leyburn Institute behind me, I missed the point. And kept missing it. I don't think my car helped either. The little red and black Smart car Mum and Dad had bought me for my twenty-first birthday was really cool in London. Out here, it seemed a little, well, gay, amongst the muddy Jeeps and Land Rovers and every other make of four-wheel drive.

I had been reduced to asking directions, not once but many times, showing people the route plan Nisha had printed out for me.

'Well, you see, these directions are only appropriate if you are travelling from Llangollen.'

'What you are looking for is not Umbo, as you English call it, but Llanchwaraetegdanygelyn, you see.'

What kind of a town is it where local people deny that it even exists?

'It's here,' I told them. 'It's on the map.'

'Well Umbo is. But Umbo isn't there, you see. 'Cos it's Llanchwaraetegdanygelyn you see.'

I didn't see.

I got someone to write it down. But then there was another snag. Pronouncing it.

Saying 'Lanch-war-a-teg-dance-gelyn' just made people laugh and snigger. In those days I had no idea how to hiss the 'll' sound through the sides of my teeth, or pronounce the 'ch' as in the Scottish 'lo**ch**'. And all that enunciation stuff.

'What I would do, if I was in your shoes would be to go back to Corwen and take the Bala road and then turn off to Trawsfynydd and come at it from that direction,' someone advised.

'But wouldn't it be better for him to carry on to Blaenau Ffestiniog and then come back over the Migneint through Cerrig y Foel-Gron?'

I had spent three days meticulously researching the problems of this town and preparing my presentation. It would be such a poor thing if I couldn't even find the place to deliver it. But I had my strategy.

Llanchwaraetegdanygelyn's problem, I had decided, was very simple. At least in theory. Your town, Gwalia, was merely the last town in Wales without mains electricity, water and sewerage. The reason: inaccessibility.

It was a purely practical problem. Obviously, the cost of laying pipes and cables was disproportionately too high (on a per household basis) for the local people to be able to afford it. (It was also in the National Park and an area of outstanding natural beauty so the pipes and cables would have to be hidden, adding hugely to the cost and making the various planning committees very nervous, (a) about spending the money, and (b) about spoiling the landscape.)

I was quite confident that, given my superior mental skills and theoretical knowledge, plus Government backing in the shape of Freddy Morgan's support, neither of these obstacles (from my theoretical position) would be insurmountable. So, obviously, I would be able to solve Freddy's little problem of potential Government embarrassment, and your town's lack of power, in just a couple of days.

There would be other, minor tactical problems, no doubt. There always were. One would probably be the community – I'd seen this sort of thing before – demotivation, interfactional disputes, people not wanting the pipes and cables going across their land – that sort of thing. And, almost certainly, this would be an impoverished, economically unsustainable community, with all the clever people gone and only the Luddites remaining. But all this could be sorted with a word to the wise and a public meeting, I felt sure.

You just have to explain the facts to people in words they understand and people always see sense in the end.

My Dad always laughed at me when I said that. But it was true. Most of the world's problems could be solved if you could straighten out people's thinking: stop them fighting over who was going to be in charge and get them to concentrate on working out solutions to their problems, what their priorities were and which was the best way of achieving them.

I believed in people and ideals – still do. But Dad was a bit of a cynic. Not nasty, just a businessman, that's all. He looked at everything through a capitalist's eyes: find out what people want, sell it to them, and get rich. And don't bother to try to do what's best for people, don't even assume you know. Mostly people actually don't want what's best for them and trying to give it to them is the way to poverty.

To me, idealism and education were the keys: if everyone in the world could be educated up to university level in social politics, there would be no wars. Guaranteed. The world was an improving place. We understood it, now, better than ever before. In universities and think tanks we had it within our grasp to solve all the problems of the world. It was just a matter of analysis and finding the solutions. Within my lifetime.

Like most young men, I was sure I was right.

In the meantime, the world needed people like me to be 'parachuted down' into places where local people couldn't yet work things out for themselves and help them sort it out. And people would be grateful.

But Dad would have been crowing with laughter if he could have seen me that morning! Mum, too, probably. I just couldn't find where I was supposed to be.

I could imagine them sitting in their penthouse flat, enjoying their fine coffee and croissants, glad to have me away for a week.

'How many more years are you going to expect to be living at home?' they often asked.

'Why can't you just find yourself a wife and be her responsibility. Or come into the family business and be like a normal son.'

Dad thought I was critical of him and his materialism and business mentality.

'And what is so wicked about making yourself rich out of property. Being a success should be something to be proud of.'

I was determined to show them. (Typical young man, you see.) Just as I was determined to show Freddy Morgan and Andrew and all my colleagues at the Leyburn Institute. One day they'd all understand. They'd have to respect me.

I wished they already understood. That they were already proud of me.

Then it popped up in my mind: did thinking about home mean I was homesick?

Of course not. But the hours were slipping away. I was already very late. And the Leyburn Institute did seem a long way away.

Why is it such a chore trying to make the world a better place?

Why are so many obstacles put in our way?

But I would succeed. I was determined.

I just needed to find Umbo or Llanchwaraetegdanygelyn – or whatever it was called.

I KNEW YOU would be lost, Jon, visitors always got lost in those days. It was part of our conspiracy. How were visitors to know, Jon, that our town is wrongly named on the map?

Umbo is merely the English version of 'Wmbo – what we say here for 'I don't know'.

Anti Gwenlais never tired of telling that story.

'Once upon a time the English mapmakers decided to make a map of the whole of their evil empire. They made maps of Africa and India, maps of Australia and Canada, and very soon the whole of the world was painted a horrible shade of pink, the chosen colour of the evil Empire.

'But when they looked at the map of the world, they found they had missed one place. And it was still white. And it was here, in Wales, right under their noses. So they urgently sent out their map-makers again. And told them to be sure not to make any mistakes this time.

'And so they came here, to the Migneint, the final unmapped corner of their god-forsaken Empire. "What's this place called?" They demanded.

'"Wmbo", the people shrugged, because, being Welsh speakers, nobody here could understand their foreign English tongue.

'"What's that you say?" The English mapmakers asked.

'"Wmbo", we told them. We don't know what you're saying. "Wmbo".

'"Oh Umbo," They said. "Umbo. Why didn't you say so in the first place?"'

So Umbo was the name that went down on the maps, Jon. Your maps, not ours. Llanchwaraetegdanygelyn remained our name for our town, the real name, the name we use. And, like every real place name here in Wales, it is fashioned out of our language, and has real meaning.

Anti Gwenlais put it more colourfully than I:

'And did you know that when the Celts first settled in Wales, Llanchwaraetegdanygelyn had a different spelling and therefore a different meaning – celyn, not gelyn – the same as the great Celyn mountain which towers over the town, meaning holly. So the name of the town would have been 'Land of fair play under the holly'.

'But, after our last great Welsh hero, Owain Glyndŵr, suffered his famous defeat at the hands of Henry IV in 1412, ending our hopes for independence, that last syllable was changed to Gelyn, changing the meaning from Land-of-fair-play-under-the-holly to Land-of-fair-play-under-the-enemy.

'Never forget now that Owain Glyndŵr's poor body was never found. He and his army went to hide with the remnants of Llywelyn's army in some secret valley, deep in the mountains, waiting for the time to be right to re-emerge.'

'Do you really believe all that, Anti Gwenlais?'

'Oh yes, Gwalia. Indeed we do. And not only that. Your Yncl Penhaearn and I are certain that Llanchwaraetegdanygelyn is that place. Why else would we have kept ourselves to ourselves for so many centuries? And kept these stories alive?'

I had been waiting on the Maes with my Taid and his pals for Anti Gwenlais to reappear and now she did, sniffing the air for gossip, striding across the rough-mown grass towards us.

'Bore da, Gwenlais. Sut dach chi?' they said.

'Bore da. Iawn, diolch. Sut dach chi.' She patted me on the arm. Despite the disagreement in our kitchen earlier, she was still convinced that I would be her ally. I knew that she expected loyalty whatever was said indoors – and that family loyalty in Wales was matriarchal.

'Will you be opening Y Fferyllfa before the meeting?' Elwyn asked, knowing the answer full well. Y Fferyllfa, her chemist's shop, was beside the Supermart across the Maes, next to the struggling butcher's shop which opened only for a few hours a day and in the same terrace as the greengrocer's with wilted rhubarb that draped over your hand when you picked it up and the bare-windowed charity shop that always looked badly in need of charity itself. The only lively shop was the hippy shop, run by the runaway lesbians.

'Indeed I am. That's why I'm hurrying. I have a responsibility. People must have their prescriptions. If I failed to open – for any reason – I am sure Mrs Driply would be the first to complain. She's bound to be needing fresh supplies of Senna pods after the weekend. Not that anything can even begin to cure what's wrong with her.'

I tried to move away. You had to choose your moment carefully to escape from Anti Gwenlais. She wasn't an easy speaker to escape.

'I don't know why it is always the English who are so demanding?' she went on. 'Take that Mrs Leakin, for example – Boudiccea, as she insists on being called – ointment for chapped thighs if you please. And pessaries, too. Well!'

I didn't know what pessaries were. But I did know better than to ask.

'Why can't the English just be ill quietly, like the Welsh, instead of demanding perfect health, as if it was their god-given right! They are spoiled their whole lives, it seems to me. They drink and fornicate their bodies to ruin. And then still expect to have the bodies of twenty-year-olds.'

'I expect you'll be late for the meeting if we don't let you go,' Taid said.

I knew that now she was going to tell me that she only needed to open the chemist's then close it again. And how, when she was a child Y Fferyllfa had stayed open all day and every day, except for Sundays and Wednesday afternoons.

'Oh. No rush. I just need to open and put the 'Closed: back in two hours' sign on the door. It's not like it was in my father's day. We were a full-time chemist's then, remember. Before everyone had cars and took their money and prescriptions elsewhere.'

Never qualified herself, she was allowed to open the modest prescription cupboard only twice a week for just three hours, when the visiting pharmacist came. But she liked to appear busy.

'Prescriptions are available from the Doctor's anyway,' I said.

'Well. I do my best, don't I? It's very difficult to please people. They complain when I don't stock particular items, and then don't buy them when I do. I expect you find the same kind of thing in Y Ddwy Ddraig. People are never satisfied, are they? Especially the English.'

Taid tried again to prompt her into going.

'It is very fortunate for you that your opening times fit so neatly around your civic responsibilities. It must be very demanding being on every committee in the town,' he said.

'How perceptive you are, for a man. People don't always appreciate that.'

'Perhaps you should be honoured with an official title,' Elwyn suggested mischievously.

'Oh, good heavens no. I'm more of a behind-the-scenes sort of person. My written Welsh is non-existent. I'm of that generation as was discouraged from learning Welsh at school. I can only read and write in English, though I have never had need of it, mind.'

Now the Welsh Not story would be coming.

'You can't imagine how it was, Gwalia. But these gentlemen can. In our schooldays pupils were forced to wear a notice saying Welsh Not in the playground if they were caught talking Welsh, weren't they not?'

The three nodded, trying to work out if Gwenlais was actually old enough to remember that.

'Yes. And the last child of the day wearing the notice would be beaten,' said Irfon.

'An encouragement to sneak on each other, you see,' said Gwenlais. 'That is the way the English mind thinks. And that is how Welsh people came to think, too, if they think in English. But we didn't, of course, we always thought in Cymraeg. And boys like your Taid were man enough to take it in turns to be beaten at the end of the day. You don't see that kind of bravery these days.'

Out of the corner of her eye, I spotted a customer lurking outside Y Fferyllfa.

'I think you might have a customer,' I prompted, 'hadn't you better . . .'

'Oh yes. Norman deLuge. Another regular. From London.'

Norman had bought the old toilet block down by the river and converted it into a second home.

'I don't approve of the English having second homes in Wales,' Gwenlais started again. And we gleefully composed our faces to listen to another homily.

'I believe it was quite a coup for Penhaearn the day the Council sold it,' Elwyn prompted.

'And I agreed with him,' said Gwenlais. 'I said to the Council, I said: "Toilet facilities attract the English tourists like flies. There must be something the matter with them." He agreed to renovate the building at his own expense without applying for any kind of grant. He even asked if he could call it by a Welsh name – Yr Hen Gotej – another mark in his favour. He was very eager as I remember.'

'Yes,' I agreed. Anti Gwenlais could be surprisingly ignorant, even for a spinster.

'Personally, I still don't understand why he'd kept the two entrances and the signs Dynion and Merched.'

'I expect he had his reasons.'

Norman had spotted us now and was coming across in his tight jeans and pink polo-neck jumper. He was trim for a man of sixty. But there was something about his walk that wasn't masculine.

'I have to say his parties are not entirely in keeping. Do you know, sometimes I've seen them popping in and out of the Merched entrance again and again in a ridiculously childish manner?'

'Bore da, Gwenlais, Sweetie,' Norman beamed at Gwenlais. He spoke a smattering of Welsh with a posh English accent. 'Ti'n edrych yn absolutely gorgeous this morning, cariad. And what a darling hat. All that exciting fur.'

It was amusing to see Anti Gwenlais flush.

'Bore da, Norman. I'm coming now.' Gwenlais rummaged

in her bag. 'Just looking for my keys. I expect you'll be wanting more of the ribbed condoms,' she said.

'You know my innermost secrets, Sweetie,' he said and winked at me. 'I need a pack of twenty at least. Tell you what. I'll pop back after I've been for my paper.'

He gave us a little wave and tripped away, swinging his hips, just a little.

'You certainly know your customers,' I said.

Anti Gwenlais touched me on the arm.

'Well, being a dealer in surgical appliances does give me a certain expertise in delicate matters, I must confess.' She pursed her spinster's lips. Then she frowned.

'But now I come to think of it. I've never actually seen him with a woman.'

She looked at her watch.

'Wicked girl, keeping me talking like this when I should be working. I'll be late for the meeting. Shame on you, Gwalia.'

And with that she marched off to Y Fferyllfa.

In a quarter of an hour, she would arrive at the meeting, late as usual, leaving her famous notice, BACK IN TWO HOURS on the door.

WEDI CAU
YN ÔL MEWN DWY AWR

The trouble was. She never said what time she'd put it there.

I waited as long as I could for you to arrive, Jon. Finally, I could wait no longer so went up to the Council Chamber where the entire Council was waiting in that bored but anxious way that people who are waiting for something important often have.

Hiraethog was sweating visibly, squirming in the huge Mayoral Chair of dark carved oak. The May sunshine was projecting the reds and greens of the dragon from the stained-glass window, through his thin hair, onto his moist scalp. Penhaearn sitting next to him, sat cool as a gravestone. Every so often Hiraethog would lean forward to whisper to him. And everyone else leaned forward to hear, pretending not to.

To me, a simple chapel girl, the whole room was as uncomfortable as an English church, too strange and echoing, making everyone cold and formal, not cosy and personal as a chapel gathering would be.

'I've never met a man from Westminster before,' Hiraethog whined. He was a large, outdoor man, ill-fitted to the Mayoral Chair and only there because his wife and brother-in-law had forced him into it. 'To be totally honest with you, Penhaearn, I'm a little nervous.'

Penhaearn ignored him as long as he could.

'To tell the truth,' Hiraethog said, 'I'm very concerned indeed.' His voice went up at the end of sentences, tipping into falsetto.

'All you have to remember, my dear brother-in-law,' Penhaearn told him finally, as if talking to a child, 'is to smile, and nod, and agree with everything I say.'

Hiraethog smiled. And nodded. And agreed. 'Yn union!'

'Don't worry,' Penhaearn commanded. 'I've got a secret plan.' He looked around the room and winked. 'We can turn round any decision made here today at the County Planning meeting tomorrow. So we can agree to anything we like with the man from Westminster today and then change our minds back again tomorrow.'

Penhaearn rubbed his hands together. He was very pleased with himself.

'I'm sorry. I'm very stupid, I acknowledge that,' Hiraethog said, his voice rising. 'But I like things tidy. You want me to vote for this plan, even though we are against it? Is that right? And what will people think of me when they read the minutes?'

Penhaearn sighed. And gazed into the infinity of the Council Chamber for a long moment before refocusing and trying again.

'You want to keep our Council charges down, don't you? And you don't want all the men employed in running our generators, and bringing in our water and transporting our sewage to be put out of work, do you?'

Hiraethog nodded and shook his head and groaned and clutched at the Mayoral Chain around his neck as if it was strangling him.

'Well, that is the level of responsibility you have on your Mayoral shoulders, Hiraethog. I'm relying on you. As Mayor and brother-in-law.'

'I do see. Honestly I do. It's just I'm not as clever as all of you. I find these things very confusing, you see. The whole town owes such a debt of gratitude to you, Penhaearn, for your cleverness. And I hope I don't have to say the opposite of what I really mean to express that to you.'

Penhaearn smiled at him indulgently. Hiraethog subsided into silence, fermenting his next little worry.

'What if he asks me to say something?' he expostulated.

Penhaearn patted him on the back.

'Leave the talking to me. You just do the formalities.'

Hiraethog nodded, miserably, his worries bubbling up like indigestion in his brain.

'Where's Boudiccea and Blodeuwedd?' He demanded. 'They haven't yet arrived either. But they were invited, weren't they?'

He looked at Islwyn.

Islwyn looked at the minutes. And then at me.

I pointed out the item he was looking for.

'They were indeed invited,' he announced. 'I sent the invitations out myself.' He knew full well that I had done it.

'You do think it is all right for Boudiccea to come to a Council Meeting?' Hiraethog asked. 'Considering The Facts.'

We were all well acquainted with The Facts. Victoria Leakin – Boudiccea – wasn't Welsh and didn't speak Welsh, though she was trying very hard to learn.

When she had arrived in Llanchwaraetegdanygelyn with big plans, five years before, she had been politely informed by Penhaearn that Council meetings took place only through the medium of Welsh, that no minutes could be provided in English. So being a Council member was obviously impossible.

Victoria Leakin had taken this all in her stride. As a seasoned community worker from London, she had simply smiled sweetly and enrolled herself in Welsh lessons.

Then she had called a series of public meetings. Then she had formed a community group.

Her titles for the meetings were particularly apt. *Lifting Umbo Out of the Dark Ages* was one, *Bringing Power to the Valley* was another.

So adept was she at persuading important speakers from the Welsh Assembly and important organisations to come, that she startled Penhaearn. If he didn't control her, the town would attract so much attention, it wouldn't be so much of a secret anymore.

In no time at all, it seemed, she had bypassed the Town Council and formed her own Town Development Group, called Antur Deg, and had even forced Penhaearn and Hiraethog to join it too. Her arguments for bringing mains water and electricity to Llanchwaraetegdanygelyn were very persuasive. Many people believed them. I did myself when I was talking to Dad, though not when I was talking to Mam or Anti Gwenlais.

Mam and Anti Gwenlais insisted Boudiccea would destroy our way of life and our language. Once our town became not secret anymore, all meaning and purpose would be gone.

'We are the soul of Wales. If we lose our identity as the last unspoiled Welsh town, then Wales itself will wither away and die,' Anti Gwenlais said one day, her voice shaking with emotion. 'Penhaearn told me.'

Anti Gwenlais had repeated those words to everyone. They were burned in our collective consciousness: 'If we lose our identity, Wales itself will wither away and die.'

They certainly appeared to be burned on Hiraethog's consciousness, though it was said that he would nod and agree with anyone who told him anything. Now, though, it was clear that the pressure was getting to him and the bubbles of intellectual indigestion in his head were becoming quite uncomfortable.

'I don't know why we ever let that Boudiccea take over the town development group,' he wailed. 'If we don't want mains electricity or water here, we should have stopped her at the outset. Now she's bringing in the Enemy.'

'Penhaearn should have buried her,' muttered some wag. And everybody laughed. Except Hiraethog who found it difficult to keep all the facts about Penhaearn in his head at the same time: brother-in-law, funeral director, County Councillor, ghost hunter.

'I don't get the joke,' he bleated. 'Really I don't.'

'Well, Boudiccea is married to Lawns, Penhaearn's business partner.'

'Yes, I know that,' said Hiraethog, miserably.

'Undertakers? Buried her? It's a joke, Hiraethog.'

Hiraethog shook his head. Then nodded. And brightened.

'You mean because Penhaearn buries people?'

'The body goes down. And the spirit comes up,' Penhaearn said, rubbing his hands together gleefully. 'I might have to bury you one day, Hiraethog.'

'I'm sorry,' said Hiraethog, looking very worried.

'Where has this wretched man from Westminster got to?' Penhaearn demanded. Then he spotted me and had an idea. 'Has he checked into Y Ddwy Ddraig yet?'

'He hadn't when I left,' I said. I could feel myself flushing. I had never been addressed directly at a meeting before.

'What if he's waiting at reception? You'd be holding up everything.'

'Dewi will be there,' I explained nervously.

Penhaearn's answer chilled me. 'Dewi!' he said, his voice like a bell tolling. 'Dewi! Do you think that's wise?'

'Do you want me to go and check?' I asked, aware of every eye in the Council Chamber on me and hating it.

'The false smile reappeared on Penhaearn's face. His voice warmed slightly.

'I think you should, don't you?'

Glad to escape that stifling room for the sky and a feeling of freedom, I hurried out to the Maes.

By now, Jon, you were already more than an hour late.

Back outside, Taid and his friends were still rueing the state of the world and the town so I could tell at a glance you hadn't yet arrived. There was no unfamiliar car on the green and certainly not outside Y Ddwy Ddraig.

'Hardly a shop left on the East side of the Maes, the whole terrace is empty now.'

'All of the banks have shut. And all of the offices. It used to be such a prosperous town fifty years ago.'

'Nor do you see door-to-door salesmen any more. The cheery insurance man, the smelly fish man or the library van.'

'Everyone goes off in their cars to the big towns now.'

'There's not a word of Welsh on any of those notices on that so-called Supermart. And this a Welsh-speaking town.' Elwyn moaned.

They watched a huge, fume-belching timber lorry advancing down the road from the top of the Maes, coming from the forestry plantations up the valley, a copy of *The Daily Sport* prominently displayed on the dashboard. The load reached up to the first floor windows of Y Ddwy Ddraig.

The airbrakes hissed and the driver hooted impatiently as it approached the clutter of stationary cars and sheep trailers outside the Supermart. I spotted Garmon Drefnus, bless him, directing the traffic in his grandfather's nineteen twenties policeman's uniform, as he was wont to do on what was still called Market Day though it was only a shadow now of what it had once been.

Anti Gwenlais always insisted that Garmon's lager can contained only orange juice 'because he prefers to be thought drunk than stupid'. I'm not so sure.

'These youngsters just stop and park anywhere. Not a thought for anyone but themselves,' Elwyn said. 'It's a good thing Garmon Drefnus is on hand.'

There was another hiss of airbrakes as the lorry juddered forward. Garmon Drefnus, can of lager in his hand, stepped in front of the monstrous vehicle.

I couldn't catch the words, but we saw the lorry driver open his cab door, lean out and shout at poor Garmon. He was a big man with a huge belly; almost bursting his dirty white T-shirt, he was. English, obviously. He brandished his rolled up *Daily Sport* threateningly.

I could imagine what he shouted, though I was too far away to hear the words.

Garmon clowned as usual, cupping his hand to his ear, shaking his head and shrugging. Whatever the lorry driver was saying, Garmon didn't understand. Why would he? He had only ever spoken Welsh.

The driver carried on shouting, waving his rolled-up newspaper, and shaking his fist, showing off his tattooed arms.

Garmon pointed at the blockage in the road behind him, Two farmers, the Maes yr Eirin brothers, had stopped their Land Rovers and were chatting to each other across their bonnets just outside the newsagent's – which was why poor Garmon had stopped the lorry in the first place.

Gareth Maes yr Eirin acknowledged the lorry driver with a cheeky wave and pantomimed hurry as he ambled over to the newsagent.

The lorry driver clambered down and walked toward Gareth's brother, Llyr, shouting again. Garmon blocked his way. The driver shouted something else. And then Garmon took out his whistle and blew it.

I saw the lorry driver raise his paper and hit poor Garmon Drefnus across the shoulders. Despite the lightness of the blow, Garmon, being Garmon, was knocked off balance, and fell, flailing like a wounded cranefly.

My hand went to my mouth. Oh Garmon! Druan bach!

I started to run across the Maes towards him. But then I stopped and caught my breath as I realised I had felt something. A spontaneous emotion for someone else. For the first time since my trauma, I had felt something more strongly than my own familiar ache, that dull emotional pain that hung like an autumn mist over my heart and mind. I had felt sympathy for Garmon. Poor Garmon! I could feel it when I said those words! I looked again. I could sympathise with the Maes yr Eirin brothers. I could even identify, in some perverse way, with the frustration of the lorry driver!

What a place the world suddenly was.

Perhaps my heart was not so completely perma-frozen after all!

I watched my whole small world unfolding, powerless as a dumb spectator, understanding everything. Tears in my eyes. A lump in my throat. Able to do nothing.

The cold Council Chamber. My own bedroom. Rooms and houses to shut in lonely days. The greed of oversized lorries rowdying up our tranquil town. Men pitted against men. All of us with our own hurts and reasons. Not even trying to understand each other.

Sympathy and frustration!

Typical emotions, I suppose, of someone growing up.

I saw Llyr shouting and running across to confront the lorry driver, shouting at him in Welsh and jabbing with his finger on the man's fat belly.

Then Garmon struggled to get up and was reaching into his pocket for something.

At that moment I too hated these lorry drivers, and saw all too well that Llyr and Gareth had more reason than most to resent them. Hillsides which had been summer pastures when Taid was young were now covered in regimented lines of poisonous fir trees. The brothers' home farm – Maes yr Eirin – had been marooned in the middle of them. Mile upon mile of spookily-silent forests, carpets of dead needles where nothing else lived.

The two men now were facing up to each other.

Garmon Drefnus had struggled to his feet and was trying to separate them, hitting the lorry driver with his truncheon and blowing on his grandfather's whistle plaintively.

I saw the lorry driver grab Garmon's arm and push him into Llyr sending them both sprawling.

I heard an old woman's scream coming from outside the Supermart. Several people were running towards the melée.

The door of the Mind Body Spirit shop opened and out came Billi-Jo and Jean, the Leicester housewives who had famously fallen in love with each other and run away, leaving their husbands behind and ending up here. (How Anti Gwenlais loved that story!)

Seeing the approaching mob, the lorry driver turned belly away and lumbered off.

In a few urgent strides, he had reached his lorry and clambered back up into the cab. There was a hiss of airbrakes and a belch of diesel. He sounded his two-tone horn and jerked the truck forward, forcing the small crowd to scatter.

There were shouts and offensive gestures as the great articulated truck with its load of a hundred Welsh trees grumbled towards the clutter of cars and people. Then, with an ominous rev of the engine, he swerved angrily off the road and onto the grass of the Maes to get around the clutter of cars and people, gouging the grass and sending up a spray of mud before swerving back onto the road, sounding his horn contemptuously as the huge lorry scraped through the narrow gap between the houses at the bottom of the Maes.

'Look at that – driving over the Maes!' groaned Elwyn, behind me. 'Someone will be killed by one of those lorries one day, you mark my words.'

'It's wicked the way they've scraped the stonework on those houses,' said Irfon.

They were counting silently but with lips moving as they stared at the point above the wet slate rooftops where the lorry would reappear.

Twenty-five seconds. Much too fast.

They followed it accusingly with their eyes, as it chugged up the steep hill along the oak and silver birch-lined road.

Then Elwyn spotted her.

'Look there! She's like the flash of a kingfisher flying low along a wooded river at dawn.' He rolled his Rs and rounded his vowels. Elwyn was the poetic one.

Boudiccea hurtled down the hill in her blue and green Lycra cycling outfit and red helmet.

My newly liberated heart sang melodies for them, as they gazed in rapture to see their vision of divinity flash past the timber lorry, weaving dangerously between the old pick-ups and Land Rovers with their trailers coming to market, surging down the hill, going twice the speed of sheep trailers, and then disappearing behind the shiny wet rooftops.

Again their lips moved as they counted. They got to only two-nines before she flashed out from between the rough-stone houses into the Maes, her nearside pedal grazing the tarmac as she swooped around the corner.

This was the spectacle they were waiting for!

Boudiccea hurtled up the far side of the Maes, a vision of womanhood from a different world.

'A magnificent sight,' Taid said. 'Look at her in her blue and green skin.'

To these dear old men, I have no doubt, Boudiccea might as well have been naked. To them she was a goddess, mounted on a silver tandem with twenty-three gears, locks of her ginger-blonde hair billowing out from under her red safety helmet and out behind her, every curve of her ample and mature body stretched out triumphantly in sports position, the rear seat vacant; a shockingly erotic sight for chapel folk.

'There is no doubt Boudiccea is a very fine figure of a woman,' said Elwyn trying to appear unexcited while at the same time goading his friends into admitting that they felt the same erotic glowing of their sexual embers as he did.

They pursed their lips and strained their eyes and

wrinkled their faces, but they were concentrating far too hard to respond, intent on memorising this vision in considerable detail.

Still travelling at about thirty miles an hour, Boudiccea sped past the Supermart and shops on the far side of the triangular Maes, swerved perilously around the clutter of cars, decrepit Land Rovers and sheep trailers waiting to turn at the Post Office, and then, still at breakneck speed, she leaned over, almost flat to the ground, and with her blue-clad thigh almost brushing the grass, rounded the top of the Maes opposite Y Ddwy Ddraig, and came juddering onto the slate cobbles of the old road on the side of the green where the three philosophers could ponder her mysteries more closely.

Juddering down the cobbles, Boudiccea slowed, but only slightly. And then, as she bounced towards them, Taid, Irfon and Elwyn rose painfully to their feet despite their arthritis, and held up their now-empty mugs of tea in salute and welcome.

Elwyn managed a wolf-whistle, and then looked guiltily towards the Supermart in case his wife was watching. Boudiccea playfully rang her bell and came skidding to a halt in front of them and dismounted as they watched her prop her tandem against the wall, remove her helmet and let the rest of her ginger, golden hair cascade around her face.

Of all the women in the world, she alone could make them forget for minutes at a time that they were old.

'Bore da, boys,' she flirted. And then, with a huge smile, she disappeared through the big oak door.

I ran across to Y Ddwy Ddraig just to be able to say that I had thoroughly checked that you hadn't arrived. And then ran back to the Town Hall. And still got back to the Council Chamber before Boudiccea arrived.

She'd had to climb up to the tiny Antur Deg office in the attic, to pick up her part-time officer, Blodeuwedd. And tell her what to say and how to say it. Blodeuwedd is a name which should conjure up a mythical girl made of flowers but, in this particular instance, the name denoted only a moody teenager with spiky gelled hair and boots. Another of Penhaearn's nieces, and cousin of mine. (We all have many cousins in Llanchwaraetegdanygelyn.) But employing Blodeuwedd was another reason why Uncle Penhaearn had generously permitted Victoria Leakin to take these liberties.

I went back to my seat at the big round table and sat down.

We all waited.

Hiraethog heard the footsteps on the stairs before anyone else. He stood up abruptly and adjusted his chain.

'That'll be him now, I'm sure. Is everybody ready?'

The door swung open and Anti Gwenlais bustled in, clucking, like one of the panicky hens my Nain kept in her back yard.

Hiraethog sat back down.

'You'll never imagine what has happened,' Anti Gwenlais clucked, dumping her smelly leather handbag down just beside me.

'Garmon Drefnus has just been assaulted by a lorry driver with a crow-bar. He's been rushed to the surgery. It's a disgrace.'

'O'r Nefoedd!' yodelled Hiraethog, jangling to his feet again. 'We must *do* something.'

'Hold yourself together, boy,' Penhaearn hissed in a very loud whisper at his shoulder and turned to Gwenlais.

'What *exactly* happened, Gwenlais?'

The faces swivelled between Hiraethog, Penhaearn and Gwenlais, expectantly.

'One of the timber lorries. The driver got out and hit him. It's terrible.'

It was at this moment that the doctor arrived.

'Sorry I'm late,' he said. 'Have I missed anything?'

Now the faces swivelled to him.

Gwenlais was still hovering over where I sat.

'Oh doctor! Thank God you're here. We've been so concerned. How is the patient?'

'What patient?'

'Well Garmon, of course.' She was beaming quite inappropriately.

The doctor stiffened slightly. 'I can't really discuss a patient's . . .'

'But I'm a pharmacist,' she said, which wasn't strictly true, of course. But then nothing Anti Gwenlais said was ever *strictly* true.

'We just want to know he's all right. We heard he had been attacked with a crow-bar,' Hiraethog said. His voice was pleading; he sounded genuinely concerned, I thought.

'Yes, yes indeed,' said Anti Gwenlais, pecking furiously at the air.

The faces leaned forward.

The doctor laughed.

'Is that what you heard?' he chuckled. 'A crow-bar?'

'Yes,' said Hiraethog, looking to Anti Gwenlais for confirmation. She nodded encouragingly, so he carried on: 'I expect it was a very vicious attack, by the sound of it. Life-threatening, I'm sure. As if poor Garmon's unfortunate mother has not got enough on her plate already.'

'Well the weavers of yarns have been especially busy this morning then, I should say,' the doctor chuckled.

'Tell us, tell us, doctor,' Anti Gwenlais clucked.

'I think he will live,' said the doctor. Then he relented. 'I suppose there's no harm in my telling you. My understanding is that he got a little over-excited after being lightly struck on the shoulders with a copy of *The Daily Sport*.'

The observers relaxed and sat back in their chairs. Disappointed.

Penhaearn chuckled, then looked at Hiraethog and shook his head as if to say: 'What am I going to do with you?' And sat down.

Hiraethog sat down, too, and glanced around. Even he thought that he was stupid.

Now the pace of parochial politics started to heat up. Boudiccea came storming breathlessly in, a vision in Lycra and perspiration, Blodeuwedd in tow, each carrying large document cases.

'Bore da, bawb.' She almost sang the words. Blodeuwedd, squinted, looking especially truculent.

'Right. Where are we supposed to be sitting then?' Boudiccea demanded in English.

Penhaearn scowled at her use of the enemy tongue in this hallowed place and nodded disapprovingly at two vacant chairs. Boudiccea dragged Blodeuwedd across to them and heaved her heavy document case onto the table, beaming. Here she was, at an official Council Meeting, for the first time. She had finally got in, albeit by special invitation, and only for an extraordinary meeting.

Once she had sat Blodeuwedd down, she moved around the table to where Penhaearn and Hiraethog were sitting.

'I think it is needed being that I should insert myself here,' she said in Welsh.

'There's no room,' Hiraethog blurted, wrestling between the embarrassment of being rude and the desire to please Penhaearn.

Penhaearn stood up and thrust his hand out.

'Oh I think we can fit another chair in for Mrs Leakin,' he oozed, and offered her his own chair. Then stared meaningfully at Hiraethog.

Hiraethog, wrong-footed again, stood up to relinquish the Mayoral Chair to his brother-in-law, and then stood lost for a few moments while Penhaearn motioned everyone to shuffle along.

So Boudiccea finally took her seat at the head of the table (if there can be a head to a table that is round) and beamed roundly at everyone.

Meanwhile, Anti Gwenlais was loudly swapping scandal with Islwyn, the Clerk and notorious womaniser in his day, a man she always seemed to find intriguing. Twice now he had invited me up to the Council Chamber at strange times of day on the pretext of discussing the minutes and familiarising me with the old ledgers. Each time I had successfully dodged his wandering hands.

Like Islwyn, most of the councillors were barely literate in Welsh, victims of that education system which had tried to drive out the Welsh language in a generation. Sometimes I got tired of being told how lucky I was to be able to learn entirely through the medium of my mother tongue – fy mamiaith.

And still we waited.

After another twenty minutes, people started disappearing, sometimes for minutes on end, and then coming back and whispering to each other. After forty minutes, even Hiraethog had noticed, but obviously didn't like to ask. Now that he wasn't sitting in the Mayoral Chair, he wasn't sure whether he or Penhaearn – or Boudiccea – was chairing the meeting.

Eventually, my Anti Gwenlais could contain herself no longer.

'Briallen has just told me that her son-in-law at the garage at Betws-y-Coed was stopped by a young gentleman – definitely not local – driving towards Maentwrog at nine-thirty, asking the way to Umbo if you please,' she crowed.

Which prompted Alun Jones Tŷ Popty to report that his daughter, who worked in the bank in Dolgellau, had helped a young man asking for directions at nine-fifty.

'Westminster was mentioned.'

So he was a *young* man!

Murmurings around the Council Chamber became a clamour.

Islwyn Gwallt Coch announced that he had better go to the kiosk on the Maes to phone his son in the heddlu – the police. We all waited expectantly.

A few moments later he hurried back, quite breathless.

Yes, a young man had been seen all over North Wales that morning. And yes, he was looking for Umbo. In fact, the desk sergeant was running a sweepstake on whether he would find it.

'My son has a tenner on it that he will. So I have to let him know when he arrives,' he declared.

Boudiccea had clearly been struggling to follow the conversation but must have picked up the words heddlu, 'video camera' and 'Colwyn Bay'. So she had jumped to the conclusion he'd been arrested.

'We must be running at the police to freedomise him and exhibit his circumstances,' she proclaimed, in not-quite Welsh.

Hiraethog looked at Penhaearn in utter bafflement.

'Perhaps you should go and phone the place yourself to ask where this young man is now,' suggested Penhaearn Tegid Foel, coldly.

'But I would have to leave the meeting to do that,' pointed out Hiraethog anxiously, even more unsure of his position. 'And I can't do that until I declare the meeting closed. I am the Mayor, you know.'

'Then declare the meeting closed for God's sake,' shrilled Boudiccea in frustration, in English.

This use of English caused a terrible silence to fall on the Council members and their sagacious Clerk. They all looked at her, accusingly.

'Mae'n ddrwg gen i,' she said. 'Euog ydw i. Rhaid i mi siarad Cymraeg. Dw i'n gwybod. I must speak Welsh, I know.'

'The trouble is,' said Hiraethog, scratching his head. 'If I close the meeting to go to the phone, there will be no meeting to come back to in order to report what I find.'

Penhaearn stared at him, icily. 'Then *adjourn* the meeting.'

They all perked up then, nodding and smiling.

'This is why County Councillor Penhaearn Tegid Foel Jones carries the authority he does,' Islwyn said. 'A wonderful head for procedure.'

Hiraethog nervously adjourned the meeting for half an hour.

I arrived back at the Two Dragons Hotel to find Dewi stacking glasses in the bar.

'Gwalia!' he said. 'Did you hear what happened to Garmon? In hospital. Beaten up this morning by a Sais of a lorry driver, he was,' Dewi spat out the word *Sais*. 'Knocked Garmon unconscious and kicked him in the head, he did. And then just got in his lorry and drove off. Right across the Maes! Right across.'

'That's rubbish. All that happened was he was slapped across the shoulders with a newspaper.'

'That's not how I heard it.' Dewi pouted.

'I saw it, Dewi, Garmon's fine.'

'You've spoken to the doctor then, have you?'

'Yes. To tell the truth, I have.'

'I heard he'd broken his skull, he had. Air ambulance to Wrexham hospital, I heard.'

'He's fine.'

In my town, stories grow instantly to fit people's needs for those stories. By closing time, that night, Garmon would probably be celebrating his own beatitude as a Welsh freedom fighter. And Garmon, being Garmon, would be telling everyone who would listen – especially English tourists – how he had been killed and resurrected and was now no less than a real-life martyr. And the story would be official and therefore true, regardless of the anomaly that Garmon was clearly alive.

'The Saeson have gone too far this time, mind. They need teaching a lesson. Have you seen all those English signs on the Supermart?'

'What has the Supermart to do with it, Dewi?'

'Well, it's their fault, isn't it? Making people shop there, it is, putting Welsh shops out of business.'

'They don't force people to shop there.'

'Wrth gwrs eu bod nhw. They've got all those signs up making people shop there, blocking the road outside. Imposing their language on us. I've decided. I'm going to raise it at the meeting tonight. Get Mr Jones involved.'

Dewi craved my approval. But I wasn't going to give it.

'You support the Welsh language, don't you? Mr Jones is an important man. You haven't forgotten that, have you?'

'Course not. But I'll be working, won't I? If you're at the meeting.'

'You can still come in for the vote though, can't you?'

'I don't like going to meetings, Dewi. You know that.'

'Yeah, I know. But you seem so . . . well, you're better now, you are.'

I looked at him.

'You remember. Wales for the Welsh. The Welsh language for all. You used to be so eager about all that stuff.'

'I have tried, Dewi, I have. You know I have. But it's just pretence. I don't feel anything. I keep trying, but it's just not there. You know . . .'

He came over and put his arm around me.

'That's fine Gwalia. You'll be fine, really you will. I can tell.'

I pulled away. What did he know?

Most of the time, I felt nothing at all. This morning, on the Maes, I had felt something. Usually I felt no love, no hate. No jealousy. Nothing. Just a vague melancholy. So I kept busy and pretended to be cheerful. If you couldn't feel it, it was better to pretend than just be lonely and miserable. Mostly, when I did feel anything it was likely to be negative. Anger. Resentment. But mostly I felt nothing. And I had long since learned how to keep that hidden.

'It's OK,' I told him. 'I support you in my head. It's just my heart I'm having problems with.'

Damn boys. Damn boys like Dewi. Damn them that they can do that to you.

'We gotta do something, though, Gwalia. The English don't care a ferret's cock about our language, they don't. It's just an inconvenience to them. Most of them don't even know that a quarter of a million people living next door to them speak a different language, that's what Mr Jones is going to say tonight.

'I'm not sure about Mr Jones? He's too – serious.'

'He's just what Gwrthsafiad needs. Some new fire in our bellies. We're very lucky to have him as tonight's speaker.' He pursed his lips and sucked his breath in through his teeth, the way all sugnwyr lemwn did. 'It's the fortieth anniversary of the first protest next month.'

'Oh, no. Not that again!'

It probably wasn't the smartest remark to have made, even to someone who worshipped me and would forgive me anything. This was the most inflammatory subject you could mention in our town. The pwnc llosg – to raze us all to the ground. I should have kept quiet.

Dewi, like Penhaearn and Hiraethog, Anti Gwenlais and my Mam, was one of the incomers – sugnwyr lemwn – one of those who forty years before had been relocated, mostly to the new estate above our town, when their village was deliberately flooded by the English to create Llyn Y Gelyn, a reservoir to slake their insatiable thirst for industry and wealth. (Dad said it was tragic how this event had been allowed to ruin and shape our lives by filling us with bitterness. And he blamed Welsh politicians for constantly fanning the embers for political reasons.)

'How can you say that Gwalia! You know how important the flooding was – and is.'

'Oh come on, Dewi, lots of people have to move house, of course they do.' Perhaps I'd spent too much time listening to Dad and reading his *Guardian*. 'They move because of wars and drought, slum-clearances, for work or for families or love. It's forty years ago. You weren't even born then.'

'Gwalia! Llyn Y Gelyn was different. You know that! The forcible relocation of Welsh people was an imperialist act of enormous arrogance and insensitivity.'

'What pamphlet are you quoting here, Dewi – Mr Jones's?'

'What's got into you today, Gwalia? This was the event that ignited Wales and roused our usually submissive nation from its quietism and relaunched the very national movement which has led to the triumph of the Welsh Assembly. We have to keep it alive. Maintain the momentum. You know.'

'Definitely not your words. Well memorised, though.'

He looked totally crestfallen now. (How I wished sometimes there was just one person I could talk to who could see things the way I saw them and understand my dilemmas!)

'I'm sorry, Dewi. It's just such an old tune, that's all.'

I didn't want to hurt poor Dewi's feelings. It was just that, like my Dad, I'd grown so tired of seeing those long sugnwyr lemwn faces every time Llyn Y Gelyn was mentioned. Pursing their lips, sucking in their cheeks and twt-twt-ing.

Dewi smiled. 'Don't give up, Gwalia. We have to believe in it. In Wales.'

'I do, Dewi. It's carved on my heart, too.'

But then he had to come and try to put his arm around me and hug me.

I paused a moment and then pulled away from him.

He couldn't hide his hurt. And I couldn't help him.

At twelve o'clock, Hiraethog reconvened the meeting. And promptly adjourned it – another brilliant suggestion from Penhaearn. I duly recorded that the councillors of Llanchwaraetegdanygelyn had solemnly proposed and seconded, then voted in favour of, making the date and the time of the adjournment: same time, same place, tomorrow. Officially.

'We shall meet here every day until the man from the Prime Minister's office – or someone else in his place – arrives.' said Hiraethog decisively, but with a glance at Penhaearn that reminded me that my Yncl was an undertaker first and that Hiraethog, for all his good intentions, was red-faced and flustered enough to become a customer before his time.

I went home thinking stupid thoughts. My little argument with Dewi, my uselessness. I was horrible. As a daughter. As a girlfriend. And as the other thing that I was so ashamed of I couldn't even bear to think it out loud.

I am Gwalia. I am an island.

I needed to bang my head against a metaphorical wall. Shake myself out of it. Sometimes I felt as if I had already dashed my brains out.

It was Monday, Mam would be at Nain's, doing her washing; I could have a nice lunch and chat with Dad. I would make him cawl and I would make something special for supper. I would make myself good. Bread and butter pudding with eggs and marmalade, as Nain taught me. It could cook in the Aga all afternoon and be golden and crisp on the top by evening.

Dad's school lunch hour was still an hour away when I got home, so I set to work. There's therapy in chopping and washing and whisking and baking. Then I cleared everything away and made the downstairs neat and tidy for everyone. I could at least pretend to be good.

Then I decided to reward myself with a cup of tea.

Unfortunately, putting the bottle of milk back into the pantry it slipped and broke, spilling milk all over the black slate shelf. Perversely, I stared at it for a long time thinking it looked beautiful. The tragedy of the white milk on the black slate; so beautiful yet such a waste. Like me.

I burst into tears. And stood there sobbing. Shaking. Everything was such a mess.

Dad didn't come. Nobody came. No one to put their arm around my shoulders. Why would they? A woman of twenty-two. Standing there stupidly in the pantry. Crying over nothing. Yet somehow unable to stop myself.

I stared for a long time at the strange pattern of the spilled milk. A lake, holding itself in shape with its own surface. An archipelago of small white pools strung out along the black slate shelf like pearls. *I am Gwalia, I am an island.* Milk. The universal food of babies. Spilled.

I hadn't meant to be unkind to Dewi. Perhaps it was a

punishment. Everything was punishment. My shattered nose, my life.

I wanted to go and get the clwt to mop it up, but it looked too beautiful. Too precious.

Dad found me standing there, took one glance at the spilled milk and my tear-stained face and took me into his arms without a word.

I sobbed again a little.

Neither of us needed to speak.

Then he gave me his big white hanky that I had ironed for him, that smelled of fresh air and love, and waited, full of kindness, for me to dry my eyes.

'I just want to feel normal,' I tried to explain. 'Not to be cold and unfeeling.' I longed for a bond with someone who didn't misunderstand and view my opinions with suspicion, the way everyone did. 'No one understands me,' I said.

'Perhaps I do,' he said, gently, 'a little.'

After lunch, I told him how I'd been mean to Dewi.

'What are you so grumpy about, today,' he asked, quietly, 'apart from yourself?'

'I don't know,' I said. I was always angry about something, as he nicely knew. Mostly I was angry with myself. And then I looked at his face and relented.

'Today,' I told him. 'I am cross with the sugnwyr lemwn. They talk about *their* problems and *their* traumas,' I said. 'Mam and Anti Gwenlais spend whole lives talking about it. And Penhaearn. And the people in the Council. How bad the English are. How unfair the world is to Wales. Yet they don't see the real unfairnesses right in front of them. And Dewi's just as bad.'

'Go on.'

'I don't know how many times I've had Mam and Anti Gwenlais moaning how they had to watch the graves of their own grandparents being dug up to move the bodies. Or having to walk to school past skeletons and rotting corpses and broken coffins left lying overnight on the low stone wall around the churchyard. It was forty years ago, Dad. Am I a horrible person?'

'No. You're not horrible.'

'Yes I am.'

'No,' he said as if it were a very gentle fact. And he looked at me with his deep blue father's eyes. 'You are not horrible. You are haunted by your own fears. Your own *past* fears. You need to cast them out. They are not your friends, Gwalia. You don't need them.'

He was right, of course. We had talked about it many times. I had to leave my precious island. My refuge, my safe place. Trouble was even the thought of it felt like a betrayal of myself. But I nodded, I had already said too much.

'I don't hate everyone,' I said suddenly. 'Today I felt really warm inside for Garmon Drefnus. And everyone. I felt that. For a minute or two I felt it.'

He hugged me.

'That's good,' he said. 'That's really good.'

I had my trauma and the sugnwyr lemwn had theirs. It didn't take a genius to see why I was jealous of them. I looked across the table into his face. My Dad's face. I wanted to hug him and I think he knew that.

'You know,' he said thoughtfully, 'you may be right to keep all those things inside you. Until you are ready. The lives of the sugnwyr lemwn have been cursed by the fact that their trauma became so important to everyone else.

'If they had been allowed to get over it and get on with their lives, they might all have found better things – good things – to talk about. But the flooding of their village was such an important symbol of Welsh oppression, such an important rallying point for Welsh nationalism, that they were never allowed to move on from it and get on with their lives.'

This was true. Even after forty years, Llyn Y Gelyn was constantly on the radio and television, and in books and newspapers. Just as my trauma was always in my private headlines. At every opportunity, every anniversary, the sugnwyr lemwn would be interviewed again. They could always be relied upon to suck their cheeks in, say what a terrible thing it had been to see the bodies of their forefathers dug up, to be torn from their native land, wrenched from their family homes, without any choice at all, the English behaving like totalitarian fascists as if Wales and its people were considered to have the rights more of animals than of people.

Had I trapped myself in such a martyr's role? Perhaps I had.

'Everyone cashes in on the cause,' Dad said. 'You know that. Psychologists. Politicians. Writers. Artists. Programme makers. No one can argue with them. If you so much as hint that a work of art is not very good or a programme less than interesting when it is about Llyn Y Gelyn you are immediately condemned as a traitor, disloyal to the cause of Wales and insensitive to the wrongs this country has suffered at the hands of the oppressor. If you are an artist or writer or politician and you aren't very good, it's a good subject. It gets you publicity.'

'Just like me,' I said, 'always in the role of victim. The role of martyr.'

He was right. That was exactly what I was doing to myself.

He thought for a moment then went on carefully.

'No. Not like you, Gwalia. The public have no choice in what they feel. They respond as the media know they will. Everybody sympathises and agrees with the lemon suckers. Of course they do. What else could you feel for that story the way they tell it, apart from sympathy and anger and outrage? The sugnwyr lemwn wring their hands and shed their tears and the Welsh can only empathise and agree. But we are trapped in that story. After forty years. After eight hundred years. And woe betide us if we try to move on from that bitter role.

'The Welsh have suffered, Gwalia, and been noble – truly noble, Gwalia – but not perhaps in the way they imagine. They have indeed sacrificed their lives, but not by dying, they sacrificed their living lives for Wales. And we carry on doing it. For our politicians, our documentary programme makers, our journalists, our writers and artists. We allow ourselves to be sacrificed by those who insist on keeping us as victims of our history.

'You have avoided that, Gwalia. You make yourself fun and cheerful and optimistic, despite what you feel inside. Do you think a father can't see that? Wales could learn a lot from you, my daughter.'

'But everyone knows my story,' I said. 'I can't escape it.'

He got up and came round the table and put his arms around me.

I stood up and cried into his shoulder while he stroked my hair.

'You can escape it. And you will. One day very soon, you will be well. And it will all come right. I promise. You have been very wise to keep your bitterness inside you. You have been so brave in avoiding turning yourself into a lifelong victim. And I do know that there is a cost in doing that, too. Quite soon now you will have the opportunity to change. You must look out for that opportunity, recognise it when it comes and seize it.'

'I know,' I whispered. 'I know.'

I pulled away and dried my tears.

I still had the white pearls of spilled milk to mop up.

In the afternoon, I went back to Y Ddwy Ddraig to work on the accounts.

There was still no sign of you, Jon. Everyone had given up on you long since. But I knew you would come eventually.

It was after three when Boudiccea came bustling in, heading for the public phone.

'Now. I'll find where that man has got to,' she said to me in English. 'You can't trust anyone these days. If Westminster can't keep their word, who can?'

A few minutes later she reported back that all your office would say, Jon, was that you were on your way.

I wanted to be especially attentive to Dewi to make up for

being horrid to him earlier (my sort of credit system) so I helped him organise the old dining room for his meeting. We moved the harp with its dirty cloth cover into a corner. I even played 'Ar lan y môr', for him when he begged me to. And then a couple of happier tunes; what is it about music that can change your mood?

'That's good,' he said.

Then we rearranged the room, putting the chipped melamine-topped table at the front on the dais and setting out our two dozen 'best' wobbly wooden chairs, in three rows of eight, to face it.

Mondays were a busy night, but only because of the activities. Y Ddwy Ddraig was the closest Llanchwaraeteg-danygelyn had to a community centre. I liked the busy nights best, working behind the bar, flitting between rooms, answering constant demands.

It took my mind off things.

Upstairs, the Welsh learners would be wanting coffees. There were eight of them this year. Dewi's meeting would probably be smaller, though he always hoped for a crowd. And the usual handful of beery philosophers would be eloquent in the bar.

I was looking forward to this evening, all of it a welcome distraction.

Yet, there was a thought lurking at the back of my mind – more of a worry than it should have been – where were you, Jon? Where on earth had you got to?

By six o'clock, I was back in the kitchen at home, busying myself toasting Welsh cakes on the Aga hotplate, giving Gethin and Awena their tea.

The scene was timelessly the same: every morning, every evening; Mam and my Anti Gwenlais at the table, smoking, twting and pecking over the day's rumours; Dad hiding behind his paper, waiting to ambush them and, once a week, going out to choir practice.

'Billi-Jo and Jean have explained it all to me,' Anti Gwenlais was saying, 'The incident with Garmon, the man from Westminster not coming. Everything. They took some soil from the Maes and did the crystal test on it. It all makes sense now.'

'Wouldn't they have been better off with the bones of a dead bat?' Dad asked without looking out from behind his *Daily Post*.

'Ych-a-fi!' Awena chirped up – that's disgusting,

'Cŵl,' said Gethin. In English.

'I wouldn't be so mocking if I was you, Artwr, bach,' Gwenlais chided Dad. 'There's a calamity coming.' Though bach was a term of endearment, on Anti Gwenlais's tongue it had the flavour of condescension.

Mam poured her sister another paned from the cracked teapot and pushed the plate of hot Welsh-cakes that I had just dumped down on the table across to her. Then I served Gethin and Awena and Dad their bread and butter pudding.

'Do tell us more, Gwen,' Mam encouraged. 'What else did the soil show?'

'Something terrible is going to happen. A crisis. I've sensed it myself you know. Fortunately, they think we can avert it.'

Anti Gwenlais had become very interested in Billi-Jo and Jean, who ran the hippy shop, and in their witchcraft recently. She had introduced them to Penhaearn and he had even invited them to join his ghost-hunts, despite them speaking no Welsh.

'I'm intuitive, but I'm not as intuitive as those two, I can tell you that much,' she confided and sat back with her arms folded as she always did when one of her stories was officially over.

Dad stifled a snort.

'What's intuitive mean?' asked Awena.

'Understanding things without having to ask,' I said.

'Not plucking stories out of thin air, then?' the voice from behind the paper enquired.

'Don't mock me, Artwr. Something bad will happen. Mark my words.'

Mam glared at him. 'Yes. Hissht, Artwr.'

'I held the crystal myself, Gwalia. On a silver chain it was.' She tugged my sleeve and pulled me towards her. 'It should have swung in a circle, you see, but it only went backwards and forwards. Something is very wrong. I felt it.'

'Rubbish,' said Dad. But it did sound rather spooky.

The talk turned then to Billi-Jo and Jean. How they had fled their husbands, how their husbands must have been very cruel to them.

'It's no wonder they turned to their own sex,' Anti Gwenlais said. 'They cried on my shoulder, you know, telling me about it. In their shop, in broad daylight. The both of them it was. One on each shoulder.'

I cleared the table.

Standing at the sink, my mind conjured up an image of Anti Gwenlais, standing amongst the tarot cards and £4.99 books of spells, Billi-Jo's head on one large breast and Jean's on the other, the wind chimes and the dream catchers swinging, hanging by their threads all around them.

'Ahhh,' said Mam.

'They're lovely people, you know. And so worried about the town. It's the ley-lines you know; Billi-Jo told me all about it.'

It would soon be time for me to go back to Y Ddwy Ddraig.

'Anybody going to the meeting?' I asked.

'I promised Penhaearn I'd go,' said Anti Gwenlais. 'So I suppose I'd better.'

'Pity 'tis that men are not more sensitive to a woman's needs,' Mam said and glanced at Dad.

Dewi had been so busy trying to lure the bar regulars into the Conference Room, he'd failed to notice the arrival of the evening's speaker.

'I should have been here to welcome him. And I still can't find an audience. What will I tell him?' he fretted. 'I feel terrible, I do, arranging for the man to come so many miles to speak to so few.'

His hand-drawn posters advertising the talk had been up for weeks: Wales, The Way Forward. Come to Y Ddwy Ddraig on Monday at 7.00 o'clock. Speaker: Dafydd Y Gwrthsafiad.

'You will come, won't you?' He looked at me with spaniel eyes.

'I have to work in the bar, don't I? In your place. But all right, I'll try to pop in. You have five there. More might come.'

The five included Mr Dafydd Y Gwrthsafiad, the visiting speaker, Penhaearn and Penhaearn's wife, Nerys, Dewi's friend Rhys and my Anti Gwenlais. Mam would have been there, of course, apart from domestic responsibilities with Awena and Gethin. Others, too, I'm sure, if they hadn't been so busy washing clothes, getting in firewood, putting children to bed or supervising their fires and paraffin lamps and generators in this land without electricity or mains water.

I popped in for a moment and saw Dewi greeting Dafydd Y Gwrthsafiad, the speaker. I saw Dewi looking backwards and forwards from the front to the back of the room, scratching his black curly hair, looking puzzled. I knew what he was thinking. I knew him more than well enough for that: if he sat with the committee they would then outnumber the audience, so he went to sit with Rhys next to Penhaearn's wife, dressed in a black fur-collared coat, make-up and pearls. It was said (though not by Anti Gwenlais) that Penhaearn made her wear his dead mother's clothes.

'Well then, I think we can begin,' Penhaearn said in his most formal, burial service Welsh. I hurried away.

Up in the makeshift classroom, Mrs Jones had already started her Welsh class.

'Now you all remember how last week we did clauses. This week we shall be doing – is-gymalau adferfol amodol yn y Gymraeg – conditional adverbial sub-clauses.'

I needed to know how many wanted tea, and how many coffee.

'Noswaith dda, Gwalia,' the teacher sang out at me for the benefit of her students.

'Noswaith dda,' I said, obediently.

'Noswaith dda,' they chorused, back. At least they could all say 'Good evening'.

Boudiccea sat in the middle of the front row, enthroned by dictionaries and grammar books, the half a dozen other English people she'd recruited arrayed around her.

'Pwy sy eisiau te?' the teacher asked. 'A phwy sy eisiau coffi?'

They all knew the Welsh for who wants tea and coffee, too.

Back in the lounge, Taid, Elwyn and Irfon were waiting patiently at the bar to order their beers. Later they would go to sit down at the table by the window where two more pints each, drunk in halves would last them the night. They were in no kind of hurry any more.

Dan Wfftio breezed in, creating his usual ripple of curiosity. The star of the town, and an erstwhile actor in Wales's favourite Welsh-language soap opera, he saw himself as a real man, a Romeo and a proud and frequent user of room 10, the bridal suite whose key – when it wasn't being used – always hung from a hook beside the line of spirits upturned on their optics. (Well, I didn't start that tradition, nor was it for me to stop it.)

By the time I got back to the conference room, Dafydd Y Gwrthsafiad was addressing his audience with a declamatory eloquence entirely disproportionate to the size and importance of the meeting, raising his voice and banging his fist on the table. Surprisingly, no one seemed to find this at all embarrassing. I did.

'Are we just going to sit back and watch while Wales is trodden underfoot once more?'

Gwenlais shook her head and Dewi said shyly: 'We are not!'

'Are we going to stand by and allow these English to march in with their enormous chequebooks and steal our houses from under our own noses? Leaving our children homeless?'

'We are not!' Penhaearn joined in this time.

I went back to the bar.

'What's going on in there?' Dan Wfftio asked.

'Gwrthsafiad meeting,' I told him. 'Top secret. So keep it under your hat.'

Taid winked at me. It was the kind of joke he would make.

Dan Wfftio frowned. Then launched off.

'I remember Penhaearn organising meetings like that years ago. Everyone went then. At the height of the Llyn Y Gelyn protests it was. Telling us why we should and shouldn't have electricity here. He fancied himself as an up-and-coming politician then, you know.'

'Strange how all the other heroes of the Nationalist movement from the Sixties are doing so well these days,' Elwyn said. 'But not him.'

'It's God punishing him, I dare say,' Irfon added.

I left them to it. Much as Penhaearn made my flesh creep, I couldn't stand there and be disloyal to him in public.

I stuck my head back into the meeting just as Anti Gwenlais was getting to her feet:

'English families move in here making Welsh girls pregnant. I had a fourteen-year-old come into the chemist wanting morning after pills last week. Fallen pregnant to an English incomer. I told her I'm not competent to sell her that. Now if that child goes to term, then – no doubt in my mind – that poor child will be brought up English-speaking. I try to persuade them to use condoms. You should see the queues I get for morning-after pills after weekends. Especially Bank Holiday Mondays.'

Dewi's hand shot up.

'I think we should take action against the Supermart,' he said. 'Someone was nearly killed there by an Englishman this morning. We should let them know they cannot come here, threatening honest Welshmen and ramming their filthy language down our throats. They deface our town with their language and their posters and their disrespectful ways. I myself am prepared to organise a protest. Tomorrow if necessary.'

He stared at Rhys expectantly.

'Yes,' Rhys said shyly, by way of support.

'That sounds like a very good idea,' said Dafydd Y Gwrthsafiad, cheered by having motivated two thirds of his audience into direct action. 'A protest. What is your opinion of the matter, Mr Chairman?'

'Yes,' said Penhaearn, with statesmanlike reserve. 'Certainly.'

'Direct action it is then,' said Dafydd Y Gwrthsafiad. 'I'll be here to help in any way I can. Now we need to mobilise as many supporters as possible.'

'Champion!' said Dewi, winking at me. I gave him a thumbs up. I don't know why.

'Is there any need to rush into things?' said Penhaearn.

'On the contrary,' Mr Dafydd Y Gwrthsafiad said. 'This is a textbook case, as I am sure you know from your own experience of activism. Immediate response. As any farrier worth his salt would tell you, you must strike while the iron is hot, wouldn't you agree?'

I went back up to the furnace of the Welsh lesson, wondering if even the teacher would know 'gof', the word for blacksmith, these days.

Mrs Jones was labouring over mutations.

'You are year six now,' she said. 'Year six. We did this in year one.

'Remember that "his dog" is "ei gi o", "her dog" is "ei chi hi". But when ci – dog – is plural – cŵn – then it doesn't take a soft mutation. Unless it is the first word after the subject – "Jon bought dogs" – "Prynodd Jon gŵn". And if it was a question, of course, the prenodd would take a soft mutation – "Brynodd Jon gŵn?" – Is everyone happy with that now?'

'It's a wonder so many come to a Welsh town to live,' I said, back in the bar.

'The English must be very thick not to be able to learn our language in six years,' said Dan. 'I could speak it fluently by the age of five. And just look around you at all the very stupid people who speak Welsh perfectly well; the English must be at least more stupid than all of them.'

By eleven they had all gone home. I locked up and trudged back to our house, feeling a great disappointment and sense of anti-climax.

But thinking of you, Jon. Imagining what you might be like. And where you might be sleeping.

I WOKE in foetal position, cold and sweaty, lying across the two seats of my little car, full of cramps and twinges. I postponed waking up completely as long as I could. Despite my discomfort, I was in no hurry to face the reality of my predicament. For all that I complained about my parents' flat, it was jolly comfortable compared with other places, like my small, cramped car, for instance.

Without opening my eyes, I tried to stretch my legs, haunted by anxious half-dreams about doing a nightmare presentation in The Hub. And being sent into exile. And being made fun of for never having a girlfriend.

There would be no hot shower or warm jacuzzi this morning; no waiters to bring up breakfast or coffee. And no escape from the fact that I'd failed even to find this god-forsaken town.

What I actually noticed first was the birdsong. And the music in it.

I opened my eyes.

The condensation on the windscreen was sparkling, a million jewels magically produced from thin air, sunlight playing on them. I rubbed at the windscreen, looked out and saw the perfection of that morning.

Twisting around, I opened the car door and felt the dawn air rush in to bathe me with its freshness. I clambered out. Above me, warm sunlight sparkled through the branches of gnarled oaks so brightly that I could see the veins in the green translucent leaves.

The shafts of sunlight made the world so bright. I still remember the greys and browns and reds of the earth and stones as being more vivid than I have ever seen them before or since. A thousand shades of green in the plants and lichens. The smell of grass and damp earth intoxicated me, made me want to take it deeply down into my lungs and feel it tingling in my blood.

I breathed in Wales.

Never had I wakened like this before.

I felt as fresh and pure and innocent as the dawn.

This was magical. Better than any Hollywood – or art-house – film, and with nature's own soundtrack! The music of the birdsong was underscored by a waterfall and overlaid by the babble of water.

I looked around. And found more food for wonderment.

I was in a little grotto with a waterfall, a pool and a stream.

Never mind the discomfort of the night, and my smelly self, I had survived the night and woken up in Eden. The freshness of the air, the beauty of the shafts of sunlight sparkling on the water, the green of . . . everything.

So I was lost. And sweaty. And dirty. And my car was stuck in a river. Well – stream. So what! It was a wonderful morning to be alive.

I laughed out loud with sheer joy.

The previous night, I had been miserable and angry, frustrated and depressed. Now, this morning, all that was gone. Nothing in this enchanted light could look that bad!

Shifting one slightly biggish stone would probably do it. I took off my shoes and socks and paddled into the water, heaved the rock aside, got in and started the car, and pulled forward onto the bank.

Then, I felt this need to tell someone about it. Andrew. Nisha. Anyone. But there was still no signal on my mobile: only the birds to share my excitement with – and they were all too busy chirruping to me about what a wonderful morning they were having.

I hadn't even bothered to roll up my trousers so they were now wet. So what? It wasn't that bad. Nothing was bad this morning. A problem to solve, that was all, and the day was still young.

The night before, I had eventually found a fish and chip shop in Beddgelert then driven on to stop and eat my steaming feast under the stars in the shadow of Mount Snowdon. Several times my hopes of finding Umbo – and a proper bed for the night – had been raised, only to be dashed again.

Eventually I had turned into yet another dead end.

That was when I had reversed into the river, trying to turn around, and got stuck. Low on petrol and tired, I had got back into the car, pulled my jacket around me, and fallen asleep, fitfully and miserably, wondering what the hell I was going to do. My logic and strategic talents useless.

This morning, everything felt so completely different.

The world, that had seemed hostile and obstreperous in the darkness, had today become benign. I don't think I had ever slept in my clothes before. And the only time I'd gone camping had been with Maria. But, actually, it was all right, I had survived. Yes! I'd survived.

I looked around. I was completely alone. Miles from anywhere. And completely free.

This was wild! Exhilarating.

It was then that I became aware of a strange smell and realised it was me.

I told myself gently that, no, there was no shower here. No hot water and no invigorating gel. I added this to my list of problems to solve. Smelly, dirty, lost. That wasn't so bad.

I had clean clothes in the car. And my washing bag. But no towel. One always expects towels to be provided in hotels.

I looked at the cold stream. And I argued with myself a little. But I knew what had to be done.

With some trepidation, I gingerly stripped off, feeling the cold air all over me, grateful for the slight warmth of the sunlight, my skin turning rough with goose pimples. I placed my clothes neatly into a pile, with my glasses on top, and paddled tentatively into the stream, trying to scoop up water onto my face and under my arms.

The stones were painful to walk on and the whole thing was so primitive and barbaric. But exhilarating, too. The water was refreshing. Like a baptism. And, since my skin was already numbed, it felt less cold than I had expected. But where I was was not really deep enough to wash satisfactorily.

I paddled towards the deep pool in front of the waterfall

and waded in, making ripples in the dark water. All around me was the reflection of the trees rising up to the green spring canopy and the blue sky. Blues and greens and the grey rocks.

To hell with being a city boy, I could do this camping lark.

As the water came over my waist, and chilled my groin, I remember yelling and whooping out loud to the pagan gods. And a couple of sheep up on the grass in the wood above, briefly stopped feeding to stare at me.

I waved at them. So this was what people meant by 'communing with nature'.

I knew what I had to do.

Taking a deep breath, I plunged my head under the water and came up laughing. And did it again. The third time, I came up behind the waterfall, the peaty taste and smell of the water in my mouth and nose and face. And all over me.

Fantastic!

I climbed up onto a ledge where there was a sort of cave and peered out through the curtain of water. This whole world seemed truly magical.

Never mind my responsibilities: the town I had failed to find, the job I was supposed to be doing, and to hell with civilization and making the world a better place. I was swimming at dawn in a pagan pool, in an undiscovered land. And the world was teaching me a thing or two.

I laughed aloud.

The weight of water was surprisingly heavy as I stepped back through the waterfall and dropped into the pool beneath the water before swimming and wading, and then paddling, out to dry land. I hauled myself up onto a huge slab of warmish slate and stretched out in the shafts of sunshine, naked in the fresh spring air feeling as if I had arrived at last – innocent and wet – at the wrong place, at the wrong time. And without a towel.

As I giggled to myself, I lay back and looked up through the canopy of rocks and trees to the blue sky, watching the shafts of sunlight filtering through the oaks above the grotto and dancing on my skin. I had arrived somewhere wonderful and unexpected.

High above, there was a large bird circling, watching me, reminding me I had things to do.

I found a clean T-shirt in my case and dried myself. It was then that I noticed something else. Halfway up the rock, daubed large in white paint in a language I didn't recognise, I saw three words: Cofiwch Y Gelyn.

EVER SINCE Billi-Jo and Jean had joined Penhaearn's ghost hunting group, Mam and Anti Gwenlais had had funny ideas. All about karma and ley lines and crystals. This month it was Angel Cards. So every morning at breakfast, each of us had to reach into an old china bowl, mix up the cards and pick one out. The Angel Cards, which sold in the hippy shop for £7.99 a packet, just had simple words on them. In English. But they didn't seem to mind that for these purposes.

Mam's said *Perseverance,* Gethin's said *Gratitude* and Awena's said *Hopefulness.* Mine said *Romance.*

Dad refused to play.

'Is it supposed to be a prophecy or advice?' he asked. 'I might join in if you told me.'

'Ah,' said Mam, quoting Jean. 'That's between you and your inner voice.'

Dad looked skywards and we all giggled, but for different reasons.

'I bet your guest won't come now,' Dad said.

'I have a feeling he will,' I said.

I got to Y Ddwy Ddraig early.

Dewi arrived full of his plans for the protest and wouldn't stop talking about it. I wasn't very interested. We needed wood for the fire and for some reason I had an urge to pick fresh bluebells for the room I had set aside for you.

'The protest is going to be hellish massive,' Dewi said, his Welsh slipping into joskin slang in his enthusiasm. 'You'll be really impressed with me this time.'

'You've organised it very quickly.'

'A few words to the faithful. That was all it needed.'

We headed up to Drws y Coed, the path that led to the oak wood across the fields behind my house.

The year felt changed to spring at last. Dai's horses were grazing on the Maes. The smell of the wood smoke hung in the air, damp above the stone houses. But there was something else, something new and different. Not something bad, as Anti Gwenlais had said last night, but good.

'I knew the name of every farm and field, and every hillside in this town,' Dewi said. 'Until the devil's English moved in. Now I don't even know the names of their houses, not after they've finished changing them to things like Rose Cottage and Dun Roamin and stuff.'

I was hardly listening.

The man from Westminster was going to arrive. I could sense it. And I had picked the Angel Card *Romance*.

It was while Dewi was collecting wood and I was picking bluebells that I peered over the edge of the chasm, from the top of the wood.

There was this vision. A perfect, naked man, lying on the flat rock at the pool's edge by *my* waterfall. Strange and beautiful. And like an exotic god.

Dewi hadn't seen him. He was still chattering on.

I had never seen a completely naked man before. But even if I had, I don't think I would have been any less bewitched. I gazed at him for only a few moments but it could have been forever. He was beautiful. Glistening. The most beautiful thing I had ever seen. Of all the millions of things in the world, why is it that we are only really fascinated by people? And of all the millions of people, why are we drawn so strongly to just one?

My spirits leapt. I knew it was you. I felt it. And I knew not to mention it to Dewi.

And something inside me unlocked.

A few moment later I found myself skipping through the wood, humming gently. No longer counting off my many chores, no longer so deadened in my heart, but gently singing.

I was still humming an hour later when I left a note for Islwyn, saying I would wait to greet the man from Westminster before coming to the meeting. I arranged the fresh bluebells I'd picked so carefully in the room I had made ready for you. And then I went to find little jobs to do at the reception desk in Y Ddwy Ddraig, in order to be waiting for you when you arrived.

I had decided to be sweeping the carpet in reception, with the push and pull. And I would be singing. And you would mistake me for the cleaner. A good role for a Mata Hari, wouldn't you say?

I knew now that I could certainly spy on you. I had every reason to. Whether it was to find out about your plans for my town or not. I wanted to find out every last thing about you.

My body was tingling.

I PUNCHED the car radio controls, searching impatiently for Radio Four. Something about bombs in Central London, but I could only get snatches of it. The reception was appalling, fading or switching to some foreign language channel every time I came over a hill or dipped down into valley.

The thought of it made me drive faster. Several bombs. Emergency services rushing to the scene.

The foreign station switched in again. I recognised the word 'bombs' and 'Llundain'. Then it dawned on me: this must be Welsh.

And back to Radio 4.

News flashes. Scant Information. Bare facts – raw and jumbled. Undigested. Over-hastily explained. News with all its birth pangs, garbled and provisional. Reporters and presenters struggling to stay calm and factual.

Six or eight bombs. Emergency services at the scenes. Central London hospitals recalling staff and preparing for a major influx of casualties. Mainline stations sealed off. Trains stopped and passengers escorted along railway lines to safety. Buses halted and evacuated. Streets in Central London sealed off. The Prime Minister would make an announcement shortly.

Statistics still coming in. A picture emerging.

Bombs had been placed on mainline trains and buses. The terrorists had chosen the morning rush hour for maximum casualties and panic. Euston Square, Tower Bridge and Westminster Tube station.

My father had an office overlooking Tower Bridge, my mother would be there too. And Westminster Tube Station was just round the corner from the Leyburn Institute. Andrew and Nisha used it.

I stopped and tried my mobile. No signal. Communication was my priority now.

I had to find a signal, had to speak to people.

I set off, driving faster, looking for high ground within line-of-sight of a transmitter, glancing at the phone display.

Three bars. I pulled over and phoned Dad's private office line. Mum answered. I could hear a TV in the background.

'You OK? I just heard the news.'

'We're watching it on screen now.'

I heard Dad shout. I could imagine him watching it on the big plasma screen that always displayed the news and stock prices.

'Are there many hurt?'

'They haven't said so. They're just saying that members of the public caught one or more of the terrorists.'

'Can you see anything from the window?'

'There are police cars and sirens going everywhere. We saw a lot of ambulances go out from Guys Hospital an hour ago but there don't seem to be any coming back. I can see lots of fire engines and flashing lights across the river. But we haven't heard any explosions.'

We said goodbye. I needed to phone Nisha now.

She answered straight away.

'Jon. How are you?'

'What's happening, I heard about the bomb?'

'I'm virtually the only one in. It's chaos. They've shut the transport system down and they're telling people to avoid Central London.'

'They'll be worried about more bombs.'

'It's still very confused.' She sounded scared.

'Is Andrew OK?'

'I think so, he was supposed to be going to a meeting.'

'Do you think I should come back to London? I expect I'll be needed there. Is Angela in?'

'Hadn't you better wait to see what she says? She may be trying to phone in. The mobile networks are solid. You were fluky to be getting through. I'll call you if you are being needed. Stay accessible, yeah? Are *you* OK, Jon?'

'Fine,' I said. It didn't seem the moment to have to explain about sleeping in the car and bathing in a waterfall and how wonderful it was. 'Are you sure you're OK?'

'It's totally chaotic. Only half a dozen of us have got into the office. We're manning the phones as best we can. I am a bit worried about Andrew.'

'Didn't you come in together?'

'He had a breakfast meeting at the Home Office.' There was a catch in her voice.

'He'll have missed it, then. He'll be fine.' I wanted to reassure her but my words were empty. I was being positive for the sake of it.

'He should be. But I hope everyone else is all right.' There was a pause. 'Jon!'

I could hear a new fear in her voice. Then sirens in the background. What the hell was I doing stuck in Wales when I needed to be there?

'They will be,' I said, looking for something I could say that might mean something. 'Of course they will. Statistically, in these kinds of situations . . .'

She interrupted me.

'I know the statistics!' she snapped.

'Look, Jon. I need to go. The switchboard people aren't in yet and there are calls coming in from all over. I'll phone you later.'

I pressed the end-call button. And looked around.

I was the only car on the road. In all directions there were only mountains rising into the sky.

I had to find my hotel and get myself sorted. Then go back to London.

I stopped at the next town I came to and asked at the Post Office.

Two minutes later, I had my AA map and a simple sketch with clear instructions to take the A2142 Trawsfynydd road to Llyn Y Gelyn. Next time I would bring Sat.Nav.

'You can't miss it, it's just on the corner, by Arenig. "Llyn" means lake by the way.'

They could have told me that yesterday!

So I set off yet again, the roads looking very familiar. Some of the drivers even seemed to raise a familiar hand of recognition.

Four miles to the west, by Llyn Y Gelyn, I took the unmarked turning I had taken the night before, across the boggy moorland with mountains and valleys all around. Half a mile further on I went past a turning I recognised, checked the map, and carried on up a long, steep hill.

A quarter of a mile past that was the turning I had been looking for, an innocuous lane that might have been the driveway to a farm, turning off between a large boulder and a field of small gnarled oaks. There was no signpost.

You don't see Llanchwaraetegdanygelyn itself until well after you take that turning, perhaps a mile further on. The road narrows to single-track, then passes between two huge rocks, like gateposts to a secret kingdom.

Then you see a view to take your breath away. The road seems to drop away almost vertically.

So there below me, Gwalia, was your town, laid out in that confluence of valleys isolated from the rest of Snowdonia by the mountains I had just come over and a gorge that carried the river, over that precipice – the waterfall, as I now know, where I had bathed.

For an instant, I felt as if I was going to launch out into clear air, but the road turned back on itself and went down the side of the hill, solid rock on one side and an almost vertical drop on the other.

I could see from there how cut off the valley was, how the town sat at the confluence of three valleys, and how, just past the town, the main valley narrowed to the chasm and the waterfall, leaving no room for a road.

That was why it had been so hard to find. That was why I had to drive to it over the mountains.

This really was a secret, cut-off place.

No wonder, twenty-first-century progress had failed to reach it!

As I descended the hill, looking down at the slate rooftops,

I could see a triangular village green and specks like ants – people moving around. Nisha's briefing notes were running through my mind. Three hundred and twenty houses. Population: seven hundred.

It was a long way away from London and the bombings. And I was holding my breath and coming very slowly round the hairpins, a rock face on one side and a drop on the other.

I edged down, feeling as if my little car would pitch forward, and roll head over heels down the mountainside. The people were looking bigger now; I could see them going in and out of the shops, and what looked like horses, grazing.

Then the road flattened out and came to a terrace of small houses before it turned between two buildings and burst out onto the village green, near a school with children playing and squealing in the playground. At the apex of the triangle of the village green, I could see a white hotel with two large concrete dragons outside, one red and one white. That must be it, I thought. The Two Dragons. (Not just a pretty face, you see.)

I drove up past the shops and Supermart, and parked at the apex of the Green.

I had finally made it. A day late. But I was there.

I took a deep breath.

I SPOTTED your funny little red and black car as soon as it entered the Maes and watched it hesitate as you looked around before driving up past the shops. The clock said ten thirty. Across the Maes the Town Council would have reconvened and Islwyn would be getting twitchy.

You lumbered in lugging one big bag, one small bag, a projector and a briefcase. It *was* you. The boy at the waterfall. Not like a 'man from Westminster' at all.

You dumped your bags down and glanced around.

You saw me, but I was only the insignificant sweeping girl, with the ugly broken nose. You rang the little bell on the counter impatiently. How typically English after all! Impatient and demanding. No doubt you would be arrogant, too.

I let you ring the bell a second time.

Then I moved round behind the reception desk, still sweeping. I was determined to be furtive, to collect intelligence for Mam and Anti Gwenlais.

I had to think like a Welsh Mata Hari now, an agent of Y Gwrthsafiad, the Welsh Resistance.

'Bore da,' I said.

'Eh?' You looked flustered. But still handsome, despite your glasses and confusion.

We had a rule at Y Ddwy Ddraig. Mam's rule: Always use Welsh first, especially to the English, to let them know their place.

'Ga i'ch helpu chi?' I said, covering my nose with my hand.

You still thought I was the cleaner.

'Er . . . Jon Bull. I have a booking.'

You didn't even look into my face. But I looked deeply into yours.

'Ah, yes. Mister Bull?' I pretended there were many entries in the register.

'Have you heard any news about the London bombings today?'

'I haven't I'm sorry. But I'm sure it'll be in the paper tomorrow.'

You looked appalled by my manner. Was I being very offhand? You stared at me in puzzlement. You seemed especially confused by my ffedog, my pinafore.

So I took it off.

Your eyes ran over my body. That was good. I'd already approved yours. Naked. But still you hadn't looked at my face properly. So I made myself take my hand away from covering my nose and took my hair band out. And shook my hair down. Now, why did I do that? Me with my ugly nose? What makes us do these things?

'I need to make a phone call.'

'There is a phone in the bar.' I pointed vaguely in the direction of the bar.

You looked in that direction. And back at me.

Then at my face but not at my nose. You smiled. And what a smile! I wanted to laugh. To sing. And I found myself smiling too. So we stood there, both smiling at each other for quite a long moment or two. I don't think you knew what was happening at all. I did. Then I think you did. Because you started acting all flustered and apologised and said 'excuse me', and went off to make your phone call.

I stood there, my head writing music for my heart.

You were beautiful. The strangest, coolest, most beautiful and exotic man I had ever seen.

You came back, a minute or so later, looking calmer. I could feel you looking at me while I concentrated on the register. I was trying not to stare at you, though I was desperately curious to. I could feel your eyes on me even when I wasn't watching you. I think it was my mouth your eyes kept coming back to.

'Ahrr yes, you werrr booked in yesterrrday, Dw i'n credu.' I said, rolling my Rs just to let you know that I was going to the trouble of talking *your* hateful language.

I ran my finger up and down the empty reservations list. I suppose it could be said that I was toying with you. Enjoying myself for the first time in as long as I could remember.

'You'll have to fill in your particulars.' I tossed a registration card onto the desk, being careful not to take the dusty one from the top of the pile.

'Yes, please. Sorry.' You seemed so much less confident that I would have expected a man from Westminster to be.

Our eyes met again

Do you remember? Your brown eyes. The way I flushed? You must have noticed. I felt so dazzled by you that I had to look away.

You filled in your name, address and phone number.

For the first time in seven years I felt truly alive. No, more than that. Ecstatic.

I handed you the keys and led you upstairs to your room. I remember feeling ashamed of the frayed carpets and the rickety stairs and floorboards. But I felt no need to help you with your bags. My heart was far too busy.

He must be used to such luxury, I was thinking. He must know so much that I do not. He must think me such a peasant. Not that he will be even thinking about me at all, I expect.

Room 12.

I opened the door and watched your face to see if you would notice the bluebells. And if you would like them. Not that it was any concern of mine whether you might like a bunch of bluebells or not.

I hoped you wouldn't notice the worn candlewick bedspread or the threadbare white towels I had placed on it. I hoped you wouldn't take one look at the room and decide to check out, the way some people did.

Men don't usually notice such things, I told myself.

'Thank you,' you said. Dismissively.

I decided not to tell you – yet! – about the Town Council sitting waiting for you just a hundred yards away. I wanted to keep you to myself a little longer, and relish the fact that I knew something – actually many things – that you hadn't an inkling about.

You obviously wanted to be left alone. So I left you to it. And busied myself tidying Room 10 next door. The Honeymoon Suite. And kept my ear cocked.

I could hear you moving around. As soon as I heard you come out of your room, I was back in the corridor immediately.

'I can't find the socket to recharge my mobile or my laptop,' you said. 'Can you show me where it is?'

'I'm afraid we don't have electricity. I think that's what you are supposed to be here to arrange,' I informed you and watched the understanding dawn on your incredible face, as you swallowed and breathed out your frustration.

'Oh yes,' you said. 'No mains electricity. That's right. So there's no television or kettle either? Is there a bathroom, by any chance? Shower?'

I pointed down the corridor.

Not as clever as I'd hoped, but certainly better looking.

You stepped back into the room and closed the door.

I could hear the hard leather soles of your black-polished shoes on the lino. Going over to the cracked basin next to the window. Discovering that only the cold tap worked. I imagined your reaction to the slow, brownish trickle. And smiled.

Would you give up now? And go and find somewhere else to stay?

I heard you go back over to the bed. And imagined you picking up one of the towels from the bed and looking at it in disbelief. I backed away down the corridor as you opened your door and came out again.

'Is the shower this way?' you demanded.

I nodded. And you headed along the corridor.

You were going to stay!

But I hadn't told you about the hot water, had I?

You found the bathroom all right. The old stained bath and cast iron shower and cracked white tiles.

I heard you shower, knowing the water would be

lukewarm – a slight improvement on the waterfall. I decided you would not be using the tablet of soap I had left there, because you would have brought your own fancy stuff.

By then my curiosity was running so wild, I couldn't stop myself. I stood brazenly leaning in your doorway, waiting for your footfall back along the corridor on the old floorboards.

You hesitated when you saw me, clutching your dirty clothes, the towel around your waist. I couldn't stop myself from smiling.

I knew I was blocking your way.

'I should have advised you, Mr Bull,' I said, reciting our standard announcement and staring straight at your wonderful flat belly. 'There's hot water only at dawn and dusk. The generator starts at six. And runs till ten. And it's six until eight at night. Breakfast is at eight.'

You looked at me quizzically.

'Are you really from Westminster?' I blurted. Unable to help myself a moment longer.

'Well. Yes. No. I suppose so. Sort of. Yes. Sorry.'

'And you think you've come here to help us, I suppose.' I asked, recovering my self-control.

'I hope I can help. Yes.'

'Good. We need improving, as you can see for yourself, I'm sure. The town, like the hotel, all needs improving. Not that we don't do our best, you understand, but there it is.'

'I see.' You looked bewildered. You were clearly not as intelligent as one might have hoped of a man from Westminster. It was not going to be difficult at all to steal your secrets. This would be fun.

'The hot water,' I explained. 'We can't afford to keep it on all day.'

'Well, I'm sure there are improvement grants available from a number of bodies.'

'Well, we've not had a penny from your Government. Not ever. Otherwise it would have been a lot more comfortable here, I can assure you.'

'I'm sorry,' you said. 'But really I do have to get dressed now.'

You have no idea how delicious it was having you there. Being inches from your nearly naked body. Feeling my own body coming alive near you.

I saw you watching the stupid smile on my lips. Did you think that I was some kind of tart perhaps? The landlord's desperate daughter? You didn't seem to have noticed my nose.

I didn't care. I just wanted to control you. The way you were controlling me.

'You do know the Town Council is waiting for you across the road, don't you?' I said.

'What? Who? What do you mean?'

In your alarm, the towel loosened and fell, so that you were left standing totally naked, holding it in front of you.

I pretended to ignore this.

'The meeting you were supposed to be at yesterday?'

My voice had gone up a few notes, like Hiraethog's.

'Postponed until today?'

You really were very dumb.

I made an exaggerated play of looking at my watch. But in fact I was looking straight past it at your groin. And your legs. They were very smooth for a man.

'They've been there twenty minutes already.'

You tried to edge past me into the room.

'Sorry,' you said.

I moved back slightly to allow you through and your chest brushed against my breasts, only the thickness of my T-shirt and bra between us.

I caught my breath. The tingle. Surely, you must have felt it too.

And then I had a good look at your buttocks.

'I'm sure they'll wait for you. They waited over an hour yesterday.'

Neat and naked. I could memorise you now. From the goose pimples on your arms, to your TB scar, and the mole nearly in the centre of your chest.

You dropped your clothes on the bed and secured the towel.

Were you wanting me to go?

I don't think so.

'Do you want me to wash those for you?' I nodded towards the carrier bag of dirty clothes.

Did I want to please you now? To be your woman? Your slave? The words just happened to my lips.

'Thank you,' you said, softly, as a boy might to his mother.

So I stepped across your threshold into the room. And picked them up

'They're a bit damp. Sorry.'

I couldn't be stern with you any longer, then.

'I know,' I smiled. 'It's fine.'

'Have you worked here long?' you asked.

'Oh I don't exactly work here. I'm sort of doing my A-levels. I do evenings and weekends to help my Dad out. Most of the time I'm studying.'

This was mostly true, but quite a lot not. Well, spies are supposed to have cover stories and I couldn't tell you all about my trauma and years of missed schooling and how I was yet again going to retake my A-levels this summer too.

'What are you studying?'

'Welsh, Welsh Literature, French and English Literature. I could do those as well if you like.' I nodded to the clothes you had just taken off which lay where you had thrown them, on the bed.

'Errrm.'

Before you could object I was there beside you reaching down, my cheek inches from your stomach.

You took a step back, I remember. I looked up at you, amused.

'I didn't mean to startle you,' I said. 'Are you nervous? I wouldn't imagine a man from Westminster would be nervous about anything!'

'Sorry.'

Then we just stood there, looking at each other. You seemed so familiar to me. As if I already knew you. And had done for years.

'I need to start thinking about my meeting,' you said.

But I wasn't going to leave without playing my trump card.

I paused in the doorway and looked back over my shoulder, flirtily.

'I hope you enjoyed your morning swim today.'

Unforgivable, I know, but I hadn't flirted for so long – and never as a young woman – that I had no idea if I could do it.

And then I swept out of the room. Hoping – no, knowing – that your heart would be totally impaled.

PANICKING hardly at all, I searched frantically through the sheaf of notes that Nisha had prepared for me till I found the list. My heart sank. Hiraethog Jones – how do you pronounce that? And Penhaearn. And everybody was called Jones. I should have listened much more carefully to Nisha.

But I was much less concerned than I would have expected to be because I was a bit taken aback by you, Gwalia. Your pretty face, your curly brown hair. And your cheekiness. I confess, I hadn't even noticed your nose. And the way you put your hand up to your face just seemed like shyness.

It was the way you had looked at me, I think. That look in your eyes. Or rather, the way we had stood there looking at each other.

What a strange, illogical day.

Shit!

The meeting. They were waiting for me.

And no PowerPoint! Not unless there was electricity over there. Probably would be. Surely. Still it was only the preliminary meeting. I could wing it. Talk about 'exciting plans'. And stuff like that. Ask them for their perspective. I wasn't feeling quite as confident here as I had in London. Now, where was Neuadd y Dre – however you pronounced it?

I would ask you at Reception. I wanted to talk to you again. But when I got downstairs, you'd gone. Had you really seen me swimming at the waterfall? I hadn't realised how close I had been to the town – as the crow flies.

I crossed the village green and went up to three old men sitting on a bench.

'Excuse me, I'm looking for 'Nay-oo-ad why dree', the Town Hall, is it?'

'Oh Neuadd y Dre, is it? You'll be wanting to meet the leaders of our community?' said one.

'Yes.' I said. 'My name's Jon Bull.'

'Indeed it is,' said another, grasping my hand and shaking it.

They solemnly shook hands and introduced themselves, oblivious of my urgency.

'They think themselves the leaders of our community. And I dare say they are as much that as you are the Man from Westminster,' said the second.

'God forgive you,' said the third.

'You are not a Welsh speaker, then, Jon,' Dai Call said, his eyes twinkling.

'I'm afraid not,' I said. 'Is that a problem?'

The other two began to nod.

'Oh no. Not at all,' said Dai Call.

And the other two started shaking their heads.

BY NOW, I had raced across to the Town Hall and run up to the Council Chamber, breathlessly telling everyone I passed that you were here. That you were coming. I couldn't understand why Taid and his pals and the councillors were not as excited as me.

Then I had to sit, waiting, with my Anti Gwenlais staring at me, far too suspiciously for my comfort. Waiting. Waiting to test the moment when you arrived. To see if my heart would skip a beat. To be completely sure I was better. Lots better. Already.

My Anti Gwenlais kept going to listen at the door, ready to alert us, like a naughty schoolgirl keeping lookout. Then, as soon as she heard you at the bottom of the stairs, she closed the door and the councillors scrambled into line, jostling for position.

Boudiccea went first to stand in front. Then Penhaearn elbowed her out of the way and pulled Hiraethog next to him.

Boudiccea sighed heavily and looked skywards, though she was just as bad.

'Peidiwch â bod yn wirion!' she said.

I stayed put. So did Blodeuwedd, though she probably didn't know the difference between affecting disinterest and boredom. She really hated being the officer for Antur Deg. It crossed my mind that perhaps she had been told to be a spy too. Penhaearn's secret weapon, designed to ensure Boudiccea's plans came to nothing by feigning incompetence, except we all knew she wasn't feigning.

I held my breath as you came into the room. And concentrated on my heart.

I definitely felt it.

A wave of something. Not just a tingle. Something.

When you were there I felt excited and contented all at the same time.

Hiraethog, on the other hand, was experiencing quite the opposite. Something approaching total panic.

He had no idea what to say or how to react.

You, the Englishman, the physical embodiment of English colonisation, Welsh subjugation, conquest and empire, were not at all what he had been expecting.

'This is totally unexpected,' I heard him whisper across to Penhaearn. 'What's the protocol?'

He used the anglicised word *protocol* as if he wasn't quite sure what it meant and didn't know the Welsh word for it either.

Like many in the room, Hiraethog had never actually had to deal with a black person before.

He'd seen black ticket collectors on trains and black people walking the streets on his occasional visits to Manchester or Liverpool or London, but he had never actually had to speak to one before.

I was being stupid. So what if I did fancy you? It was probably just a crush. Just because I had seen you naked a couple of times. And just because it was my first crush on someone since my trauma didn't make it true love, did it? And anyway, a sophisticated man such as you would not be interested in someone like me. Especially someone who kept covering their nose with their hand.

The most important thing was not to let anyone know that I might be in love with you, especially not you. You were the very last person who should know. And the other most important thing was that you had decided to stay. And that you hadn't complained about the room. But the most important thing of all was that you were splendid and you made my heart beat, the way hearts were supposed to beat. And that was, most importantly, a secret, too. At least until I had – also most importantly – calmed down.

I knew exactly what you must be thinking of this place with its old-fashioned oak table and panelling and stained-glass window. And of Hiraethog with his clanking chain and Mayoral mumblings in Welsh. And all the others.

You'd be thinking exactly the same as me. Obviously. Because that's what people in love do.

But, on the other hand, what was it to me what some English Jon Bull might be thinking?

The English only ever wanted one thing. Control. Well if you thought you were controlling me by tricking me into thinking I was in love with you, you could think all over again.

I watched you very carefully, as it was my duty to.

It was obvious that you didn't understand a word Hiraethog was saying to you.

I felt this urge to help you. I wanted to translate. To stand next to you, my mouth close to your ear. Your cheek. Your neck. Whispering the English translation of the rubbish Hiraethog was gabbling.

But why should I have thought that when all you English had only ever brought for us was harm? But you weren't a bit like all those English that Anti Gwenlais was always warning me about, were you?

THE COUNCIL CHAMBER seemed gloomy after the sunshine outside. And I remember my glasses were a little steamed up from rushing. So I must have blinked quite a bit.

'Good afternoon, everyone,' I said as brightly as I could. 'Sorry I'm late.'

It was important to be positive, especially when you didn't feel it.

The Mayor mumbled something I couldn't understand. So I stood there like a prat. Unsure. Was this Hooray-thog? Or the other one? Pen-*something*. And where was Mrs Leakin?

Another man stepped forward, brandishing his hand and smiling avuncularly.

'Bore da! Y dyn o Westminster dach chi, dw i'n siŵr. Penhaearn Tegid Foel Jones, Cynghorydd Sir Y Migneint ydw i.'

I shook the proffered hand.

'Councillor Pen-high-urn,' he smiled.

'Faswn i'n hoffi'ch cyflwyno chi i'r Maer, Mr Hiraethog Jones,' Penhaearn continued.

'Mayor Here-ay-thog? Isn't it awful about this morning's bombs in London?' I said. One could hardly talk about anything else. 'My radio reception was terrible. You haven't heard anything, have you?'

Penhaearn said something I didn't understand and started propelling me down the line, shaking hands, like royalty.

'Hello,' I said.

'Sut dach chi,' Islwyn mumbled back..

Then I became aware of a cheerful, red-faced woman in parrot-coloured cycling gear lunging purposively towards me.

'You must be Mr Bull.' She seized my hand and pumped it vigorously.

'Victoria Leakin. Chair of Antur Deg. It was I who arranged your visit.'

The assembled line dissolved before her.

'We have a rule here that we only speak Welsh. But don't worry, I'll translate,' she beamed.

At last, I had found a friendly face.

SOMETHING had definitely changed. Yesterday I would have registered Hiraethog's panic and discomfort only with complete detachment and no sympathy at all for his embarrassment and confusion. Today, I felt for him. I checked the feeling inside my chest to make sure: yes, a definite feeling of concern, even for Hiraethog.

It was like coming out of the cold and dark cellar at Y Ddwy Ddraig into bright sunlight on a summer's day. Every time I looked at you I felt my whole world brighten.

And I could feel things.

Sense people's feelings.

I had come alive.

I couldn't wait to get home and try out my newly rediscovered powers on little Awena. And Dad. And Mam. And even Gethin.

I sensed your nervousness, and how brave you were in hiding it. And Penhaearn's morbid suspicion and calculated cheeriness. And I could have written a book on what you thought of us – you, a sophisticated, broad-minded young man from the big wide world.

You could smell our suspicion. Even though we tried to mask it. Especially Hiraethog's. He stared at you, his mouth open, mesmerised by your dark skin, your wonderful teeth, and your lovely, clean pink tongue. Then he turned to Penhaearn.

'Ydy o'n Sais neu o Affrica?'

I felt the word for Africa hit you, even though you had no idea what else he had said. I wanted to tell you that Hiraethog was a good man, a fine, hard-working man, though a stranger to tact and subtlety. In his view, being honest was only being truthful, saying what you felt; it would never have occurred to him that his feelings might be wrong. Hiraethog was famous for three things: his painful longing to return to the flooded village under Llyn Y Gelyn where he believed he would have had a perfect life; driving his Jac Codi Baw; and being very stupid.

You turned to Mrs Leakin and extended your hand.

'Ah. Yes. I believe it was you who initiated my visit,' you said, 'So pleased to meet you.'

I saw Hiraethog staring at your trousers.

'They call me Boudiccea – nickname, you know – after the Icenic Queen. I'm not as warrior-like as the name implies. You made it, then? In the end. Did I mention I'm chair of Antur Deg?'

She sat you down at the large, round table, facing Hiraethog, and plonked herself next to you, while everyone else went back to their seats. Hiraethog reclaiming the Mayoral Chair with a sly glance at Penhaearn, who was back in his old seat.

Despite this triumph, Hiraethog looked very confused, his bald head shining wet. Before he could resolve this confusion into words, you had lifted your briefcase onto the table and started to pull out your laptop and projector.

'Is there anywhere I could plug this in?' you asked, beaming around expectantly. 'And perhaps a screen? Possibly?'

Boudiccea shook her head. And whispered loudly to you, as if whispering English was all right: 'There is no electricity.'

You cleared your throat and started to address us. You hadn't looked in my direction.

'Of course. Thank you. I do have some print-out versions of the slides.' You pulled out a sheaf of papers. 'But, firstly, may I . . . er . . . apologise for having missed the meeting yesterday.'

'O, na, na, na. Byddwch ddistaw!' Hiraethog spluttered.

I died a thousand deaths for you. How could you know Hiraethog was trying to shut you up?

'No matter,' you smiled, and reached into your case and produced a sheaf of papers. 'Although I haven't yet had the chance to see much of the town, what I have seen looked cool, really cool.'

You paused and looked at Boudiccea, waiting for her to translate. She didn't understand, so you whispered to her.

'Oh no,' she laughed. 'They don't need a translation. Everyone speaks English.'

'Oh. I see.'

I felt your confusion and embarrassment as if it were my own.

You smiled and soldiered on, dealing your papers around the table.

'I am,' you told us, 'confident I can find funding to develop and implement your plans for electricity, mains water and sewerage – which I have summarised here for you to peruse at your leisure. I assure you I will do everything I can to help you develop the strategies and plans to bring all your hopes to fruition and generate the outcomes you envisage.'

Your voice! So noble. So musically spoken. And you still hadn't noticed I was there.

'We can also look at the feasibility of a satellite relay and broadband,' you glanced around the room, finally taking in your audience.

Then you saw me! And stared momentarily. I felt everyone glance towards me and realised I was grinning and nodding very, very stupidly.

You raised your eyebrows and looked expectant. Were you expecting me to speak? I was only the unofficial Assistant Clerk. I wasn't even allowed to speak. I shook my head and felt the blood rush to my face. I looked away and heard you carry on.

'All in all, I think we can be confident of satisfactory outcomes in all exigencies.'

Boudiccea clapped her hands.

'Brilliant, young man,' she said. 'How long will all this take?'

'Like everything, there are certain procedures we must go through. Public consultation, feasibility studies, funding applications. But I am confident that if we expedite everything this end, we can look to setting an implementation start date of, say – best case scenario – six months from now. Does that sound OK?'

There were murmurs around the room.

'The first step is to demonstrate to the authorities that you as a community are united behind the plan.'

Penhaearn coughed, said something in Welsh and handed a piece of paper to Hiraethog who looked at it then handed it across to Islwyn to read out.

I was already cringing for what I knew was coming next.

Islwyn cleared his throat.

'I'm afraid we have a procedural difficulty. Constitutionally the business of the Council can only be conducted in Welsh. Therefore we cannot accept any of your presentation in English.'

'But surely . . .' protested Mrs Leakin.

The members of the Council had obediently started handing their documents back.

I looked at your face and our eyes met. I wanted you to know that I was not like them. I was a friend. I could help you. But not here.

That look between us made me start to tingle again.

Penhaearn commanded Hiraethog to close the meeting.

Mrs Leakin said something incomprehensible in her worst Boudiccea Welsh.

The voice of Penhaearn 'Tegid Foel' roared out in thick, clumsy English, rumbling around the old room and shaking the coloured glass in its lead. Now that the meeting was closed he could speak in English.

'Our language, Mr Bull, is very precious to us. You should know that it is the oldest living language in Europe. Only a few are left who speak it. Part of our duty in this town is to preserve it at all costs. We have sacrificed a very great deal for our language, including all these . . . *modernisations.*' He spat the word out. 'I ask you to respect that.'

You closed your eyes for a moment and then said, rather wearily, 'Please forgive me for my ignorance in not having had the forethought to have had these documents translated into Welsh.'

So beautiful! So magnificent! You rose above them effortlessly.

Here you were, offering us a gift of several million pounds to help bring labour-saving devices to our tiny community, our washing-weary mothers and hand-hewing men, and we were quibbling about the language you were using to offer it. God knows how we needed that money. You had seen for yourself just how badly my Dad's hotel could have done with it.

But we have principles. We Welsh don't like to think we are being bought. Especially not by the English.

'IS IT JUST ME. Or was that weird?' I asked Mrs Leakin as we walked back across the green to the hotel, London and the bombings nagging in my mind. There seemed no interest at all in development here.

'I'm very sorry, Mr Bull,' she apologised. 'People who don't live in Wales just don't appreciate the importance of the language here, you see. It didn't occur to me for a moment that they might refuse to let you speak in English. You must understand, I haven't been completely in control here. Believe it or not, this is only the first time I have been allowed in a Council Meeting.'

We passed the three old men on the bench who grinned and waved.

I lowered my voice so they wouldn't hear.

'Language would have been uppermost in any project with a non-ethnic UK community, naturally. I just didn't think that with an indigenous people, communicating in English would be an issue.'

'Please don't be angry with us, Mr Bull.'

'I'm not angry.'

Actually I was disorientated. I wanted her to go away. And then I wanted to run away back to London. I just wasn't equipped for this. My lack of Welsh was reason enough on its own. But I was desperate to speak to Mum and Dad and Nisha and Andrew to make sure no one was hurt. I hadn't heard any news since the initial reports of the bombs.

'Impatient then. I have apologised.'

There was a catch in her voice which made me glance at her. She looked distressed and I realised I was striding rather fast and she was having difficulty keeping up and talking at the same time. We stopped.

'You do understand, don't you? I'm awfully sorry. This project is very important to me. To us. The town.'

Out in the daylight she looked an older woman than I had assumed; her face was lined and there were tears in her eyes.

'It's no one's fault,' I said. 'You just need a Welsh speaker instead of me, that's all. There must be people in Wales.' It had been a cock-up from the beginning. I needed to be back in London. I needed to know that everyone was all right. To be with them.

'Oh no, it's you we need. Please don't give up on us.'

We were back at the hotel. Mrs Leakin led me into the dining room.

You were there again. You seemed to be everywhere, Gwalia. Up waterfalls, at reception desks, in my room, in the Council Chamber. This time you were a waitress.

'That is going to be very difficult given that the key players refuse to talk officially to me in English and I don't speak Welsh,' I said.

I remember thinking: why does that girl keep appearing everywhere? And staring at me like that? And smiling so sweetly? I feel as if I should know her, like an old friend, but I don't.

I needed to phone the office again. What was I – an expert in immigration and the problems of ethnic integration – doing here? I was worse than useless. This was a simple economic development project. Someone from Cardiff should be doing it.

I needed to find out about the bombings? Professor Lain would probably need me back in London. The bombers were almost certainly from one of our indigenous immigrant communities. They'd need my expertise to go and set up a liaison group in whatever cities were involved. I knew how to do that. *Salaam aleikum*. Two words more than my Welsh. Surely she would need me to advise on trouble spots, liaise with the police.

Mrs Leakin was talking nonstop.

'It's a disgrace that no one told you, Mr Bull. Mind you, I didn't know either, until I met my husband. It's not something they tell you at school. But I've been learning the language, you know. I go to classes twice a week. I think it's very important. I encourage everyone who moves here to do that. It's the least one can do.'

I was hardly listening. I needed to talk to Nisha again. And you seemed to be hovering around the table, Gwalia.

'I can hardly believe it myself, Mr Bull. It must be very embarrassing for you. However, I'm sure it's an easy mistake to make. When I first moved here I had not the slightest conception of what being in "a Welsh-speaking area" meant.'

'Well I think we know now, don't we, Mrs Leakin? It's a place where people actually speak Welsh as their main language. I need to make a phone call, I'm afraid. Would you please excuse me?'

I got up. You made a sort of motion, Gwalia, as if you were going to lead me to the phone, even though I had already used it once and did know where it was. But Mrs Leakin wouldn't let me go.

'Quite right, Mr Bull. Quite right. People assume it's like Latin or Cornish or something, you see, there's a lot like that. They assume it's a dead language for people to do at evening classes. I'm so sorry I should at least have mentioned it.'

'Don't worry about it. I'll probably have to go back to London this afternoon anyway.' If I phoned and spoke to Professor Lain now, I could probably be back in London for dinner.

You led me to an office this time, behind the reception desk.

'There's an extension phone here,' you said, moving some papers and revealing an ancient handset. I thanked you and you went and stood at the reception desk.

I got through to Nisha on a direct line.

'Is everyone all right there after the bombs? I haven't been able to hear any news at all. Does Angela need me to come back?'

Nisha assured me that I was not needed back in London and that Andrew was OK. It was a little disquieting, knowing that you were obviously eavesdropping, Gwalia. It didn't occur to me that you were spying on me. I thought you were just nosy. I'd never had any reason to fear being spied on before.

'You did find the place in the end?' Nisha asked. 'Andrew and I had visions of you sleeping in the mountains.'

'Oh yes, I'm fine,' I lied. I could explain about sleeping in the car when I got back. 'You wouldn't believe this place. They're refusing to speak to me in English. They speak only Welsh.'

Nisha laughed very hard.

'Well then, that will be being in the nature of a predicament for the Englishman,' she said, exaggerating her slight Indian accent by way of mockery. 'You'll just have to be talking louder and slower.'

'Very funny.'

'I'll get onto the Welsh Assembly and see what they suggest. Are you online yet?'

'No electricity. And certainly no wi-fi. And the phones are all hard wired in to old-fashioned boxes with no plugs.'

'I'll text you then.'

'I doubt it. There's no signal because of the mountains.'

'Snail-mail then. I'll check the post code with the service provider. Phone me later.'

'Thanks Nisha.'

I went back to the cold chicory coffee – of the sort that you get for breakfast in cheap hotels – then Mrs Leakin spent forever telling me the history of the project and what seemed like most of her whole life story: from being raised in middle-class Surrey to marrying an East End boy to being head of some community organisation and then a humiliating divorce. Dating via a newspaper soul mates column and moving to Wales. And how now her whole life had been turned upside down and inside out by inexplicably falling for Penhaearn's business partner, Lawns, so that now she felt like an outsider in both the Welsh and the English communities and an insider nowhere. And how her mother would have been horrified to think that she had moved to Wales and married a mortician. And how the Welsh were so po-faced about everything. And she could barely stand living in such primitive conditions. And something had to be done. And she wasn't just sitting back waiting for someone else to do it, she was getting on with it.

Insofar as I was having difficulty coping with the primitive conditions and po-faced obstructiveness, I think she sensed a kindred spirit in me. But I also felt wary of becoming her ally and losing my objectivity.

'You must call me Victoria – or Boudiccea if you like – because that's an ancient Welsh version of the word Victoria, you know. It's how I sign myself now. The Prime Minister's office sent me a letter addressed to Boudiccea Leakin this week, but then, I expect you know that.'

While she told me everything, Gwalia, you hovered in the background. Did you already feel like my guardian angel?

'You won't believe the frustrations and disappointment I've suffered, Mr Bull. It's so nice to be able to talk to another professional. Of course, my officer, Blodeuwedd, is a complete disaster. I sometimes think she does it deliberately.'

'I've read through the papers. You seem to be doing all the right things, strategically, Mrs Leakin.'

'You don't know what a trial it's been. I've had to take this town by the scruff of the neck and literally drag it into the twenty-first century. Single-handedly.'

Then she announced that we were going on a tour. Unfortunately, I was far too tired and dispirited to argue. Did I see you smirk, Gwalia, at that?

She led me outside and ordered me onto the back of her tandem, then mounted in front of me. I was conscious that half the town seemed to have stopped what they were doing and turned to watch. The old men on the bench, waved.

We set off past the hotel and out of the top end of the town. I guessed we'd be going up one of the tributary valleys I'd seen from the top of the hill.

I don't think she stopped talking all the way, though I

caught only occasional words and sentences, flying over her shoulder on the slipstream as she pedalled furiously.

'We're going to see the Ingresses, my dear. Wendy and Guy are desperate for mains services, you see.'

'Yes,' I shouted pointlessly at the Lycra-clad buttocks gyrating in my face.

'They want to build a four-star holiday village . . . power showers . . . jacuzzis . . . visions, the lot . . . could be the making of this town, Jon,' were words I did hear. 'But you don't power that on fresh air, do you.'

'No, Mrs Leakin, you don't,' I mumbled, though it did occur to me that, with wind farms, you possibly might.

'We'll have tourists flocking here. Million pounds a year . . . two . . . four . . . such plans. But we must have power . . . fundamental . . . Nothing must stop us now.'

Long before we were even half way up the valley, I had weakened. I'd shrugged off sleep deficit, lack of food and everything else – no problem, but Boudiccea was exhausting me.

'You'll have to pedal harder,' she ordered, as we came to a steeper hill. 'It's a lot heavier with you on it.'

Riding a tandem, I discovered, was – and yet was not! – a bonding experience.

By the time we reached a cluster of buildings at the head of the valley, I felt I knew her intimately. I did not especially like her, but, there was something about Boudiccea!

Turning off the lane and up the unadopted forest road to the Ingresses' property, I caught the sound of a rough petrol engine rasping above my own breathing and the thump of my heart.

A man in his late thirties was standing naked to the waist in the yard, next to a concrete-mixer, directing three other men heaving buckets of slopping cement into an outbuilding obviously being renovated.

'Victoria!' A woman standing at the front door, neat and trim in a summery frock, waved. Amidst the chaos, she was fastidiously collecting dirty mugs from the wall, being careful not to chip her nail varnish.

We dismounted.

The man looked up and acknowledged us. And then came over.

I was introduced to Guy Ingress and his wife, Wendy.

'What happened to you then, yesterday?' Guy shouted over the noise of the mixer.

'I couldn't find the signs to the town,' I shouted. It is best to be concise when you are shouting.

He raised his eyes heavenwards.

'Those bloody Welsh nationalists,' he shouted. 'They're always sabotaging the signposts. Pulling them down, making them point the wrong way.'

'It's because they only recognise the Welsh name Llanchwaraetegdanygelyn. They don't accept the name Umbo,' Victoria shouted back.

'Umbo is the name on all the maps,' shouted Wendy. 'It's so silly.'

'How are we supposed to bring tourists here with all that nonsense going on?' Guy shouted.

He jabbed with his finger.

'I've got to get this lot sorted before the mix goes off. I'll join you later.' He turned back to the cement mixer and Wendy led us round the stack of breeze blocks, pile of sand and bags of cement to the front door.

'I think you've come just in time,' Wendy said, flashing me a wan smile and leading us through to an impressive room with ingle-nook fireplace and tarred oak beams.

She looked at Boudiccea, smiled bravely, then suddenly her face collapsed into tears and she pulled a paper tissue from her sleeve and dabbed at her eyes.

'I'm sorry,' she said. 'I'm sorry.'

'Is everything all right, Wendy?' Boudiccea asked, putting a yellow and blue Lycra arm around her, revealing the sweat patch under her armpit.

'Oh Victoria. I'm so worried. It's everything. It's chaos. Guy's just furious. I don't know. You do your best . . . and then those bastards on the Council.' She looked at me. 'Victoria knows the story.'

Boudiccea gave her an encouraging hug and sat her down.

'Jon Bull is the man from Westminster I told you about. He's come to hear your story. He's going to sort all this nonsense out, aren't you, Jon?'

I confidently assured her I was.

With Boudiccea's arm locked around her shoulder, Wendy composed herself.

'We sold our house in Wilmslow, you see. We fell in love with this place. And the people. We made our commitment, we invested all our money. And we're doing our best to help improve the local economy. We really are. We thought they wanted that.'

She dabbed at her eyes and was going to start weeping again but Boudiccea squeezed her sharply to her senses.

'Everything's turning completely tits up,' she blurted, crying and talking at the same time, her blond hair stuck to her face by tears. 'We've run out of money. And we owe so much! And it's all obstacles.'

She looked at me imploringly.

'We've got obstacles with planning permission, obstacles with the National Park, obstacles with building regulations . . . It's all just obstacles. Everywhere.'

She looked at me. 'I don't know if I can take it anymore,' she wailed.

'You see,' said Boudiccea. 'You see.'

The tissue had disintegrated.

'Take no notice of me.'

She got up and fled from the room.

'It's terrible to see such a brave woman reduced to this,' Boudiccea said.

We sat in silence for a while. A minute later Wendy was back, her face washed, her hair brushed, clutching a whole box of tissues, her brittle confidence restored at least for the moment.

'You poor thing,' Victoria said. 'I'm sure it'll work out in the end, now Jon is here.'

Boudiccea leaned over to give her another hug, but Wendy jumped up and escaped.

'It's so unfair. I feel we've worked so hard. We've done everything – we've always employed local people – kept the bed and breakfast to generate a little bit of income while all this gets done. But this really has disheartened us, Jon. You must understand that. And thank you so very much for coming to see us and helping.'

She came over to where I was sitting and touched me on the shoulder.

I muttered something else and forced a smile.

'Aren't you going to take any notes?' Boudiccea demanded.

I pointed ambiguously to my head. I was too tired to begin to explain how tired, hungry and exhausted I felt.

Wendy carried on. She was a very pretty woman. Seeing inside relationships was still a novelty for me. She seemed very wifely, I remember thinking. Not like Nisha or Maria. Half-way between a girlfriend and a mum.

'Guy's so angry that people are trying to undermine him when we've tried so hard to work for the town and help by employing local people and buying materials locally. Everything.'

'Don't despair, it'll all work out. Once Mr Bull has organised our mains electricity and water.'

'Oh, Victoria! You're such a star!' said Wendy, clapping her hands. 'But I don't know. Sometimes I doubt it'll ever happen. I'm sorry, Mr Bull. I don't know what you must be thinking.'

'I'm noting everything you say,' I assured her. 'I can appreciate why you need outside intervention.'

'Intervention!' screeched Boudiccea. 'Yes. That's a good word, Mr Bull. Intervention. That's exactly what we need. You have no idea quite how frustrated with these Welsh Nationalist people we are.'

'Oh, I think I do,' I said.

Then Guy came in, the smell of sweat coming off him whenever he moved. I stood up. And we shook hands. I found him slightly menacing. Wendy looked at him with what I suppose was pride.

'All I've got to say is this,' he said, jabbing his finger on my chest. 'We came here to run a business – like many other English people here. Understand?'

I smiled and nodded.

'We wanna make some money, right? And then move on. We're not here to retire or just to mark time like these Welsh buggers, happy to earn a few piffling thousand a year. I'm not here to piss about. If you can't get these projects moving, then we're selling up and moving on. And plenty of others feel the same.'

He stared hard into my face to make sure I had understood, then started to pace the room.

'We are sick to death of these Welsh idiots getting in the way. Prissying about with Welsh language *this* and Welsh language *that*. You can't even go and talk to their committee unless you speak their language.

'Well, let me tell you something. We have rights. This is our country too. And we have a right to speak our language here and do things our way. They can't stop us having mains services any longer.'

He paused. Always a mistake in Boudiccea's presence.

'We understand that this is their town,' she interrupted anxiously. 'We do understand the importance of their language. And we do respect their right to speak it.'

'Do we shit!' said Guy.

'Oh Guy,' said Boudiccea, with the tone of a disappointed governess. 'That's not true. Wendy and I both take Welsh lessons.'

Wendy flinched and Guy exploded.

'Why! Why should we? They all speak English, don't they? What difference does it make to them what language we speak? The world moves on. It has to move on. Look at this town. Shabby run-down shops. Earth toilets in their back yards. This is the twenty-first century. Why should we respect their fucking sensibilities? They don't bloody respect mine.'

Wendy was glancing anxiously between her husband and Boudiccea and me.

'We do understand it from your point of view, Victoria,' she said. 'Married to a Welshman. But it's different for us. We've invested our life savings. We have children . . .'

'Don't worry about my feelings, my dear' said Boudiccea. 'You won't offend me.'

'That's another bloody thing,' Guy started up again. 'Insisting on teaching my kids in Welsh. What about my rights, eh? I don't want my kids to learn Welsh. I don't want them to speak a language I can't understand in my own home.'

And then he turned back to me.

'This is a third world country here, Mr Bull. And it's the fucking language that's keeping them in the third world. That's what you've got to tell them! Welsh is a fucking joke . . . is what it is. A dying language.

'I need to get these outbuildings converted, make my money, and get out. I'm not staying here a minute longer than I have to. I've had it up to here with fucking Welsh. We're going to Spain. They know how to look after their investors there.'

AS SOON AS you'd gone, Jon, I had these strangely joyful urges to please you. Normally, all my little jobs were chores. Tasks to be undertaken, duties to be discharged. Self-discipline to improve my soul.

But not today.

Today I was doing everything for you.

I had always laughed at other girls who fell into a strange awe of boys just because they fancied them. Yet here I was, ecstatic to be washing your clothes in the tub, putting them through the mangle, and hanging them up to dry. Singing. Grateful to have the clothes that had been next to your skin in my hands. Glad to serve you. The nearest that I could get to you until your blessed return.

I had no idea, really, what you thought of me. Some instinct made me keep my joy a secret. A delusion, perhaps, to savour in silence.

And all the while I kept explaining it away to myself by thinking I was spying on you. I'd had another thought, too. The things you'd said about getting grants for the hotel – you probably didn't even remember saying them – they'd got me thinking. Maybe if I could persuade you to help me, we really could modernise Y Ddwy Ddraig.

My imagination was running rather wild, wasn't it? And you were gone so long!

What fuel there is in absences for fantasy.

When you finally did arrive back, I feigned nonchalance. Indifference. I brought you a measly cup of tea and two home-made Welsh cakes.

You looked deliciously grateful, and wolfed them, two bites each.

'How was your cycle ride?' I asked, with dreadful coyness, unable to help myself.

'It was very hard pedalling uphill. And very fast pedalling down,' you said carefully.

'And did you find that – thrilling at all?' I persisted.

'We did seem to corner very fast and low.'

'I expect you'll be ready for something to eat then, by now, I should think.'

Another look of child-like gratitude swept your face which was tingly for me, too, but in a different way.

'I've only had a muesli bar and fish and chips in 24 hours. Do you know where I could get something?'

You were asking my advice! I hadn't felt like this since . . . since forever. Oh you! The myth of you that I was creating in myself. Of course I knew exactly where you could get something. But I had to play with you. I had to, Jon. I had to! You can understand that, can't you?

'You're a bit late,' I said, surprising myself with my own bossiness. 'Caffi Cyfoes'll be shut. And we don't really cater for visitors at this time of year.'

You looked crestfallen. But I was full of my plans. If I could get you home with me . . . I checked myself. If I could get you home, it would be a triumph. Mam would think I'd brought you home to steal your secrets, but I could get you to talk to Dad about the grants, then maybe we could make Y Ddwy Ddraig successful again. Also, you and I would have to spend quite a lot of time together, especially if I asked you to help me fill out all the forms. There would be bound to be lots of forms. And then . . .

'I'll have to drive somewhere else, then.'

'Well,' I said, feeling myself cocking my head and doing something unaccustomed with my eyes. 'You could come back to my house, I suppose, if you really wanted,' I said, trying not to sound as eager – or as vulnerable to your possible refusal – as I felt.

'Oh no. No no. I'll find somewhere,' you said. But I think your eyes were saying something else.

'You do look tired out,' I shrugged.

Did I wiggle my shoulders? Was I being very girly?

'Low sugar levels,' you said, alarmingly.

'You're not diabetic are you?' I asked, a little too

concernedly. *Nain* was diabetic, I knew all about diabetic. 'Not that it's any worry of mine.'

It must have been obvious to you by now that I was totally in your power. Any fool could have seen it.

But you were not just any fool.

'I was just rather incompetent with my directions,' you said. 'It took somewhat longer than expected to find you.'

To find me? No. To find us. Because Dewi and I had moved the signs. It was all my fault!

And then you looked in my eyes. Which caused an enormous shiver.

I took a deep breath. 'It wasn't your fault you couldn't find us.'

Suddenly I saw those nights that I had gone with Dewi and Gwrthsafiad, taking down the signs with Umbo on, in a different light.

'The signposts are rather confusing,' you said. 'Anyone would think you didn't want people to find you. Besides I have loads to do. Look. Maybe I could get a sandwich or something from the shop.'

You got up to go.

'I could translate for you,' I blurted in desperation, tucking my hair behind my ear, lowering my face and shaking my hips and shoulders at the same time. Where had I learned all that? 'I could help you in all sorts of ways.'

'But you're . . . It's not just the odd sentence. It's a long piece.'

'Show me.'

You pulled the plan from your briefcase. And I leafed through it. Three pages. Mostly bullet points with a paragraph of introduction to each section.

'It looks straightforward enough to me.'

'They wouldn't even look at it at the meeting.'

'I know,' I said. 'I was there. You probably didn't notice me.' Did that sound sulky?

'Oh yes I did. I mean. Of course you were,' you flustered. 'I was a bit confused. It was rather disorientating, I'm afraid. Sorry.'

You looked at my hair and my face. I worried for an instant that your gaze might stop at my mutilated nose. But you seemed more preoccupied by my mouth. Aren't boys funny?

Yes! I would get you home. And you would talk to my father. And you would sort the town out. And the hotel. And I would be your translator. And your Mata Hari. And we would sit together. And . . . But I could think not a *meddwl meddal* further than that for now.

'You'll have to come back to my house,' I said decisively. 'I have to be home in quarter of an hour. You can have dinner with my family. I'm only waiting for Dewi.'

'Oh I don't want to be any . . .'

'You wouldn't be. You can talk to my father. He enjoys visitors.'

'That's very kind of you. I'll pay you, obviously.'

'I would be most insulted if you did,' I said firmly.

FOOD! Home cooking! I wanted to put my hands on your bare shoulders and kiss you. Your neck looked kissable. And your mouth was very kissable. And your shoulders, obviously. But, for reasons of professionalism, I put that out of my mind. Completely. Well, as much as possible.

To be honest, you mesmerised me. Bedazzled me. No girl had ever gazed so directly at me before. Not the clear, warm, smiling way you were gazing at me. I hardly dared look back at you. I was dazzled by how beautiful you were. Many, many unprofessional thoughts were zinging through my think-tank mind. And my stomach was asserting its own, more basic, needs. It was as if my body – my biological self perhaps – had its own independent agenda. It had made its own decisions, I think, without consulting me.

'That sounds great,' I heard myself saying. 'I don't suppose I could have another cup of tea, could I? And maybe some toast or something.'

'Certainly, Mr Bull,' you said, jumping up. You had a lively way of moving which kicked the hem of your skirt up, and made me respond somehow, as if my body wanted to dance with yours.

'Please,' I said. 'Don't call me that. I'm Jon. What's your name?'

'Gwalia. It's the ancient name for Wales.'

You said it over your bare shoulder as you went out to the kitchen.

Gwalia. Ancient name for Wales.

You came back with two mugs of tea and a piece of cake and sat down beside me.

'This will keep us going.'

You shuffled closer.

Another wave of gratitude swept over me. All the same, it seemed a little forward of me – and of us both – my brain was noting. And yet, I felt so pleased and flattered and grateful.

'You can unwind now,' you said, your dazzling face less than a foot away.

Unwind. I was practically unravelling.

The cake was delicious. Probably the best cake anyone had ever made anywhere in all of history (subjectively speaking, obviously).

'Wow! Brilliant,' I said, wolfing it.

There was no problem being friendly, I told myself. Or grateful. Just so long as I stayed professional.

'You were hungry then?'

'Ravenous.'

'Come on then.' You got up, obviously wanting me to follow.

'What about this place?' I said. It seemed incredible that you could just leave the hotel wide open with no one in charge.

'It's all right. Dewi'll be here shortly. He's in the bar tonight.'

So I picked up my laptop and briefcase, and let you lead me out through the kitchens, across the rough chippings in the little car park, through a gate, and across a small orchard to a terrace of detached stone cottages standing on their own by a rough track.

There was one question nagging at me, which I had to ask you.

'What did you mean,' I said carefully. 'When you asked me if I'd enjoyed my morning swim today?'

You looked at me and smiled. Your eyes were shining. There was an interesting crease at the corner of your mouth.

''Wnest ti ymddangos o 'mlaen i fel rhyw fath o dduw y bore 'ma,' you said.

'What does that mean?'

You laughed out loud then. But you didn't answer.

It was only later that I found out what you had said that day. Something about me seeming to you like the vision of some god who'd come to save you.

Your house was so completely different from my own parents' penthouse flat in Putney that it threw me. I was used to minimalism, remember. Mum and Dad have bare white walls, white carpets, white cupboards and mirrors. Nothing on display except the London skyscape through the huge picture windows. Even the massive television folds away into the ceiling at the touch of a switch.

Your kitchen was a clutter of old furniture and books, an old sheepdog (who pestered my crotch incessantly) and several cats. The air was heavy with the smell of casserole and baking bread.

You said something about me to your mother in Welsh. She looked at me irritably, nodded, wiped her hand on her pinafore, eyed me suspiciously, and shook my own proffered hand. Then I was introduced to Awena, who told me proudly in English that she was six and a half.

Finally, you parked me in the dog's smelly chair beside the Aga while you helped your mother with the chores, arguing in Welsh with each other. About me, I expect. In my belly the smell of all that food was making my gastric juices gurgle.

I distracted myself by trying to listen to your Welsh, admiring the musicality of your language, trying to decipher some kind of meaning. Strange how there is always meaning in human voices, whatever the language.

Then you apologised for being rude and talking Welsh.

And your mother scowled and twted.

'Not that we need to apologise for talking our own language, as I am sure you will agree, Mr Bull,' she said.

'I should have realised, but I really didn't know that people actually spoke Welsh, like all the time, till I arrived here today,' I confessed.

You looked at me sharply.

'I'm not against it,' I said hurriedly. 'Just intrigued. It's great that a region of Britain actually speaks its own language. I just hadn't realised, that's all.'

Your mother rounded on me then.

'A region of Britain! Another language! And I'm astonished that you are sent here with such a level of ignorance! Have you never heard of Gaelic? Or Manx?'

'Well, yes. I'd heard of them. Most of our interest centres

on Urdu and Hindi and Bengali, that's all. And Polish is getting more important these days. And Chinese, of course. But the Chinese seem much more self-sufficient somehow. That's all I meant.'

'That's all you meant!'

'And I'd heard of Welsh, of course. I just didn't sort of realise that communities – I don't know – you know, spoke it. Like, on a daily basis.'

'Well we do. As you see. That's the snag, you see, Gwalia, no one knows. And no one cares, do they? And if anyone should know and care it is the people at Westminster, who are supposed to know how to help us. Don't you agree with me, Mr Bull?'

It wasn't quite the moment to explain that I wasn't exactly from Westminster.

'They should certainly know about Welsh-speaking communities,' I said. 'How many are there?'

But she ignored that.

'I'll have you know it's an older language than English. Did you know that? I would have thought a man with your position would have known more than me about it. But I expect that is stupid of me. For thinking that a man from England, an advisor to Government, might be bothered to have learned the single most important fact about us. Welsh, young man, is our *first* language. Our *mamiaith*.'

You gave me a look, Gwalia, which I'm sure said 'I'm so sorry,' you were cringing for me at your mother's abruptness, trying to signal to me with your eyes to ignore her. I saw the prospect of my dinner evaporating before me. Along with any hope of getting the translation done before tomorrow's meeting.

'I'm sorry,' I said, apologising for all England. 'It is very remiss of me. But I will do whatever I can to remedy my deficiency, I do assure you.'

You rolled your eyes then. Even to myself I sounded very slimy. Like Freddy Morgan or something! I can only attribute it to hunger.

Your mother eyed me suspiciously.

Then she threw me a tea-towel and commanded me to make myself useful and dry some saucepans and cooking pots while she prepared vegetables in the stoneware sink and attempted to remedy all the deficiencies in my knowledge about Wales at once. I'm sure she would have taught me your whole language in one lesson, if she could.

'Part of the Brythonic family including the languages of Cornwall, Brittany and, more distantly, the Gaelic languages of Ireland and Scotland.

'Celtic was spoken all over Europe before the Romans,' she told me.

Fortunately, your father arrived home just in time to save me. He stood at the door, waiting for an opportunity to speak.

'Leave the boy alone,' he said in English and winked at me. 'We must welcome him properly to our hearth.'

'He wasn't aware that half a million of us here speak Welsh. Twenty percent of us. And sixty thousand people in Scotland speak their language.'

'Well, that's a shame,' your Dad said, breaking in as she paused for breath. 'We are fortunate, then, that you have been able to rectify that gap in his knowledge.'

We shook hands. He seemed a kindly man.

You came to his side then, Gwalia, and announced that I had said I might be able to offer some advice on getting grants for the hotel. I didn't quite remember saying this, but it had been a very confusing day.

Over supper, I heard the whole story: how your father had inherited Y Ddwy Ddraig from his father, and he from his, going back to the coaching inns and the drovers' trails of medieval times when shepherds would drive huge flocks of sheep and herds of cattle hundreds of miles to market, stopping to graze on the common lands and village greens, and taking travellers with them, to the great meat markets of London. And how it had fallen on harder and harder times as the population of the town had shrunk and aged.

'I only keep it going as a service to the town. I'd like to see it pass on to Gwalia, Gethin and Awena,' your Dad sighed. 'But I fear it is more of a liability than an asset.'

He was a wise and patient man, I decided. And probably an excellent headmaster.

'That was wonderful,' I said when we had finished the home-made rhubarb pie and proper custard, made with egg yolk. 'How do you say thank you in Welsh?'

'Diolch. Or, Diolch yn fawr.'

You seized a piece of paper from one of the piles on the table and scribbled it down..

'Well, diolch yn ffawr, then'

'No, not ffaw – vaw – F is always pronounced as a V unless its double F – vawr. And roll the rrrr.'

I tried again. You laughed and clapped your hands.

'But you don't need to frown when you speak Welsh, Jon. There's nothing to frown about.'

I felt you touch me momentarily on the forearm, with your fingertips. And I carried on feeling the place where you had touched me for moments after. I remember your eyes reflecting the soft light from the lamp; your face was only inches from mine. Inches from my lips. I remember how pores in your soft, perfect skin made delightful patterns as they ran across little creases to your eyes and mouth. And your not-quite-perfect-but-lovely-anyway teeth. Your lips seemed to quiver slightly.

And you seemed to be watching me just as intently, attentive to my every word. Once or twice, when I spoke, your mouth moved slightly as if you were kissing my words. I'm sure you knew what I was thinking.

Then you realised your mother was watching you and the way you were looking at me, so you laughed and looked away. And then glanced back.

I laughed too.

Your mother got up and began to clear the table and your Dad went off to choir practice.

'Next time,' I said, 'I'll bring a bottle of wine.'

Your mother turned towards me sternly.

'Oh no,' she said. 'I'm very glad you didn't. We're totally teetotal here.'

I think there was a note of disapproval in her voice.

'Well, diolch yn fawr for a brilliant dinner,' I said. 'Let me help with the washing up.'

She softened a little then, and while you busied yourself upstairs, with Gethin and Awena, I think, helping them with their homework. She washed, I dried, the way I did sometimes when I was at my grandmother's. I wasn't very good at it, but I did feel less like a spare part.

Finally, when we'd finished our chores, you came back downstairs and wiped the table. I got out my laptop and you pulled a chair up next to mine.

You translated for me, laughing at me when I couldn't find the accents for the Welsh alphabet on my laptop. You knew where they were, though, amongst the special characters and symbols.

With the hiss of the paraffin lamp in the background, we worked through the print-out of the proposal I had taken to the meeting, line by line, word by word, you writing it out in longhand Welsh, bullet point by bullet point, for me to tap laboriously into the keyboard, letter by letter, hesitating over the unaccustomed accents, like the to bach – 'little roof' – as you called it on some ŵ's.

'I hope my battery will last,' I said.

'Well let me do it then, I'll be much quicker.'

So you pushed me aside, sat in my chair and took over.

You sensed my affront.

'Why did you imagine I wouldn't know how to use a computer?' you demanded, typing away much faster than me. 'Just because the town has no electricity?'

'But where do you get the opportunity? Where do you practise?'

'I learn at school,' you laughed. 'They're letting me take my A-levels this year.'

Several times our shoulders touched, and twice our hands brushed against each other. I can still picture us that night, our faces only inches apart, you laughing, wrinkling your nose, so engrossed in me and everything I said; and me fascinated by the light dancing in your eyes and the creases at the corners of your mouth.

Every now and again you'd ask me to clarify what I meant by a certain phrase. Some of the official expressions, like 'tactical' and 'strategic', puzzled you and two or three times you had to ask your father, by now back from choir practice. He lowered his paper, smiled kindly and delivered his answer, pleased to have been consulted, I think.

It took much longer than a couple of hours, and I once had to run back to the hotel to fetch the spare battery pack for my laptop, hurtling through the darkness, across the field, completely intoxicated by you. Coming back, seeing the yellow light of the paraffin lamp through the window panes, I was filled with an excitement that tightened my chest and made me run like a little boy.

We were touching minds, touching worlds.

I made myself stop running and slowed to a walk. I must be entirely professional, I told myself. Think only about work. The town project, nothing else.

More than once, when you had reached across in front of me to touch the keys, your hair had brushed my lips. Our faces had been so close that I had felt the warmth of your cheek against mine, so close I could have counted each of the fine golden hairs on the back of your neck. How easy it would have been to kiss you. In less than a centimetre, I could have kissed your neck. Instead, I had closed my eyes and filled my breath, and my whole being, with the sweet Welsh smell of you.

I was even picking up a few words from your language: 'y' for 'the', 'cyfarfod' for 'meeting', 'cynllun' for 'plan'. And 'diolch yn fawr', of course, for 'thank you.'

I lingered long after it was obviously time to go. You didn't mind. You seemed amused. I saw your mother looking at me doubtfully. It would be unprofessional to overstay.

So I packed away my things and thanked her once again for saving me from death by starvation. I don't think she got it. Your father did though. He laughed, got up, and shook my hand.

'Diolch yn fawr,' I said, wishing, for some strange reason, that I could have said something eloquent and adequate to him in his own language – your language. 'I wish I knew a little more Welsh. It seems a fascinating language, all these strange mutations and elisions.'

You scowled at your mother, smiled at me and came to show me out. Just then your Dad appeared again and pressed a small packet into my hands. And said 'Nos da' and disappeared again before I had time to thank him. Rather absent-mindedly, I put it in my pocket, I was preoccupied with you, I suppose.

'Take no notice of Mam,' you said. 'She's a bit old-fashioned about some things. They worry about me.'

'They seem lovely,' I said. 'You're lucky.' I meant it. You seemed closer to your parents than I felt to mine.

We walked across the field together, the first time we had been alone together since arriving at the house.

'Thank you,' I said. 'You've been incredibly kind to me. I don't know what . . .' and then I realised I hadn't even paid you for your translation.

'How much do I owe you?' And I reached into my pocket for my wallet and took out £50.

'I don't want your money,' you said, totally insulted.

I'd spoiled the mood.

I'd ruined everything.

'I'm sorry. I'm sorry.'

Did you sense the panic in my voice?

You grasped my arm.

'Please. Don't try to pay me.'

I felt completely awkward now. Dazed. Confused.

And the next thing I knew was that you were standing on your tiptoes, your lips brushing mine so lightly and so briefly it had hardly happened. And then you were gone. And I was left watching you skipping back through the almost-darkness across the field towards your open front door with its yellow light spilling out into the night.

'I really like your family,' I called after you, thinking, even as I said it, what an idiot I was.

Your door closed, trapping the light back into the house, leaving me in darkness, your kiss still tickling like a feather on my lips.

All night, Gwalia, I could think of nothing else but you. That inconsequential touch of your lips on mine. Pathetic as it was, my brain kept going back to every detail of you and that evening. Long after I had more than exhausted every possible fact and memory there was to think about you, I still kept thinking of you.

I woke the following morning still thinking of you. My mind intoxicated by you – your people, your language. Your stone-walled fields climbing up the mountains to the cloud-filled skies. The soft, sweet smell of you lingering in my nostrils. And an inexplicable urge to be with you.

It was only then that I remembered the packet your Dad had given me and fished for it in my jacket pocket. Inside your dad's carefully recycled brown paper bag was a 1950s cloth-backed booklet, discoloured with damp and frayed. *Welsh Phrases for Beginners.* I flicked through it and tried out some of the simple sentences aloud.

I would surprise you. Impress you. It would not be that difficult to learn a couple of dozen words. I leafed through the book.

'Mae'n ddiwrnod braf heddiw,' I repeated, trying to remember to roll the r's and pronounce the f's as v's and the dd's as a voiced th, as in 'the'. 'It's a day fine today.'

'Rhaid imi ddefnyddio'r tŷ bach – I need to use the little house.'

I had a lot of lost time to make up for. And, yes, I could

advise your dad on grants for modernisation and *en-suite* facilities. Today I could do anything. 'Mae'n ddiwrnod braf heddiw.'

I was still reciting these phrases as I opened my door and set off for the tŷ bach.

'Mae hi'n ddiwrnod braf heddiw. Rhaid i mi ddefnyddio'r tŷ bach.'

'Esgusodwch ni, Mr Bull,' said a deep voice .

It came from a whiskery character in dirty corduroy trousers and yellow road safety jacket. There were five of them, standing in the corridor outside my door. How long they had been there I had no idea.

'We have come to make our representations to you,' said the whiskery one. The next man tugged at his sleeve.

'Twm Slwtsh is who he is, Sir. And I am Jo Botel, and this is Gwyn Mantel and Jac Dŵr. We are honest traders. And we need a word with you.'

In London, I can look at people and judge immediately what sort of people they are, no matter where they come from. Not here. This country seemed very foreign to me. And I felt very close to naked.

Twm slowly turned to Jac.

'Be ti isio, Jac?' he asked and, for my benefit, added in English. 'I'm asking Jac what he wants me to say.' He was clutching a piece of paper. 'Shall I read it now?'

'I think perhaps Mr Bull is on an urgent errand,' Jac Dŵr said in English.

'What kind of errand?'

'Mae o isio mynd i'r tŷ bach.'

'Oh yes, I see,' said Twm, scratching his head. 'Please carry on, Mr Bull. We'll wait here.'

'Thank you,' I said. And fled to the tŷ bach.

When I returned, they were still assembled. And followed me into the room.

'Errrm. I think I need to get dressed,' I said, trying to be tactful.

'Don't mind us,' said Twm. 'We're men of the world like you. We've been in the rugby team.'

'Twm deals in shit, you know,' said Jac.

'And Jac deals in dŵr,' said Gwyn.

'Water, you twpsyn,' said Jac. 'You have to say water not *dŵr*.'

'Dŵr is water.'

'But Mr Bull doesn't know that, do you Mr Bull?'

'I do now,' I said, struggling to get into my pants without dislodging the towel.

'There you are,' said Gwyn, 'he understood perfectly.'

They watched fascinated as I pulled on my trousers and shirt.

'Now, gentlemen. What can I do for you?'

Twm lifted up his hand with a piece of paper in it and began to read.

'We are here to express our concerns about the ongoing viability of our businesses. We fear the adverse effects from mains electrification and water that will have its impactation on our businesses.'

He stopped.

'We are none of us rich, of course,' Jac went on. 'We have wives and children to support. Grandchildren some of us.'

Gwyn carried on the pleading.

'Twm Slwtsh here makes a reasonable living emptying the earth closets at the backs of the houses and cottages. Jo Botel, is the Calor Gas man. He is very worried that no one will buy Calor Gas any more, once they have electric cookers and ovens. And I have sold paraffin lamps and mantles for them all my life.'

'Ydy. Mae o.' Twm took up the baton. 'Gwyn Mantel, here is very concerned for the effect of mains electricity.'

The other man coughed.

'And Dai Nyts here is a very important man in Llan-chwaraetegdanygelyn. He maintains the generators.'

'We are all extremely concerned, Mr Bull,' said Twm. And the others nodded.

I looked at their worried faces.

But how could I surrender my mission and the whole of modern technology progress to protect their livelihoods, just like that?

'I'll make a careful note of what you say,' I said, trying to herd them towards the door. I was starting to sound like a politician.

'Then you must at least let us take you on a tour of the town,' Jac said. 'It will not take long.'

I decided I had little choice, considering the determination of these men and their occupation of my room. This was what public consultation was all about, I told myself.

So I was led across the green, past the supermarket and up past the market and through the small maze of streets which went up the hill at the side of the town.

There, they proudly showed me what looked like an awful mess of raised ditches, fashioned by hand in rough concrete, running down the sides of the roads and branching off in all directions into the houses and cottages.

Then they took me up to the spring which fed the system. Ein ffynnon, they called it.

'You can appreciate, I am sure,' said Twm. 'How much work and effort goes into building and maintaining this intricate network of watercourses.'

'I do indeed,' I said. But it was a third-world solution in a twenty-first century British town. I could see why Freddy Morgan wouldn't want these pictures in the media, come election time.

'I think you must agree that the town is very fortunate to have such a very well-developed system,' said Twm.

I looked around me. You could see across the rooftops of the town from here. A large house, up to the left, with carefully manicured gardens, caught my eye.

'Whose house is that?' I asked as we said our goodbyes.

'That,' said Jac, 'is the house of Mr Penhaearn Tegid Foel.'

There was a crowd of people outside the Supermart when I got back to the Green, or the Maes, as I was told to call it. I recognised Dai Call and his friends sitting on the bench outside Caffi Cyfoes. They acknowledged me, so I went across.

'Bore da, Sut dach chi,' Dai Call said.

I recognised that greeting from *Welsh Phrases for Beginners*.

'Bore da to you too. Dach chi'n iawn?' I attempted to say, pronouncing it all wrongly.

'Da iawn,' said Dai Call.

'You are a fast learner, young man, I should say,' said Elwyn.

'What's happening here, then,' I asked.

They shuffled uncomfortably and looked at each other.

'It's a protest,' Elwyn muttered.

'Did you say protest?'

'Ay,' said Dai Call. 'A protest against the English signs on the Supermart.'

'And the violence of the English lorry driver yesterday.'

'Oh, I see,' I said. 'And against me coming, do you think?'

'Ooo, no. Not at all,' said Elwyn.

'As God's my witness,' Irfon added.

'Are you sure?' I said. 'It does seem quite a coincidence.'

'Maybe, then,' said Elwyn. And Irfon nodded.

'You can't wash your hands without getting them wet,' said Dai Call.

I noticed graffiti then, on the walls of the Supermart and went across to look.

Slogans had been sprayed in red paint on the windows in the night and over the garish plastic signs on the Supermart windows.

Now all I needed was someone to translate them for me. I looked around for a friendly face.

YOU COULD NOT have imagined the embarrassment and horror and mixture of emotions that I felt to see you coming across the Maes towards me, your skin shining in the sun. A black diamond in my world which was no longer grey.

I had only agreed to take part in Dewi's stupid protest to keep him quiet. Now I had this strange feeling that I was betraying you. But why should I feel anything for you? I was already hiding my face – and hideous nose – from the TV camera. Now I was shrinking from you.

Outside, Hiraethog's wife, Dwynwen, Llanchwaraeteg-danygelyn's Mrs Media was working hard. She had already interviewed her stepbrother Penhaearn four times – in Welsh for Radio Cymru; in English for English-language Radio Wales; in Welsh to camera for S4C; and, in English to camera for BBC TV Wales. Now she was repeating the process interviewing the protesters.

Meanwhile Dewi was organising an orderly queue for her to talk to the mandatory vox pop of outraged local residents. At the front was Garmon, heavily bandaged for the camera, his face stained with iodine, leaning on an old World War II crutch.

Her husband, Hiraethog, absenting himself from his hedge cutting, was also standing in the queue, resplendent in his Mayoral Chain over his yellow safety jacket, but anyone could have told him he would not be called upon by his wife to speak about such important issues, even though he was concentrating very hard, his lips moving as he rehearsed his lines.

Behind Dwynwen, Dewi was now marching backwards and forwards with last night's speaker, Dafydd Y Gwrthsafiad and his two friends. They carried all-purpose Brodyr y Ddraig placards with the famous dragon's head logo at the top and a wipe-clean whiteboard at the bottom which they changed for each take: Cymraeg yn unig, for filming the Welsh version, 'Wales for the Welsh' for filming the English.

I noticed my Taid, Elwyn and Irfon following you across the Maes to contribute their considerable wisdom.

'They beam this into people's houses, you know,' I heard Elwyn say. 'Into their living rooms. And into their bedrooms, even.'

'I should not like Dwynwen beamed into my bedroom,' said Taid.

'In my day only the Angel Gabriel could beam himself into people's bedrooms,' said Irfon.

Penhaearn was starting on his English language interview.

'As County Councillor for this parish, I want to assist your viewers in having a rare glance into the gravity of this moment for the history of our wonderful town and its vital necessity in the evolvement of Wales,' he said.

Dwynwen beamed at him. No one could inspire her like her stepbrother.

'Here, in one of the very few remaining Welsh-speaking strongholds, we stand at our battle lines against the English invaders who have been intruding into our country for centuries and very dreadfully indeed in the immediate recent history of this town.

'We will not allow them to be taking from us the one thing that has united us as a nation for many hundreds of years and through which we cherish our cultural heritage and two-thousand-year-old inheritance.'

Dwynwen chatted to Penhaearn while the crew dismantled the camera from its stand in order to reposition for a panorama shot.

You hadn't yet spotted me, so I tried to make myself as small as possible. I was full of worries, Jon. That you would disapprove of me being with the protesters. That you would not be as glad to see me as I was to see you. Worried that, in the cold grey light of a Welsh day, you might suddenly become aware of my true ugliness.

Gwenlais sidled up to me.

'Look at poor Hiraethog. Imagine how he must be feeling, Cr'adur bach. Standing there in his Mayoral Chain. Doing his duty. And being only ignored.'

Hiraethog was standing on his own, a little away, shuffling his feet. Sighing.

'He ought to know by now that Dwynwen never interviews him.'

I didn't reply. I hoped she'd go away.

She tried again to provoke a conversation.

'To be treated like that by your own wife. Well!' She twted. Gwenlais was possibly the loudest twter in Llanchwaraeteg-danygelyn, though my mother came a pretty close second.

'Perhaps it's a matter of protocol,' I suggested, unable to control my tongue. 'I expect her bosses probably don't like reporters interviewing their own husbands.'

I felt my Anti Gwenlais's hackles rise.

'Well she interviews her stepbrother all right. Your Yncl Penhaearn – such a hard-working man, dedicated to the town – it's only poor Hiraethog she ignores. If I was in his shoes, I'd be feeling hurt. Very hurt indeed.'

I wished she would go away.

'Look, you can see it in his face. He looks as though he wants to run away. He's much happier back at work among the hedgerows in the cab of his Jac Codi Baw.'

'Why doesn't he then? Go and tell him, Anti.'

'It's his duty to be here, isn't it?'

I so badly wanted her to go away. Not only were you going to find me there. I was going to have to introduce you to my Anti Gwenlais.

'This will cause terrible ructions in the town,' she said. 'You can be sure of that.'

I wondered if my Anti Gwenlais had been chosen by God to bring hysteria to the world. Such a rare talent she had for turning minor upsets into feuds and feuds into wars.

'Don't you think you should go and open Y Fferyllfa, in

case anyone is going to need medical supplies?' I suggested. 'Mrs Driply perhaps.'

But she was reading the placards, now, with a mounting sense of excitement. There was going to be trouble. There would be rumours and clecs to carry for weeks.

'This will be a day to look back on. You mark my words.'

Dewi was now leading his small group around the checkout tills in a kind of conga, chanting:

'Be am be am be am . . . Be am be am be am . . . Be am – ein Cymraeg?'

Gwenlais started clapping her hands in time with the chanting, then grabbed my arm and tried to drag me in. I pulled back. I knew exactly what you'd think of me.

Customers had stopped shopping and were standing around with their shopping trolleys and baskets. Some were clapping in time with the chanting. Garmon had discarded his crutch and was doing a little jig.

At the tills, the shop manager was scowling at the protesters sitting on the floor.

Finally you spotted me and came across. I disentangled myself from Anti Gwenlais. You were beaming. That was good. Except that this was in front of *everybody*. That was bad.

'Dw i ddim yn gallu siarad efo ti yn Saesneg,' I said. And then repeated it to you as a whisper in English. 'I can't talk to you in English.'

You smiled. 'Mae hi'n braf,' you said. And I felt the urge to giggle. Just being next to you, lifted a weight from my heart.

The conga ran out of steam and Dewi came to a halt a few yards away. He was glaring at you. And at me. Horrified that I was standing with you. I thought for a moment, he might hit you. But Gwenlais plonked herself between you and Dewi.

'It is a very strange coincidence that you should be protesting about the Welsh language here,' she told Dewi in Welsh. 'Considering that I was myself the victim of a racist remark in just this very shop less than a week ago.'

I was very glad you couldn't understand.

'Really,' said Dewi, his concentration still more focussed on you and me.

'Well, I don't know if I should be telling tales, you know.'

'Oh, I think you should,' said Dewi. His acolytes had started gathering around him now, nodding their heads in agreement. 'In fact, I think you have a duty to tell me.'

You stood there smiling, Jon, not understanding a word, fascinated by the sound of our language.

'Well I was paying at the till, you see. And I was talking to the girl on the till – Rhiain, it was – in Welsh.'

'Yes. Go on.'

'And the manager said to us – rather rudely I thought – "What did you say just then?"'

'And . . .?'

'Well, he couldn't understand, you see. So then we had to turn to talking English.'

'You had to turn to English!'

The acolytes all looked at each other.

Gwenlais nodded. She had expected a stronger reaction than this.

'I'm sure there was something more to it than that, Gwenlais.'

'Oh yes. He said it quite aggressively. This *English* manager.'

'He was quite aggressive?'

'He was very aggressive, Dewi. He said he was sorry but he couldn't understand Welsh.'

'He admitted that he couldn't understand Welsh, then, did he?'

'That was what he said.'

'Did he say anything else, Gwenlais?'

'He apologised to me because Rhiain had forgotten to key in the discount on one of the special offers, and because the top of the counter was dirty. He said she was a little stupid. And he told her off.'

'He said she was stupid, did he?'

'Yes. That's it. I'm sure that's how it was.'

'Because she had been speaking Welsh?'

'Well, yes, I suppose so.'

'So – in effect – what you are saying, Gwenlais, is that this very rude English manager told off Rhiain – a good Welsh-speaking member of staff, mark you – for talking our stupid language.'

'In effect, yes. It sounds so much better the way you put it, Dewi. I think you have the gift. You should be a publicity spokesman.'

'Thank you,' said Dewi, looking at his acolytes to make sure they had heard.

'Well it has been very nice to talk to you,' said Gwenlais, moving away.

'Oh no,' said Dewi. 'You and I have some work to do now, we have. You are a keen supporter of the Welsh language, I know.'

'Indeed I am, young man.'

'Well it just so happens. You are also a very important person today. Because we have a man coming shortly from the *Liverpool Post* to interview us, we have. And I think you should speak to him. And you are looking so smart today.'

'Oooh,' said Gwenlais coyly, a little unsure as to what exactly she had done to deserve this honour. But very pleased.

'But first,' said Dewi. 'I want to go through your story with you. Just once more. And then perhaps we'll get Dwynwen to interview you, isn't it?'

'Does that mean I shall be on television,' Gwenlais asked.

'I shouldn't be at all surprised,' said Dewi, winking at me. I think he thought he was impressing me.

I was so very glad, Jon, that you had not been able to understand a word of this.

IT WAS FRUSTRATING not being able to understand your language, Gwalia. I had this sense of political intrigues going on which became more certain as the day progressed.

I felt completely cut off from the rest of the world; I hadn't heard the news since those garbled snatches in the car. Normally news was a constant. I phoned Nisha and my Mum. The bombs had been badly made, no one had been killed. Members of the public had even caught two of the bombers. I sensed there was a feeling of jubilation, back in London, that I was missing out on.

'Ah, there you are!' shrilled Boudiccea, arriving just in time to save me from my thoughts of home. 'I've been looking for you everywhere. I have lots more people for you to meet and somewhere very important for you to go today.'

So, that afternoon, Victoria Leakin, Guy and Wendy Ingress and a certain Mr Donald Flood arrived to whisk me off to a meeting of the Migneint County Council's Developments Committee in Mr Flood's huge four-wheel-drive, telling me, with a lot of winks and nods to each other, that I would have the chance to see County Councillor Penhaearn Tegid Foel in action again.

It was the first time I had met Mr Donald Flood, one of those overgrown English public school types I knew so well, born to lead – captain of football, captain of cricket and head boy. And still like that twenty years on, in middle age.

'This will give you an insight into the workings of our local community,' he told me as he ushered us into his Land Rover, keeping up a constant diatribe against the Welsh. 'I don't think they have any idea how much English people dislike them,' he said.

The County Council offices were an hour away across the Migneint. I realised again how bleak and beautifully desolate the mountain moors were and how the verdant valleys cut into them, with their stone-walled fields and trees and huddles of houses. By the time we arrived at the County Council offices, most of the councillors were already there,

Penhaearn in the chair, conferring with everyone. We took our seats in the public gallery and were pounced on by a bouncy little man who handed us earphones. I noticed a lot of the councillors staring at me. Black people don't get that in London, though you do sometimes in the villages of Surrey.

'You lot look as though you need translation equipment,' he said busily and watched us put them on before disappearing into a portable booth.

'I shall be translating from Welsh to English. If you can hear me, please raise your hand now.'

We shuffled awkwardly and obeyed. A few councillors looked across to see the non-Welsh speakers with their hands up like naughty children.

'See how they try to belittle us and smirk at our headsets with the little red diodes, our badges of shame,' said Guy. 'It's worse than the coloured triangles of Auschwitz, forcing us to advertise our ignorance of the Welsh language as if that is something shameful.'

He winked at Donald Flood.

'Guy!' Victoria Leakin, hissed. 'Don't you dare be so horrid. We should all learn Welsh. And if we can't manage that, we should show respect. It's their right.'

Guy Ingress and Donald Flood sniggered. Victoria looked pointedly ahead. She wasn't wearing any headphones.

'You don't need these then?' I asked. 'Your Welsh must be very good.'

'I don't understand everything, but it's very good practice for me,' she said.

In the Press bench, I recognised Hiraethog's wife, Dwynwen, doodling in her notebook and adjusting her hair in case she was called to beam herself into people's bedrooms.

Penhaearn rapped his gavel on the desk and looked around the room. He noticed me and gave an almost imperceptible nod. This was clearly an entirely different class of meeting to those in the Town Hall in Llanchwaraeteg-danygelyn.

The first item of any substance on the agenda was about what colour to paint the bus shelters.

'They decide this every alternate six months,' Guy whispered. Blue to match the County's buses. Then the other alternate six months, they have a meeting of the National Park, to decide to paint them green – because that's the correct colour for a National Park. And Penhaearn chairs both committees. Good use of public money eh?'

I said nothing.

According to the commentary on my headphones, the motion to paint the bus shelters blue was passed unanimously.

Next, he asked the Planning Officer, a Mr Gordon White, to lead the committee through the list of planning permission applications. One of the councillors indicated that he wanted to speak. I heard the translation over the headphones.

'It pains me – as I am sure it pains other members of this committee – to see so many of these developments and improvements driven by English money. It is always the English who buy these barns and derelict houses. You could tell them by the names. Only the English can afford them.'

The planning officer interjected something but Penhaearn shushed him.

'The officer is reminding the chairman of the committee's responsibilities under equal opportunity legislation,' the translator reported.

'Political correctness again! Are we to be gagged now!' Another councillor exclaimed. And several others nodded and concurred.

Someone else cut in: 'In my view it is entirely wrong to allow non-Welsh speakers to settle here. Or to employ non-Welsh speakers in Welsh-speaking areas. It deprives our own native Welsh speakers of jobs that are rightfully theirs. And houses.'

Dwynwen looked uncomfortably in our direction.

Another councillor, who was also wearing headphones, stood up and said in English. 'I object to this line of discussion, Mr Chairman. And I move progress.'

The officer shuffled uncomfortably.

'Unfortunately, Mr Chairman, your decisions as a committee cannot be made on the grounds of racism. You have to make your decisions on the basis of legislation.'

A ripple of disquiet ran through the chamber. Penhaearn banged his gavel.

'There are rules to follow. I am sure you will all agree that it is important to follow them.'

Donald Flood leaned towards me. 'What he means is, they need to be careful if he's to go on getting his fifteen thousand a year for this farce. It's a disgrace. Ten thousand in attendance allowances and an additional five thousand for chairing this rubbish.'

Penhaearn seemed to look pointedly at me: 'We will ensure that the rules are followed to the letter. Especially where the English are involved,' he said in English.

They came next to the question of the Llanchwaraeteg-danygelyn Summer Fair – Gŵyl Llanchwaraetegdanygelyn – the planning officer was recommending a health and safety study.

'As you will have seen from the report that was circulated with the agenda, we have an obligation to consider all risks in relation to possible claims for negligence,' he read.

Penhaearn bristled visibly, but the officer went on.

'Members will appreciate that up to twenty large timber lorries go through Llanchwaraetegdanygelyn a day. Why, only this week, there was an incident . . .'

Penhaearn interrupted.

'I think this has been exaggerated,' he began.

Another councillor got to his feet.

'These forests are a blight on the Welsh landscape. It's a disgrace it was ever allowed. Our land bought by English millionaires and pop singers to take advantage of tax concessions, taking our wood to English timber mills when we so badly need jobs here.'

Penhaearn nodded and smiled and held up his hand.

The officer went on.

'There is a clear health and safety danger here. Pedestrians could be killed. With market stalls set up along on the road, and mothers with children and pushchairs, I would be failing in my duty if I didn't advise against it. And I should also advise that the fairground on the Maes poses a number of health and safety concerns too.'

Penhaearn interrupted again.

'Am I right in saying that this fair has been perpetuated for four hundred years without incident? Why do we need to change things now? That is what members want to know.'

The officer frowned. 'In my view it is only a matter of time before someone is injured or even killed. I must advise you to urgently agree that an independent expert be appointed to appraise the situation. You may be personally liable if you fail to safeguard yourselves and the Council.'

'I think we should oppose that,' said Penhaearn.

'I'm not sure that would be advisable,' the officer persisted.

'We would much prefer a report on the damage these lorries are doing to our town.'

There was a general murmur of agreement and the motion was adjourned.

Mrs Leakin caught my attention.

'This is our motion, next,' she said.

The translator's voice whispered in headsets that the English electricity company was applying for planning permission for a line of pylons and a sub-station to bring electricity to Llanchwaraetegdanygelyn.

Penhaearn began to speak.

'I think we are all agreed,' the translator reported him as saying, 'as agreed last year, this would be totally against planning policy, and very destructive of an important visual amenity of international significance. And I think I can say with some confidence that the people of Llanchwaraeteg-danygelyn are not interested in destroying their beautiful valley with pylons.'

Victoria Leakin, Donald Flood and Guy Ingress stood up and started shouting.

'Rubbish.'

'Nonsense.'

''Dan ni angen trydan,' shouted Mrs Leakin in a high-pitched voice.

I sat quietly, trying to stay neutral.

'Tell them,' she told me. And Messrs Flood and Ingress looked at me expectantly.

'This is not the appropriate time,' I said, but aware they would feel I was betraying them.

Dwynwen frantically started making notes.

The officer motioned to them to sit down and held up a letter.

'If I may point out, Mr Chairman, we have received a petition from a Mrs Victoria Leakin, signed by some fifty residents of the town, asking the committee to reconsider this proposal.' He passed the petition to Penhaearn. 'Mrs Leakin is chair of Antur Deg, the community development group for Llanchwaraetegdanygelyn.'

'I know very well who Victoria Leakin is,' said Penhaearn, snatching the document. And glaring across at us.

'I'm here!' she shrieked. 'Dw i yma.'

'Please sit down, Mrs Leakin,' Penhaearn said in Welsh. 'You are not permitted to speak.'

Several councillors turned to look at us. Penhaearn brandished the letter as the translation of what he was saying came jauntily though my earphones.

'And this is only signed by English people.'

'They, nevertheless, have certain rights,' the officer pointed out.

'You know very well,' Penhaearn told him. 'We have decided many times over the years that the only way to bring electricity to Llanchwaraetegdanygelyn is by underground cable.'

Many of the councillors nodded agreement. The few with headphones shook their heads.

The officer looked towards us and shrugged, then he spoke again and I had the feeling he was directing his remarks at me, albeit through translation.

'The cost of running pylons to the town would itself be the equivalent of £40,000 per household. Putting the cable underground – which would involve blasting through rock, negotiating rights of way across miles of countryside, going through dry stone walls and hedges, et cetera – would multiply that at least tenfold.'

'Why has no feasibility study been done on that?' demanded a headsetted councillor in English.

'Because it was considered that the cost was out of the question anyway,' Penhaearn explained.

On the Press bench, Hiraethog's wife, Dwynwen, was still making copious notes.

'Well,' said Penhaearn, addressing the committee. 'As you all know, I have to declare an interest here, so I cannot vote as chairman and I cannot speak on the matter, only seek clarification, as I have tried to do.' He glared at the officer, adding, 'Against almost insuperable odds.'

'Does any member wish to speak?'

Silence.

'Anyone wish me to leave the chair in the interests of disinterest?'

Silence again.

'Are we all against it?'

There was a murmur.

'Anyone for?'

The hands of the few councillors with headsets went up.

'Right, then. All those against.'

Hands were lethargically raised to shoulder height.

'Agreed then!' Penhaearn declared.

As we were getting up to go, I saw Penhaearn rubbing his hands.

The drive back was spent in a tirade of angry protestations and pontifications from Guy Ingress and Donald Flood.

'It's a farce. That's what it is. Now you have seen it for yourself.'

'Look at them, sitting there, in broad daylight . . .'

'That's what you've got to overcome.'

'The man's insane. They all are.'

'Ignorant and backward, that's what they are. The lot of them.'

'That's what we have to contend with, you do see, don't you?'

Yes, I did see. It wasn't just a problem of strategy.

I WAS SITTING with Taid and Elwyn and Irfon outside Caffi Cyfoes, wondering where you might have disappeared to, when Mam came striding out toward us from Y Ddwy Ddraig, looking very serious.

Taid put his arm around me. 'My son married a stern woman,' he said under his breath to me. 'Perhaps some men need stern women, but children never do, cariad.' He always called me cariad.

'Bore da Gwênfer,' Taid called to Mam, pronouncing it so it sounded like gwên fer – short smile – not like Guinevere, the legendary Arthurian queen, which was obviously what my grandparents had intended.

'Bore da, ddynion,' she replied to them, glowering at me.

Elwyn and Irfon giggled.

'I need your help with something in the house,' she said to me.

I had a feeling it would be to tell me something I didn't want to hear. Taid gave my shoulder a little squeeze and winked. Elwyn and Irfon winked too. I smiled back, but I had a growing feeling of unease.

As soon as we were alone, Mam made a cup of tea and sat me down at the kitchen table.

'I know you are grown up now,' she said. 'And I know you are getting better. But I have been lying awake all night worrying about you.'

'Oh, Mam.' I reached out to touch her.

'No, I am going to have my say.' She twted. 'You never listen. Today you will.'

'I always listen!'

'I saw the way you were looking at that man, Mr Jon Bull, last night. And I don't mind telling you I am very concerned.'

'I'm only spying on him. Like you told me to.'

She looked at me coldly.

'You're doing rather more than that, I think.'

I didn't answer.

'I don't know if you realise how ill you still are. How

damaging any kind of relationship could be to your long-term well-being. Your father and I have tried . . .'

'Mam. Stop! Please!'

There was silence. And Titania the white cat jumped up on my lap.

'I'm sorry Mam. I didn't mean to shout.'

'It's all right. I understand. But that only goes to show how distraught you still are.'

'I know, Mam. I'm not sure I can explain it to myself, even.'

'He will be gone in a few days. Never to return, probably, whatever he might promise you now. And your father and I will be left to pick up the pieces. It is not that he is black, though that is not something that makes it easier. But I have discussed it with your father. And he agrees with me.'

'Does he?' I asked, surprised. I doubted that: she would have told Dad what she intended to tell me and taken anything he said as minor quibbles; she would not have discussed it. Dad was always on my side. And Dad wasn't racist.

'Completely. If this man was a Welsh speaker, it would be different. Or even just Welsh. But we don't want to see you getting hurt. Neither of us do. We want what's best for you. He's not even of our race, is he? Let alone Welsh.'

'I don't know what I feel yet, Mam. I like him, that's all. He's good for me. I feel better than I've felt since my breakdown.'

'Oh Gwalia. I think he knows all right. I saw the way you two were looking at each other. Have you kissed him?'

'You talk as if I am a child. Nothing's happened. I just want to feel that I could make my own mind up. That's all. If I wanted to. You know. It's nothing. A little crush maybe. A sign that I'm getting better perhaps. You know – awakening. Why can't you see it that way!'

'Gwalia. Don't deceive yourself. You are very fragile. Very vulnerable.'

'Well stop putting pressure on me then! Anyway, he's

fantastic. He's so clever and he knows so much. And he could help get grants for Y Ddwy Ddraig and everything.'

'Believe me, Gwalia, I have agonised over whether to say this to you. Why do you think I lay awake all night? You know nothing about him.'

'I know that he is wonderful. And I know I might think something completely different tomorrow. And I know that what my heart says and what my head says are two separate things. And you can only speak to my head.'

'He probably leaves a girl like you in every town. And I'm sure you haven't told him anything about yourself. Have you told him about . . .'

'Hissht, Mam. Don't say anything.'

'He doesn't know, does he?'

I shook my head and felt the pain of it. And the old depression and panic crushing down on my mind and my body.

'Mam! I hate you!'

'Please, Gwalia.'

'I'm not listening!'

My name is Gwalia. I am an island.

'Gwalia! Listen to me!'

My name is Gwalia, I am an island. My name is Gwalia, I am an island.

She let me be then.

And with the old words chanting through my head, I started to cry.

But that was only the start. Soon I was shaking with my whole being.

Then Mam had her arms around me, comforting me.

Do parents always hurt you just so they can comfort you?

After a long time I calmed down enough to voice my worst fear.

'I know I am hopeless.'

'No. No, Gwalia, you mustn't think that at all.' Mam got up and went to fetch tissues.

My body was shaking in great sobs.

'Hush. There there. It will be all right.'

I lifted my head from my hands and looked at her.

'You must let me go,' I said. 'I will be better. I am better.'

'If that's true then you must prove it to me.'

'How. How do I prove it?'

'You must tell him. You must tell him everything'

'I can't.'

She was triumphant then.

'Because you can't. That's why, isn't it? Or is it because you think it will scare him away?'

'No. It won't.'

She looked at me imperiously, with all her maternal authority in her eyes. 'I'm only telling you for your own good you know.'

And that was when I made my decision.

'All right then, I will. I will tell him. I will tell him everything.'

'I don't think you will.'

My body had stopped shaking.

'You're confused. Of course you are. Think about what I say. And don't be hasty.'

She kissed me on the top of the head, said 'Good girl'. And went out.

I wiped my eyes and looked at myself in the mirror.

What a sad, sad creature I was.

My name is Gwalia, I am an island.

But I don't have to be.

IT MADE NO SENSE, I'd met you only days before. We'd spent barely six hours together. Hardly any time alone. And by next week, I would be back in London, back to normal in Westminster. Yet I was totally fascinated by you. You seemed already so familiar. It wasn't logical. How could this country girl, who I'd only just met, be so suddenly important to me?

Looking back, I think perhaps I did sense there was some great shadow over you. Perhaps my heart knew more than my head. I just hadn't had much practice at listening to it before.

When you came to my room, I wasn't surprised. And when you said: 'Let's go for a walk', it seemed such a natural thing to do.

As soon as we were in the fields, our hands seem to reach for each other. My heart leapt at that and my mind was jumping. I kept thinking of you as *this girl*. This girl who seemed to have taken me over without my brain having been consulted.

This girl!

The softness of your hand. *That I was holding it.* The sweetness of your mouth. *That it was talking to me.* The fascination of your eyes. *That they were drawn to mine.* I didn't need to be told that I could kiss you if I wanted to. That you would welcome that. I guessed perhaps my own eyes were telling you the same. Smiles were dancing back and forth between both our lips, irrespective of our minds and spoken words.

It did cross my mind to wonder what Professor Angela Lain, my boss, might think. (The need for impartiality is pretty much number one in the social research Code of Conduct.) And whether someone might accuse me of being unprofessional in spending so much time with you.

But actually, I decided, I was being more than sufficiently professional: I was consulting everyone, wasn't I? Meeting lots of people? Doing lots of things that were less enjoyable than being with you. OK, so we did occasionally hold hands, and kiss, but a new strategy for Umbo was my number one priority. I thought about it constantly. Really I did.

And I spent a lot of time asking you about Penhaearn and why you thought he was obstructing Mrs Leakin's plans to bring power to the town and things like that. And you were answering. In-depth research was what it was. Valuable in-depth research.

I remember very clearly, Gwalia: I needed to understand everything, I told you. So that I could do my job properly and fairly.

'Oh yes,' you said. 'I understand that perfectly.'

'You are my only real ally here,' I said. 'The only person I feel that I can really trust and talk to.'

You flashed me a smile. And the cute little crease at the corner of your mouth did what it did to me.

'I'll give you all the help I can,' you said.

'Great,' I said. 'Fantastic. You see, I need to bounce my impressions off you.'

I took a deep breath.

'You see, to me Victoria Leakin is only really supported by the English. And Penhaearn doesn't really want the town to change. And I don't know what the rest of the townsfolk think, but I did have a very concerned delegation of tradesmen who are clearly very worried about losing their jobs if mains services come in.

'Meanwhile, the English are growing very frustrated at the delays. And the Welsh are historically hostile to the English anyway. I saw that at the supermarket. And your mother probably isn't alone in worrying about the threat to the Welsh language if English people move in.

'But the economy – and bear in mind I haven't seen the factory yet – the economy looks as though it needs a real injection of new businesses. And maybe that could not be done without English people moving in.'

It was quite hard walking uphill, over rough ground,

holding hands and talking at the same time. And you seemed to have gone very quiet. I hoped it wasn't too complicated for you. But I sensed that this could be a very important moment for my project. And that was probably more important for you and your family than it was for me and my career. So I carried on.

It didn't occur to me that perhaps you might have something important that you badly needed to say to me.

'Really it's classic text book stuff in community relations. Once we understand why, we can try to address the problem. And the key is to get the whole community to understand the dilemmas and the choices the town faces. Is this making any sense?'

You pulled me up over a stile leading to some woods, your light body nimble under your simple yellow dress and your bare, white legs running down to neatly-matching ankle socks and blue plimsolls.

'You see, I have very little idea, as yet, about what the townsfolk think. So I've drafted a questionnaire. But I would need you to translate it, of course. Maybe you could help me find some volunteers to help me circulate it through letterboxes, yeah?'

'This is Drws y Coed,' you told me, 'it means Door to the Wood.'

And you made me turn around and look back over the town. We'd come further than I thought. Umbo nestling in the bottom of the valley, with the mountains all around. It was a very charming sight and all that, but I was rather perplexed that you hadn't responded to a word I had said.

Two birds were circling over the town. At about the same height as us. And then they swooped towards us and were over us in only a few seconds.

'Don't worry,' you said. 'They're not vultures.'

I looked at you. Although we had held hands and our lips had brushed. We had not yet kissed properly, as I remember it. You know, a long snoggy kiss.

I realised in that moment why you needed to poke fun at me and saw you looking at me, watching it dawn on me. Smiling. We were both smiling, then both laughing. The same romantic possibilities flitting through both our minds. Although I was still determined not to make the first move – for professional reasons – we both knew it was inevitable.

By now, I had thought about kissing you so much that it had come to seem like my right. A fact, like your soft skin, your gentle hands, your delicious shoulders and that little crease on the corner of your mouth when you smiled that had become a complete obsession. I was thinking about them most of the time.

I had this nagging feeling that I should have been thinking about real things. Strategy. Plans. To regain my professional perspective. But there would be plenty of time for that.

I checked my watch. Four thirty.

In the Leyburn Institute offices Nisha would be processing the day's news and cross-referencing it to current research data; Andrew would be sitting at his terminal lamenting a world which had lost its idealism. In his head, he would be reciting the familiar woes of a young social researcher being battery-farmed for theories and statistics. And, in her office, Professor Lain would be peddling ideas to ambitious politicians cynically looking to increase their influence and power.

And here I was. With you. In this beautiful, simple place. On a bright, spring afternoon, with the grass wet on my shoes and birds – which were not vultures – circling above me.

We sat on the stile for a while and you interrogated me about my family, my life, and my job. Did I have any girlfriends? What were my ambitions? Your eyes darted over my face, flitting from one topic to the next. So distracting! But distracted, too. I wasn't sure if you were actually listening to my answers or if you were really very interested. You seemed miles away.

Then, suddenly, you kissed me. A long passionate kiss. But

just as I was starting to take the initiative, you jumped up and pulled me after you.

'You must know so much in your head after spending eight whole years at university . . . And you say, that place you work – the Leyburn Institute – is like a battery farm for ideas. I imagined that you worked behind that big black door in Westminster, and wore a bowler hat . . . And what about your hobbies?'

'That's an odd word – *hobbies.*'

'You do have hobbies, am I to take it?'

'I go to art galleries and poetry readings sometimes, with my friends Andrew and Nisha.'

Art galleries and poetry readings. Had I admitted that? Now you would think me a complete nerd.

'We have a lot of good artists in Wales,' you said. 'And fantastic poets.'

'I saw a Welsh poet once in London,' I said, 'RS Thomas. Have you heard of him?'

'I wouldn't exactly call him Welsh. He wrote in English. But, as it happens, yes, I have heard of him.'

'And do you like his work?'

'We are the lost people,' you recited from memory.

'Tracing us by our language.

you will not arrive where we are

which is nowhere.

The wind blows through our castles;

the chair of poetry sits without a tenant.

We are exiles within

our own country . . .'

'Do you know it,' you asked.

I shook my head.

You clapped your hands delightedly. 'I know it! And you don't! "The Lost People". One of his later poems, you know,' you said, imitating my posh English voice.

And you danced around me, chanting.

So I had to reach out and stop you.

And then you were in my arms and we were hugging and kissing again.

And I remember wanting that moment to go on forever. Wanting our bodies to melt into each other so that our hearts could actually touch the way they seemed to ache to do.

'It's strange,' you said, still in my arms. 'I feel as if I've always known you.'

'That's just what I was going to say.'

'Do you feel it too?' you said. 'I knew you did.'

But then neither of us knew what to say next.

'I hope you will help me with the questionnaires,' I said very earnestly.

And you stared at me in disbelief.

And we both burst out laughing.

If it hadn't been for how we felt, it would have been completely stupid. What a miracle it was that you were feeling it too!

We kissed again and hugged for a long time. Then you took me further into the woods. To where there were bluebells. A vast blue carpet of them, spread out under a canopy of great beech and oak trees.

'Clychau'r gog, they're called in Welsh,' you said. 'The bells of the cuckoo.'

'Clychau'r gog,' I repeated. 'That's easy, I could learn Welsh.'

'Just like that, I suppose. For a man who is so clever, that he cannot even find a town to arrive somewhere on the right day.'

'Why not, though? At twenty words a day, I could acquire an everyday vocabulary of six hundred words in – what? – a month. A bit extra, maybe, for irregular verbs and grammar. Then I could talk to you in your language!'

You turned and skipped away.

'Here are some words for you, then. If you are going to learn Welsh.'

You stooped and picked up a little white flower.

'Botwm crys – shirt button. And suran y coed – wood sorrel'.

'Botwm crys and suran y coed. Wow. Great. That's five words I've learned already!'

'Drycha!' you said delightedly. In one of the flower heads was a bead of water.

'See! It's like a crystal ball,' you said. 'Look into it, tell me what you see.'

All I could see was the beauty of your perfect hand, gently holding the flower without breaking it from its stem, the fragile petals holding a crystal bead of water in which the light you had brought into my heart danced.

I cupped my hands around yours.

'Look at the flower in my white hand in your black hand,' you said. 'I can't believe you can be so black and yet so – English. Are your mam and tad black too?'

'Mum and Dad? Of course.'

'And are they as – English.'

I laughed.

'Yes. Of course. Dad tries to put on this jive accent sometimes. But he can't really do it.'

'What do you see in the crystal ball,' you asked.

'Light,' I said. 'Refracted light.'

You pulled your hand away.

'Ti'n anobeithiol,' you said. 'You're hopeless.'

'What do you see, then?'

'I see the whole world and a happy future.'

And then you jumped up and skipped away through the wood. And I followed you through a world of wild flowers and bluebells. A world I wouldn't even have looked to notice a day before. And all beneath a great high canopy of rich green beech leaves and the young yellow oaks.

We stopped at the edge of a small gorge.

You took my hand. And we kissed again. Then I looked down.

Below us, I saw a waterfall with a big black rock beside it and a ribbon of tarmac leading up from the pool.

'This is where you spied on me!'

You laughed out loud now.

'Where I fell in love with you. My naked black god!'

You laughed again. And pointed along a short ledge just above the waterfall to an opening.

'My secret cave,' you said. 'This is where I came to play as a child. My secret place.'

I tried to kiss you again. But you pulled away and started walking back through the woods, me following.

'I need to get back,' you said.

'But this is such a beautiful place.' I tried to take your hand. 'Such a beautiful country. I want this afternoon to go on forever.'

'I know, Jon. So do I. But I have to look after Awena.'

'I really liked your mum and dad. And your sister.'

You stopped dead, then. And the colour drained from your face. You looked away.

Your whole body was tense and stiff.

'What have I said?' I begged. 'What have I done?'

I felt as if my entire universe, had frozen.

You turned away from me and kept turning away. When I finally got in front of you, you put your hands up to your face and I saw tears were streaming down.

'What is it? What's the matter? What have I said?'

You said something very quietly. Which I didn't catch.

You said it again.

Again I didn't hear.

I cupped your head in my hands and pulled it to my chest, to my heart.

You started to cry. I could feel your body shaking and feel your tears wet on my shirt.

After an age, the sobbing subsided. You seemed to make a decision and looked up at me.

'Awena's not my sister.'

My eyes searched yours, but all I could see was your awful pain. Some crippling hurt. I felt it, as if in some strange way, it hurt me, too. As *my* pain, in *my* chest.

'I'm sorry.' I said. 'I . . .'

I don't know why I was apologising.

Then it came.

Then it came.

'She's my daughter.'

'What do you mean?'

'Awena is my daughter.'

It seemed to take my brain a very long time to process this simple piece of new information. That meant you were a mother. A single mother.

You had turned away and were looking back up towards the wood and the bluebells. The red light from the setting sun filled your hair with red and gold.

The Gelyn valley was already cold and turning from twilight to darkness.

I put my hands on your hips and turned you gently around.

'There!' you said, bitterly. 'That's changed it, hasn't it? You can't overlook that like you can my broken nose.'

And then you said something else in Welsh I didn't understand.

'Changed what?'

'Changed your opinion of me.'

'No,' I said, carefully. 'I don't think so. Lots of girls are single mothers.'

'I shouldn't have told you. I should have waited. Now you'll think . . .'

'Hey!' I took your hands and made you look at me. 'Let's take this one step at a time, shall we? We've only known each other a few hours. We haven't even been out together yet.'

'You won't want to now.'

'I don't know what I want yet,' I said, softly. And saw your eyes cloud over.

'Is it Dewi?' I asked. Somehow, if it was Dewi it would be different.

'What!'

'Awena's father, is it Dewi?'

You slapped my face.

Hard.

And then, the tears welling in your eyes again, you started off, running down the hill.

I caught you easily and pulled you to me. I tried to hug you but you beat feebly against my chest with your clenched fists. And tried to pull away again.

I refused to let you go.

'Tell me,' I said.

You tried to pull away again, but I held you firm.

'Not Dewi,' you said.

We looked into each other's faces: you defiant, me willing you to come to me. Neither of us saying anything.

'Hug me,' you said. 'If you could love me – with my ugly nose and ugly history – as much as I could love you, then hug me.'

So I hugged you.

'I love your nose,' I said. 'And you hardly cover it with your hand with me these days.'

'Kiss me,' you said.

I hesitated. Then I kissed you on the nose. And then the mouth. You were salty with tears. And I was almost crying too. I have no logical reason why.

'Please,' you said. 'Gods aren't supposed to get emotional.'

'And princesses aren't supposed to cry.'

'Just kiss me.'

So we kissed until we were breathing each other's breath, deep into each other's lungs and hearts.

'Our air will be circulating in each other's blood now,' I said.

You looked at me and shook your head.

'Ti'n weird. Do you know that? Weird.'

'So are you.'

And – finally – we were both able to laugh.

'I will answer your questions,' you promised. 'Just not today. Not just yet.'

197

That night, I read and worked.

And wondered about you.

The following day I had been due to meet Iwan, my contact from the Welsh Assembly Cultural Unit, at eleven. But he arrived early and found me sitting at a table in the deserted dining room, trying to turn all the documents and notes which surrounded me into a coherent report.

'Dr Bull, I presume,' he said, striding forward, hand outstretched. 'You've got yourself a job on here then, boy.'

He had the kind of South-Walian accent I had originally expected to hear in Umbo before I discovered that the North Wales accent is completely different.

'How was your drive?' I reciprocated.

'Gor-jas,' Iwan told me. 'God knows how I love my country. Coming up the old A470 this morning, boy, up through the valleys and the mountains. Beau-ti-ful. Who could wish to live or work anywhere else?' He looked me up and down. 'What's your speciality then?'

'Regeneration, mainly,' I recited. 'Rural. Metropolitan. Changing social structure. Impact of economic and social policies. That sort of stuff. I've been working on alienation in Muslim communities recently. How Al-Qaeda recruit vulnerable young men from poor, inner-city Asian communities. That kind of thing. But my PhD research was on the impact of social policy on third generation poverty in former pit villages in county Durham.'

He slapped me on the back.

'Well done, boy. You're the man then. I'm more of a general dogsbody, me. Masters in Social History and Politics at Aberystwyth.' He paused. 'What have we got here then?'

He nodded towards my papers.

'Would you prefer the Welsh or English version?' I offered one of each.

'Good on you, boy. How did you get these done? I heard the Welsh Nationalists were maulin' you.'

'Oh, you know,' I said in the way men do to each other, 'fieldwork contacts.'

'Da iawn,' Iwan said. 'This is good stuff.'

'Diolch yn fawr.'

Iwan looked at me quizzically.

'Picking up a bit of Welsh, too, then? Are you sure you know what you are into here? This is Welsh Nash territory. Big time. The Middle Ages had their Gwylliaid Cochion, we've got Gwrthsafiad. Tora Bora of Wales this is, round here.'

I looked at him blankly.

'You haven't heard of the Gwylliaid Cochion? Or Gwrthsafiad.'

'No.'

'Paid â phoeni,' he laughed. 'Gwylliaid Cochion – wild red men – they were brigands who lived in the hills just south of here, near Dinas Mawddwy in the Middle Ages, see. Like the Welsh terrorists and Robin Hood all rolled into one. I was thinking about them as I drove over that great lonely pass to Dolgellau only this morning.'

Iwan had the way of a storyteller about him.

'The Gwyll . . . what?' I knew to get the 'll' sound from the sides of my tongue.

'Gwylliaid Cochion, boy. The wild red men. Some say they were descendants of the original Celts, others that they were remnants of the army of Owain Glyndŵr, last Prince of Wales and that the Gwylliaid Cochion was just a cover story. Myself, I think they found a secret valley, and hid away, biding their time through the generations, protecting the royal blood of Wales, awaiting their moment to return.'

I blinked.

'A secret valley like this one?'

'Course not! That's all fairy stories, boy. But then again . . .'

He laughed at my alarm and then went on.

'No, these days, the guerrillas are all political and their weapons are bureaucracy. Except for Gwrthsafiad. They're the most militant of the Welsh Nationalists. They think of themselves as the Welsh Resistance Movement, you see. Operating against the occupying forces of the English. They have a big following here, I warn you. Graffiti and protests mainly. They were the ones behind that protest here at the Supermart the other day. I thought you'd have known that.'

'It looks as though I have a lot to learn.'

'Don't worry.' He reached into his briefcase. 'I've got loads of background info for you here. You've probably got all these, but I thought it might be useful to make sure. Population profiles. Economic statistics. Death rates. Employment rates. Birth rates. Immigration and emigration rates. And there is a bit somewhere about Gwrthsafiad.'

'Yeah,' I said, slowly letting my breath out and picking up the bundle. 'Thirty percent elderly. Sixty-two percent mothers with children under sixteen. And of those age groups in between, an incredible eighty-two percent of the potential childbearing population have left. It's unsustainable. The whole community will have disappeared in a generation.'

'You've got it. The young adults leave. Go to university, fall in love. Don't come back. Who's left?'

'The not-so-clever. And the elderly English,' I suggested. 'Not so different from the old ex-pit-villages up North.'

'The elderly *racist* English,' Iwan said pointedly, 'moving here to escape the mass immigration into English cities and towns . . .'

'We call it "The White Wave",' I said. 'Immigrants grow more prosperous, move out of their original ghettoes into the suburbs, and the English start to move out to the country and towns like this.'

'Great name! White Wave. I like that! You London chaps have a way with words. The silver hoards fleeing the cities looking for the English idyll in the English countryside. Well we've got 'em in Wales big time. Moving out of Birmingham to escape the ethnic minorities – and they come here and find they're the immigrants.'

I nodded.

'And not just retirement homes, it's second homes, too. Our research is showing younger couples leaving the cities now. Buying second homes as fast as the mortgage companies will let them. It's not just immigration that's driving them out. It's crime. It's drunken teenagers. Brawling louts. Hoodies. It's not just the elderly who are frightened to go out. Young parents are increasingly concerned. They're fearful of letting their children out of their sight for a moment.'

'It's all perception, Jon. You and I know that. Fuelled by the media. And radio and television as bad as the tabloids.'

'Maybe, but that perception is a significant social trend. That's why so many are wanting to move to the countryside and Spain and France and so on. Not that there aren't those who choose multiculturalism, of course. A lot of graduates and intellectuals see that as very cool, but they tend to live in the trendy areas.'

'So what do you make of Wales, then, Jon?'

'Beautiful country. Bit dramatic in places.'

He laughed.

'It's obvious the English that are seen as immigrants here,' I said. 'The Welsh speakers have nowhere left to go. And the English can't see the problem.'

'You got it in one, boyo. Language and culture. The people here believe they have to protect their language. Keep it safe. Keep the English out.'

'Even if it means doing without mains electricity and water?'

'Even if.'

'Like that secret valley of the – what was it?'

'Gwylliaid Cochion.'

'Gwylliaid Cochion. So poor old Mrs Leakin hasn't got a chance?'

'Probably not.'

'What am I supposed to be doing here, then?'

'That depends on whether you think the language is worth preserving or not. What's your view, Jon?'

I shrugged. 'What do I know? I've learned a few words. It seems like fun.'

'Listen, Jon. People are prepared to go to jail to protect the Welsh language. *Have* gone to jail. You've seen the protests here. I saw your Councillor Penhaearn Tegid Foel on TV. And heard him again on the radio on my way up. He is very determined to block the English and keep them out. And he's got a point. The English are a pretty insensitive bunch.'

'It's not intentional, though, is it. They're only trying to assert their rights as UK citizens, aren't they?'

'Rights don't matter, Jon. Welsh speakers have their backs to the wall. As you say, they have nowhere else to go. Most English incomers think of native Welsh speakers as backward and narrow-minded and ignorant and living in medieval conditions. Think about it: one-fifth of us speak Welsh – though the number who actually live and work through the medium of Welsh, as they still do here, is much, much smaller.

'Every time a new English family moves in, it weakens the language. It only takes one English person in a room, for everyone to have to turn to English. I've seen it happen, boy. Golf clubs, choirs, dramatic societies – you name it – let an English person in and before you know it, you're not speaking Welsh any more. That's what Penhaearn believes he's fighting.'

'But you've just given me the figures. The bright people leaving. Agriculture being superseded by cheaper produce from abroad. The economy stagnating. They're on the road to nowhere.'

'That's why we need a clever lad like you, see. To sort it out for us.'

'They need power.'

'But they need Welsh power. Not English power.'

'I'm talking about electricity.'

'I'm not.'

You seemed to be avoiding me that lunchtime. But I was busy with Iwan anyway. After I had been through my strategy with him, and he had left, I had a much clearer idea of what I needed to do. I had already arranged to visit the factory that afternoon. But I urgently wanted to see you. Talk to you. Make sure you were all right.

I was tempted to go to your house, just across the little orchard behind the hotel. But I knew the next time we met, it would have to be in private. I wasn't sure what was changed by me knowing about you being Awena's mother. Not our attraction for each other. Not the fact that we were from different worlds. But something. Who said we were going to make our lives together anyway? It was just attraction, that was all. But it had happened to me so rarely, and seemed so precious, it didn't even cross my mind that I could not respond.

The way to the factory was almost past your house. I looked at the windows as I went by. Someone was moving about, I couldn't see who. But I felt as if I knew in my heart it was you. And all the way there, I was thinking what you might be feeling and how I might reassure you.

I found the factory up the valley behind the Two Dragons, in a row of sheds. I was directed across the yard by a group of women in overalls, smoking what smelled like dope and giggling to a forklift truck driver.

The office was in a large, Victorian, double-fronted house where I was greeted by a strikingly pretty girl, dressed like a night club hostess.

'Hiya, you's lookin' for me, aint yer?' Every item of her clothing, from the black pvc boots through the leather mini-skirt to the strangely-shiny white vest had company logos stuck on them – 'Jones Brothers – The Welsh Company' encircling the head of a cartoon dragon.

'You're Jon, aint yer? They said if you was to come I had to take care of you. So 'ere we are then. My name's Trêsi. What's yours then?'

'Jon, then.'

'*Then?* Oh yeah. Cos I just said that, didn't I?' She giggled prettily.

A display case along one long wall of the office showed off the company's range. Teddy bears, caps, table-mats and toys – all with a Welsh dragon and some with slogans such as I love Wales. Wales is wild. Wales is woolly.

'We don't make any of them 'ere. Ye' naaa. We just buy 'em in, see. China. And then just sticker 'em up, see. Have you seen my logos? Do you like 'em? I've got one on my bra too. Oi. Shouldn't be looking, should you? Tell yer wot. I'll get you a paned – coffee all right, is it?'

She thrust a brochure at me so I dutifully leafed through it.

''Av yer read that then? Dull, innit? 'Ere, I know. Come an 'av a look at these pic-chers on the wall over 'ere. I'm in some of 'em.'

Music was obviously important. Some photos showed the factory choir, others showed the brothers in a pop group. In others they were clog-dancing, dressed in cloth caps, breeches and scarves. In some Trêsi danced, too.

We went through to a kind of boardroom.

'Thing is, they aint back yet. But there's more pictures here – with their wives and children.'

I dutifully inspected these too. She was obviously wracking her brains about what to do with me.

'Ere, I know,' Trêsi said, suddenly having an idea. 'You look like a cool geezer – being black and all – do want to see my personal gallery?'

I wasn't sure what she had in mind. My week had already got the better of my professional judgement once.

'You can 'av another paned, too, if you fancy it.'

I followed her through to a kind of canteen with an oil-fired cooking range and four tables littered with dirty mugs. The walls here were covered with unframed, curling snapshots of staff outings, nights in the staff clubhouse and presentations to staff.

Trêsi, clearly the company mascot, was in the centre in all of them, like a page three girl, between the two brothers.

''Ere, this is my favourite.' She showed me a picture of the brothers posing with a group of customers and what looked like a team of American cheerleaders.

'I took that picture: our top clients. Good innit? We did that for the company's hundredth birthday. Centenary they call it. Didja know that?'

I was unsure what to say. I nodded.

'Look. Don't get me wrong, right. We works hard and we plays hard. An we don't half have a lot of fun. An' that's good innit?' she said.

One of the brother's legs looked strange. I looked more closely at the picture. From the knee down, it was silver.

'That's Dedai, that is. He's got an aluminium foot, ain't ee? You mustn't mention it, though. Promise? He's really sensitive.'

I promised.

'Knew I could rely on you. You got a kind face, aintcher?

'What exactly are *chosen girls?*' I asked, not really sure I wanted to know.

'Oops.' Trêsi dipped her knees, raised her finger to her lips and looked skywards in a pantomime gesture of naughty-girl caught. 'Hush my mouth!'

'My name's not really Trêsi, you know. It's Patricia. They just call me Trêsi, see, cos they say I look like a Trêsi. They wanted to call me Aderyn cos it means bird in Welsh. It's like a joke, see. Cos of my London accent and that. Cockney sparrow. Geddit? But it didn't catch on. They're gorgeous with their names, the Welsh, aren't 'ey? And kind with money and that. They looks after us. Everybody loves 'em.'

'Aderyn means bird, then?'

'I don't talk Welsh really. It was too late, see. I came here wi' me Mam when I were fourteen. Like ten years ago. Mam came running after this Welsh geezer who was daaarn saaarth werkin on the railways. Then she found out he had a wife and two kids an' that. But he chucked 'em out, see. There and then.

Just like that. On the spot. And we moved in with him anyway. So that were all righ', weren't it?

'They only spoke Welsh in the school, see. So I couldn't understand a bloody word, could I? It was horrible. Everyone talking this gobbledygook stuff and I couldn't understand a bleedin' word. Scwuse my manners. Corse, I can say "paned" and "bore da" and stuff. And that's enough for me, innit?

'Dedai was really sweet to me. I knew what he was after, mind. Just cos I aint ejicated don't mean I'm stupid. But them's OK with me, see, coz them's honest about it. There's no front with them. And I was really upset when he shot 'iz foot off that time. But that's just 'im, see, innit?

'They're like the celebs of Umbo, if yer get me. And they're the only ones round here who know how to have a good time. Well the locals are a real po-faced lot. Tea-total. Lemon suckers they calls 'em. An' they're not wrong neither.'

'So you're happy in your work, then?' I asked. I wished the brothers would come.

'Oh yea-eh! I'll say. I got a fantastic life aint I? I'm like *the* local model, see? I bin on the Chrissmuss gift calendar seven times. I modelled a Welsh dragon thong last year. That was a larf. Top seller that iz. 'Cept I caught a chill on the shoot. In the snow.'

She lifted up her skirt and showed me the thong emblazoned with a smiling dragon's face.

'I'm, like, you know, locally, really famous. I get to go to all the corporate hospitality stuff with the clients and that. An' all I 'as to do iz hand out drinks, bit of fetchin' and carryin'. I'm made up, ain' I?'

I wasn't sure what to say.

'Ere you're such a good listener, aincher. And here's me yak-yakkin' far too much. Dedai and Huw say they really like that. They think I'm a larf see.

'I don't always get the chance to talk much 'cos everyone else talks Welsh and I carn't really join in that. I can understand what they're saying tho'. D'ya know what I mean?

You know, even though I couldn't say what a particular word meant if you woz to ask me.'

Before long I knew most of Trêsi's life story. That she'd caught VD off of Dedai when she was fifteen and he was thirty-four. That they'd decided to abort the child because of the infection.

That she'd then had a miscarriage with another pregnancy off of (she thought) Dedai but it could have been Huw Môr.

''Ere. You're really sweet. D'you know that?' She gave me a little peck on the cheek. 'I feel I can really talk to you. You must think I'm a real tart But I've only ever slept with them two. And, like, some people have slept with 'undreds, ain't they? So I'm not really that tarty am I? Not compared with most girls these days.

'It's like I'm sort of pledged to both of them, see. It makes me special. Even though they keep going off and getting married to other people. That's sort of for formalities, if yer can understand me. And I don't mind about Dedai's foot. Cos I love 'im.

'See, I carn't have kids now, after me abortion. So sex is just recreational innit? And coz I'm special to them they'll always love me, won't they?'

The brothers arrived smelling of drink. They shook my hand a little too vigorously and herded me into their office.

'I'm sure that Trêsi's been looking after you,' Huw Môr said, while Dedai winked.

They offered me Welsh whisky. I tried to decline but they wouldn't accept my *No*.

'This is one of only a very few bottles of genuine Welsh whisky, not made for a hundred years. If I tell you that it is worth over a hundred pounds a glass, I'm sure you'll be able to appreciate it,' said Dedai.

'We'd be insulted if you said "no",' Huw Môr added.

They poured me half a tumbler-full.

'Iechyd da!' they said.

'Iechyd da.'

'Now,' said Huw Môr, 'what can we do for you?'

I began my spiel.

'As you probably know I'm here to help the plans to bring electricity and mains water to your town. So I need to know what effect the proposals would have on your business.'

'None at all,' said Dedai. 'What do you think of the whisky?'

'Very nice. Thank you. Would it help you to expand, sell more, create more jobs?'

'No. But would you say it was worth a hundred pounds a glass?'

'Well I'm not an expert.'

'Take another sip then. You will be shortly.'

I did as I was told and rolled it around my mouth.

'Now say what you think.'

'It's very unusual. Dark golden colour. A thick and heavy viscosity, clinging to the side of the glass. Almost like honey.'

'Da iawn. Da iawn. I like it. Keep it coming, boy . . .' Dedai sounded like a sports trainer urging his athletes on.

'It's very special. You can tell that. The taste is almost – kind of smoky . . .'

'Yes. Yes. Ewch ymlaen.'

'. . . with a sweet smell but a sharp, almost medicinal flavour.'

'Medicinal!' Huw Môr seemed a little affronted by this.

'Well . . . yes in the sense of being herbal. Therapeutic. You know.' I paused wondering if I had said the right thing.

Huw Môr equivocated

'Iawn. Iawn. Ewch ymlaen,'

I thought it best to carry on.

'. . . an extravagant taste which changes in the mouth to mead and vanilla, leaving a rich aftertaste of . . .' I searched for the right word. '. . . raspberry.'

'Da iawn! Write that down for us. We like that, don't we, Huw?'

Dedai thrust a pad and Biro at me. And Huw Môr came and sat on the desk, towering over me, watching as I wrote it down. This was how quickly they had reduced me to the role of performing monkey.

'Now then, Mr Bull. What were you saying?' Dedai was looking down on me.

'Do you have any opinion about bringing mains electricity and water to the town?'

'Fantastic idea,' said Huw Môr. 'I've supported it from the start.'

'And mains gas, too, if poss. We could get rid of our oil-fired generators, introduce mechanisation. We could probably save a fortune.'

'Good, good.' This was encouraging. I pulled out one of my questionnaires and started to fill it in.

'What effect would it have on staff, do you think?'

Dedai shrugged and looked at Huw Môr.

'Might you be able to employ more people, perhaps? Or maybe it would enable you to get different machinery and employ fewer people? Would you benefit from advice on additional grants to expand the company?'

'We don't want your help,' said Dedai.

'What my brother means is that we haven't really thought about it yet.'

Dedai raised his hand threateningly and was holding his forefinger just a couple inches from my nose.

'Think of it as confidential,' he said.

'Oh, yes. Of course. It is,' I said. 'Completely. Just to help you achieve good governance.'

Dedai kept his finger there for a long, threatening moment before moving it away.

'Electricity and water would be good, of course,' said Huw Môr.

'But there's a lot of people in the town who don't like change,' said Dedai. 'You talk to them, you'll see.'

'We very much appreciate your help, don't we Dedai?'

Dedai took the hint and heaved himself off the desk. Then went back to his chair.

'That was a very good verdict on the whisky,' he said, moving the pad. 'Now then. Let's drink to that – what was it you said?'

'Good governance?'

We picked up our whiskies.

'Good governance.'

I took a sip, then realised that the brothers were gulping theirs in one and I was expected to do the same. I followed suit.

'Good man,' said Huw Môr, glancing at his brother, who nodded. And then stood up abruptly.

'We really support what you are doing for the town. We want you to know that. And we'd like you to come and talk to one of our business partners. Would you be happy to do that?'

'Maybe,' I said, instinctively standing up too. 'When?'

'Good man. A few weeks, actually. We have some Chinese interested in putting some business our way. But they want official reassurances from the Council. And you know what the Council people are like. It would be better if you could come. OK?'

'If I can, I will.'

'Great.' I wasn't sure what I was agreeing to, but before I could speak, he was taking the empty glass from me and shaking hands.

The other brother had stood up and was shaking my hand and smiling.

'You're a good man,' said Dedai. 'I expect you've got a lot of people to see. It's been very good talking to you. I hope you'll pass on our compliments to the Prime Minister. And assure him that everything is under control.'

Huw Môr gave a look to silence him.

Trêsi gave me a cheery wave as I was bundled out.

I COULDN'T THINK. How could I think?

How can a person who feels marooned like an island see further than the water which surrounds her? And think about anything other than whether it is calm or stormy? And wonder what the shapes mean that she sometimes sees on the horizon?

But you, Jon, had turned my little island world into something else.

What was I supposed to think? What could I think?

Were you my causeway? Appearing magically from the depths to reconnect me with the world? Or were you – my black god, the most beautiful man I had ever seen – some kind of trick of life? A clever, wonderful, gentle man come to escort me to my happiness? Or, as my mother believed, a man intent on deceiving me?

What if I was deceiving myself?

I had worked out one thing. Or so I thought.

You could not be my causeway back to Awena. Your causeway could lead only to your land, not to mine. My damaged, troubled land.

I thought about nothing else.

How my love for Awena was still buried in bitterness and stupidity. How her love for me was dormant and unknown to either of us, if it was even there. My love for Mam and Dad still strained by my incompetence as a human being. How would falling in love with you help me or Awena with that? (You see, Jon, how it was possible for someone to learn my diagnosis and the whole psychological manual yet be quite unable to use it?)

How can someone who believes she is an island fall in love? Or experience that happy fusion of two people in (as you once called it) perfect symbiotic selfishness? How could our self-interests ever coincide?

You had your job, your life in London, and your mission

to change the world and make it a better place. You could not abandon your life any more than I could abandon mine. And even if – in some great moment of madness – either of us did decide to surrender our life and culture and individuality to the other, how could either of us become the different people that we would need to be to fit into each other's worlds?

How could the momentary illusion of joy in each other be anything other than doomed to disappointment?

Only a fool would dare to think otherwise.

I could not.

THE VISIT to the factory had been a minor mistake, the whisky a bigger one. I needed to walk, to think, to clear my head. I took a path along a hand-cut stream full of green aquatic plants. It led into the back streets of the town, little terraces of houses, but it was the streams that fascinated me. At each new terrace a ditch branched off it. This was the water system Twm and his gang had shown me. But they had only shown me the good part.

In some places the conduits had been ploughed into the side of the road in others they had been built up in hand-shaped concrete, with pond weed in them and clear water flowing. But, in others, there was sheep dung and dog dirt and they stank.

I followed a random tributary down one back alley, aware of the growing noise of petrol engines and smell of exhaust fumes. Sculleries opened onto back yards. I glimpsed a woman standing washing clothes while another wrung them out through an old-fashioned mangle. Only then did I realise that the noisy thrum of motors was generators. A cacophony of them, heating water, essential to power all the equipment and gadgets I, in my city life, had always taken for granted.

I couldn't see at first where the dirty water went.

In some places pipes led into the ground, perhaps to septic tanks; in others they ran into another system of ditches, this time covered with paving slabs. I hoped this was only for rain water and dirty washing water. Not for sewage, surely!

It was like a scene from how I imagined the early Victorian slums in London might have been.

My next turn brought me out onto the Maes. I saw this, too, in a different light now. What had seemed quaint and charming before now looked run-down and dilapidated. The shops with their sad, sparse window displays, and long-expired attempts to draw in customers. The Post Office. The clothes shop. The chemist's.

The only shops that seemed to have any life, were the Supermart and a curious gift shop, dealing in herbal medicines and the supernatural.

But my day of fact-finding visits was not over yet. This evening I had scheduled a visit to Clwb Pori Rotri, a sort of gentlemen's dinner club.

I hoped you would be in the hotel, but you weren't.

I wanted to phone you, to text you. But it seemed that wasn't possible here. It seemed inappropriate to come knocking at your door.

MOST OF THAT DAY I busied myself in domestic chores. For Awena.

'What are you doing,' Mam said. And tried to help me.

But I wouldn't let her.

'I must do it myself,' I said. 'I must. I must.'

I had to demonstrate to Awena that I loved her. To prove it to me, to her, to all of us.

All day I tidied and cleaned her room. And half of me hoped that you would come to find me, see me wearing my ffedog, and understand.

I laundered her bedclothes by hand in the galvanised tub in the scullery, pushing the happily bubbling suds through the cloth until my hands were red and sore, and then rinsing each one in fresh water until it was completely clear. And then I hung everything out in the sun to dry. I ironed her clothes, heating the two flat irons alternately on the Aga, until I was satisfied I had taken out every crease.

And then I cooked her tea.

Mam watched me, saying nothing.

'Leave me alone,' I said. 'I want to be alone with Awena. I am never alone with her without you being here, taking over everything.'

Again, she didn't reply.

'I want to have tea with Awena on my own. You and Dad and Gethin can have yours later when they come in. Don't worry, I'll prepare it all. I just want to be alone with Awena. For once.'

So Mam went over to Nain's and left me on my own.

Awena's nursery school, just round the corner, finished an hour and a half earlier than the big school. So I had it all planned.

As if a mother can prove her love in half a day!

I fetched her, took her satchel, helped her with her coat and sat her down and asked her about her day and what she had been doing.

And then we had our tea – her favourite cheese on toast –

but she refused to eat it. 'I don't like it,' she said. 'Where's Mam? Why isn't Mam here to make my tea?'

'Mam's at Nain's,' I explained. 'But I've made your Welsh Rarebit just the way Mam does.'

'I don't like it,' she said.

So then I shouted at her, tried to make her eat it. But she refused and sat there with her mouth tight closed.

I cleared away feeling cross with myself for shouting. And telling myself how useless I was as a human being and mother. Thinking is good, Jon, but introversion is terrible. So I tried to stop thinking about myself.

I offered to read her a story.

'I don't want you to read me a story,' she told me. 'I want Mam to read it to me.'

I tried to insist and pulled her onto my lap.

But she wriggled off.

And then I shouted at her again and pulled her back and tried to hold her there.

And then she bit me.

'You're horrible. I hate you. I love Mam,' she shouted.

'I am your Mam,' I screamed. 'That's who I am.'

'You're not. Not. Not. You're not my Mam. You're a liar.'

And then I hit her.

A slap across the head. I don't think it was hard, but I'm not sure. She stared at me, mouth open. And I was frightened I had hurt her. Damaged her.

As she opened her mouth even wider, I could see in her eyes her astonishment and horror at my complete betrayal of what little trust we had had. The disbelief. I saw the wracking cry come silently up from deep inside her and then burst out.

'I'm sorry,' I said. 'I'm sorry.' And I tried to hold her and comfort her. But she cringed away from me.

'Go away. I hate you. I hate you. I hate you. I want Mam.'

And she ran under the table and sat there looking out at me, afraid of me.

I went down on my hands and knees, but every time I

tried to reach out and touch her to pull her to me, the crying went ten times louder. And I was crying too. Horrified by what I had done. Fearful that someone would come in and I would have to explain.

I was shaking as I went to clear up the dishes, throw away the uneaten cheese on toast and finish preparing the meal for Mam and Dad and my little brother.

It was Gethin who came in first. Awena came slowly out to him, giving me a long, suspicious look to see if I would make another grab for her. In a few minutes, he was reading to her and they were chatting happily.

When Mam came back, she saw at once that I'd been crying.

I wanted to tell her what a failure I'd been and how I'd hit my daughter. How I'd told her I was her mother and she hadn't even believed me. And about how hurt I was. And how it was never going to change. Never be any better. But I couldn't. I don't know if it was for me or them or just for fear of disturbing the other stinking, rotten things inside me. So this became yet another dollop of shame to bury away and leave to fester and grow poisonous inside me.

Instead, I went to my room, lay on my bed and cried.

Soon, I would have to go and work the evening shift in Y Ddwy Ddraig. Nos Fercher – Wednesday night. It would be Clwb Pori Rotri.

I was an island, marooned in a sea of my own stupidity.

Neither you nor anyone else could help me.

I had my home, I had chores to do, I wanted for nothing. What right had I, little Gwalia, to ask for more? I had been stupid to think that someone like you could love me.

No one but a fool could love me if they knew what I was really like. And what would I want with a fool?

Mam came in to see me a little later.

'You know,' she said. 'You can't make her love you.'

I DROVE OUT to Donald Flood's range-style house and arrived exactly at seven, as he had instructed me, expecting a chat before we went off to the meeting. I rang the bell. He appeared at the door in shooting jacket and green waxed cap. I was glad I'd worn my suit.

'Recovered from that bloody meeting?' he asked, sticking out his hand. 'Good to see you again.'

'Yes, thank you, Mr Flood,' It was uncanny how my voice seemed to mimic his. He reminded me of Freddy Morgan.

'Call me Donald.' He looked across at my little Smart car. 'Is that comfortable?'

'It's great.'

'I think we'll go in mine.'

Instead of inviting me in, he led me across the gravel and opened the passenger door of his Land Rover. I climbed in, wishing I'd had more time to prepare. 'I'm afraid I haven't had access to a photocopier so I only have skeleton data sheets. Some of the local statistical variations are very surprising.'

'It's only Clwb Pori Rotri,' he announced. 'They'll just want a quick talk. Not more than fifteen minutes so just run us through the main points of your strategy, if you don't mind. It's a social night.'

'Fine,' I said.

'You're probably a member of the Round Table or something yourself, aren't you?'

'Actually, no,' I said, 'I'm not.'

'If y'ask me, best way to get into any community. Join their club. Give 'm a bit of cash, volunteer for everything, show willing. They'll follow you to the ends of the earth. First thing I do when I move somewhere new. Join the club. Never fails.'

'Right,' I said.

I realised then that I was being driven straight back to the Two Dragons.

In the dining room, twenty men were crowded around a small table paying for their food. The language was English, though a small knot of Welsh speakers stood talking quietly together in their language, sipping their pints.

I was introduced to the secretary, the treasurer, and the chairman, all wearing badges or chains of office and then escorted to the bar where Dewi was frantically pulling pints.

'Is this a men-only club?' I asked the chairman. (The Leyburn Institute had done a lot of research into the social effectiveness of equal opportunities legislation.)

'Some Pori Rotris have ladies,' he said. 'But happen we don't. Umbo ladies have lots of clubs. But for us lads, there's nowt else.'

Donald Flood thrust a glass of red wine into my hand as a bell rang and everyone took their places for grace. I was ushered to the 'top' table, between the secretary and Mr Roberts.

You appeared suddenly, with two other girls, bringing in trays of soup and placing them in front of everyone with no fuss. I saw the old men's eyes on your body. Our eyes met momentarily. A shadow of a smile flitted across your lips.

'If you want to make a lot of money, you need two things,' Mr Flood was saying. 'Money and good people. All the rest is just hard work. I know. I've been there. I've done it. How many men can say that? Eh?'

I mumbled something but I was watching you, Gwalia, worrying about how you looked.

'You'll probably spend your whole life working for other people. Me? I've never worked for anyone else in my life. I have other people working for me. If you work for other people, you're making money for them.'

It sounded like a speech he had made a thousand times.

'I have a thousand men working for me around the world. And I make damn sure every one of them is making me a minimum of two pounds a week, every week. The good ones make me more. Much more.'

He laughed, delighted at his own cleverness. Happy to be (as he thought) impressing someone new. Around the room men who were obviously familiar with the story, were concentrating on their soup.

I watched you standing in the doorway, Gwalia, waiting to clear the dishes.

'So you see, young man. There's not much you can tell me about money. And that's what's important. Never mind politics. Most of the men here are retired. But they'll tell you. Never mind social theory. You need to look after yourself first. Once you've got enough for yourself. And your family. Then you can start thinking about doing something useful for other people.'

I don't know how he managed to talk so much and still finish his soup first.

I kept my talk to the fifteen minutes exactly as prescribed. And ended by asking who was in favour of mains electricity and water. Surprisingly, not all the hands went up.

'The thing is,' Mr Flood said. 'We've all got generators now. That's all you need. A good generator.'

'You must understand that it's different for the Welsh people,' said one. 'We haven't got the money that the English have.'

'Would Clwb Pori Rotri be willing to help raise money towards bringing mains services to the town?' I asked. 'Or actually support the project in some way?'

'Shouldn't think so,' said Mr Roberts.

The secretary looked perplexed.

'We're mainly a social club,' he said. 'We're just old men.'

'You might be,' quipped someone. 'We're very sprightly.'

And they all laughed.

And, with that, my talk was forgotten. Next item on the agenda was The Quiz.

The chairman gave out pens and paper while the men sorted themselves into teams of four. It would have been rude to leave so I sat with the Welsh group. Perhaps, in your eyes, Gwalia, I wanted to distance myself from the English.

'Bore da,' I said, completely inappropriately. 'Don't feel you have to talk English on my account.'

'Now then pop pickers . . .'

And Donald Flood turned into a wooden caricature of a DJ and quizmaster, playing snatches of sixties and seventies pop songs without the slightest change in personality. I had the feeling that he'd done this show in every new town he had lived in.

I was amazed to discover that the Welshmen at my table knew virtually none of the songs, all of which had been enormous hits. Even I knew them and they were the songs of my Dad's and Grandad's generations.

'I know them. And it's twenty years before I was born,' I protested.

'We were listening to our own songs,' they told me. 'In Welsh.'

'People like Dafydd Iwan and Edward H Dafis.'

I shook my head.

'Those names mean nothing to me.'

I tried especially hard after that. And, as it happened, we won. The Welsh were particularly jubilant at that.

'Why do you join a club like this?' I asked. 'Don't you mind the English crowing about knowing their own culture better than you?'

'To be honest. Clwb Pori Rotri is good for business, ynte?'

'But people keep telling me that your language is disappearing. Wouldn't you prefer meetings in Welsh?'

'The English are the people with money you see.'

'We like to keep in with everybody, we do.'

The man next to me tossed his head impatiently.

'You sound like a Welsh extremist. We're not all like that. We can talk Welsh at home and in the choir, and English here, isn't it?'

Later, I asked some of the English members if any of them had thought of learning Welsh.

'I went to lessons for a year or so, but there's no point really,' said one.

'Yeah. People talk English to you anyway.'

'I don't know a single English person who has learned it properly,' said another. 'They crack on that you can learn it in a year. And they have these programmes, Welsh in a Week, and so on – but I know people who've been learning for ten years, and Welsh people still prefer talking to them in English.'

I saw Donald Flood's ears prick up and he came over.

I was aware of you, Gwalia, collecting dirty glasses on a tray. I was constantly aware of you.

'Talking about Welsh?' he asked. 'Waste of bloody time. Dying language. I've been all over the world, negotiating complicated business deals, international contracts, financial transactions. For a lot of money in a dozen languages. I've never needed a word of anything other than English. That's the language of money, you see. And it's money talks. Not people. Money's international.'

The glasses crashed to the floor.

Without being able to help myself I rushed across to make sure you weren't cut.

Our eyes met. Your anger was almost palpable.

Donald Flood was standing over us, grinning.

'Leave the Welsh wenches to do the work, Jon. There's a good lad.'

'Don't you think that's a little insensitive and sexist and anti-Welsh?' I bristled, standing up.

'Insensitive! Anti-Welsh!' laughed Mr Flood. 'I am Welsh. Born and bred in Pembrokeshire. A hundred percent dragon's-blood Celtic I am. I just don't speak the dying language, that's all.'

I bent down again and helped you clear the broken glasses.

'And I had the sense to move to Birmingham and make money. Frankly, my boy, I think it's the bloody Welsh speakers who are insensitive. Over eighty percent of us speak English. And, actually, if you count the number of conversations in Welsh and the number in English, you'd find Welsh is infinitesimally unimportant.'

'I've heard a lot of Welsh here.'

'It's like farming, old boy, ask people round here what

percentage of the Welsh economy is down to agriculture and people will tell you sixty or eighty percent. Do you know what the real figure is?'

'Actually,' I said. 'I do.'

'Then you'll confirm that it is less than one per cent. And what is the biggest single economic generator?'

'Tourism,' I said. 'At just over thirty-seven percent.'

'Exactly. Without tourism, this town will die. And it has none. Cos they keep taking down the signs.'

'But with tourism, the language will die.'

'It seems to me, Mr Bull, that according to both those scenarios, the language dies anyway. At least my way, we keep the town alive.'

As the meeting broke up, I thanked Donald Flood politely for his hospitality. But I think we both knew we were no longer on the same side.

'If I were you I'd walk up and collect your car in the morning,' he instructed.

I went back to my room.

I waited half an hour and came back down to the kitchen where I guessed you would be washing up. I helped you dry the dishes and put them away. Then we went for the inevitable walk. This time along the river on the other side of the town. There was a full moon, low in the sky so it looked blood-red and enormous.

And something kept swooping around us.

'What's that,' I asked.

'Bats.'

As my eyes accustomed themselves to the darkness, I could see them circling above the water, and circling us. And there was an owl, too, except that you had to explain to me that there were two, calling to each other 'One goes *tywit* and the other *tywoo*.'

We kissed for a long time. Then – surprise, surprise – you pulled away.

'I am a hopeless cause for you,' you said. 'You know that, don't you.'

'All I know is how I feel. And I think I know how you feel.'

'You'll be gone in a day or two.'

'I can come back. You can come to London.'

'You know so little about me.'

'I know your heart.'

'Yes,' you conceded. 'You know my heart.'

And my heart leapt.

We stood hugging each other, the bats circling around us.

'I don't ever want more children,' you said.

My voice answered for me, without my brain being asked for its opinion.

'It doesn't matter. I don't want children.'

'I can't offer you sex. I can't bear the horror of even thinking about it. You understand that, don't you. I am useless.'

'It's OK.' I heard myself saying. 'It doesn't matter.'

You turned away.

'I'm useless to you,' you said. 'And you are useless to me. You should go and leave me alone. We can only make each other miserable.'

'You don't know what you are saying,' I said.

'Yes. I do.' You looked so deeply into my eyes. 'I do. I do. I do.'

'OK, yes, there have been a few problems but I'm optimistic. In fact, I feel absolutely confident,' I told Professor Lain on the phone. It was important to be positive when talking to your boss. That was one difference from academia.

'You seem to be rather out on a limb there, Jon,' she persisted.

'Not at all,' I said. Now that you'd let me use the room behind the reception desk as a temporary office, I wasn't out on a limb at all.

'I've done everything according to the text book,' I assured her, 'used all received wisdom – as well as a good deal of my own personal flair – to make the Llanchwaraetegdanygelyn project a success.'

'You mean Umbo?'

'Llanchwaraetegdanygelyn is the Welsh name.'

'I see.'

'I've had extensive meetings with local people. Consultations with local pressure groups. Discussions with the Council. And I've recruited local helpers to push questionnaires through every letterbox.'

Actually, that was a slight exaggeration. It was just you and me, Gwalia, who had pushed the questionnaires through every letterbox. But it was four hours well spent.

'And you should have received the plan I posted to you yesterday.'

'I've seen the plan. It's very well written. And I'm impressed that you had it translated into Welsh. But you don't seem to have been able to work very closely with Mrs Leakin.'

This was true. I didn't want to tell her that Victoria Leakin's constant talking made my ears ache and her assistant Blodeuwedd was useless. And there wasn't room for me in their cramped little office in the attic above the Council Chamber (thank goodness). And I was much better off working here, at the hotel, with you.

'I had to maintain a balance,' I said. 'The reason her initiative had stalled was because she is English and had alienated the Welsh community. And there was a lot of mutual suspicion between the two. I've been working to reassure them both. Develop a consensus. Reconcile the two groups.'

'That's a tall order for less than a week.'

'I'm fairly confident, Angela. All we need now is for the people of the town to come together the day after tomorrow and say yes.'

'Have you got plenty of local support, do you think?'

'I think the women will all be in favour. I've seen how hard and cold it is to do the washing in the back yards. And how much trouble it takes to light the lamps. They must all be desperate for electricity and progress.'

I had discounted that Penhaearn seemed to be against it. Just one man's voice. Faced with a public meeting neither he nor the Gwrthsafiad could possibly carry the day. I had also discounted that you had been part of the Supermart protest, Gwalia. Why does love always assume automatic loyalty?

'Are the movers and shakers coming?'

'Absolutely. I've lined up a top team of experts and executives from the electricity and water companies, I've got Iwan Roberts from the Welsh Assembly, and I'll outline how Government and European funding will share the costs.'

'Very good,' said Professor Lain. 'You seem to have thought of everything.'

'And I've decided to make my opening remarks in Welsh,' I added proudly.

There was a short silence.

'Well you know best.'

And she hung up.

I was determined that the meeting would be a success.

You had helped me translate the first two hundred words – and spelled them out phonetically for me and spent hours schooling me in correct pronunciation. How to ynganu – pronounce – yn Gymraeg.

They would be so charmed by my flattery and dazzled by my faultless logic they would – despite all evidence to the contrary – say 'Yes' to self empowerment. And 'No' to living in medieval poverty.

In my scenario I would return to London in triumph, with you on my arm, parading down Whitehall to be offered a job in Freddy Morgan's Westminster Policy Unit, inside No.10 Downing Street, the following week.

'We can't fail now,' I said, coming back through to the reception area where you were ledgering the accounts for last night's meagre Clwb Pori Rotri takings. 'Every house in the town has had a bilingual copy of the strategy and a questionnaire. They can't possibly say no, can they?'

'You know, Jon,' you said. 'It will mean huge changes. Don't be too upset if it turns out people don't want that.'

I wasn't listening to you. Or anything but my own ideas. Not *listening* listening.

'Think of it! Electricity. Mains water. Proper sewerage arrangements. It'll make life so much easier. Your people can't want to go on living like a third world country forever.'

'Maybe we don't want to be like every other English place.'

'But think how much healthier it'll be. Think of the risk of pollution in the water. I've walked round Twm Slwtsh's water system. You're lucky the town hasn't had an outbreak of dysentery.'

'But isn't it having everything so easy that makes so many people's lives seem so meaningless? Isn't that why so many people who seem to have everything get depressed?'

Again, I wasn't listening.

'Look. All this back-breaking work is pointless and meaningless. It's medieval. It's as simple as that.'

You looked crossly at me then. Or was it disappointment?

It was the first time we had not seen eye to eye.

'Maybe that's why we quite like the idea that Twm Slwtsh empties all our septic tanks into Llyn Y Gelyn reservoir – for the people of Liverpool to drink.'

'Would you like me to take you out somewhere tonight?' I asked. 'We could drive out to a restaurant. To Chester or somewhere.'

You shook your head.

'No, don't think so,' you said. 'Better not.'

'Well I suppose I should be working on my speech and things for the big meeting.'

So that's what I did.

It didn't occur to me for an instant that you might be plotting against me to subvert the meeting you had helped me organise.

I don't think I had ever spent so long out of contact with Andrew and Nisha and Mum and Dad. Usually, I was texting them or sending them e-mails several times a day – and I was seeing them and talking to them all the time as well. Here, I couldn't do that. But there was so much to tell them.

Not just about you, Gwalia, and what an astonishing thing it was that I had come here to this remote and wonderful place and found you here, but about other things, too. You can really think out in the remote countryside, can't you?

I wanted to tell them about the difference between living in a place like London and a place that was really rural. Like Wales. And how you can really get a different perspective on things in the country.

About people.

And about how life works.

And what I'd been thinking was . . . you know how, in London, we live and work in the so-called 24-hour culture? You know, constant news, endless ambition, and all of that. From the middle of the country that all seems just hot air and relentless, about as relevant to real life as a disco, all that dancing and competing and showing off.

Here, in the country, there was another way: accept life as it is. Don't judge people by their cars and houses and what they earn or what they bought in some exclusive shop somewhere.

And I was thinking, maybe I could do that. Come to live in a place like this. Get back to studying. To books. Maybe write something. Try to make a difference that way.

Pretty profound, eh?

But what floored me most was the realisation that even the people who want to make the world a better place can never agree on what to do to make it better – and usually end up making it worse, sometimes fighting wars and killing each other. Especially people who say they believe in gods.

It all seemed very clear to me.

Here, in the mountains of Wales, I felt away from that, able to look at it with the benefit of distance.

Yet, even here, Penhaearn had one vision of how to make the world a better place and Guy Ingress another.

Penhaearn wanted to keep Llanchwaraetegdanygelyn purely Welsh-speaking and was prepared to sacrifice all progress and economic development to achieve it; whereas the English saw the town as underdeveloped. And a way to make money.

Boudiccea was trying to balance culture and economics for the social benefit.

Not even your own family, Gwalia, could agree.

Everyone had their own view.

It was all so clear.

I went to sleep, feeling contented, as if I understood the world in a way that I previously hadn't.

Forgive me, Gwalia. I was very young.

YOU HAD NO IDEA, did you, Jon, that I was meeting Dewi at midnight? Gwrthsafiad had been my one excitement since the incident. My one way of knowing I was alive. Dafydd Y Gwrthsafiad was there, of course, bossing us about.

We called at Rhys's house first. There was no need to knock. Rhys was waiting for us wearing pathetic dark clothes and a woolly robber's hat. We laughed a bit at that, until Dafydd Y Gwrthsafiad reprimanded us.

'This is a military operation. Don't laugh! Maintain your discipline at all times. You're a proper operational unit now.'

We set off, keeping to the shadows, eyes darting everywhere, making sure that nobody saw or heard us. The risk of getting caught had always been part of it, I suppose.

Dewi and Dafydd had it all planned.

Dewi rummaged under a stone on the wooden window sill and produced the key to Hiraethog's corrugated iron Council shed at the top of the Maes, And then they bossed Rhys and me about, supervising us borrowing stepladders and pots of black paint and carrying them over to the Supermart.

'I don't know why I'm doing this,' I said.

'Yes you do,' said Dewi. 'It's for Gwrthsafiad, for the language. And for Wales.'

It took less than ten minutes to cover the white pebble-dashed wall with foot high slogans. I kept look out.

'Cadwch Gymru yn Gymraeg,' Dewi daubed.

'DIM SAESNEG.'

'Ffasgwyr Saesneg Allan.'

And he added a 'Dal dy Dir' and a 'Cofiwch Lyn Y Gelyn', just for good measure.

It was like a children's game.

Then the work was inspected and Rhys and I were ordered to fall in, pick up the stepladders and paint and carry them in an orderly fashion back to Hiraethog's hut.

Then we all lined up, saluted, and Dafydd commanded us to fall out.

And I went home full of adrenaline.

THE FOLLOWING MORNING, I was working hard, while panicking gently and rehearsing the Welsh section of my speech, trying to memorise it, when Boudiccea stormed in to my room, clutching a copy of the *Daily Post* in her hand. She was even redder in the face that usual, and already sweating.

'It's a scandal,' she said. 'I don't know what we're going to do. My dear young man, don't you realise? It's a propaganda war. You'll have to cancel the meeting.'

'Let's have a look then, shall we.' I affected an air of cool academic detachment.

One glance at the front page headlines showed she had a point.

Pictures of Gwenlais and the Supermart manager glared at each other across the words: **How dare you speak that DIRTY WELSH LANGUAGE HERE!!!**

Underneath was a picture of Dewi and his friends waving their wipe-clean placards. I noticed you, Gwalia, standing with them. Even then the penny didn't drop.

'Ah!' I said.

'I have to say, Mr Bull, you are taking this very coolly. Frankly, I am rather disappointed. You do understand, you'll have to cancel everything.'

'Oh. I don't know,' I said. 'How relevant is a row about the Supermart to our public meeting? We have a good chance of winning the day I think.'

'They're not going to let that happen. Listen to this, Mr Bull. Listen!

'"An English shop manager caused uproar in a Welsh-speaking town when he told staff: 'Don't you dare speak that dirty Welsh language in my shop.'"

'And a few paragraphs further down, it quotes the store manager.'

She read on, trying to imitate the store manager's voice.

'"How can I be in charge of my staff if they are talking a language I can't understand? People can talk whatever language they like when I'm not there, but they might be telling me to **** off or go and have a **** or anything.

'"How am I to know what's going on in my own store if they don't talk in English?"'

She hurled the newspaper down, scattering my speech across the floor.

'You do realise this is all because of you, young man? I hope you do.'

I opened my hands to her in bewilderment.

'They've staged all this for your benefit, you know. That Gwalia girl and her spotty boyfriend, Dewi. They're the ones who've organised this to ruin my strategy. I thought you'd been sent here to sort all this out. You've made it worse.'

'I don't think that is true,' I said. 'It's certainly not true of Gwalia.'

'Well you've been totally seduced by her, haven't you? We can all see that. Walking around the town hand in hand with her. In broad daylight. She's a nationalist. She has convictions for it. Did you know that?'

'Convictions? Court convictions?'

'Yes! For pulling down roadsigns and painting graffiti. I thought that I had difficulties with my committees, with my Welsh not being good enough. But you have really upset the applecart. I never had this sort of problem in London.'

'I can only say I think you are completely mistaken.'

Her eyes bulged. And her bad breath filled my face.

'Well I bow to your superior intelligence,' she spat sarcastically. 'But I must say, personally, I see absolutely no hope of this project working now. I offered you my help, made myself available to you. But you've avoided me all week. We could have worked together. But, oh no! You had to please yourself. Be taken in by that little strumpet and her Welsh Nationalist boyfriend. Well, I hope you see them now for what they are. I take it you've seen what they've done to the Supermart this morning.'

'What do you mean?' I had been too busy working to even look outside my room.

She strode across to the window.

'You'd better come and look then. You can read the bloody insults from here.'

And so she dragged me across to the window. And pointed out the graffiti.

'Do you still think you're not making matters worse? You had better be bloody good at the meeting. That's all I can say.'

I didn't know what I felt. Humiliated? Challenged? Undermined? Very confused about you, Gwalia. Pretty terrible actually.

'Personally,' she said. 'I'm going to go and shoot some rabbits.'

She stormed out.

And half an hour later, I heard the sound of a shotgun echoing around the surrounding hills.

'YOU WILL HAVE TO CHOOSE,' Dewi told me as dramatically as he possibly could. 'It is either him or me.'

If I needed proof that my true feelings had come back to me, this was it: real anger and frustration.

'How can you be so unfair, Dewi?'

'We are made for each other, Gwalia. You know we are.'

'No, Dewi, I don't know that. All I know is, I am, starting to get better, my feelings are returning to me, and two of the people who claim to care most for me start giving me silly ultimatums. First Mam, now you.'

'You should listen to the people who know you, then, isn't it? We're the ones who care about you, ynte?'

'I'd have thought you might have been glad for me, If you really loved me. Glad that I might have found someone. Anyone, however temporary. But no, you just want me for yourself, Dewi. You just want to push me into playing the roles you've chosen for me.'

'I'm sorry Gwalia, but that's the way it is, ynte? I can't help my feelings either. It's just the way I feel.'

I had been so patient with Dewi for so long. I had been kind and careful, but I hadn't really been honest. This morning I felt strong enough that I could be.

'Listen, Dewi. You have always been very kind to me.' I really didn't want to hurt him. 'You were wonderful to me when I had Awena. And I'll never forget the way you walked out with me that first day with her in the pushchair when I had to face the world . . .'

'Don't say "but", not here Gwalia. Not today. I can sense what you are going to say. But you don't know what you are saying. I'm only going to accept one answer, you know.'

'I do very much appreciate you, Dewi. And I am very fond of you. But I'm not in love with you, Dewi. I'm just not. I'm sorry.'

I had expected this to be a bombshell for him. I'd avoided saying it for as long as I could remember.

Now that I had said it, Dewi seemed unaffected by it.

'You will be in love with me, though. When your feelings come back properly. It is me you love, Gwalia. I know it is, I do. You're in – what do they call it? – denial. That's it. You're in denial now. I understand that. Totally. You've been out of your mind, haven't you? You don't know what you're saying. I'll be there when you come back into it again. I will. Then you'll see.'

'Dewi. I'm not sure that is true.'

'You don't love him, do you? Can't do. He is black for a start. And he's English. You have to love one of your own kind, don't you? Have to. You got to love me, you have.'

'Dewi, Jon has awakened something in me. He will be gone tomorrow. I don't even know if I shall ever see him again. But I have been changed by him, you see. In here.'

I put my hand over my heart. And honestly now, Jon, I felt I was touching part of you.

That was too much for Dewi.

'I will not allow it. You are going to be mine. You are mine. You are! I've seen you two together. I've seen how you look at each other. I won't allow it.'

I didn't answer.

'Don't think I will just stand by and let you throw yourself away on him. Make a fool of yourself. Behave like a tart. And make a fool of me. Not after all I have done for you.'

I didn't have the strength to deal with Dewi's rage. I didn't have the strength to deal with any of it.

I turned away and ran home, crying. And up to my bedroom, lying on my bed sobbing.

I am Gwalia.

I am an island.

But, after only a few minutes, I started to feel ridiculous. That mantra no longer worked its maudlin magic. I needed a new solution now.

Perhaps I could just run away somewhere.

Or come with you back to London.

There was nothing for me here.

Nothing.

WHEN I PHONED into the office, Nisha's voice was sardonic.

'You *have* been putting the cat amongst the pigeons,' she said, ominously. 'It is all over the newspapers today.'

'What is?' I was already in a rising state of panic – my hormones preparing me for fight or flight or some redundant primitive rubbish like that.

'Didn't you hear the *Today* programme this morning? How did they put it? "Don't speak that dirty language here. In your town with an unpronounceable Welsh name."'

I groaned. My mind should have been racing but is wasn't.

'You've got the Welsh and English at each other's throats.'

'Has Angela seen it?' I was bound to be sacked now. Finished. Back to university. Or going to write books in the country.

'She has indeed. And not just Angela. Freddy's on the warpath too. His bow tie practically rotating. I'd lie low for a bit if I were you.' Definitely writing books in the country.

'What does Andrew think?' Not even Andrew's cool, cynical logic could help now.

'He thinks you'll be fine if the public meeting goes in your favour.'

'Really!' Maybe there was hope.

'Yes. He says it's results that count in the end. If you can win them over, all this will be forgotten.'

We talked a little longer. Then said goodbye. I had to think. I had to make a plan.

But, really, there was only one thing filling my mind.

You, Gwalia.

I needed to talk to you. That would make it all right again. I knew that.

But I needed to read the papers for myself.

That's when I got another shock.

Coming into the reception hall, I saw you and Dewi standing there. Him with his arms around you. And you crying.

Neither of you had seen me. Which was a pity because it meant I had a choice. Cough noisily. Or run away.

I had other choices. Punching Dewi's nose. Or being furious with you for seducing me and ruining my project. Had I imagined all that intimacy between us?

It was you who had made me feel like this. And now I was thinking like an idiot. I was determined not to behave like one.

What had I done?

How could I have been so stupid?

I was in love with a woman who was in the arms of another man.

I'd been deliberately seduced by a Welsh Nationalist. A spy. A Mata Hari.

I'd read enough books, seen enough films, about this kind of thing. But, of course, these things didn't happen in reality.

Idiot!

Parts of my body seemed to be working without my consent.

I was half way back up to the landing by the time I noticed and forced myself to stop. I didn't want to be upstairs, I needed to go and buy papers. But I didn't want to go downstairs either.

You're behaving like a stalker, my brain told me. As if you owned her. And you are supposed to be smart. You've cocked up your assignment. Cocked up any chance of ever working for Freddy Morgan. And you'll be lucky to have a job at all, if you don't get back to work and get this emotional coup by your stupid heart under control.

Okay, so I had misread the situation. Apparently. I had thought you liked me. Surely instinct couldn't be that wrong.

Superstitious clap-trap! You don't believe in psycho-kinesis, do you? Or thought transference? Or ghosts and fairies? Or UFOs? Of course not. So why do you believe in instinct, then? Or love?

Good questions.

I was shaking slightly.

I managed to get myself under some kind of emergency control.

Fine then. Now stop behaving like a stalker!

Right, go to your room, smarten yourself up. Pull yourself together. Be professional. Never mind being duped by romance (if that was what it was); Jon Bull has a job to do; so pull yourself together.

I got to my room only to realise my key was still down at reception.

What a jerk. What an idiot. What a loser. (Maybe she goes for losers. Hadn't thought of that, Mr Megabrain, had you?)

I quietly retraced my steps, keeping to the wall to stop the floorboards creaking. You and Dewi were still there. But, if I could just creep by unseen . . .

I escaped out into the fresh air, heart pounding, brain incredulous at my lack of emotional fitness. I had to think harder about this. Much harder. And I needed coffee.

A cappuccino grande with chocolate and a macaroon would be good. I headed for Caffi Cyfoes. The place was afog with steam and smelled of bacon. The choice was between stewed tea from the huge aluminium teapot or instant coffee from a catering-sized tin, hot milk or cold. In the steamed-up window display, the icing on the one lemon slice ran with condensation.

I went up to the counter where two large women in stained floral pinafores were working furiously, one smearing margarine on ready-sliced bread and dolloping on spoonfuls of tuna mixture, the other slicing the sandwiches in half with a huge antique carving knife and wrapping them in cling-film. They didn't acknowledge my presence.

I was still trembling. Perhaps I had become invisible.

I looked around. The café was half full but no one was looking at me. Be calm, I told myself. No one else knows how you feel. All you have to do is act naturally. No one will know.

Except that Boudiccea had probably already discussed my seduction by the girl from Gwrthsafiad with Guy Ingress and Donald Flood and every expatriate Englishman within shouting distance. How many rabbits had she killed today?

Of course they would have done. Everyone would be talking about it.

Including Gwrthsafiad.

They were bound to all be supporters of Gwrthsafiad in Caffi Cyfoes!

I watched the woman with the huge knife deftly slit the final sandwich in two, wrap it in cling-film, and toss it into a wicker basket. Then she looked up questioningly. She looked as though she knew.

'Bore da. Ga i'ch helpu chi?'

Even the grubby dishcloth festering on the Fablon-covered counter seemed to be telling me something.

I was suddenly very aware that I was about to speak English on enemy territory. So I didn't.

'Ga i goffi please, os gwelwch yn dda.' I had no idea where that came from. Your Dad's phrase book probably.

She pulled out a chipped mug, spooned in a lump of the coagulated coffee powder, held it under the steaming iron water heater, then plonked it down in front of me.

'Helpwch eich hun i laeth a siwgr. Pumdeg ceiniog, os gwelwch yn dda.'

I proffered a two-pound coin and was given a pound and something change. And turned to the plastic jug of milk and a cereal bowl of sugar with four used plastic spoons on the counter. I needed to calm down. Act normal. Compose myself. I found a seat and sat down. I was still shaking. But I had just conducted my first transaction totally through the medium of Welsh.

'You look as though you have the world on your shoulders.'

A kindly, white-haired old lady was standing beside me. She had that look of wisdom and knowingness which old people are supposed to have but so rarely do. She seemed somehow completely familiar.

'May I sit down with you for a moment?'

'Of course.'

I tried to stand up out of politeness, but the bench and table were bolted to the floor and it was too difficult to slide out.

She smiled. 'You aren't from around here, are you?'

'London,' I said.

'Da iawn,' she said. 'I couldn't help notice that you used a little Welsh just now.'

'Ermm. Yes. I . . . I'm afraid I only know a couple of words.'

'You know at least eight,' she said. 'And you have only been here two days.'

Her eyes were laughing.

'I'm Marged,' she said holding out a powder white hand, the skin like tissue paper, so fragile I was worried it might tear.

'Jon Bull.'

'You must have a wonderful teacher.'

An image of you, Gwalia, flashed into my mind, and my horrified brain heard my garrulous mind saying: 'Yes. I have.'

'Come and see me,' Marged said. 'Bring her with you.'

She patted me on the arm. 'We need people like you here.'

I felt suddenly calm. The trembling seemed to have gone. My jangling spirit was stilled.

I felt as if I had been touched by a saint.

That was all she said. We need people like you here.

Then she got up and went to the door.

I slid out, stood up and held the door for her. She was dressed immaculately in a pea-green suit, pea-green coat, pea-green shoes; parked outside was a little pea-green car, which had to be hers.

As I held the driver's door open for her, you appeared, Gwalia, across the Maes, and waved and came skipping over.

Our eyes reached for each other and I felt a huge surge of relief and joy. Your eyes looked a little red. But they were clear meeting mine.

'Shw mae, Gwalia.'

'Sut dach chi, Marged? Dach chi'n iawn?'

'Da iawn, diolch, Gwalia. Sut wyt ti, cariad?'

'Iawn, diolch.'

You gave Marged a hug.

'Rhaid iti gadw gafael ar y dyn 'ma; un da ydy o,' said Marged.

'Peidwch â phoeni,' you laughed. 'Dw i'n bwriadu gwneud hynny.'

As Marged started the car, you linked your arm into mine. You seemed very happy.

I wanted to ask you why Dewi had had his arms around you, but I didn't.

'What were you saying? Just then.' I wanted to know. 'What were you saying?'

'She told me I had to look after you. Not to let you go.'

Your eyes were twinkling. I didn't need to ask you if you loved me or if you didn't. You were here beside me, and that was enough. Whatever demons had cast their shadows over me were gone.

'And what did you say?'

'Fy musnes i ydy hynny,' you said. I could work out what 'fy musnes i' meant.

'She knew everything about me.'

You laughed. 'Of course she did. Everybody knows everything about everybody here. Including you.'

'I DON'T KNOW what it is attracts you to this hunting for ghosts,' Dad was saying. 'You're worse than mad the whole lot of you.'

'You have to be there, bach. And you have to believe in it or you won't ever experience it.' Mam never tired of trying to win Dad over to her cause.

'You're always hankering after something that might have been. If it's not your drowned village, it's the ghosts of the past,' Dad told her. 'Always looking for things that might have been different if you'd lived your lives differently. Capel Y Gelyn would have had no fascination if it wasn't gone.'

'You've never understood,' Mam said. 'And probably never will, will you?'

Anti Gwenlais was here to tell us about her latest adventure. I had my Gwrthsafiad, she and Mam had their ghost-hunting with Penhaearn.

'It was very exciting, Gwalia. You would have had to have been there. You should come with us. I do keep telling you.'

I glanced at Dad.

'No thanks,' I said. 'I don't believe in ghosts.'

'Ooohah,' she twted. 'You never know when you might need to converse with the departed.'

I gave a nervous laugh, she was a bit chilling sometimes, was Anti Gwenlais.

'I won't ever need to contact the dead,' I said.

'Are you sure?' she asked. 'If someone you loved very much was taken from you, before you had the chance to explain or to find out how much he loved you?'

Another little chill ran down my spine.

'No. I don't believe in it,' I said more decisively than I felt. 'But do go on telling us about your ghost hunt, please.' I didn't want the talk to turn to being about me. Not today.

'Well,' she said. 'We had to check no one was watching, then we climbed over the gate into the field. As quietly as we could. I've never seen your Yncl Penhaearn so, you know, *edgy*, as they say in English.'

'Anyway, here were the seven of us in all. Your Mam, me, Dwynwen, Jac Trydan and Penhaearn, wrth gwrs, and Billi-Jo and Jean.'

Mam busied herself with the cooking. She knew what I thought so she never bothered to tell me about it.

'Why didn't you wait till midnight when there was no one about?' Dad asked.

'Oh no. We had to go at twilight, you see. Billi-Jo and Jean said – they know about these thing. In Celtic mythology, one day changes to the next, not at midnight, but at sunset, ynte. So that's why we had to do it at twilight.'

'Owain Glyndŵr wasn't a Celt though was he? Weren't the Celts before the Romans?' I asked. Dad nodded. He didn't like the way some Welshmen claimed to be Celts as well as Welsh. To him, as a history teacher, *Celts* meant only Bronze Age.

'I think you'll find we're all Celts here, Gwalia,' Anti Gwenlais said. 'And in Scotland, Ireland, and Brittany too. That's what Billi-Jo and Jean said. But if you don't want me to tell you the story, I don't have to.'

'I'm sorry, Anti Gwenlais. Please do carry on with the story.'

'All right. But don't interrupt me. I lose my train of thought, you see, bach.' She stared at Dad.

'Iawn,' he said, in a resigned kind of way.

'So there we were, by Owain Glyndŵr Mount, with these big two-foot candles, and we had to climb up, didn't we? Like a mound, it was. But quite a big one, though it only looks small from the main road. You do know it, don't you, between Corwen and Llangollen?'

We all nodded.

'A bit of a snag wearing those long robes, if you ask me, in the mud. Well, we all kept slipping, didn't we? It was a lot harder than it sounds, you know. A lot harder.

'Anyway, we were filthy by the time we got to the top. I noticed Penhaearn kept looking round, I think he was a bit worried that we didn't have permission, but he hadn't told us that.

'He was very nervous when Billi-Jo and Jean started lighting our candles and started chanting. Billi-Jo and Jean had made us stand in a circle, you see. Except they said it was a pentacle. With Penhaearn in the middle. And Jac Trydan was somewhere with his headphones on and all his sensors and gauges and things.

'To be honest, Gwalia, I think if your Yncl Penhaearn had had his way, he'd have preferred to go ghost hunting on his own. But he has so fallen under the spell of those – can I whisper it – lesbiaid – that he does whatever they tell him. He even talks to them in English.'

'Carry on with the story.'

'So there we were each of us as the corner of this pentacle arrangement, holding up our candles and chanting. And Penhaearn loses the button.'

'I'm not following, Anti Gwenlais. What button?'

'Well, *the* button, of course. An actual button worn by Owain Glyndŵr himself. Penhaearn took it from a costume on display at the last Welsh Parliament building in Machynlleth.'

'I've seen that display, Anti Gwenlais. I don't think it was the actual clothes of Owain Glyndŵr. I think it was only a replica. On a shop window dummy.'

'P'raps that was what the problem was, then. Anyway, we all had to cluster round with our candles while your Mam and Penhaearn went down on their knees in the mud to find this button. It was your Mam who found it, needless to say.'

Mam twted at the sink. She was obviously listening to every word.

'Then, we all went back to our places and started again. You know chanting, walking slowly in a circle and banging our candles up and down on the ground.'

'And what were you trying to accomplish exactly?'

'To summon up Glyndŵr's ghost, of course. That was where Owain Glyndŵr was born. And where he was proclaimed Prince of Wales by his followers on September 16, 1400. Penhaearn told us.'

'But did his ghost appear?'

'What Billi-Jo and Jean were worried about was that it was also the site of an iron-age hill fort. They were very concerned that we might raise the ghosts of Iron Age warriors. You have to be very careful, you see. Though we had deliberately chosen the Spring Equinox – a most significant Celtic day – in order to exclude them.'

'But did his ghost appear.'

'I don't really know. Billi-Jo and Jean said they saw something on the paranormal plane and Jac Trydan said there was a strange occurrence on the green line on his screen. He was lolloping about with his headphones on saying there was a disturbance in the ectosphere.'

'But you didn't see anything.'

'No, dear, not then. It was later that Billi-Jo became possessed. It couldn't have happened then because I slipped in the mud, you see, and broke my candle.'

'Penhaearn didn't see anything?'

'Not then, no, Gwalia. But he was very pleased.'

'Billi-Jo and Jean said it had been very successful. They assured Penhaearn that by combining the better astrological knowledge of the present day, with the inaccurately scheduled pagan feast (which had been distorted by Roman calendar changes, you see) they really had contacted the other side.

'Jac Trydan said he wanted to pack up then, on account of his batteries were starting to run low. But Jean and Billi-Jo insisted we carry on. They explained about it being a very propitious day, you see. It was a matter of judgement, they said, about whether it was better to use Beltane – the ritual Celtic spring day – or May Day, May the First – or St David's Day. But they had worked out that the spring Equinox, which was scientifically the day of transition, must be the right one. Equal day and night, you see, the year's regeneration back from death to life.'

'It's OK, Anti. I think I get it.'

'So I had to stick my candle back together with melted wax. And we began walking around chanting again.

'Penhaearn took the button in the palm of his crossed hands in the centre of our circle and started to read the invocation Billi-Jo and Jean had written in English and he'd translated into Welsh, so that the ghost of Glyndŵr could understand it.'

Mam did the sound effects from the sink, chanting in a weird voice: 'Glyndŵr! Glyndŵr! We call upon your spirit to come back to us. We are your true servants. We await you.'

Anti Gwenlais glanced at her younger sister oddly, and carried on.

'That was when Billi-Jo went into this kind of trance, you see. She turned her candle upside down, extinguished it on the ground, and walked to the centre of our circle, facing Penhaearn with a strange look on her face.'

'What sort of strange look, Anti?'

'Haunted,' Mam said from the sink.

'Yes, indeed,' said Anti Gwenlais. 'Definitely haunted.'

'Master! Master!' Mam cried out from the sink, and turned round, looking a bit strange and started coming towards me. 'What ails you?' I wasn't sure if Mam was pretending or not.

'Just like that it was,' Anti Gwenlais said. 'And Penhaearn was looking round not sure what to do. Jac Trydan was very excited and gave him the thumbs up. So then Penhaearn shouts out. 'Who goes there? Name yourself.' I had goose pimples all over, Gwalia, I can tell you.'

Mam was bending over me now, still acting very strangely.

'You know me, master,' Mam said, looking very spooky and putting her face close to mine, but not looking as though she was seeing anything. 'It is I, Gwen, your servant girl.'

'Stop it, Mam. Stop talking in that funny voice. You're spooking me.'

'And the strange thing was,' said Anti Gwenlais, 'she was talking perfect Welsh. And Billi-Jo doesn't speak any Welsh.'

'Go on, then.'

'Tell me Gwen, Penhaearn said. Who am I?'

'Why you are you, Sir. You know who you are, Sir.' I shuddered. Mam was playing the part a bit too well for my liking.

'Tell me now, Gwen.'

'Don't be cross with me, Sir.'

'Of course not, Gwen. But I must hear you say my name.'

'Why you are Owain, Sir. Owain, Lord of Glyndyfrdwy.'

'And then Billi-Jo fell on the ground and Jean went rushing across to her on the ground. She was rolling around and mumbling and Penhaearn had to kick the candle away from her to stop her robe catching fire.'

'She was making it up, Anti Gwenlais. Play-acting. Just like you and Mam are now.'

'You had to be there. Jac Trydan rushed across. "That was incredible," he said. "The gauge was off the scale and the temperature dropped ten degrees."'

'Your Mam's eyes were shining as if she too was possessed. She went over to your Yncl Penhaearn and kissed him. 'It's true,' she said. 'You are the reincarnation of the Welsh Prince. All the Welsh princes.'

'Billi-Jo came-to then. But she was a bit groggy on her feet. 'What happened?' she asked. 'You did it, you did it,' your Mam said. And we were all jigging around, in a sort of celebration dance.'

Mam stepped out of her part now.

'Jean explained it all to her properly on the way back to the van. Penhaearn was very quiet after that. Lost in thought he was. It was only after we got back to the Maes and Billi-Jo and Jean reminded him about payment that he came out of it.'

'How much did he pay them?'

'Fifty pounds, I think,' said Mam. 'I was thinking we might club together and raise my Grandmother at Christmas.'

'No Mam. I don't think it's good for you, this ghost hunting.'

'Penhaearn thinks it's good. You know what he wants next?'

'Go on. Tell me.'

'He wants us to go to Cilmeri to raise the ghost of Llywelyn himself.'

I didn't need to ask Dad to know what he thought about it.

And I certainly didn't want to think that one day I might want to contact someone from beyond the grave. As if someone like me would ever come to believe such a thing!

I WAS WORKING on my laptop when you knocked on the door. You knocked very softly as if you were hoping I wouldn't hear you.

'Esgusoda fi.'

'Come in.'

I wasn't sure if I wanted to see you, now. Romance seemed so difficult. I think I had decided that any chance a romantic fling was now just stupid and impossible. That it was only the binge-drinking disco types that can have those carefree one-night stands. For me, seeing any kind of logic in people's emotions has always seemed quite impossible. I felt safer reading dry papers on social science and working.

And yet, when you came in, there was obviously something I hadn't considered. My heart did lift whenever I was with you.

'You do know you have done an extraordinary thing for me, don't you?' you said.

'I know,' I said. 'But maybe it's just boy meets girl. It's easy. Everybody does it. Lots. Except me.'

'And me. Dw i'n dy garu di, Jon. You know that. So there's things I have to tell you.'

'Tell me what?' I know now that Dw i'n dy garu di means I love you. I didn't then.

'Things I have never told anyone before apart from the police and doctors and my parents.'

'Whatever they are, Gwalia, I shall be gone tomorrow. I guess we had our chance. I'm really glad I met you. You've been such a fantastic help. And teaching me all about Wales.'

You came over and stood by the bed where I was sitting with my laptop. I needed to concentrate. If I was going to redeem myself at the Leyburn Institute, I needed . . .

'Knowledge changes things you know,' you said, stepping gingerly across the papers and files.

'Absolutely.' I heard myself saying. 'You've certainly changed me.'

'I don't know who Awena's father is.'

Was that it? Was that what you had come to tell me?

'That's OK. It's not unusual,' I said dismissively. 'The world is full of single mums who don't know who the fathers are.'

You stared at me, unable to speak.

I realised I'd said the wrong thing. And suddenly it mattered.

You turned to go.

And then I didn't want you to go at all.

All I'd said was that the world is full of single mums. What was wrong with that? Subtext – you shouldn't feel bad about it. Why should I have felt guilty about saying that?

'How bad can it be, Gwalia. A one-night stand with a stranger? A guest in the hotel – like me? I don't care. I'll take you as you are. As you take me.'

You stopped, facing away from me.

Waiting.

I got up and went over to you.

I stood behind you, put my hands on your shoulders and turned you round. We stood, faces so close, staring at each other. Neither of us knowing what to say or where this was supposed to be going next.

'What are you trying to tell me?' I said. 'Just tell me!'

'It's not what you think.'

Something told me this moment was some kind of turning point. You had some terrible thing you needed to unload from your heart. And you had chosen me to help you. Whatever dark and dreadful thing it was, I had to help bring it out into the world, and shine the sunlight on it so it didn't eat away at you anymore.

I pushed aside some of the papers that were strewn across the bed, and patted it.

'Sit down. Tell me everything.'

You sat down gingerly.

'It's okay,' I told you.

'You,' you said, almost sadly, 'are the first person I've told who isn't a doctor. Apart from Mam and Dad. And the police. I haven't even told Dewi the things that I want to tell you now.'

Your blue, innocent eyes were beseeching me to be gentle.

'It was a school trip to an international festival at Cardiff. You know, intended to expand our horizons. A group of half a dozen of us, invited to play at this important Eisteddfod with music and dancing and young people from all over the world. I was to play the harp. The others were there to sing to my accompaniment. And they were all a little older than me.'

I was watching your face. You looked so hurt. So noble. And so beautiful. Part of me longed to take you in my arms but I knew not to.

'So we ended up arriving early evening at this bed-and-breakfast place. Branwen and the others wanted to be out on the town immediately. It all seemed terribly exciting after Llanchwaraetegdanygelyn; it always did when we went away.

'They were so excited. They'd been getting changed and doing each other's make-up on the coach. And going on about how they would be hitting town big style, finding boys and going to exciting bars. Mam had told me to stay with the teacher because I was younger – it's what I usually did – but this time they encouraged me to go with them. Hearing them talk and getting ready made it all sound so exciting. It seemed ridiculous for me not to go. I wasn't a child anymore who needed a babysitter.

'So I said yes. And they were great about it. They lent me clothes and insisted on making up my face and everything.

'"I haven't got any money," I told them,

'"Don't worry, we'll soon find boys and they'll be more than willing to buy us whatever we want," they told me. We were all laughing and giggling. It all seemed such fun.'

You paused then, as if you were expecting my disapproval.

'Well, I'd never had the chance to look like that before, had I?' you said defiantly. 'It was the first time in my life I felt – you know – sexy.'

Again you watched for my reaction.

'Anyway, off we went to hit the town. Round all the bars and everything. The city seemed full of young people taking part in the festival. Branwen and the others had been right, it wasn't hard to get boys to buy us drinks; the hardest part was restraining them. But being a boy, Jon, I expect you'd know quite nicely all about that.'

'Not really,' I said. But it wasn't about me.

'It was Branwen who attracted the attention of the English steel drum band – you know Branwen, she works in Caffi Cyfoes, but she was at school then, a couple of years above me – Branwen said they were really nice. From a boarding school somewhere near Birmingham. She and the others flirted with them outrageously, in a way they'd never have done at home. So then these boys invited us back to the international head-quarters, which they said was like one huge party. Branwen and the others weren't so sure about going, but I insisted. I don't know what came over me really. I suppose it was the drink. And finding that I had power over boys. I'd never experienced that before. They seemed to be so fascinated by me.'

You paused, staring at the wall. Then you shrugged, as if to some invisible jury, and carried on.

'They all seemed very posh and English – bois y crachach – and I thought that meant that I could trust them.'

You got off the bed and started to pace the room.

'You don't have to tell me if you don't want to,' I said.

'No, I want to.' You came back to where I was sitting and took my hand.

'Cusan!' You commanded. And kissed me. Then you frowned and said: 'But you won't want to kiss me again after I've told you.'

'I will,' I assured you. 'Of course I will.'

You started pacing again, closing your eyes as if it was very important to get everything in the right order. And as if that wasn't easy for you.

'They say my memory of that night will always be a little shaky. I feel panicky just to think about it, a bod yn onest.'

252

I went to get up and go to you. But you put up a hand to stop me.

'I can remember sitting and laughing with the others. And enjoying myself. And Branwen telling me that I was so lucky. That these were not like the boys at home. They were cool and rich and cultured. And imagine how it could change our lives to marry one and never have to worry about starting the generator, lighting the paraffin lamps or emptying the outside toilets ever again.

'And there were two of them that seemed to fancy me who were both quite good looking.'

Watching you, Gwalia, I could feel this tightening sensation in my stomach. And my breath shortening in sympathy with yours.

'They made fun of our accents a bit, and the fact that we all spoke Welsh (they'd never heard Welsh before). So we said what did they expect coming to an international event in Wales. They laughed at almost everything we said. And we laughed, too. And there was a lot of touching and kissing going on. And Branwen was snogging one of them. All of it was very exciting, I suppose.'

You paused and looked at me. I couldn't tell what you were thinking.

'I don't remember exactly how I got upstairs. I wasn't forced to go. I remember saying to Branwen that it was OK. And then I was on my own with the two of them. Safety in numbers I thought.'

You turned round then and banged your fist against the washstand.

'Stupid me!' you shouted angrily. And punched the wall. 'Stupid me!'

I was worried you were going to hurt yourself.

I jumped to my feet and went to you to hold you.

'It's OK,' I said. But you pushed me away roughly. And you were breathing hard.

'Go drapia! No! It's not all right. It's not.' And then you

stared hard at me, wildly, as if you hated me. 'Gwranda! You've got to listen!'

I backed off, alarmed. 'OK,' I said. 'I'm listening.'

And you calmed down a little. And carried on.

'The doctors told me afterwards there must have been at least five of them. But I can only remember two. They say my brain is mixing up the details to protect myself.

'Mam won't have it, but the frightening thing is, Jon, at first I wanted them to have me. They were the two most beautiful boys I had ever seen. And I had the drink in me. And I didn't want to be a virgin anymore. And I'd heard about everyone else out there having sex and how wonderful and free it was. I was drunk. But I knew I wanted them. Can you believe that Jon? Both of them. What kind of woman who is a virgin would want that? What does that make me!'

I shook my head. I couldn't quite take in what you were saying.

'Mam and my Anti Gwenlais have their own versions. Mam says I was raped by all five of them. Forced against my will. And Anti Gwenlais, in her version has them all shouting "Let's have the Welsh bitch".'

You seemed to be talking more to yourself than me.

'I've been through it all so many times, I hardly know anymore what's true and what isn't. I don't even care anymore. Because none of it makes any difference to how I feel.'

Your eyes were shut, tears streaming down your face. You were in a place I couldn't be.

Something in me recognised something very brave and noble in you. And in that moment my heart went out to yours – whatever that might mean for us.

'I don't know how many hours later it was,' you were saying. 'I woke up alone, in a pool of my own vomit in a laundry basket in some cupboard in the hotel. I must have lain like that for hours, dizzy and hurting, and with a terrible headache. I was sick a few more times. But all of that seemed trivial.

'It was the chambermaid who found me. An East-

European with very little English and no Welsh. I must have frightened the life out of her, *gr'adures*, poor little thing. Gabbling and crying out to her in my mamiaith. First she screamed and then she thought that I would get her into trouble and was cross with me. Then, when she realised what had happened, she was very kind.

'They said that I'd been raped many times.

'Apparently, after I'd had sex with the two I'd gone upstairs with, the story had got round. Others had come and plied me with more drink. And Mam reckons I was drugged. The police took statements from some Norwegians and some French boys. Sometimes I have nightmares about every race you can imagine. And I am trying to fight them off me.

'They found their sperm on my face and in my hair. My clothes had been torn from me, leaving open wounds on my skin. My breasts were bruised and one of them was almost bitten through. There were teeth marks, too, on my buttocks and the blood had been sucked to the surface of my skin all over my body.'

You were talking at the window now, I was only an observer. I shut my eyes and wished I could have shut my ears. But most of all I wished – as I still wish – that none of it had ever happened.

'My anus was bleeding and my vagina was so badly bruised and torn, it hurt for me to move. Even my cervix was bleeding. From a stick they thought. But, worst of all, my nose was broken and torn. I have no idea why.'

You were silent now, except for your breathing.

'I am an island,' you said. And looked at me. 'I feel like an island.'

'Yes,' I said. 'Surrounded by stormy seas.'

You smiled ruefully at that. And gave a little laugh.

Slowly, as I felt your storm subside, I moved towards you till I was standing behind you, looking out over the town. The Supermart daubed with graffiti, the Town Hall, facing it implacably across the green. I put my arms around you.

You held my hands against your stomach. I put my chin on your shoulder and you touched your cheek to mine.

'The strange thing is, Jon, you've never mentioned my nose.'

'Well, you've never mentioned mine.'

'But there's nothing wrong with yours.'

'Exactly.'

You turned round then, laughing, the tears still in your eyes and all over your face. And you hugged me and held your cheek on my chest. And I hugged you and gently rocked you so that we were moving together in the same standstill dance, thinking only about that moment.

After a long time you lifted your head and kissed me on the lips. Our tongues touched and we breathed each other's breath, backwards and forwards, as if that made us one.

'Jon. These are things I have never been able to say to Dewi.'

My heart was breaking for you. All the confusions in your head. All the conflicting loyalties and ways you felt that you'd let each person down. And hardly half a thought to protecting yourself.

'Oh Gwalia! Gwalia!' I kissed your face. Your tears, your eyes, your cheeks, your hair. 'You poor, poor thing.'

'You see,' you said, trying to pull away. 'Now you pity me. You think I'm such a mess.'

'I don't think you're a mess,' I said, pinning you to me. 'I think you're amazing to have coped with such a dreadful ordeal without turning into a total recluse or hating the world. No one would guess from looking at you.'

'Yes they would,' you said. 'It's all here in my broken ugly nose. You must have seen it. Even though you're too polite – far too much of a perfect gentleman – to mention it.'

'Did they catch the boys who did it?'

'Yes and no. Everyone insisted that I make a complaint. Tell the police everything. And you know the strange thing? The real horror wasn't the rape. I couldn't really remember any of that, I had drunk so much. It was what followed on from it. They told me they were trying to help. That it was all for my own good. But ... But ... Minute by minute it just got more horrific. I wanted someone to make it go away. But it just got worse.

'The hotel manager. Teachers. Mam and Anti Gwenlais. Police. Forensic examination. Full medical examination. Admission to hospital. How can I begin to explain to you? I hardly knew what had happened to me. But they tried to make me piece it all together. What was I thinking this moment? What did I do the next?

'Can you imagine how many times I have been through it all? Over it. And over it. Trying to remember. How if only I hadn't done this or that. Or been so stupid.

'The first thing they did was give me a pregnancy test. The doctors suggested a morning after pill. But Mam and Anti Gwenlais wouldn't hear of it. Stupid stupid stupid! And I can't really even remember it.

'Think of it! I can't remember my daughter's father's face!'

'It must have been horrible.' It was as if I felt the echo of your horror inside me.

'I felt completely numb. Emotionally numb. And the worst thing was, at the end of it, they said there wasn't enough evidence.'

You looked at me imploringly. I had to reassure you.

'You'd become a helpless victim. You had no control. You tried to distance yourself from your own experience – mentally. Did it feel as if it was all happening to someone else?'

'Yes, that's it. How did you know that! It was as if I was inhabiting a body that was nothing to do with me. The police questions, the doctors stripping me and taking swabs and stitching my wounds, it was as if I was outside my body, looking down on it.'

I was helping you now.

'That all makes perfect psychological sense,' I said, as if I really knew about such things.

'But then I looked in a mirror and saw my nose. My own stupidity and shame was written all over me, forever, for all to see.'

'It's a beautiful nose, Gwalia.'

'No, Jon! It's bent and horrible. Look at it.'

'OK. I will.'

I examined it very closely.

'It's a sweet little nose,' I said. 'I think you've been very unfair to it. It hasn't had it easy, we can see that, but I think you have to stop blaming it. Give it a break. Start being nice to your poor little nose.'

'Mae o'n afiach!'

I didn't know what that meant.

'I'll kiss it better, then,' I said. 'It's an ancient voodoo remedy.'

And I kissed it symbolically three times, three seeming like a magic sort of number.

You smiled at me ruefully, gratefully. 'That won't do anything.'

So I kissed it again. Ten times. Twenty times.

Till you began to laugh.

'It's still not going to make any difference.'

'Then we will have to find other ways to make you love it again.'

We were standing facing each other, now. I was holding both your hands in mine and raising them to my lips and kissing them.

'You can start to let it go now, Gwalia. I'm here. Those things were just your strategy for coping. You can let them go.'

I felt your body tense. You tried to pull your hands away, but I held them.

'How do you know all this?'

'People are damaged in the same way as communities. It's my job to know. It's why I'm here.'

You looked puzzled.

'You're here to help me?'

'Finish your story, Gwalia. Tell me about Awena.'

You started pacing up and down again.

'She hates me. Poor little innocent Awena. I should have been there for her. I should have been her perfect mother. I should have sung to her and read to her and taught her songs and how to play the harp. But I can't. I used to be so bright and cheerful, Jon. You should have known me how I was before all this.'

'You always seem bright to me.'

'It's a pretence, Jon. It's an act. The doctors told me if I behaved like that, then one day I would forget I was pretending. And anyway, it makes life better than it was when I was sulking in my room all day and being miserable. But Awena isn't fooled. She won't accept me.'

'Maybe the doctors were right. Maybe it is all starting to work out for you.'

'Oh Jon. You're being so kind to me. I wish I could have given you my old self. Always happy and laughing, always with music in my head. Mam and Dad were always so proud of my singing and harp playing. Awena was robbed of that. And so I was robbed of her. Now I can hardly bear to hear those songs and tunes I used to love. And I hate myself for playing them.

'You have to forgive yourself, Gwalia.'

'Forgive myself! What does that mean? How will that make it go away. It is me, Jon. You should have seen the newspapers: Headmaster's daughter raped. I hated them. I hated everyone. I hated me. Months of guilt and self-recrimination. The look in Dad's face. Mam's. The days of shame turned into weeks. And months. It never goes away. Imagining what they thought of me. Wanting to die. Wanting to kill myself. The months turned into years. It'll never go away.'

'You can't say that, Gwalia.'

'Oh I've heard all that. I've seen psychiatrists. Taken tablets. A day's worth at a time. They kept a very careful eye on me.

'I remember driving back up through the Rhondda Valley from one of those psychiatric visits, a couple of weeks before Awena was born. Seeing all those girls with prams in those god-lost little towns with their closed chapels and churches. And realising that it wasn't all going to be better just because my baby was going to be born.

'They didn't dare let me be alone with her. They couldn't trust me with her with my nightmares. Nights of shouting and screaming. Hot sweats, cold sweats. Scratching my skin to open scabs and – once – banging my head against the wall, trying to dash my brains, Mam said.

'Once when Mam was trying to calm me in my fitful, sleeping rage, I lashed out, punched her in the face. And wouldn't stop. The town thought Dad had beaten her.

'One night, I tore my pillowcase open and awoke, hysterical, in a snowstorm of angry feathers. Feathers sticking to my sweat-drenched body, fists clenched and with Mam crying, her arms slippery with my sweat, trying to hold me.

'I probably would have killed myself that night if she hadn't been there. Sometimes I wish I had. I hated her sometimes.

'After that I'd only stay with Dad.

'Dad talked to me. Talked in the same calm tones he uses in school and in chapel. When I first came home, I wouldn't let go of him for a week. He sat with me day and night, reciting poetry, the psalms and telling me Bible stories, as he had done when I was very young.

'When I was pregnant, I thought about the baby as "it". "It" inside me, moving and feeding on me. A memento of them. An alien. The ultimate victory of the conqueror.

'I got it into my head that "it" was English. That "it" had been planted there and was trying to rape me from the inside as "its" English fathers had done from the outside.

'They decided not to prosecute. I was too unstable to give evidence, they said. An unreliable witness. So not enough evidence. Thank god.'

You had finished now.

I took you in my arms, and cradled you gently, rocking you like a baby.

I wanted to hold you and protect you like this forever. Sort out everything for you.

And never let you go.

Except that then you said you had to go. And let me get on with my work.

So I was left on my own in that awful room, my bed strewn with papers, your story filling my mind.

Unable to make sense of anything.

The deputation of farmers arrived an hour later. I fancy I could smell the whiff of slurry even before I saw the convoy of Land Rovers making its way up the Maes. It didn't occur to me they might be coming for my benefit.

I was still supposed to be working on my speech. I had my notes and laptop spread out over one of the larger tables in the dining room. But my mind still filled with the enormous hurt you had suffered. As if, in sharing your story, all that pain and anger had now become partly mine too. It was not just my speech to the town that I was rehearsing in my head, it was what I wanted to say to you.

'I understand how Wales has been hurt by the English over centuries,' I wrote. 'I understand why you, the people of Llanchwaraetegdanygelyn are reacting to offers of help as you are. Like any living thing who has been abused – evasive, defensive, and aggressive. Taken in the sweep of history you have been conquered, overrun, exploited and ignored. But it is not just your town this has happened to. Every town and country and people has suffered from its history. We are all hurt. This was what has made each one of us what we are. It defines our character. But only in part.'

I deleted it.

I couldn't say things like that!

I tried again.

'The domino effects of cruelty and injustice cascade down through history from one damaged generation to the next. Bitterness and hatred generating more bitterness and hatred, each act being justified as revenge for the last. We see it all over the world and all through history, like Greek tragedy. Our challenge being always to rise above it.'

I deleted it again. Better not to mention Greek tragedy. How could I, a young black Englishman, still viewed as a foreigner by many of his fellow Englishmen, stand up and lecture this town – or you, Gwalia – on your morality?

I knew what I wanted to say. But how to say it . . .

The whiff of manure and diesel was inescapable now. The tractor engines grew louder. I got up and went to the window. They were stopping outside. The penny was starting to drop now.

By the time the deputation of farmers arrived rowdily in the lobby, I was there to greet them with an outstretched hand.

'Sut dach chi?'

'Iawn, diolch. A chithau?'

'Fine, thanks.'

The sweet-sour smell of manure forced me back a step. One of them shuffled uneasily forward clutching a piece of paper he began to read from.

'We have come here today to see the young man from the Government whom we are given to understand is here to help us in our needs,' he said, reading very slowly.

He paused and looked at me.

'I'm very glad to see you,' I said.

'Mr Bull, we are in dire circumstances. We are losing many grants. Many of us cannot now afford to carry on farming as our fathers and our grandfathers did.'

'I see,' I said. 'Please go on.'

'Many of us have to work part-time – or even full-time – at other jobs in order to support our livelihoods as farmers. Our children go away to college, and they can earn much more money than us in even menial jobs.'

He glanced up and then carried on reading.

'Farming is the backbone of the North Wales countryside. The local economy, in the form of shops, and banks, and all those working at livestock marts and agricultural suppliers, are all dependent on us.'

He looked up.

'Without us, these towns here in North Wales will die, Mr Bull.'

'I am only here to bring power to your town,' I said. 'My remit doesn't extend to agricultural policy.'

'But it is agricultural policy, Mr Bull. We've been told. There's only a limited amount of money. If they put money into bringing power to Llanchwaraetegdanygelyn, they will take it from the farmers, like they have for all these new town developments and industrial estates.'

That puzzled me. 'You think that the money to pay for bringing mains water and electricity here will be taken from the agricultural budget?'

'Definitely, Mr Bull. That's what happens. We've been told.'

'Who told you that?'

'Mr Penhaearn Tegid Foel Jones. He's our County Councillor. So he knows about these things. I don't think he's supposed to have told us. But he did. So we've heard it from the horse's mouth, you see.'

'But that's completely wrong,' I told them. 'Please. Sit down. I think I need to explain to you how these things work.'

'You're wrong there, Mr Bull.'

'We know the Government don't admit to it. But that's what happens.'

'We know it's true. We've seen our incomes going down and down.'

For the next ten minutes I tried to assure them as best I could, that funding for the project to bring power to Llanchwaraetegdanygelyn was completely independent of farming subsidies or anything else. But they wouldn't believe me.

'Bringing power to your town will help your economy, make your lives better not worse.'

'It won't help us, Mr Bull. We've read your leaflet and questionnaires. You make no mention of farming. None at all.'

'And farming is the most important thing in *our* local economy. We represent the cefn gwlad, you see.'

I hadn't heard of cefn gwlad before.

'Asgwrn cefn y wlad,' he explained. 'We are its language, its culture, the very lifeblood of its heritage.'

'Actually,' I told them. 'Agriculture is no longer the most important factor in the local economy. It's tourism.'

I'd checked my figures with Iwan.

'Well that just shows how ignorant you are of our community here,' the spokesman said. 'We don't allow tourists here. We discourage them. So they can't be important, you see. Farming is what is important here. Very important indeed. So, you see, you are completely mistaken, Mr Bull. Completely.'

They looked at each other. Then one of them nudged the spokesman and whispered something to him. He pulled out a document.

'There is obviously no point in discussing this further,' he said. And they all stood up. 'We have written down our concerns for you. My advice to you would be to read it carefully. And take notice of what it says.'

I took it. And thanked him.

After they had left I checked my notes again. The largest single economic generator in North Wales was tourism. Thirty-eight percent.

The contribution of farming to the local economy was nought point nine percent – less than one pound in a hundred earned by the area came from farming.

Did that make it less important?

Or would that be seen as just another hurt to create yet more resentment?

'PAID, DEWI. PLIS!' I didn't have the strength to argue with him.

'I have told you.' He wagged his finger at me, in my face.

'This is your choice. You must choose me. Now! Isn't it?'

I tried to turn away.

'I have to go to the meeting.'

'No, Gwalia. Now. Before the meeting. Once he's gone back to London, you will pine for him, you will. He will become bigger than real life and you, as a girl, will not have the opportunity to see all his faults as I can see them. I know the way girls can be about such things. I am not stupid.'

'Please, Dewi. Just leave me alone now.'

'I mean it, Gwalia. He's a bastard of the worst sort. I can see it in his eyes. All he wants to do is get you into bed. After that, he will forget about you. Whereas I have been constant to you. And get no reward.'

'Dewi,' I pleaded. 'Please don't!'

'No. I will say it. You can't see it, you see, because women cannot understand these things as men do. I know how your mind works, Gwalia. I am the one who has always helped you. Isn't it me that stayed with you when you came home? All through those long years when you were getting better? Isn't it me that got you playing your harp again? Got you interested in politics again. I understand you. I've been waiting for you. I have. You can't go off with him after all we've been through together. It's me and you, see. We love each other we do.'

'Cer! Dewi. Cer!'

'You don't see it, do you, you don't. It's like the animals, see. This is what rams and bulls do. Fight to control their flocks and herds. The females have no say in it. They just go with the winner, they do. I'm respecting you, you see, by discussing it with you, I am. You've got to look at it that way, haven't you?'

'I don't know what you're talking about, Dewi.'

'I'm talking about me and him, Gwalia.'

'I'll talk to you after the meeting.'

'He hasn't waited for you like I have. I've waited for you and looked after you for five years now. That's how long I've loved you. No, before that, I did. Now I'm asking you to come with me. I want you to marry me, Gwalia. That's what I'm asking. Will you marry me, Gwalia? Will you?'

I burst into tears.

'Oh, Dewi. I don't know.'

I ran from the room.

I wanted nothing to do with you, Jon, or Dewi. I wanted everyone to go away.

Why couldn't I be just an island again?

I THOUGHT the meeting was going pretty well, really. It had started all right, anyway. My Welsh introduction rolled nicely off the tongue. Only eleven words, I admit, but I think the pronunciation was pretty good for someone who had only been learning it for a few days. That was down to your good tutoring, Gwalia.

'Noswaith dda, bawb, i chi i gyd. Diolch am ddod heno.' See, I can still remember! It was a bit irritating, of course, hearing my own words translated back to me in English through my headphones: 'He says: Good evening everybody, to all of you, Thanks for coming.'

Then I had to revert to English. And I still didn't know if I was going to say that stuff about understanding what history – and the English – had done to Wales.

'The women, I know, are tired of maintaining generators, washing by hand and having to fetch in wood and coal. I know that you all have an attachment to the daily routines of lighting your Tilley lamps, replenishing the candle-holders. And I understand how hard it is to have to clean without vacuum cleaners or electric polishers, cook without electric cookers, microwaves, electric bread-makers, food processors and manage without fridges and freezers to store the food in. Well I am determined to break this cycle. I am here to help you.'

'What have cycles got to do with it?' shouted Jac Olew, the oil man. And several of them laughed.

'You know nothing,' Gwyn Mantel, the Tilly lamp man, shouted at me.

I ignored the murmurings and soldiered on. I had a duty to the executives from the Electricity and Water Boards and from the County Council and Welsh Assembly sitting beside me. Especially Iwan. And the spectre of Freddy Morgan lurked in the near future, along with its fellow spectre of failure.

'All your queries will be answered,' I said. 'And there will be plenty of opportunity for comments and questions at the end.'

'Hissht,' shouted Iwan, imploring them to listen. 'Gwrandwch!'

I hadn't said more than a couple of sentences more before the murmurings started again – louder.

'Please,' I said. 'If you'll only let me explain.'

I could see you, Gwalia, sitting next to your parents, looking very sad and red eyed, worrying about me.

Then Penhaearn Tegid Foel slowly rose to his feet and the meeting went quiet.

'What you say is very interesting,' he said, speaking in very slow, difficult English. 'But who is going to pay? That is the question.'

There was a chorus of approval and a lot of nodding and agreeing.

Wendy Ingress stood up at this point and said in a tremulous voice. 'I agree. I think we should all be very grateful and support this kind young man from the Government. And for the enormous hard work done by Victoria Leakin.'

There was a smattering of English applause.

'Well said, Sugarbun,' said Guy, very audibly.

Hiraethog rose to his feet next. Much to the consternation of Penhaearn and Dwynwen. They pulled him back to his chair before he could speak.

I tried to soldier on.

'I am sure there are some here that are in favour of this modernisation. And I am equally sure that there are those who aren't. The question we have to ask ourselves is whether we are happy with the town the way it is.'

Jac Dŵr piped up next: 'If Mrs Boudiccea wants bright lights and jogging and cycling, I think she should have moved to New York rather than come to live here,' he said in English.

Titters and a smattering of applause. A shout of approval from the back.

'Can we just be quiet for a moment and hear what some of the experts have to say,' I pleaded, gesturing towards the executives seated along the table beside me. 'You need to hear what the Electricity Authority and the Water Board, and the Tourist Office have to say.'

Mr Johnston, from the County Council stood up and tried to speak. But he was shouted down.

Then the Electricity Board man, whose name I don't remember, had a go.

It had become quite rowdy by now and I think it was then that I abandoned the script.

At some point, someone started throwing things.

I caught a glimpse of Dewi, standing at the back, pulling things from a sack and handing them out.

Then I was aware of rotten cabbages flying towards me. And of one hitting Iwan.

IT WAS NOT going well for you, Jon. We could all see that.

Sitting between my father and my mother, between their enmity and love, I thought my heart would break. I tried to stand up and stop them. All of them. I tried to go and shout at Dewi to stop. But Dad held me, shushed me, kept me calm. He had seen me like this before.

I felt helpless. Hopeless. Lost.

You were improvising now, Jon. The cabbage leaves – not one of Dewi's better ideas – fluttering around you in a storm.

'You have to understand that your perceptions of your situation are corrupted by the position from which you are viewing it,' you persisted.

Above the rising commotion, I heard the shrill voice of Boudiccea shrieking in nearly-fluent Welsh: 'How do you expect to be getting any power here, you peasants, if you don't stop fighting amongst yourselves, you joskins.'

Her words were still being translated into English, by the cheerful, bouncy little man from Welshpool for the benefit of the few English still sitting with their earphones clamped to their ears, uncomprehending of the taunts in Welsh against them, only now beginning to be aware of the bedlam breaking out in the rows behind, ever confident that English good manners and decorum would be reasserted by the powers that be and would prevail for ever more.

Where I was sitting, the shower of cabbage leaves had become a blizzard.

You were still pleading with us.

'Please! Please! If you could see it from where I am standing, you would see how very much better you would be with mains power and electricity. Take it from me . . .'

But the shouting was starting to drown you out completely now and so many cabbage leaves were being flung around you, you had stopped trying to dodge them. They were settling on your head and shoulders and one was stuck in your glasses.

I wanted to laugh. You thought you were being so brave

against the silly cabbages. How was it that only I could feel this enormous love for you? What was wrong with everybody else that they could not see how marvellous you were?

The different factions in the audience were starting to throw cabbages at each other now. The lemon suckers against the Dan Gelyns, the Joneses against the Robertses. The Welsh against the English.

Dad was starting to become anxious for Mam and me and had made us stand up and was shepherding us out. So I lost sight of you. Some people had started to brandish wooden chairs. And I saw shepherds crooks raised in the air. Some of the older men seemed surprisingly handy with their walking sticks.

Many must have come prepared, sensing the opportunity for old scores to be settled.

Hiraethog, resplendent in his Mayoral Chain, was looking anxiously at his responsibilities, the cogs of his mind laboriously turning. No point in throwing yourself into the thick of it; that would merely be joining in. But, as civic leader, he could hardly stand aside doing nothing.

The English, finally grasping what was going on, were now trying nervously to make themselves invisible until they could sneak quietly out, as soon as half an opportunity arose. Perhaps it was just as well that, unaware of the local importance of tribal loyalties, it had not occurred to them to sit together.

I saw my Anti Gwenlais standing by the stage, taking all of it in: there would be histories to be invented, legends to be created.

Just in front of me Twm Slwtsh, Ifor Olew and Jo Botel, were nose to nose with the man from the Water Board, with Gwyn Mantel trying to separate them.

On one side Jac Trydan was wrestling the Electricity Board executive to the floor. And on the other Jac Dŵr, and Gwawr, who runs the ironmongers' shop, and his younger brother Dai Nyts, who maintained the generators, were flailing their fists against anyone wearing a suit and tie.

Dan Wfftio, mab John Cigydd, was watching carefully from the sidelines, shadowing some of the fight moves in case he had to use them for a scene in his next big role.

Up in the balcony, Norman deLuge and half a dozen friends were applauding, delighting in the young farmers brawling as if they were an annual pantomime.

Dwynwen, of course, was in her element. Bossing her camera crew around in order to be pictured making her report from the thickest of the action, on one occasion interviewing an old man flailing at the bottom of a pile of bodies.

'And what do you think of falling standards of public behaviour amongst the young,' she asked insightfully.

'I think it's time we taught them a lesson,' he said, shrugging off the bodies above him for a moment.

Not quite all the English stayed aloof.

In the front of the stalls, Jean and Billi-Jo were wrestling together, their eyes alight with lust. Hiraethog, looking for achievable objectives, arrived on the scene to separate them.

'You two don't want to be fighting each other, now, do you?' he said, reasonably enough, in English. And four hands reached up and pulled him down into their breathless mêlée.

Boudiccea, by now, was standing on her chair shouting alternately in Welsh and English. No doubt frightened that she might fall, Taid had his hands around her thighs to steady her and his left cheek pressed against her right buttock, from where he could see and feel every sweat-stained fibre of her Lycra-clad body straining for attention.

The last thing I remember before Dad pushed me out was seeing Dewi hurling himself out of the pandemonium – at you – a murderous look on his face.

My parents ushered me out.

'I suppose you noticed how the lemon suckers had started it,' Dad observed.

'Rubbish,' Mam replied. 'It was your people who take that dubious honour.'

'Llanchwaraeteg was never rowdy like this before the lemon suckers came.'

'Without us you would let the English walk all over you. Taking our houses, raising house prices. Killing our language and our culture. You should stand up for yourselves.'

'But, Cariad, they mean no more harm than you lemon suckers did when you came, evacuated from Y Gelyn after allowing the English to flood your village.'

'You see, Gwalia, your father is a traitor.'

It was half an hour before I was able to slip away from them and come to find you.

You were loading your bags into your car. Were you going to leave without saying goodbye, Jon?

'Look,' you said. 'This is hopeless. I'm just going to go back to London.'

'Yes,' I said. I couldn't help you. I was starting to feel dead inside again.

We sort of hugged.

Dead.

Inside.

Again.

And I stood there while you got in that funny little car. And drove off.

And I was left looking out over the Maes.

Alone again, in a sea of darkness.

It was with a cold heart that I worked in the bar alongside Dewi that night, serving celebration drinks to Llanchwaraeteg-danygelyn.

In the events room, the cold buffet you had ordered, Jon, out of misplaced optimism before the meeting, stood like a funeral breakfast: sausage rolls, cold chicken legs, crisps and coleslaw (the best the Supermart could offer, I'm afraid) was all that remained of your grand plans for our little town.

There was a sort of gap in my being where you had been.

But you had left so suddenly. Was there nothing to stay for?

I went upstairs and wandered the empty corridor of Y

Ddwy Ddraig, looking for traces of you. In your room there was still the lingering smell of you. I pulled the sheets from the bed and tossed them into the laundry basket.

You had brought me back my sense of joy. I had taken it for granted.

Now it had gone again.

Poor, foolish me.

Down in the meetings room I lifted the cover from the harp and touched the strings. Sad melodies.

I caught a glimpse of myself in the mirror. That awful nose. That awful, broken me. But there was no sense in feeling sorry for myself.

I looked at the buffet and made a decision.

Back in the bar, where they were all busy rewriting the history of the day, I grandly announced a free buffet in the meetings room.

There was a whoop of approval and they started rushing through.

After that, I pulled the pints and took their cash in English pounds, and traded in their currency of ignorant jokes, vainly inflated tales of their own deeds, all of them heroes, all sides claiming famous victories.

How quickly the old skills – pretending to be happy – reasserted themselves. Helo, Gwalia, sut wyt ti? I'm fine. Are you? Wrth gwrs! An island in an archipelago. Let no one know! Some Mata Hari I had been.

Collecting glasses, serving pleasantries, I could pretend to be as wrth fy modd as any of them. I, who had sent you off without a proper kiss.

What was there to feel bad about, anyway? It would never have worked. We were from different worlds. I had something to celebrate. I'd been a successful Mata Hari.

And I'd never seen Dewi happier.

Touching my hips each time he manoeuvred around me behind the bar, his eyes constantly looking into mine, smiling and chatting and being oh! so sweet.

I swear to you Jon, if I was laughing and joining in that night, it was all put on.

Around the tables, I caught snatches of their conversations.

Penhaearn Tegid Foel, in fine form, holding court. The king and his courtiers gnawing on their chicken drumsticks, swilling their ales, gleeful and merry in their triumph.

'Mark my words, now. Wales will rise again and be a great and independent nation with its own flag in the United Nations . . . The ghost of Owain Glyndŵr himself has told me.'

A succession of disjointed images inform my memory of that lonely night.

Boudiccea was out, dressed for once in skirt and blouse, with her husband, Lawns.

'I think it's remarkable that everyone is so resilient. So cheerful after such a setback. Don't worry, though. We shall come back from this. We shall fight again.'

While Lawns looked slightly embarrassed, wiser in our ways, of course, than she.

'It'll be for the best, Victoria. It wasn't meant to be. You'll see.'

I remember Twm Slwtsh sitting there, in his whiskers, with scruffy Jac Dŵr and skinny Dai Ôd, the three of them beaming at each other and clashing their beer mugs together and slopping their frothy ale with every last celebratory swig, always with two or three full pints in hand.

And Blodeuwedd in fine form. Resplendent in a totally inappropriate floral dress and wide-brimmed matching hat, her face looking as if nature had freshly scrubbed it with pumice stone.

Jean and Billi-Jo, more open in their love for each other than we had ever seen them, bought a bottle of Cava and sat at Penhaearn's table, exercising their learners' Welsh and prophesying more great exorcisms to come, with Hiraethog between them.

Y Ddwy Ddraig was so full that night that they were

standing, jam-packed together, people overflowing from the bar.

It was out in Reception that the English sat, on the old sofas and carved oak benches. Apart. Talking recklessly in their own tongue with only me, the invisible serving wench, to hear them, catching snatches of their insurrection as the tide of their opinion turned.

Guy and Wendy Ingress were in deep discussion with Donald Flood and his wife Olivia.

'It goes to show what I've been saying all along. There's just no sense to these people. They block us out from all their committees and councils on the grounds we don't speak Welsh. And then they make incomprehensible decisions like this!'

'I think it's racist.'

'It is. It is racist. It's keeping us out of local democracy. We're being disenfranchised. That's what it is!'

'Shush dear. Somebody'll hear.'

'I don't care if they do. We're in our own country here. We gave them the chance to vote for devolution in seventy-nine and they didn't want it.'

'They voted for it in ninety-seven.'

'Yes but only in a very watered down form! Most Welsh people are happier being part of Britain. They can't go on excluding us. It's racist.'

'English is the official language in Britain. We're entitled to participate.'

'Victoria is trying so hard.'

'She's drinking with the Welsh. She's married to one of them. Penhaearn's business partner, in fact. It's my business I have to worry about. That's what's suffering.'

'Mine too!'

'We could be making a lot of money here.'

'We should be!'

'I know Victoria means well. But she's had her chance now. I don't think we can go on indulging her. Or them.'

'You're right, we have to bite the bullet. Bring it to the attention of the authorities.'

'Nepotism is what it is. Corruption.'

'Totally.'

'They're running a closed shop here.'

'Cabal, dear. It's called a cabal.'

'Cabal, then. They're running a cabal.'

'Can I get you something?'

'So that's another double, gin and tonic, two large glasses of that dreadful vin ordinaire and a large whisky on the rocks.'

And back to Penhaearn's table. And Penhaearn holding court.

'We saw them off today! We've fought them off again.'

'We've kept Llanchwaraetegdanygelyn Welsh.'

Norman DeLuge breezed in.

'Wasn't it a darling cyfarfod, darlings? So exciting! I've got half a dozen friends staying at the cotej tonight. Can you imagine. I'll be dead to the world tomorrow.'

Though nobody in the town had been able to see the TV broadcast because such technology was still far beyond the means of our little valley, Dwynwen had once more excelled herself with another stunning dispatch from the front line of nationalist revival.

The culmination of a week of rural unrest in which the Welsh-speaking Welsh had stood firm and proud against the invading hordes of English incomers wanting to drive out the language and take over our homes.

I had heard her radio report, though, her voice rising in glee as the public meeting turned to riot.

Poor you, Jon!

Poor Dewi.

Poor Llanchwaraetegdanygelyn.

PROFESSOR ANGELA LAIN had not been at all pleased with my efforts in Umbo.

'Freddy's been pestering the hell out of me, after all he's seen in the papers. Asking me what on earth you think you've been playing at. So, Jon: how did you get on?'

I felt like a naughty little child standing in front of the headmistress in a terrifying study, fearing for . . . I knew not what.

'Come on, Jon. It isn't like you to be reticent? Where's your report?'

'Errm . . . pending,' I muttered.

'Pending what exactly?'

'Pending outcomes. I need to get the questionnaires translated. I need to find out why the town acted so illogically.'

'I need your report, Jon,' Angela said curtly. I was clearly not the rising star I had been just ten days ago. 'And I need an explanation for all that bad publicity while you were there.'

She thrust a ream of newspapers into my arms.

Oh shit! I knew that I had to get this mess sorted out.

I needed to find a Welsh translator. And moral support. And a little comforting reassurance. I went to Nisha at the Hub.

'You should phone Gwalia,' Nisha said, radiant in a gold-yellow sari. 'Ask her to translate. She'd love to help you. And you could help her. That would mend your spirit.'

Nisha knew everything. It was a mistake to always unburden myself to her.

'I need a Welsh translator in London,' I said.

'You're angry with yourself,' she told me. Yet again I felt like a silly little boy. Telling people things gives them power over you.

She put her fingertips together and closed her eyes. Nisha could look so mystical in her sari. 'And I sense a deep longing in your karma.'

This time she was joking. We both relaxed.

'Do I see a little smile? That's better.'

'Gwalia and I inhabit different worlds,' I said defensively. 'We have nothing in common. We don't even speak the same first language.'

'Ah,' said Nisha. It was an irritating *Ah*. The sort of *Ah* designed to breed self-doubt in the feeble-minded.

'No. I refuse to let my life be dictated by emotion.'

She put her brown fingertips together, so that her red fingernails, gold rings, and rubies made a critical mass, and raised them to her lips in a gesture of greeting.

'Namaste.'

Even surrounded by the computers and screens and wires at her data bank, Nisha had the infuriating ability to look serene.

'You're not going to influence me,' I insisted.

So I got the big brown eyes treatment.

'You have her soul in your heart, I think.'

She was partly right, of course, Gwalia, you *were* certainly in my head. But if you were in my heart, it was just temporary infatuation at the most, I had decided.

'Do you go on like this to Andrew?'

'Sometimes. So tell me what you think about when you think of her.'

I shrugged.

'Her curly brown hair, the way her mouth crinkles in the corner when she smiles. Her voice. Her Welsh. And her hurt blue eyes. Mainly her hurt blue eyes.'

I could feel my voice grow softer. And something softening in my chest.

'You see!' said Nisha, triumphantly. 'You melt when you talk about her.'

'I do not! I'm just sensitive to her situation. She had a very bad experience. She had never talked it through with anyone before. I'm just empathising. A standard biological mechanism. It shows I'm a nice person.'

'Ah-hah! I thought you were supposed to rise above such feelings. Intellectually.'

'Let's stick to facts,' I said. 'I am not infatuated with anyone. Once I sort out these questionnaires, do my final report for Freddy, I can forget Wales and get back to the urgent business of solving society's important problems.'

Nisha lowered her head. And gave me the big brown eyes again.

'It's no good giving me your Eastern scepticism look. I just need to find a Welsh language translator. Here in London.'

Nisha snapped back to Data Manager mode and punched the return button on her keyboard.

'Very well then. London Welsh Centre in Grays Inn Road.'

And then she was suddenly very busily immersed at something else.

The taxi driver gave me *his* opinion as soon as I got in.

'Wot you wanna go there for, then? I'm telling you, it'll be shut? Not much call for Bloody Taffy Nig-nogs these days.'

'The world's full of them, innit?' I said sarcastically. The man was too absorbed in his own shallow eloquence to catch a hint of my black irony.

'Tell me 'bout it, mate. Paki nig-nogs. Chink nig-nogs. Poles. And wot gets me is that you blacks complain about the Pakis and the Pakis complain about you. But if *we* bloody complain, we're racists, aint we?'

'Too right,' I said.

He rode his hobbyhorse up Whitehall.

'Can't bloody win, these days, can yer? D'you know, mate, if I refuse to 'ave a disabled fare in 'ere they can do me. In my own cab. I can't discriminate anyone. But they can discriminate me.'

He ranted all the way through Bloomsbury to Grays Inn Road. We pulled up outside a nineteen-thirties, red-brick building looking a bit like a small school. It seemed somehow homely.

'I nivver brung no one 'ere before. Bloody Welsh. If yer want my opinion, the building looks like the country. Totally un-fucking-kempt. Fuck the lot of 'em I say.'

Inside, the hallway was deserted. A notice board. A list of male voice choir performances, Welsh evening classes and an appeal by the drama club for new members.

A frail old lady appeared carrying a tray of chipped mugs.

'Are you the new boy for the Welsh class?' she asked in a South Wales accent. 'They're in the Winstay room. I'll 'ave to make an extra one now, won't I?'

I carried the tray for her, to a high-ceilinged room where a white-haired man was teaching a dozen people of different ages.

'Dyma Mrs Morris gyda'r paneidiau te a'r bisgedi,' he said. 'Amser toriad.'

'Mae'n ddrwg gen i,' I said, surprising myself. 'I'm not here for the lesson.'

As they milled around the coffee tray, I brandished my sheaf of questionnaires. And introduced myself.

'I'll be happy to go through your questionnaires with you afterwards,' said Mr Dai Edwards cheerfully. 'But, obviously, I have a class at the moment. You might like to sit in, efallai.'

So I took a spare seat. Just another dreary evening class on another rainy evening.

It was only when Mr Edwards politely handed me a photocopy of a Welsh magazine article extolling the virtues of Wales and the Welsh language that I realised I would be joining in and reading aloud. It wasn't difficult. A vocabulary sheet listed almost every word.

I was reminded of that learners' group in Llanchwaraetegdanygelyn, and another decrepit building. And of you, Gwalia. As if at any moment it might be you who might come in to collect the empty coffee cups.

'Your pronunciation is excellent,' Mr Edwards told me, and moved on to the next student, who struggled through the article extolling all things Welsh. Welsh was the language of heaven. All animals spoke Welsh. Welsh was the language of poetry in the land of poets, the most ancient living language in Europe.

Then it was my turn again to read and translate aloud. Easy, given the vocabulary list on the back, but not everyone had seen that.

'Wales has the finest coastline, the most beautiful mountains, and the prettiest valleys. It is a land of the most wonderful home-made cooking, the softest rain and the kindest people.'

I confess I was a little bored

'Isn't this a little questionable?' I asked.

The tutor smiled.

'We destroy the myths which glorify us at our peril,' he said. 'They are part of our identity.'

I was so impatient, I found myself volunteering answers to rather too many questions, Mr Edwards' patient sing-song voice, his shock of white hair and his shapeless tweed jacket, endeared him to me. I suppose he epitomised that dishevelled personality of academia that I had left behind.

After the class, he and I sat down together and he patiently took me through the questionnaires, not just translating but delighting in the words, and generous with his time and patience far beyond my expectation.

'Thank you so much,' I said, 'you have been very kind.'

'I've enjoyed it,' he said, 'You have no idea how a Welshman exiled from his home grieves for his mother country. We have a word for it, you know.'

I heard your voice in my head.

'Hiraeth?' I offered.

'Da iawn!' said Mr Edwards. 'You should join the class. I could teach a student like you so much, so quickly. You know, they are so lucky on the Migneint still to have the mother tongue, the mamiaith. Where I come from, in Mid Wales, it has all but disappeared. You don't know how it makes my old Welsh heart sing to see documents like this.'

I grasped him warmly by the hand. These translations might go some way to salving something of my reputation at the Leyburn Institute.

'Have you ever heard a Welsh choir singing "Ar Lan y Môr?"' he asked.

He started to sing. 'Ar lan y môr, mae rhosys cochion.'

I smiled.

That summoned up another damn memory of you, Gwalia. Do you remember? By the waterfall.

The waterfall!

'Did you hear any Welsh poetry while you were there? Or a harp played on a Welsh hillside?'

I shook my head.

'You *must* go back then; you have many joys to come.'

He laughed. Despite myself, I felt a spark of joy shoot down my spine.

'I made the mistake of marrying an Englishwoman,' he said. 'Don't get me wrong, now. Lovely woman. Forty-five years we've lived in London. Very happily. The Wales I grew up in has long since gone, I know that, but it is still here, see, in my heart. It must be the same for you with your country.'

'I have no country but this one,' I told him. (My standard reply to people who think because I'm black I have some loyalty to another country.)

'I'm not interested in the past,' I said a bit too sharply, 'only the future.'

'You're a young man, Mr Bull. That view may change.'

He was a good man, he'd been very kind.

'Can I pay you for your help, Mr Edwards? Would a hundred pounds be reasonable?'

'Perhaps as a donation towards the centre . . .?'

I walked back up to Kings Cross feeling somehow discontented, incomplete.

TWO WEEKS LATER, you returned to Llanchwaraeteg-danygelyn for the day. A flying follow-up visit you called it. But neither Penhaearn nor Hiraethog, nor any of the Welsh had bothered to come. I'd asked Boudiccea if I could do the minutes, in case you didn't come to the hotel, or the house, to see me. No one else liked doing them and Blodeuwedd was hopeless, so I knew she'd say yes.

I don't know what I was thinking. I suppose I had this idea that you might need me to translate for you.

But then I felt very nervous at seeing you.

Part of me wanted to talk to you, to explain that I had missed you. And the other part saw how pointless that would be. Neither of us had been in touch.

In the end it was all very formal. You did look at me, a sort of questioning look. But we just shook hands and smiled awkwardly.

You handed your report across to Boudiccea and outlined your conclusions with friendly professionalism. You'd obviously found someone else to translate the questionnaires.

'The feasibility reports by the major utilities are included in appendices four to six. There is no technical reason why these projects should not be taken to fruition. In short, the infrastructure could be in place within eighteen months, but you would need to demonstrate the support of the town.'

You shrugged. I think it was a shrug about the support of the town.

I wanted to tell you how I felt. How I'd missed you. How I'd even decided I could come to London for a weekend or something, if you wanted. Or for the day. I'd found that, from Chester, I could be there any day, by lunchtime. And, almost any day, I could get a lift to Chester. But instead we talked about developments that would probably never happen.

How pathetic and stupid we can be, Jon!

'I have also sought and obtained an assurance from the Secretary of State for Wales that planning approval would almost certainly be granted. (That's Appendix One.)

And I had decided I would learn to drive, London being only four hours by car.

'Appendices two and three show positive indications from your funding partners. Financial Aid European Capital Into Essential Services, the Welsh Assembly, with guaranteed match funding from the Mains Infrastructure National Government Integrated Necessary Grants Fund.'

I don't think any of us in that room believed in anything now. Boudiccea seemed deflated. Rumour had it that she'd fallen out with her husband Lawns.

'However, the main body of the report deals with the community development required to create a sea-change in local public attitudes towards the scheme. At present you have only twenty-one-point-five per cent of the population in favour of the scheme.'

Even Victoria Leakin seemed merely to be going through the motions. And no one except my Taid and his friends seemed to call her Boudiccea anymore. She was just Mrs Leakin now, married to Penhaearn's brother, Lawns, and no happier than anyone else.

'So, converting that figure to a majority must therefore be our main strategic aim, you think?'

'Yes. There is clearly a great deal of misinformation, combined with understandable suspicion and concerns about loss of jobs and costs to individual households of connecting to the mains and paying electricity bills in the future.

'I have outlined various ways you might seek to allay those suspicions, correct the misinformation and turn that negative disposition into a positive one. Thank you.'

Anyone could tell that you believed that power would never come.

'Wonderful report,' Boudiccea said. 'We're working hard now to rekindle the initiative. We will come through in the end, don't you worry. God help Umbo if we don't.'

You had done your job. Told them the findings of your research. Your analysis of our situation. Your recommendations for our future. All in impeccable English. But you had made no mention of what I thought was in our hearts. Of what I had sensed you felt for me. I could not believe that you felt nothing.

You finished with these ominous words: 'Llanchwaraeteg-danygelyn is entirely dependent, economically, on one factory. And on farming. Current changes in European agricultural subsidies and international industrial trends towards off-shore production leave this community extremely vulnerable in the short, medium and long terms.'

I could see now how ridiculous I was being. What a child! Why would an important man like you be interested in a simple girl with so many problems, like me?

So after the meeting I avoided you. Pretended to be busy.

In the afternoon, you met a delegation from the Town Council – Penhaearn looking every bit the professional mourner that he was, with Islwyn and Hiraethog. You saw me sitting there and eyed me sadly. Had you been looking for me? Wanting me to find you? I didn't know.

You handed Penhaearn his copy of your final report. He handed it to Hiraethog. Hiraethog handed it to Islwyn. And Islwyn handed it to me.

'I hope my time has not been entirely wasted,' you said, looking directly at me. 'I, personally, have learned a very great deal.'

Did you think I no longer wanted to see you?

Islwyn seemed grey and distracted.

'I do assure you your report will be handled with the utmost respect. It will not be filed away and forgotten.' He whispered to Hiraethog who repeated the words to you. Then looked to me to translate them into English for you.

'You will not be filed away in the Council Archive and forgotten,' I said.

You glanced at me, I think you caught my meaning.

Then Hiraethog read his thanks from the sheet of paper.

'On behalf of the Council, I and the members present would like to thank you most sincerely and earnestly for the attention you have given to this town and our problems here. We have welcomed you into our hearth with an open mind. And we will deliberate on these recommendations fully in the due course of time. In the meantime we do thank you from the bottom of our hearts for your indulgences to us.'

So that was it.

Llanchwaraetegdanygelyn had rejected power.

Afterwards, I followed you out into the sunshine.

I would have liked us to go for a walk, but we stood on the Maes outside the Town Hall, talking of trivialities. The project. The weather. And you explained how you had got the translation done.

'I'd better go,' you said.

'Yes,' I said.

You hesitated. I decided to risk my heart.

'Unless you'd like to go for a stroll.'

'Ok.'

We went up to the waterfall, of course. It wasn't many steps before our hands reached out to each other as if they had an independent will of their own.

We grinned at each other. Our hearts were back in charge, at least for now.

Above the waterfall, we kissed. But it wasn't passionate. Not really.

Tactfully, our brains marked time and pretended not to think.

'I'm sorry that your plans didn't work out,' I said. And I meant it for your sake, not the town's. 'It's just the way the world is. There's nothing people like us can do about it.'

You took me by the shoulders and held me very firmly with your hands.

'But there is, you see. We just have to believe that.'

I wanted to believe you. But I couldn't. I think that you could see that. And I could tell that you were disappointed in me.

'So how's your Dad getting on with the redevelopment

287

plans for *Y Ddwy Ddraig*?' you asked in a very businesslike tone, as our hearts disengaged.

'I'm sure he would like to discuss it with you,' I said. 'If you want to come for supper.'

Dad looked pleased that I had brought you home. Mam scowled. And piled your plate with boiled cabbage, mashed potato, mince and dumplings in a way, I knew quite nicely, you would hate.

Throughout the meal, you were as charming and polite and kind and earnest as you always were, brimming with enthusiasms I didn't have. Enough for all of us. You even ate it all, without betraying the slightest lack of joy.

'I think Y Ddwy Ddraig just has so much potential. It's a fantastic place for people to come. And Llanchwaraeteg-danygelyn is a wonderful location.'

'I don't know about that,' Mam said. 'It has its snags you know.'

'This is magical,' you enthused. 'The location, the mountains, the people. The language. I feel it every time I come down that hill. It's a secret place. It's fabulous.'

'Well I don't see how any of that can help us,' Mam said.

'I've taken the liberty of writing a draft feasibility study for you, Gwalia.' You reached in your briefcase and pulled out a folder thicker than the one you'd prepared for the town. 'I hope you don't mind, I've filled in the grant applications I think would be most appropriate. And there's a list of funding bodies, architects, structural engineers, contact names, addresses and phone numbers. I've marked the ones I'd recommend.'

You looked at me. My mind was running round and round a ring of irreconcilable thoughts. You were being so kind. You had spent hours doing all this for us. For me. How could I have doubted you! Or doubted the tingle and the warmth I felt inside when I was with you. That you were from a different world and far away, a place that I would never want to be. The coldness that I felt when you were not there. The kisses that always stayed with me on my trembling lips.

I looked at Mam. I knew what she was thinking. She saw in you so many sins. Temptation for one. My temptation.

How unfair life is!

How could she fail to understand that you were a fine and noble man burning with idealism. That was what I saw. A man who yearned to make the world a better place. A man who had caught me in the headlights of his yearning and had me shaking like a rabbit, wide-eyed, dazed, confused, not really caring if I lived or died but wondrous of the brightest light I'd ever seen.

How could you understand Mam's view? That even letting you try to help us was submitting to you. The conquest of your sly, insidious ideas. You tempted us with noble thoughts of a better life and making the world a better place. But what good had all that conquest ever done the world? It led only to exploitation, wars and, now, the awful, unimaginable prospect of mankind being choked by its own gaseous excrement through global warming.

How could you understand that just by being here you undermined our life. We could never be together.

The warmth. The difference. The kiss. The coldness. The tingle. The lips.

Why couldn't you see how impossible it all was? Why couldn't you just leave us all alone? Why couldn't the world just go away and leave the two of us together?

And then I saw Dad's face.

He stood up like a king and held his hand out.

'You have been very kind to us, Mr Bull. I'm sorry if we appear not to have been entirely able to reciprocate your enthusiasms.'

'I just want to see you succeed, that's all.'

Mam flustered and started to remonstrate: 'Artwr. I think you have said enough.' Then she turned to you: 'I don't know if we are able to accept your very kind offer, that's the thing. I don't know what impression you've had from Gwalia. But we're only a very modest sort of business you know. That's the snag. We're not really deserving of loans and grants.'

You laughed at this.

'Of course you are.' And looked at me, your frightened, helpless rabbit. Your eyes met mine and I sensed your confidence. Your power. Then you turned to Dad.

'You do understand, I'll guide you through all this, every step of the way. Really all you have to do is sign the forms. You won't let this opportunity go, will you?'

Mam stepped forward, twting. 'The snag is . . .'

'Hisht, Gwênfer!'

Dad stepped forward and held out his hand.

'I'm sure we will not look a gift horse in the mouth a second time, Mr Bull,' he said. 'I think we have a great deal we can learn from you.'

'And I from you,' you said, glancing towards me.

Mam had to shake hands with you then, despite herself. And Gethin and Awena joined in the ceremony. I hung back awkwardly, wanting to hug and kiss you, not wanting to reveal that part of me.

'Well, just take it stage by stage,' you enthused. 'Y Ddwy Ddraig is a treasure. A rare example of an eighteenth-century coaching inn. Converted, I am fairly sure, from a seventeenth-century drovers' tavern. This is a very deserving application. Don't let anyone tell you otherwise.'

Then you turned to me.

'This is for you,' you said. And handed me another file. 'This is a list of fast-track business courses, and funding bodies. If you are going to oversee the renovations and run the hotel, this is the training you will need.'

'Gwalia has her studies, Mr Bull. That's the snag.'

'If I were you,' you said softly to me. 'I would forget about catching up on your school exams – I think you're bored with all of that – and concentrate on this. I think you'll be a wonderful manager and find it very exciting. You'll be a new person in six months.'

I helped you lug your bags out to the car.

But for a word, I could have jumped in with you. Instead I handed you a book. *The Mabinogion.*

'What's this, then?'

'A book of Welsh folk tales. Our tales. The tales of Cymru.'

'Diolch yn fawr.'

'Croeso.'

We kissed goodbye. Our lips just brushed.

Watching your red and black Smart car go up the hill, I waved.

My head was full of harp music, the tunes filling my mind, making me hum aloud. I went to the meetings room at Y Ddwy Ddraig and played and played until my fingers were sore.

I HAD HOPED, Gwalia, that I could have proved to you that the world could be a better place if only we believed that we could make it so. And yet, what right did I have, in my arrogance, to think that I could make your world a better place? Your town had raised great doubts in all my certainty.

Looking around the Leyburn Institute, there were as many researchers tackling the problems caused by our previous visions of progress as there were trying to create our contemporary vision of progress now. Redundant industrial towns, discarded colonies, hundreds of thousands of people transported around the globe for slavery or exploitation, or as economic refugees, or to colonise foreign lands or exploit natural resources. And the mess left behind when those resources were exhausted. And what had all of it achieved? Heat and light, travel and transport. And the nightmare of perhaps unstoppable global warming.

My failure had left me demoralised and so negative!

That's what we at the Leyburn Institute were for – to sort it out. Untangle the threads of all that greed through careful research. And then encourage people to take control of their lives, their planet. To show them how to do all that. How to plan. How to make it work, politically.

What kind of arrogance was that! But what alternative could there be?

Your face was constantly in my mind, Gwalia. If we couldn't solve the problems in a little place like Llanchwaraetegdanygelyn, how could we hope to solve huge problems in the enormity of the world? We couldn't even solve the one-to-one problem of you and me.

I'd read that book you gave me, Gwalia, *The Mabinogion*. It was getting into my dreams. In one, I saw myself seated on a wooden stool in a medieval hall playing a harp – a poor minstrel poet in a fool's costume, a virtuoso at an ugly banquet. The smoky air was heavy with drunkenness, rape and violence.

Every now and then Penhaearn would laugh and

command everyone to dance and make merry. And send a servant across to me to demand jollier tunes, and songs to his magnificence. I knew that if I refused I would be dragged out and slaughtered.

As this pretence of fun raged around me, I played on.

In the dream, a small bird landed on my shoulder, and whispered in my ear, saying: 'Vengeance will come! Vengeance will come! Follow quickly!'

So the little bird led me out of the palace, into the darkness, and away across rough land, on a secret path through dangerous bogs.

At some point on this exodus, the bird turned into a girl, who, of course, was you Gwalia. Always you.

I tried to catch up with you but, as it is with dreams, the faster I tried to go, the deeper my feet sank into the bog, weighed down by my harp.

You danced ahead in front of me, urging me to be quick, urging me up, out of the valley, into the hills. But I kept falling behind.

By the time I reached the top, you had disappeared. And I had lost my harp.

In my dream, I fell asleep.

When I woke the following morning, and looked back over the valley, I saw only water. Where the palace had been there was now only a huge lake.

And my harp was floating on the water.

I HAD MANY rash thoughts of running away to London to come and see you. My spirit hungered for that strength you brought me and the way you made my heart lift. Thanks to you, Jon, I'd had a glimpse of how my spirit could come alive. But, still, I tricked myself from believing this was love, my one true love.

All that you had done was awaken my feelings. If I could feel that way with you, then I could feel it with others. It was impossible that you and I could make a life together, so what else could I think? You, I decided, would approve that logic. It was modern thinking. Feminist thinking. Our emotions are inside ourselves. We only project our love onto other people. We must not tie ourselves to others or allow ourselves to become their puppets.

It consoled me greatly to think that you would approve this thinking. You had proved to me that I could live! And you would be so delighted for me to learn that this was exactly what I was going to do: live my life, but without you.

It was Dad who upset the applecart.

'I have a number of queries about this application. I want you to phone him, get him to help you fill in the forms. If we fail to take advantage of his offer, we will be failing the responsibilities of our generation.'

'If it's your generation, you should phone him, Dad,' I told him grumpily.

'I am only asking for your sake, Gwalia. And for Awena's. I thought you would be glad of the chance to ring him up and talk to him.'

'It makes no difference to me whether I phone him or not.'

No matter that the mere mention of your name made my whole body more alert. There was no future in it. We had all agreed that. And yet . . .

'I'm not sure I want to, Dad. I have a routine.'

This was true. I knew now how to work at it: be attentive to my moods, resist Mam's urge to gwarchod me.

'You'll regret it if you don't.'

'Will I?' Things had settled down. Gone back to normal. I was able to guard myself against my own self-pity and pointless anger. And I was slowly clawing my way back to where I ought to be.

'I think you should take his advice about the business course. I've booked an interview for you in Bangor for next Monday.'

'I never said I would do that!'

'I want you to. And I want you to phone him.'

I turned to argue with him, the fury bubbling up from inside me and about to break free. But Dad took me in his arms and smothered it. His arms hardly strong enough to control his grown-up girl. It seemed – I don't know – so inappropriate – being cuddled by my Dad at my age. I tried to pull away and started to say something. But he held my head against his chest, refusing to let me go. Until I surrendered into his arms and I felt my whole body shudder.

He kissed my head.

'My baby, my little baby,' he said. And I could hear the catch in his voice. And I let him hold me, rocking me back and fro as if I was still young. I felt the tears welling in my eyes. 'My little Gwalia. Poor, poor Gwalia.'

He said it over and over. And his body started to shake, too.

I could hear him sobbing and feel his tears dropping onto my head. I didn't want to pull away and look at him. He had been hurting too. This was for him as much as me.

I had hardly noticed Dad, in all my thoughts. Mam's views were so strong. It had been Mam who had assumed mother's love for Awena when that had been so cruelly still-born in me. Dad too had had a love. It hadn't occurred to me until this moment that Dad's gentle view of the world also had its passion and its price.

I wriggled my head up without opening my eyes, so we were cheek to cheek. Father and daughter. He needed my comfort, too, just as I needed his. We hugged each other for a long time, until the dialogue of pain began to soften and subside.

He patted my back.

'You could phone him, if you want to,' I said, trying to reassert my pose of defiant daughter and the mood of before. But it sounded hollow.

Dad laughed.

'Oh no, cariad, I think it would come so much better from you.'

I feared to ring you, Jon. To hear your voice and reawaken that dragon in me. The dragon of lust and selfishness.

'I need to concentrate on Awena, Dad. To be the Mam that I always should have been.'

My Awena!

He nodded.

'Something in you has changed, Gwalia. Learning is never easy, and relearning is painful. But you are very brave. You will do it.'

'I want her to stop calling me *Gwalia* and start calling me Mam.'

'This man, Jon, has helped you to be brave, Gwalia. You must go on being brave. You have a life to lead. You must make it yours.'

It was a little later when Mam came in, all bright and bustling with her latest plans for me.

'I've just been talking to Dewi, I have. He was asking if I thought you'd be interested in going to the Young Farmers' Dance across in Llanrwst next Saturday. You should go, Gwalia. It's time you came out of yourself. You're so much brighter these days. He's a good boy, Dewi is.' She lowered her voice to a confidential whisper without the slightest need. 'I'm sure he'd be wrth ei fodd to be Daddy to Awena, if you did agree to marry him. Awena likes him, you know.'

She was trying to bribe me! But on this day I was not as cross with her for trying to organise my life as I usually was.

Truth to tell, that thought was not as repulsive as once it might have been.

Since your visit, Jon, Dewi had been much more sensitive. Considerate even. Attentive in the right ways. He had gone out of his way to behave, not presumptuously, as if we were a couple, but hesitantly, as if he were a courtly knight, wooing me with little pecks on the cheek when we met and parted, the way he had seen you do. And giving me little gifts of posies and chocolates.

I wondered sometimes if I had been in love with him all along but hadn't been able to feel it, numbed as my feelings were against everything.

'But do you love him, Gwalia?' Dad insisted. 'Is that all you want from your life?'

'Leave her alone, Artwr,' Mam said. 'She's been so much calmer and better lately since that black man went away.'

'I need to phone Jon about the grants,' I perked up.

'Hisht, Gwalia. You'll only go upsetting yourself if you start organising grants and renovations and things. Best to leave sleeping dogs lie in my opinion.'

Dad shrugged. His shoulders slumped.

And that was the moment I finally began to understand something about my parents. And how they were.

Mam had been so good and yet so bad. She had taken the hard role, Dad the kindly one. I doubt they had discussed it. Both had done what each thought was needed as they saw it.

Mam had taken on Awena when I couldn't bear to look at her, still less bear to feed her, change her, love her. She had lifted the problem away, leaving me with only my dragons to confront.

I could see now how stupid and selfish I had been: thinking that in my daughter's face I could see the faces of my enemies who'd raped me. That when Awena cried, it was the voices of those boys screaming at me. And that when she laughed, they were mocking me. All madness! Self-centred madness!

It was no wonder Mam had come to resent – as well as love – me.

I felt so grateful, for Awena's sake, that Mam, not I, had become Awena's spiritual mother. It frightened me to think how else we might have ended up, if I had not rejected her. If I had run away with her.

That act of generosity on Mam's part had been selfish and unthinking too. In helping she had indulged her own maternal instincts and her urge to control. She had taken my daughter away from me. And – yes – stolen her love from me.

Now things needed to be put right.

I needed to win back my daughter's love for me. I owed that to Awena. And win back Mam's love and respect for me, I owed that to her, too. Mam and Dad must become proper grandparents now. And that might take away the strain that was between the two of them.

Why hadn't I seen all this before?

No mother should blame her child for being born, even out of virgin rape. I had always known that. Now I felt it. How do we help our feelings, Jon, except by understanding? You taught me that.

Since your visit, I had begun to think of Awena as my daughter. To talk to her. And be with her. And help her. I had started to love her as if I had always loved her. We had even started to go for walks together. To play together. You had conjured up a love in me that was deeper than what I felt for you. Yes, I was still angry. I'm sure Awena sensed that. And it made her recoil from me. Her father – whoever he was – was still a half of her. And that repelled me.

'You're weird,' she told me when I tried to hug her.

Even to me, my love felt somehow wrong, forbidden. But it was a need in me and in her, even though she always pulled away, and ran from me, when I came close.

Love is therapy, Jon, you taught me that. It was time to end that big sister lie.

After you, Jon, it was as if that hate and anger thawed, and love started to grow in me again. I no longer felt I had always to pretend to cheerfulness. More and more often I felt it. Actually felt it.

Now when Awena came skipping in from school a tingle of happiness ran through my heart to see her in the light of my new resolutions. I knew how to greet her like a mother: 'Sgen ti waith cartref?' But still she thought of Mam as her Mam, not her grandmother.

'I've got to make a cake,' she told me one day, in that bossy way that little girls sometimes learn from their teachers.

'I'll help you then. We'll do it together.'

'I'm not going to do it with you, Gwalia. Miss Evans said I must do it with Mam.'

At one time I would have backed away at that. Now it made me feel more determined.

I *would* control my life. I *would* start being a proper mother to my daughter. You had had enough belief in making the world a better place to go to the trouble of bringing all those forms to us.

I would start making my personal world a better place.

And I would begin with Y Ddwy Ddraig.

So, a week or two later, Jon, I tried to telephone you.

First I got Nisha.

'I am so sorry to say that Mr Bull is out of the office today? But who am I to say is calling?'

'I'm Miss Jones.'

'And do you have a first name, Miss Jones?'

'Gwalia. From Llanchwaraetegdanygelyn.'

'So you are Gwalia! I am Nisha. I'm sure Jon will be very pleased to hear that you are phoning for him just now. Should I say that you are well?'

I was very well, I told her.

'Jon mentioned that he might help my father with the grant application for the renovation of our Two Dragons. That is why I am ringing.'

'Do you want to speak to him?'

My heart stopped.

'Yes please.'

'I'll have to transfer you to his mobile. He's working back down in Wales at the moment.'

There was a click and a pause and another click and I heard you say 'Hello?'

'You're working in Wales!' I said.

'Bore da, Gwalia. What can I do for you?'

How can I begin to tell you how it felt to hear your voice? Like sherbet in my blood. As if every vein and artery around my body had music flowing through it, sweetly fizzing, joyous and wonderful. And my head conjured up the image of your naked body lying by the waterfall.

'My father asked me to phone. He wondered if he could send you the grant applications to check over as you promised.'

'Of course. I'm working in Gwrêngham at the moment. You could bring them across.'

Gwrêngham was less than an hour away by car. Our nearest town for chain-store shopping. How had you been working so near and me not knowing? How were you able to be so close and not wanted to come to me? Why hadn't you called?

'That's very close by,' I said.

You told me a little about your work and asked about the town. Your work was very important. Much more important than I had imagined. Priorities are strange things, though. We both knew that bigger questions lay between us. And they were anxious to be discussed.

'I would have wanted to come to see you,' you said carefully. 'But, you asked me not to get in touch again. Remember?'

'I didn't suppose you'd want to come here and remind yourself of our troubles and the inconvenience we put you to.'

'I'd like to be reminded of you.'

'Come here, then. Come to see me.'

'I'd like to, Gwalia, but that might be difficult. You could come to see me here, though. I'd be very glad to see you.'

There was a silence.

'I've missed you.'

'And I have.'

'It's agreed then.'

I had no car and it takes almost two hours to go to Gwrêngham on the bus. I tried on every dress I owned and spent an hour doing my hair. Mam was scathing but I forgave her. I could have forgiven everybody everything that day. Even myself.

'You're not getting all dressed up and going all that way just for afternoon tea at the Fusilier Hotel. Isn't he even going to take you out to dinner?'

'It has to be afternoon, so I can catch the last bus back at six.'

'Why isn't he coming to pick you up?'

'I'm not sure quite. He can't leave the town. Or something.'

What I didn't tell her was that you were advising the police. In fact, you were sitting with a policeman at a table when I was shown in. Then he went and stood by the door. It seemed strange and ominous.

'So this is why you are in Gwrêngham,' I said stupidly, glancing towards the policeman.

'That's right – the riots,' you said.

I hoped that the policeman wasn't watching me.

'He's supposed to be protecting me.'

I kept glancing from your eyes to your lips. And back to your eyes. And to your hands. I wanted to touch you, but I wasn't sure if I was allowed to.

'Have you not heard about the riots here in Gwrêngham?'

'Not really.'

I could barely stop my eyes from feasting on you. My heart was so intoxicated by you, I could count its beats. Your voice. The heat of your body. Your breath hanging in the air.

'Two immigrant workers dead. Four policemen hurt, one blinded and badly burned. Cars set on fire. Shops attacked. Seven nights of rioting across three weekends. You must have heard.'

'Yes.' I said. 'Of course. I just hadn't connected it.'

The version I had heard of the story, sounded different. The English Government had drafted extra police from England into Wales.

It was at that moment that I had this image of you as a sort of spy master. What did that make me?

'The English colonialists are at it once more,' Mam had said. 'Subduing Wales yet again.'

I decided the policeman probably thought I was your informer.

You gave me a look as if you knew what I was thinking and I put all thoughts of spying from my mind.

'Do you like my dress?' I babbled. 'We don't usually dress up to come to Gwrêngham as we do for Chester.'

You laughed. Was this no more than just low-level intelligence to you?

I didn't want to talk about the riots. I had had lots of things I wanted to tell you. I wanted to throw my arms around you, and for you to lift me in the air and for me to kiss you and smother you with my great news. How I had already enrolled and been to the first few lessons of the courses you'd suggested. And I'd loved it. And how Dad and I had filled in all the forms and had a preliminary meeting with the funding officers and the planners. And a meeting was already arranged with an architect and builders. And how everything was going to be wonderful. And thank you. But now, here, with the policeman, I couldn't say any of it. And you were talking about you.

'I've been drafted in to advise the Social Task Force.' You

seemed very proud of that. 'The police couldn't stop the riots. Fact is, their presence usually exacerbates any situation. So they finally realised they needed a social scientist.'

I wished I hadn't worn my pretty dress. For a fleeting moment, it crossed my mind that maybe I was like one of those girls in occupied countries. The ones that get their heads shaved for making up to enemy soldiers. I could imagine you in a leather overcoat. Or is that the Russians?

'Have you succeeded?'

'We've brought it under control, yes. An intensive week of emergency community intervention. Emergency meetings in key streets with key members of the aggrieved communities. Letting them air their complaints and convincing them we know how to change the economic climate for them.'

'Ardderchog!'

'Street riots follow a couple of standard patterns. They would have stopped at some point anyway. What we have done is create a community strategy where everyone now wants to work together to make life better for everyone.'

'But why did they call you? I had no idea you were so important,' I blurted.

You laughed at that.

'I've read a lot of books on this sort of thing. And I've done my own case studies in Oldham, Birmingham, Leeds. We know quite a lot about it now. What sparks it. What calms it down. What sort of police behaviour is more or less inflammatory.'

It crossed my mind what Mam, and many others in Llanchwaraetegdanygelyn, would have thought of you – an interfering Englishman. All I saw was the man I loved. A clever man. Doing his best to make the world a better place. Such a waste that I was not the girl you needed.

Perhaps you sensed my sadness. Your hand across the table tempting mine. Our fingertips touched.

'But people have been killed here!'

'One thing I have learned is not to judge situations by their headlines. Sometimes people die for silly reasons. Narrow streets and petrol bombs. They couldn't back away. There wasn't room for them to get away.'

My fingers crawled up onto yours.

'That's horrible!'

'Actually, on the scale of things, it's not that horrible – fewer casualties than on the roads each day – it's just that they've been killed through civil disorder. And Governments can't be philosophical when policemen die.'

You pulled your hand away.

And then you put it back on top of mine and squeezed.

We were holding hands again.

'Why you?'

'Iwan asked me. You know – from the Welsh Assembly.'

And then you explained how Gwrêngham Council started off by welcoming Polish immigrants to keep its industries running on cheap East European labour.

'When the riots started, Iwan was called in from the Assembly office. He realised straight away that the problem was expanding their multi-cultural communities too rapidly. And remembered that's my area of expertise. So he phoned me. The police were glad of any help they could get.'

Talking to you that day, my hand in yours, it was as if curtains were being opened in my mind and sunlight flooding in. I'd been living in the dark and hadn't known it. My mind boxed in by mountains where the sun rose late and set too soon.

Now I wanted to know everything. And understand it all. And understand you. And what you did. And how.

'Why do people do this? Don't they realise they will be hurt and killed?'

'People feel desperate.'

'But why don't they listen to what people like you tell them?'

'They didn't listen in Llanchwaraetegdanygelyn.'

'They listened. They just didn't understand.'

'Understanding is pretty boring, I suppose.'

'But why Gwrêngham? Why now?'

'Historical reasons.'

You looked at my face and laughed. And I laughed too.

'OK. Ancient medieval settlement, turned small market town, then rapidly expanded when coal was discovered in the nineteenth century. Moderately prosperous, in a working-class sort of way, for a hundred years or so. Then the coal mines shut, and now industry is declining. And everyone who can leaves.'

'And that's why the Council starts looking to attract immigrant labour?'

'Exactly. Eastern Europe joins the Common Market. And you've got Estonians, Latvians and Lithuanians, Poles all eager for work and money. Airlifted in by so-called agents, billeted in the old terraced houses, every room converted into dormitories. East Europeans are now almost fifteen per cent of the population.'

'Really!'

'Yes. I've seen rooms where men are sleeping fifteen to a floor.'

'Why do they put up with it?'

'Even with extortionate rents, and agents' fees, they are still earning ten times what they could earn at home. They live frugally, work long hours, and they send as much of their cash as they can back to Eastern Europe; our pennies are worth literally pounds over there.'

'Yn wir!'

It had never really occurred to me before that this was what you did. And so handsome!

'Then, a couple of years on, they pay off their debts to the gang masters and bring their families over for a better life. Elwyn took me to one school where the headmaster was trying to cope with seventeen different languages, and where English-speaking children are in the minority. It's bound to cause resentment.'

'And we are worried about Welsh!'

'Oh, they are teaching Welsh, too! You should see the kids. Sweet little faces, hard-working, eager optimistic kids. Some of them are trilingual in Polish, English and Welsh.'

'You don't think immigrants should be sent home then?'

'Lordy no! Where would that leave mah own sweet black ass, sister?'

I didn't know how to respond to this.

So we both laughed.

'You've cheered me up no end,' you said as you walked me to the bus, your policeman walking fifteen paces behind. 'It's just a precaution,' you whispered. 'I've been negotiating with the British Nationalists. How long does it take your bus to get back?'

'Two hours.'

'And you came all the way in this to see me? I should have thought.'

You took me in your arms then. And kissed me.

'If you could have any wish,' I said. 'What would it be?'

You looked at me very uncertainly.

'End world poverty,' you said.

'I mean for you personally,' I said.

You shrugged.

'I wouldn't dare wish for anything personally,' you said. 'What about you?'

'For you to come and visit me.' I saw your eyes light up a bit. 'To help my father get more grants,' I said.

You laughed at that.

We kissed again.

'So will you?' I persisted.

'Will I what?'

'Come and see me.'

You didn't answer straightaway.

'Yes,' you promised. 'OK. If there are no riots Friday or Saturday, I'll come Sunday.'

I hoped there would be no riots Friday, Saturday or

Sunday. All the way home I hoped it. And four days later when I saw your funny little car come up the Maes I already wished I'd wished for more.

'Dw i yma,' you said, in a dreadful accent, and mutating badly, 'i ymarfer fy Cymraeg, and to see what I can do to help you smarten up this place.'

'Wyt ti wedi bod yn dysgu Cymraeg?'

But you didn't answer.

FOR EACH OF US, Gwalia, I am sure, there is one summer we look back on for the rest of our lives as *that summer*. For me, this was that summer. But how could we have known that at the time? And what difference would it have made if we had? For those few months, everything seemed charmed.

I grew to know and love that drive from London. The snail-paced crawl out of the sprawling city, the M40 and the claustrophobic tailbacks past Birmingham, followed by the sheer relief of turning off on the M54 at junction eleven and the rising optimism of a clear road out past Telford, Shrewsbury. Then seeing the hills of Wales rising up in the West.

Whatever my mood leaving London, it was always with mounting glee, that I hit that B4396 turnoff at Knockin onto minor roads. Across the border, up Tanat Valley as it narrowed and narrowed, through past Llanrhaeadr and on to Llangynog.

Then the exhilaration of the climb up over the Berwyn Mountains into what I liked to think of as my secret Wales. How treacherous and threatening that remote pass must have seemed in medieval times!

Then down into the remote valley of the Dyfrdwy, past the magic lake, along the Gwerin and finally up and over, through the gap between the rocks, and down into the really secret valley of Cwm Y Gelyn, to you, my Gwalia, and Llanchwarae-tegdangyelyn, a town so secret that it wasn't even on the map under its proper name!

Llanchwaraetegdanygelyn was such an enchanted place.

You were thrilled that I was learning Welsh.

'Ti'n ffantastig!' you told me. 'Mae dy acen di yn fendigedig! Isn't it, Awena?'

'It's all right,' Awena said. 'His accent isn't that good.'

'Have you been taking lessons?' you asked suspiciously. And started to laugh. 'You have, haven't you? You can't be getting all this from that book Dad gave you.'

We both laughed then and I admitted I'd been going to

weekly lessons at the London Welsh Centre in Grays Inn Road and had some extra private sessions with a tutor on top.

'You've been cribbing,' Awena said.

'No, Awena,' you told her. 'I think he did it to impress us.'

Awena tested me then, on nouns and verbs and prepositions.

She made me translate sentences such as 'I've got a Welsh girlfriend' and 'I'm an Englishman from London', clapping her hands when I got the answers right and correcting me kindly – like you did her – when I got them wrong.

'Do I pass my test?' I asked her.

She thought very seriously for several moments with her finger on her chin.

'I think you have done very well and you deserve a gold star,' she announced, very solemnly.

'Diolch yn fawr,' I thanked her. And she went skipping away, twirling her skirt out as she went.

'Do you know,' I told you, 'I don't think I've ever really talked to Awena before. Nor she to me. She's wonderful. She has a laugh like . . . like . . . like water babbling through a sunlit brook.'

'You should tell her that.'

'OK.'

So I did.

Awena appointed herself my personal Welsh teacher. She taught me nursery rhymes and little poems, showed me how the music of the language comes from putting the emphasis on certain syllables and certain words.

'We don't say "The cat sits on the mat," like you do in English, with the same boring emphasis equally on every word. We say: 'Mae'r <u>gath</u> yn eistedd ar y mat.' Or '<u>Eistedd</u> y gath ar y mat.'

It was she who taught me that I should always put the emphasis on the last but one syllable of a word.

It seemed like a very long way round of speaking to say 'He was John doing shopping this morning' and for a while I was puzzled as to why Welsh translations of bilingual brochures and things didn't take up twice the space of their English versions.

That was until I realised that Welsh saves words by conjugating its prepositions and other tricks. Written Welsh is like a completely different formal language from what is usually spoken which has barely changed for centuries and has an elegant beauty that entirely explains its astonishing survival.

Awena enthused me so much, I went on a Welsh course at Nant Gwyrtheyrn, the National Language Centre on the Llŷn Peninsula, curving out from the top of Wales.

It didn't occur to me at the time that, perhaps subconsciously, I was trying to prepare myself for something.

I THOUGHT for a while that you had fallen in love as much with Wales as you had with me. That maybe I could lure you here to settle down. We changed each other, Jon. Both of us changed that summer. That's how it felt to me.

I loved how you came to visit almost every weekend, helping Dad and me to supervise the hotel renovation. 'Getting the Two Dragons all fired up' you called it, as if we didn't get the joke.

Dewi didn't like it, though. He stayed polite, but sullen. Biding his time, I think. Nothing, I knew, would shake him from his deep conviction that he and I were destined for each other. And I was fond of Dewi. I knew him like a brother. He had been kind to me and had been with me through my difficult times. I wanted to stay friends with him. I believed he understood that.

You were right about those business courses. And never once did you mention my nose. Not till I brought it up.

'How can you love me with a nose like this?'

'I love you as you are. But if it bothers you, we can get it fixed.'

'What do you mean by get it fixed?'

'You go to a plastic surgeon and have it changed. It's no big deal.'

'It's a huge big deal.'

'No, it isn't. It could be done in a day. Two or three weeks for the bruising to clear up.'

'But it would need a specialist. It would cost a fortune. What if it all went wrong?'

'It's routine these days. Come and stay in London in my parents' flat. No one here need see you till it's done and mended. We'll get the top plastic surgeon in London. I'll pay.'

'No,' I said. 'I couldn't.'

'Why?' you asked, incredulously.

I think you guessed I still needed my trauma to hide behind.

'Deception and lies only cause sickness and neurosis,' you said. 'Both in individuals and communities.'

Dad agreed. You and he agreed about a lot of things.

It was you who suggested that Mam and Dad and I should sit down with Awena and explain to her properly that I was really her mother, not her sister.

'She's a very intelligent girl; it will make sense to her.'

And so we did, around the kitchen table.

'So Mam is really Nain, and Dad is Taid.'

'Yes.'

'Who's my Dad then? Is it Jon?'

'No,' Mam told her quickly, before I could speak. 'You haven't got a father.'

'I want a Dad. You're my Dad,' and she ran to Dad.

'If you want me to be,' he said. 'But really I'm your Taid.'

'I'm your Mam,' I said.

'No you're not,' she said. 'You're my sister.' And she hit me and ran away.

'I warned you,' Mam said. 'I told you it would be a mistake.' And she went after her.

'Don't worry,' Dad assured me. 'It all takes time. You've done the hardest part. It will come right.'

'Are you really my Mam?' she asked the following day.

'Yes,' I told her. 'And I love you very much and I wouldn't lie to you.'

'Well you lied to me before, pretending to be my sister. Why did you lie to me? I hate you! Why?'

I couldn't begin to explain about the rape and trauma to an eight-year-old.

Still she refused to call me Mam.

You, Jon, could do no wrong with her, though. Do you remember how entranced you were when we introduced you to the world of wild flowers? Awena teaching you the difference between the vetches and the trefoils. And their names in Welsh. And which ones could be remedies for ancient ills.

And how much we laughed that day Awena told you we used navelwort to treat a dafad, which is a wart – because you didn't realise dafad also means sheep.

That was it, you see, you could never just be one of us. There was always something that set you apart. So I could never quite relax completely and take the fact that you were there with me for granted.

Like the time I told you we would be going mountain walking. I should have said nothing. I wanted you to meet my friends, you see. I tried so hard to get you to be part of my life. I wanted Dewi to see you as I saw you. I thought maybe that he could at least respect you, now that you were learning Welsh and everything.

I'd been waiting outside Y Ddwy Ddraig for an hour. Mared, Branwen, Rowena, Llyr and I all standing about in our usual jeans and T-shirts while Dewi sat impatiently in the driver's seat .

'Am I overdressed?' you said, turning up eventually with your brand new storm jacket, rucksack, hiking boots and flask. Apparently your Mam had made a list of kit that you would need for hiking, and sent you off to Harrods.

'It's not that big a mountain,' I said. 'And you're late.'

'Sorry.'

But I was glad to see you. I just wished you understood sometimes how embarrassingly awkward you were in so many English ways.

I REMEMBER being bustled into Dewi's mini-bus with a load of people I didn't know. And seeing the six Welsh flags protruding from the windows, three each side. Dewi driving like a lunatic. And, being slightly anxious that I was in what looked like a troop carrier for Welsh Nationalists.

''Ti'n iawn?' Dewi asked. 'Dwi 'di clywed ti'n siarad Cymraeg 'wan.'

'Ydw,' I said. Obviously I was going to be expected to speak no English today. Unfortunately, I didn't know how to explain that I'd only been learning for four months and my vocabulary was still sparse.

'Ti'n iawn, cariad?' you asked and kissed me.

I could see Dewi staring at us in the mirror as he pushed the lever crossly into gear and we jerked forward.

You solemnly introduced me to your friends. I shook their hands and said a rather formal 'Sut dachi', the way Mr Thomas had taught us in Welsh class.

'You look as though you are ready for Everest,' Dewi said in Welsh.

'Take no notice,' you whispered in English, in my ear.

'Dw i'n iawn, diolch,' I answered. I was quite determined. Well, what was the point of learning your language if I didn't use it?

'Da iawn,' you said.

'Wyt ti'n deall Cymraeg?' Branwen asked me.

'Ydw. Dipyn bach,' I said warily.

Ok, Gwalia, I know, I looked ridiculous in my brand new hiking outfit, and you looked such a dainty thing. But what was I supposed to wear, a city boy like me?

So off we went, everyone chattering away, and me trying to pick out words I recognised and get the gist.

The reality of all of you speaking only Welsh was that I turned into an eavesdropper, unable to participate, painfully conscious that every time I opened my mouth I was liable to make a fool of myself.

I was slightly fearful of Dewi. Why else would I have been

there with you, learning Welsh, enduring all this, if not for you, Gwalia – to take his girl?

Climbing up out of Llanchwaraetegdanygelyn, with the town and cwm spread out below us, it crossed my mind that, if Dewi missed a gear, we would roll back and over the edge and plummet right down to the school yard.

'Today we liberate the peak of Cadair Idris from the English,' Dewi joked.

Branwen was the first to notice I wasn't speaking much, so then she started to treat me as a child, saying everything first in Welsh and then in English, with patronising little asides almost in stage whispers: 'Are you understanding this all right, Jon'. 'You are following what I am saying, aren't you?'

Dewi took the road past Llyn Y Gelyn and insisted on stopping and having a minute's silence staring into the grey waters. And Branwen took a picture of us all, the minibus with its flags flying, in the background. That also gave me an uneasy feeling: what would they have said at the Leyburn Institute!

Then Dewi asked me to take one, handed me the camera, and went and stood with his arm around you. That also bothered me, though I was relieved not to be in those pictures.

'We've all got family buried under there,' he said, and made a big deal of checking that the slogans daubed on the rocks around the reservoir were still all there. Cofiwch Lyn Gelyn. Cofiwch Y Gelyn.

Then we all piled back in the minibus and lumbered off again, along the great valley, shouting encouragement to Dewi each time he crashed the gears.

'This is the great watershed between the Dyfdwy and the Mawddach rivers. This is Cadair Idris.'

The view from the head of the valley looking down to Tal y Llyn was breathtaking.

'Wow,' I whispered into your ear, my breath shaking the little golden hairs on that perfect neck. 'I don't think I've ever seen anything quite so beautiful.'

On the far side of the valley, the whole mountainside was purple with bluebells.

'Drychwch ar glychau'r gog,' said Llyr.

We hurtled down the narrow ribbon of tarmac cut into the cliff-face, rock on one side, a drop to the valley floor on the other, Dewi barely in control. A bird of prey, perched on a fence post between us and the great drop, watched us and then took off and swooped beside us for a moment and then banked away across the valley.

'Drycha!' you said. 'Hebog.'

We parked at the foot of the mountain, and I put on my haversack and the others grabbed their bags while Dewi locked up.

You led me through the gate to a staircase cut in slate, going up the mountain. A bilingual notice informed us that the path had been created using European Parliament money.

'Wales should have its own seat there,' said Dewi. I think he meant the European Parliament. I was already climbing robotically in my brand new walking gear.

'Wyt ti'n chwysu?' Branwen asked. 'It means are you sweating.'

I was too busy breathing to answer.

We passed an English couple coming down who told us they had started from the other side five hours before, at dawn.

'The view from the top was wonderful.'

A squad of soldiers, running with backpacks, overtook us.

'Two. Three Four. Hup! Two. Three Four. Hup!' Despite their backpacks and their running, they were panting and gasping less than me.

Dewi said something in Welsh that I didn't understand and turned to me.

'You English have no conception of how offensive it is to us to see English troops here in our country,' he said loudly.

One of the soldiers glanced around.

A little higher up, there was a stopping place.

The squaddies were taking a breather. Branwen and Llyr and Rowena had stopped too, to allow the rest of us to catch up.

The soldiers glared at us.

Dewi pulled a Welsh flag from his pocket, knotted it around his shoulders and marched up and down in front of them.

I tried to let go of your hand. But you held it tight. You didn't want a fight.

I smiled at the corporal who appeared to be in charge. I had this vague hope that a friendly smile might avert the impending trouble.

'Oi. Watchoo larffin at?'

The corporal got up and came over.

'Yeah you. Nigger. Ahm tawkin tchew.'

Everyone had gone silent. You were all watching me. The squaddies too.

I prised my hand free of yours and stood up.

I was slightly taller than the squaddy. But he was tougher and fitter.

'I beg your pardon?' I said in my public school voice.

'You larffin at me?' he said. But there was doubt in his voice this time.

'How exactly do you mean,' I asked him.

We stared at each other for several seconds.

'Nuffin,' he said. And turned and went back to his mates.

You took my hand and squeezed it.

The corporal stood up and started jogging on the spot.

'Right lads, fall in.'

They all got up and joined in step.

'Forward!'

And without changing step, they moved off, up the hill.

At the next refreshment stop, I found myself standing next to Dewi.

He took a swig of his water, looking me in the eye as he drank. Then, very deliberately, he offered me the bottle without wiping the top.

I took a swig and handed it back to him. Again without wiping it.

Dewi took another swig straight away.

Then we found ourselves grinning at each other.

'Da iawn,' said Dewi. 'Ti'n ôl reit.'

We moved on. One brow gave way to another and several times the path seemed to veer away to go round crags and small cliffs. After a long time climbing, we came to a plateau. A sheer cliff of several hundred feet encircled one end of the plateau, rising up to the mountain.

In the distance, specks of people, one group jogging, headed along the cliff top against the sky, towards the summit.

I turned to follow the path but you took my elbow and guided me a different way, across rough pasture towards the base of the cliff, then you ran on ahead while I walked with Dewi, trying to decipher his uncompromising Welsh.

Without me realising it, we had come to a lake; the dead calm water perfectly reflected the dark cliff face of the mountain and the blue sky and a few white clouds above it.

Mared, Branwen and Awel were already stripping off and running in, squealing and shrieking, their cries echoing up the black cliff face, their splashes arching up out of the calm reflection into the spring sunlight. Their shouts echoed off the cliff face behind them. When they stood up their naked bodies were wet and shining, their breasts glistening.

The perfect vision of maidens bathing in a remote and rugged landscape. Andrew and Nisha would never believe this. A scene that still seems magical, romantic and mythical in my memory.

Then you appeared, Gwalia, and plunged in after them. I don't think I had ever been a part of anything more beautiful.

I stood for a moment watching. Then I stripped off and plunged in too.

'Nofia cyn rhewi,' Branwen squealed.

'Rasio ti i'r canol!'

I watched the two of you, the soft Vs of your bow-waves

rippling the blue reflection of the sky as you swam into the black reflection of the cliff.

At the centre of the lake, you tipped up your naked bottoms and dived down into the water, leaving only black, oily ripples. I held my breath and counted silently for ten seconds, then you came up again, almost together, ten or fifteen feet away, in the blue reflection of the sky, heading for the shore.

You rose out of the water, my own goddess. Your flat, smooth stomach and your hair, dark and heavy from the water, hanging down your shoulders and to your breasts. It was the first time I had seen your breasts. The first time I had seen you naked. We stood together. My skin black. Yours white.

Our lips touched and our cold bodies came together for a moment.

If only we had been alone!

But then there was a shout and a splash. And Dewi and Llyr came crashing in.

'Rasio di ar draws!'

'Joskin ydy'r ola!'

And they splashed off noisily for the other bank, sending up plumes of spray and exploding not just the tranquillity of the lake but that moment of magic between us, too.

We dressed and made a feast of bread and cheese and Welsh cakes. It was only another hour to the top, you said.

From the summit we looked out over the coast, the rugged mountain ridges and maze of valleys. And Snowdonia's ancient volcanic mountains and U-shaped valleys, a landscape surrendered by the ice age a mere ten thousand years ago.

Dewi pulled out his flag and insisted we all have our picture taken with it, yet again. I knew that I should not have been a part of it, but what could I do?

Back at the mini-bus, Dewi was re-installing the flags to stick out of the windows, and we were changing our boots, when the squaddies reappeared. The corporal came across to me and stood in front of me, staring me in the eye.

'I hope you know what you're getting into here,' he said.

He let the words sink in, saluted, executed a right turn, and marched away.

'What was that about,' you said, running across.

'I've no idea,' I said.

I was already thinking of having to be back in London the next day and of some project, I think on Teesside.

YOU'D SEEN THE POSTERS, Jon, but you hadn't read them properly, had you? And I had mentioned it, but you hadn't listened. So Gŵyl Delyn Y Gelyn took you by surprise. Awena was nagging, impatient to be out to join in the carnival.

'Hastiwch! Dewch! Come along. Brysiwch. Quick.' But you were tired from your drive the night before.

Awena led us out into the sunny June morning, holding both our hands and swinging between us.

'Un, dau, tri . . . whî!'

'Eto!'

'Un, dau, tri . . . whî!'

'O, mae'n hyfryd,' you said. And it was true, Llanchwaraetegdanygelyn did look beautiful. You'd arrived too late to see it in the dark, but the Maes had been transformed, covered with marquees, tents and stalls.

'It's some kind of festival,' you said, as if that wasn't obvious.

'Yes, Gŵyl Delyn Y Gelyn,' I said, patiently. 'I told you about it, Jon. It's what Llanchwaraetegdanygelyn is famous for – throughout Wales.'

I think you felt particularly glad to be in Wales instead of sorting out community problems in some inner city somewhere. Your laughter matched the carnival atmosphere. Even the grass and ferns up on the hills above the town were drying to festive summer golds and reds.

Nothing had started yet, Awena insisted on leading us round the stalls where people were setting up. Under all the different coloured tents and awnings, there were crafts and produce of all kinds, from all over Wales. In the large marquee, there was a stage with the harps and microphones.

Awena stopped and pointed up.

'Drycha ar y gwenoliaid du, Jon!' she squealed.

'I can't see anything,' you said.

'Drycha! Drycha!' she insisted, pulling your arm. 'Drycha! means look.'

'I know what edrycha! means,' you protested. 'But I have no idea what gwenoliaid du are.'

She crossed her arms and looked at you, tapping her foot impatiently.

'Paid â dweud,' you said. 'Let me work it out. It ends in -iaid, so it's probably a plural noun. And du is black, so it's something black. Am I close?'

'How anyone can learn a language thinking like that, Jon, is quite beyond me,' I told you. And we both laughed.

Awena was shaking her head and rolling her eyes, and laughing, too.

'So beth ydy gwenoliaid du?' you persisted.

'Me! Me! Can I tell him?' shrieked Awena, dancing in front of us.

'Wrth gwrs, cariad,' I said, and kissed her on the top of her head without even thinking about it. She came and stood in front of you, and you sat on your heels and looked into her laughing eyes, yours the same height as hers.

'Well, you see,' she explained, 'gwenoliaid du are swifts. And there is one up there, trapped in the roof.' She pointed up

'Gwenoliaid du,' you repeated.

'Da iawn, well done,' she clapped.

And then, she threw her arms around your neck and kissed you on the cheek in a way she had never done to me. And insisted on holding on to your hand. But not mine.

Did you guess that I was jealous of you, Jon? Was that why you put your arm around me?

I wanted so badly for her to be my daughter, my little girl!

I swept her up in my arms and tried to hug her but she kicked and struggled down. Each twist and kick a little punishment for all the hurts I'd made her suffer.

We walked around the stalls, saying hello to everyone, your arm around me, that soft romantic look on your soppy, smiling face.

Awena kept running off to see things, then running back to tell us what she'd seen. And whenever people complimented you on learning Welsh, she proudly told them she was teaching you.

322

'Ga i hufen iâ?'

'I know what that means,' you said, digging in your pocket. 'Can I have an ice cream. It looks nice. Wow! Welsh honey ice cream. I'll have some of that!'

You were so innocent sometimes, Jon. And I felt so in love with you.

That was when Awena took my hand, when we were eating honey ice cream.

She had taken my hand! We were like a proper family, almost.

'I've never seen so many people in the town,' you said.

'It's the Gŵyl Delyn Gelyn,' I teased. 'Haven't you English ever heard of it? It's very famous.'

'No, I haven't, as you well know. Does anyone know what it means?'

Awena looked skywards.

'Gŵyl means festival, and delyn means harp. And celyn means holly. But gelyn means enemy.'

'Or it could just be short for Llanchwaraetegdanygelyn,' I said.

'So it's the enemy's harp festival, then?' you said, pretending to be very puzzled.

'Mae 'na rai yn deud – there are some who say – that the festival was first held to celebrate the hiding of the town from the English when they wrongly named us Umbo. You know that story don't you?'

'Wrth gwrs mae o'n gwybod,' shrieked Awena, rolling her eyes and winking at me. 'He's not stupid you know.'

'There are others who say it goes right back to the age when wandering poets would come with jugglers and minstrels, bringing tales of the world to our little town.'

It was a perfect day.

We stopped at the Merched y Wawr stall – you couldn't pass all those home-baked cakes and biscuits – home-cooked was a novelty to you – and made me explain how it was Wales's answer to the Women's Institute.

You helped Awena win prizes at the coconut shy and

shooting gallery. And all of us went together on the steam-driven roundabout.

Lunch was a spit-roast pig over a charcoal fire at the top of the Maes.

Word had got around that you were learning Welsh. Lots of people greeted you with 'Bore da,' 'Sut dach chi?' or 'Sut mae?' You could talk about what a fine day it was or how excellent the gŵyl was but you didn't quite understand when they asked you if you were looking forward to the perfformiad that night.

In the afternoon, you were charmed and bemused by the sheepdog demonstrations, log-chopping contests and the sheep-shearing.

Then we all got dressed up for the evening.

You helped me into my black backless evening gown. You couldn't take your eyes off me. Nor I off you.

'I can't believe the way you look,' you said. 'With your hair up and those elegant pearl earrings and matching necklace.'

'They were my Nain's. But you need to look smart, too,' I warned.

'I wish you'd told me when I packed my case. I only have my jeans and shirt.'

'It doesn't matter. You buy expensive jeans.'

'You look a million pounds in anything.'

Our seats were in the front row of the marquee. You still couldn't take your eyes off me. I had to keep nudging you and hissing through my teeth: 'Paid â syllu!'

The Noson Lawen started with a male voice choir.

You had never heard a male voice choir before, had you?

'The singing, and power and control,' you whispered. 'It's just fantastic.'

And Awena shushed you.

You liked the soloist, too, who sang three arias – which you said were wonderful – but not the comedian who you couldn't understand. It must have been uncomfortable to have everyone else laughing when you didn't understand the jokes.

'Are all these people amateurs?' you asked. 'The standard is amazing.'

So Dad tried to explain to you how music and drama and poetry were taught in schools. And everyone with any talent would compete in the Eisteddfodau. And all of the performers had been on Welsh television at some time or another.

But you had never heard of Eisteddfodau.

You looked most shocked when they called my name. And I stood up to go on stage. And play the harp. And Awena came up with me to turn the pages.

I was so glad that I had kept it all completely secret from you!

I still have the picture that you took on your new digital camera. The huge harp tipped to my shoulder, my cheek caressing it, my fingers straining at the strings. My brown curls half across my face, cascading down my shoulders. And my awful nose. And Awena, pictured through the strings, turning the sheet music.

I had wanted to surprise you and I had. Gwalia could do something you hadn't dreamed of. And – yes – this was my first time playing in public since before the rape – yes, I could say that word now.

And then I sang.

I sang to you, and to Dad and Mam, of course. And to the whole of my little world. I'm sure I saw you wipe a tear from your eye, Dad too. He had his large red-spotted handkerchief out. It was very moving for me, as well, to be able to sing again. To sing for those I loved.

'It was amazing how all your pain and suffering was in the music, cariad,' you told me afterwards. And I suppose that was true.

The applause was wonderful. It felt like being bathed in sunshine after a long, hard winter.

After I had finished playing, I had taken Awena's hand. And, as we took our bows, she whispered something to me. Sweet, sweet words.

'Roedd hwnne'n wych, Mami.'

Mami! She had called me Mami!

What I never told you, Jon, was that I still went out with Dewi in the night, painting slogans and taking down English signs. So that Sunday night, after you had left, while you were still driving back to London, I was my other self. Can you understand that, Jon? I think that as well as loving you, I also needed to be Welsh?

Dafydd Y Gwrthsafiad liked to dramatise it all, of course. He was rather militaristic. And Dewi was completely in awe of him. So we had to wear black, with black woollen hats, and creep about looking like what he thought was the French Resistance. It was very romantic for Dewi, I think, creeping about the hillsides in the dark, sabotaging the English occupation and subjugation of Wales, with his girl in tow. For me it wasn't the fun it had once been.

I'm sorry now that I kept that hidden from you. But I had to, didn't I? Not just because you were working for the Government and this was Y Gwrthsafiad, the Welsh Resistance, but because I knew how jealous you and Dewi were of each other.

It seemed such a minor thing at the time.

I was hardly awake, fumbling to prepare breakfast for Awena and Gethin, when Anti Gwenlais came bustling in. She fixed her eyes on me.

'Dreadful news,' she said and dumped herself down with a twt and a sigh in Dad's chair. Mam and I, and Awena and Gethin, stared at her blankly.

'Wil Corffyn had a visitor before first thing, four o'clock, if you please. Then he sent Meiri, his wife, to get me out of bed to open up especially and fetch round extra gauze and lint and TCP to the house. At that time! All before dawn. Can you imagine? As if the dead are in any hurry.'

She held out her hand to show how it was shaking.

'See! You see! Look at the state I'm in. I haven't even had breakfast. And no make-up.'

'Who's died?' Dad said, coming in.

'Islwyn,' said my Anti Gwenlais, finally coming to the point.

Mam poured her a paned and put a plate of toast in front of her. 'To calm your grief, Gwenlais,' she said. 'It must be so upsetting for you.'

'It is. It is. But not for me, you understand. It's the family I always grieve for.'

She stifled a sob and dabbed her eyes with a hanky from her sleeve. Mam twted and went to put her arm around her big sister. We all knew Anti Gwenlais had had a soft spot for Islwyn.

She pulled herself together.

'It's all the same for Islwyn now.'

And then she was back to normal.

'It's confidential, mind. But you should have seen the body.'

She leaned forward

'Died straining at the toilet, he did. Mind, that can put an awful strain on the heart you know. Especially in the night. That's why you need plenty of roughage, see.'

She twted and shook her head in disapproval at the shocking nature of her revelations. Mam joined in, twting in harmony.

'How are Mari and the children?' Dad inquired.

'I had to go to fetch the smelling salts for Mari, I did. She couldn't bring herself to go near the body. He was such a womaniser you know.'

They twted in unison again at that.

'Best if everything is kept confidential then.' Mam looked up to heaven.

'Oh. Yes. It's such a comfort to live in a community where you know that you can trust your neighbours not to gossip about a man's indiscretions.'

I wondered to what extent Anti Gwenlais might have been one of them, but put the thought from my mind. It was far too scary.

She had only just left when Penhaearn arrived in his undertaker's weeds, black hat and gloves and chalk-striped suit.

'Terrible news,' he told us, wringing his hands. 'Terrible.'

'Yes,' Mam said. 'Indeed.'

He was rubbing his hands together particularly hard this morning. As if he was washing them. But his demeanour did not suggest to me that he really thought the news was terrible.

'Oh, yes, yes, yes.' He sucked his cheeks in and then proceeded to practice his rhetoric by giving us a short teyrnged.

'Islwyn will be sadly missed. He died doing the Council minutes, you know.' (Not what Anti Gwenlais had told us.) 'Such a punctilious man he was. Dedicated. The likes of him will not be seen again. I propose to organise a monument. A plaque in the Council Chamber. I will unveil it myself.'

'Isn't it perhaps too soon to be talking of such things?' Mam suggested.

'Nonsense,' Dad said. 'The secret of power is to seize the initiative. Leaders must not be squeamish, isn't that right, Penhaearn?'

Penhaearn hesitated, suspecting he was being mocked, but insufficiently sure to respond. He paused. Then cleared his throat – a sure sign he was beginning another speech.

'Succession,' he announced, 'that is the immediate issue now. And I think you will be pleased by what I am about to propose. We are very fortunate I think in having you here, Gwalia, as someone who has already been apprenticed to the job, and already knows and understands the work.'

He rubbed his hands together vigorously.

My heart sank. I knew what was coming next.

'There is a small gratuity, I believe. A thousand pounds a year. I'm sure that that would help you with your studies.'

My studies were almost over. The renovations at Y Ddwy Ddraig were almost ready to start. The final planning permissions were just going through. And I had just started being a real mother to Awena. The last thing that I wanted was the weight of the responsibilities of Council Clerk.

'I'm not sure,' I told him.

'Ah,' he said, rubbing his hands together very vigorously indeed. 'That's where I think that I can help you in particular.'

'Oh yes?'

'I believe you have some applications coming before my committee this month and I am very friendly with the chairman of the grants committee, you know. I am sure you would want to help me, just as I am very eager to help you. I have always tried to help you, Gwalia. I'm sure you appreciate that.'

So I became Clerk to the Council officially, a job I had effectively been doing for two years anyway.

You weren't so happy about me becoming part of Penhaearn's inner circle, Jon.

'Reactionaries like Penhaearn are never good news,' you told me. 'He's a petty tyrant. A little dictator. He thinks he knows best for everyone but he has no experience of anything beyond this narrow valley.'

'I had not realised you were so much against him. He's being very helpful to me over the grant for the hotel.'

You were cross at that.

'Don't you see, Gwalia, how he controls people. That's what's so corrupt. He withholds and grants his favours for personal reasons. Not on principles.'

'He works very hard for the community.'

'It's not *that* I'm against, it's his lack of principles. His favouritism and his complacency about it.'

'Perhaps I can help him make better decisions,' I said. 'Anyway, if it means we can now get planning permission for Y Ddwy Ddraig . . .'

'Exactly!' you exclaimed. 'You see how it works.'

'What?'

'It's nepotism, Gwalia, he's running a cabal. You do me favours, I'll help you. Let's all be nice to each other. Except that it's illegal.'

'I think you're wrong there, Jon,' I snapped. 'It's different when you have to live with people in a small place.'

'No I'm not wrong. He's acting *ultra vires*. Tell me why I'm wrong.'

'I would, if I knew what those words you're using meant.'

'You don't know what a cabal or nepotism or acting *ultra vires* is?'

'I would probably know them in Welsh.'

'Wel, te. Cabal ydy clic, nepotism ydy ffafrio perthnasau, ac *ultra vires* ydy uwchlaw awdurdod. You see. You still don't understand, do you?'

'Iawn. Iawn. I do. More or less.'

You had to explain at length then.

'Penhaearn is running a cabal, a closed clique of friends who keep people they don't agree with out. When those people are relatives, and they're getting pay or privileges that are denied to people who aren't in the family, that's nepotism.'

'I don't think he's doing that,' I said. 'I think you are being mean to say such a thing.'

'Gwalia! Penhaearn controls everything. His sister Dwynwen controls the media. You – his niece – are Clerk to the Council. How many councillors on the Council have been elected?'

'No one. It's a job to persuade people to come on to the Council.'

'So all the members are invited.'

'It's not like that.'

'Are English people ever invited?'

'They can't be. They can't speak the language.'

'And that doesn't bother you.'

'No. Why should it? They're not local.'

'They're legally entitled to vote, Gwalia. They're legally

entitled to know what's going on. It's only a matter of time, before they realise that. You're excluding non-Welsh speakers who are legitimate voters and taxpayers. That's how Penhaearn stopped Victoria Leakin from bringing electricity in. He blocked your planning permission till it suited him. He blocked my project. He's a petty potentate, Gwalia. It's medieval. It shouldn't be happening in this day and age.'

I recognised the truth in what you were saying, Jon, but I didn't want to acknowledge it. And I resented you pointing it out. Though I had never liked Penhaearn, he worked so hard for the community.

'It's not really illegal, is it?' I said.

'Of course it is. And it's morally appalling! He's behaving like a dictator. A tyrant. Just think how much effort, time and money in Westminster goes into elections, developing policy, trying to influence public opinion through radio, newspapers and television. Think how much politicians worry about winning arguments, beating the opposition. Getting elected. My job – the whole of the Leyburn Institute, and all the other think-tanks like it – it's all there to serve democracy to try to find better ways of running things.

'Penhaearn behaves like a feudal king who thinks he has been appointed by God and has divine wisdom in his ignorant common sense. And your town is stupid for putting up with it.'

I slapped your face.

'How dare you speak about my town like that! That isn't fair.'

You rubbed your face. And looked at me, shocked. It felt as if something between us had changed.

'Look, Gwalia. I love your town. I love your people. I love you. But it isn't a question of loyalty or love. It's a question of honesty. Look around you. Llanchwaraetegdanygelyn is stuck in a time warp. Before electricity and running water. Your people are living hard lives in poverty. And Penhaearn is determined to keep it that way. Why?'

'I don't know why.'

'Well ask yourself.'

'He wants to protect the language.'

'And how is he going to do that against the huge silver wave of English people leaving English cities, moving to the countryside?'

'You could help us!'

'I tried, Gwalia. I tried.'

I went quiet then, thinking about what you had said. Sulking a bit. Not wanting to believe it. Not wanting our relationship to have changed but feeling somehow it had.

And then I remembered something else you'd said.

'What does *ultra vires* mean?'

'It means he's acting beyond his legal authority. Sooner or later, someone is going to catch him out. I can't believe the English people here have allowed him to hold them back so long.'

'Why have they, then?'

I wanted so badly for you to be wrong, to be mistaken. And for us to agree, to be on the same side. Was this what being a Mata Hari felt like?

'Because they're nice, intelligent, educated people, Gwalia. They have money. Too much to lose. If they didn't, you'd already have had race riots here. Like Gwrêngham.'

'Democracy is not about what one small group of people want, it's about what the majority want. Those questionnaires showed clearly that people wanted electricity. Penhaearn stops them getting it.'

'Only because he wants to protect us.'

'No. Because he wants to protect himself. He lies to people. Tells the farmers they will lose their grants, tells people like Jac Trydan that he and his fellow tradesmen will lose their jobs. All he is concerned with is his own and his family's petty power and paltry county councillor's perks and pay.'

I was always a little nervous and apprehensive whenever we talked about Welsh politics with you after that. I knew I was being deceitful either to you or to Wales. Disloyal, too. But we were still in love. It was just a more mature sort of love, that was all.

After Gŵyl Delyn Gelyn you often asked me to play the harp for you. So much sometimes that my fingers had blisters. And you wanted to take me out to every Welsh-language performance within an hour's drive: plays in village halls and little theatres, or concerts. I took you to a Noson Lawen, the Welsh answer to a variety show, you called them. With music and sketches and comedians. Like something out of Victorian times, you said. I think you found the jokes a little bawdy for your taste, but you laughed enough.

'To think that I knew nothing about Welsh music and poetry and drama,' you told Dad earnestly when he asked you if you had enjoyed something, I forget what. 'It didn't occur to me that there would be a whole Welsh culture behind the language. And you can't even know about it, let alone appreciate it, if you can't speak Welsh.'

'You haven't seen the half of it,' he told you. So Dad took you to the school Eisteddfod to show you how the young ones competed to represent the town, and then the county, in singing, playing instruments, reciting poetry and acting.

'Many English parents and teachers think they've done well if they manage to get their kids to sit through a piece of music or a drama once a year,' you mused that night. 'We English are merely trained to be good audiences. And we're not even very good at that. Television has ruined us. The Welsh are a nation of singers and musicians and poets! Talented performers.'

You couldn't believe the poetry.

'It's all so technical,' you said. 'Like the englyn with its fixed number of syllables, and rhymes and internal rhymes. And a tradition going back at least a thousand years. And can you really understand Welsh poetry written in the sixth century?'

'Yes.'

'Could I?'

I showed you the poems of Taliesin from the sixth century. But it was a little hard for you. Especially the vocabulary.

'There's quite a difference between modern spoken Welsh and written Welsh,' I explained.

And then you made me get my poetry book out and read to you, explaining the different sorts of internal rhyming patterns and metres. And I had to translate the words. You were more exhausting, Jon Bull, than Awena!

There was no question but that we would have to go to the National Eisteddfod that year, though I must confess, Jon, that you made me nervous.

You were too keen. You had to be in the thick of everything. Camping on Maes B, buying the biggest, brand new tent especially.

Did it never occur to you how that might make me feel?

My friends were making fun of you. And those cheery, Sut dach chi greetings to shy chapel folk as you stood bare-chested in your pyjamas waiting for the showers and toilets.

I cringed at how you drew attention to yourself. And me. Letting the whole world know: Jon Bull was learning Welsh.

And, even though the Eisteddfod field is big, how could we not keep running into Dewi and his friends, or my old friends? And I knew exactly what they were thinking.

But you just kept going on and on about it all.

How Welsh pop music was a revelation to you. 'A whole music industry through the medium of Welsh! And it has its own style.' As if we wouldn't have our own style! And you didn't know if you preferred Maes B, for the young people and excitement, or the main field for its 'authority'. How it was like the Gŵyl Delyn Gelyn on a massive scale.

'Two theatres, a dance pavilion, another pavilion devoted wholly to poetry and literature. An exhibition of Welsh books and hundreds of stands all selling Welsh products, advertising

Welsh activities and societies. There's even a pabell for Welsh learners.'

As if we, who had been coming all our lives, didn't know all that.

And the way you reacted to the cameras!

'How do I say in Welsh: "It's absolutely incredible. A tented town of a hundred thousand people. All talking Welsh, with Welsh cafés and coffee bars, Welsh shops, Welsh exhibitions and everything in Welsh," just in case they interview me?'

You made me write it down so you could learn it. Then hung around until they could ignore you no longer.

'Mae'n anhygoel. Pentre mawr o gan mil o bobl i gyd yn siarad Cymraeg. Siopau, arddangosfeydd, popeth yn Gymraeg,' you said. And then you added: 'A stiwdio teledu gyda chyflwynwraig bert iawn', making Carys the presenter blush.

You became a minor celebrity. Not just an Englishman but the *black* Englishman learning Welsh. You were everybody's darling then. I remember how amazed you were by how many people said they'd seen you on the video screens around the Maes, or on their televisions at home. 'The Eisteddfod's more popular in Wales than the Olympics!' you said. And you were probably right.

I don't know how many scores of competitions in the Pafiliwn you made me sit through – singing, music, drama. Translating words for you, writing down phrases. Then you discovered the literature tent. You loved that! And the art exhibition.

You enthused to everyone. As Mam said, acidly, 'He has the zeal of a born-again Christian and the whitest smile.' But I have to hand it to you, Jon Bull, you kept it up.

On the third day, you discovered the political party stands, Welsh agencies and pressure groups. And you spent hours talking to the Welsh Language Foundation, the Welsh Assembly, Menter y Iaith, and Cymuned. Then I would see Dewi going by with his Gwrthsafiad mates, scowling at me.

And the invitations! By the end of the week you had bought a barbecue and made our tent a place for everyone who was anyone to come in the evenings for Welsh beer and whiskey, Welsh Black steaks and chat.

You didn't ask me. And you didn't think once about people I might want to see. I knew that Dewi wouldn't come.

But, for all the embarrassment I felt, Jon Bull, I still adored you. You were still that god I had first seen naked at my waterfall.

At night, we lay together in separate sleeping bags. And more than once I wished that I could properly be yours. Wished that I could be woman enough to be the companion you needed and the woman you craved, instead of the stupid girl who felt embarrassed by your difference and your earnestness and awkward at my own traumas and fears.

You didn't pester me. Once I'd made it clear we would sleep alone, you just accepted it, and seemed to put it out of your mind. How I wished you understood me better! And I understood you better. Wished that you were a simpler sort of man, like Dewi.

Dad told me once: 'You will know if true love strikes you. It will consume you, drive you. There is no choice when you are truly in love. Luckily for some, it never touches them. You just have to hope that you are one of those.'

I needed you to say it to me. To say you loved me. So I could say it back to you. But all you wanted to talk about, Jon, was the Eisteddfod.

'Culture is all so middle-class in England. In Welsh it is – classless.'

'You're a snob, Jon Bull,' I told you. 'You don't mean to be. But you so completely are.'

That week did wonders for you. You didn't want to be heard talking English so we struggled to talk Welsh together, even alone. You trying to say difficult things, often in a garbled mixture. While I struggled to correct you without overloading you or being a schoolma'am.

'For a land of tair miliwn, with jwst a hanner miliwn Cymraeg speakers, it's anhygoel how much culture yn mynd ymlaen through the medium of Welsh. Bobl English just don't know about it. They have no idea. Dim syniad o gwbl'

'It's not for them, is it? It's for us.'

'Strange though that there is nowhere else apart from this tented village for one week in the summer where people can come to experience all this incredible . . . Y Pethe.'

And you did wonders for me, too. Being with you forced me talk to people and join in things I wouldn't normally have done. You even insisted I enter one of the harp competitions and came to every prelim to watch me. How thrilled you were when I made main stage in the pafiliwn, but I didn't win, of course.

'Probably because I'm not pretty enough,' I said. I'm not sure why.

'You know, Gwalia, you might be right. Your hang-ups about your nose probably affect your confidence more than you think. Let's get it fixed.'

'What do you mean? How?'

'I've told you before. Plastic surgery.'

'I couldn't possibly; it must cost thousands of pounds. I would have to go to some special hospital. I couldn't.'

'You could. Easily. It'll only be a day job. I'll arrange it and pay for everything. Top surgeon. Stay at my home till the swelling goes down. Do you want me to do that for you?'

I hesitated. I remember thinking: 'He must *really* love me'. And that you *did* understand. And you *would* do anything for me.

'Would you like me to have it done?'

'I love you as you are. But I if it would make you feel better about yourself, then you must.'

You'd said it. Said you loved me. A bit casually, but you'd said it. And so generously and kindly. A true knight. At that moment, with you, anything seemed possible.

'For my birthday present?' I asked.

'If you like.'

How could I refuse such an offer?

'Iawn, 'te.'

'Iawn.'

But something inside was warning me: I must be careful how I told Dewi.

I HAD THIS LONGING to be with you, Gwalia. A hiraeth, as you say in Wales. Weekends were great. I wanted to be with you all the time. But, of course, I couldn't be.

Looking back, from where I sit now, it's so very easy for me to be nostalgic for that time. In retrospect, it seems so innocent.

Coming from London, yours was an unspoiled land to me where McDonalds and Starbucks, and *strategies, priorities* and *outputs*, were all, as yet, undiscovered. Your town was uncorrupted even by television. And you were the town's princess. So pure and innocent, despite – or perhaps because of – your own self-doubts. And, like the mountains and valleys of your kingdom, you were kept pure and mysterious by your inaccessibility, your myths, and your frequent, cleansing tears and rain.

If I dreamed that you and I could somehow make a life together, I was too young to question how. I took our love for granted, I suppose. Love makes us a little crazy, we both now know. And I had also fallen crazily in love with Wales – your history, your language and your literature.

'Where,' I remember asking Andrew and Nisha once, probably in that little pavement cafe, off Victoria Street, where we used to go to. 'Where would you find a town built entirely on a fiction?'

Andrew sighed.

'Jerusalem? Lourdes? . . .' He offered facetiously.

Andrew was impatient with me. He saw my learning of ten new Welsh words a day as totally irrational. ("Why not learn something useful like Polish or Chinese?") 'Nope. Not Jerusalem or Lourdes.'

'Well they are,' Andrew argued. 'Religious fiction. Medical fiction.'

'Sorry, wrong track.'

'OK, then,' Nisha tried. 'the Brontës' Haworth, Dickens's London. Are we getting warm?'

'Warmer. But still wrong. I'll put you out of your misery: Beddgelert in North Wales. And it's about a dog.'

'Wales! You're getting obsessed with the place!'

'He's in love,' said Nisha, flashing her perfect teeth.

'No, listen. I was reading this last night. In early Victorian times, when railways brought the countryside within travelling distance of towns and tourism was starting to take off. Right? This man in Beddgelert created a brand new myth to bring tourists to the town.'

'Where?' asked Andrew.

'Never mind where. The myth is what's important. Want to hear it?'

'I think he is going to tell us a story.' Nisha clapped her hands. 'My Gujarati grandmother used to tell us stories back in India.'

'Tell us a story, then, mah boy.' Andrew would have preferred an intense discussion about social iniquities and the politics of eradicating them.

'A prince goes hunting – yes? – and leaves his baby boy in the care of his trusty hound called Gelert. When he returns home, he sees blood and chaos everywhere. The cot is overturned, and the jaws of Gelert are dripping with blood and gore. And Gelert comes to him, with sad, sad eyes.'

'Another bad error by social workers,' Andrew scoffed.

'Shhh!' Nisha scolded him. 'It's a story.'

'Anyway. The Prince immediately sees that the dog has killed the baby. So he takes his hunting knife and kills Gelert, his trusty hound, in a single stroke.'

'Instant justice then,' says Andrew.

'Only when Gelert is dead does he hear a cry from under the overturned cot. He turns it over and finds the baby safe. And next to him is the body of a wolf.'

I turned to Nisha. Nisha was a woman. Nisha understood.

"So . . . the dog was covered in blood because he killed the wolf?'

'Exactly. And the prince realised this. And he felt so distraught and guilty for killing his brave and loyal hound, and treating him so unfairly for saving his son's life. So he built a grave for him. And, every year, thousands of tourists still visit Beddgelert to this day and walk to the grave – Bedd means grave, by the way – Bedd Gelert, see?'

'That's a lovely story.' Nisha clapped her hands.

'A story of rue,' I said. 'But the most interesting thing is that it's a fiction, made up by a Victorian hotel owner to bring visitors to the town. The grave is empty.'

'Then it's a story of cynical commercial exploitation,' Andrew said triumphantly.

'It is the creation of a myth. Many people believe the story to be true. The interesting question is: why do they want it to be true? This story of a loyal and self-sacrificing friend unjustly punished?'

'So?'

'Don't you see? It chimes so brilliantly with the Welsh character: being misunderstood, being unjustly punished, being wronged. As exemplified in that other more contemporary myth, the unjust flooding of the valley and drowning of the village to create a reservoir.'

Andrew's eyebrows raised.

'Don't you see!' I said. 'The Welsh identify with the underdog. Futility and betrayal are deeply ingrained in the Welsh psyche. This is the price they have paid to preserve their language for hundreds – no, thousands – of years. Especially in Gwalia's secret valley.'

'Brilliant,' said Nisha, 'you are finally getting emotional about something, Jon.'

'Yes, it's worrying,' Andrew said. 'The Jon I know doesn't do emotional. Jon only does logical.'

'So, how do you characterise the personality of the Welsh, then, Jon?' asked Nisha, 'following your recent in depth research into the subject.'

'Well. It's precious, introverted, defensive, hurt, don't you see? That's where the appeal of myths such as Beddgelert come from. The Welsh have several myths of lands being flooded through carelessness or wantonness – which may be based on actual floodings at the end of the ice age ten K BC. There's another myth about someone called Blodeuwedd, a beautiful but unfaithful girl made out of flowers, who tricks her husband so her lover can kill him.'

'An interesting theory,' Andrew said. 'And what do you think has shaped the English national personality?'

'Mixture of things. Post-colonial arrogance and bullying. Ruling classes brutalised by cruel boarding schools. Tendency to be a bit strident and loud-mouthed sometimes. Though there is also a softly-spoken aristocratic side, based on absolute self-confidence and unassailable power and authority. All of which we are trying to escape.'

'You are totally forgetting multiculturalism,' Nisha exclaimed. 'Look at us! The new Britons. Every colour and creed, mostly laughing and joking and arguing together. Carrying our old cultural personalities proudly with us.'

'United by consumerism,' Andrew sneered.

'Speaking personally, I'm a citizen of the world,' I said. 'My allegiance is to logic and reason. And making the world a better place. Not to history or a flag.'

'Me too,' said Andrew, suddenly remembering that he worked for one of the top think-tanks in the country.

'And we should never forget how lucky we are to be living in a country which lets us do that and doesn't put us in prison or into a gas chamber or shoot us for being different or questioning things,' Nisha said.

And we had no answer to that.

'Let's raise a toast to being British,' she proposed, raising her wine.

'Yes,' said Andrew. 'Whatever that might mean.'

We chinked our glasses together.

It didn't occur to me at that time, Gwalia, but it seems so clear now, looking back: the problem wasn't that you and I came from different backgrounds but that we had different ideologies. I wanted the world to leave its history and cultural baggage behind and start afresh, free of all past bitterness, resentment and distrust. You seemed destined only to drown yourself in yours.

And that, of course, was bound to lead to trouble.

EVERYTHING was wonderful. By now all the grants were in place for the improvements of Y Ddwy Ddraig. Boudiccea was hopeful that her revised plan for bringing power to the town would succeed this time. And I was in love. Not just with you, Jon, and Awena, but with life.

There was so much to do and organise.

Clearing out the rooms at Y Ddwy Ddraig, putting everything in storage. We would seal off the bar and keep that open till the rest was done, and then when that was open, move the bar across. It wasn't just new roofs and windows, *everything* was going to be redone. There would be a new restaurant and kitchens, *en suite* bedrooms with straight walls and ceilings that didn't sag and have leaks and water stains. And the floors and squeaky floorboards would all be sanded and varnished and made like new.

Even the dragons and the front steps were going to be smartened up. And Dad and Mam were so proud of me. It didn't occur to me for a moment that all of it could come crashing down in a season.

My life was so exciting. I loved it. Working on the costings, getting all the estimates, meeting the planning and building regulation people. And putting lots that I had learned on my business course into practice. I had such plans.

Once Boudiccea had sorted out the grants and planning problems (just as we had done for Y Ddwy Ddraig) the whole town would be revived.

It was an optimistic time.

That tingle when I thought of you. The joy of your letters and little gifts between visits, not just for me but also for Awena, and never less than twice a week. And, strangely, things like – I don't know, just greeting the postman together – had created a new mother-daughter bond between us.

Then, one day (I think I was arranging your latest bunch of flowers), completely out of the blue, Boudiccea came in to see me.

She smiled and said hello, then suddenly her face just crumpled and she burst out crying.

'I'm so sorry, Gwalia. You have to help me, I don't know who to turn to.'

So I took her through to my temporary office behind the dining room and asked Branwen to bring tea.

'What is it? What has happened?' I asked her in Welsh, out of respect for all the efforts she had made to learn it.

'It's very dreadful. It's not so fair, isn't it. They have been forcing me to retire myself. After all I have been doing for the town and all my big efforts. And it is discovering itself like this.'

I couldn't understand what she was talking about. She looked defeated.

'Tell me slowly,' I said in English. 'You've had to resign? Is that it?'

'They've accused me of being discriminatory,' she said resorting to English. 'Told me we could be taken to an industrial tribunal. And then Hiraethog phoned me up and told me I should resign. He didn't even have the courage to tell me to my face.'

She burst out sobbing again and sat there, tears running down her cheeks, a far cry from the noble kingfisher swooping around the Maes in her Lycra, on her tandem.

I put my arm around her.

'Diolch yn fawr, Gwalia. Ti'n glên iawn i mi.'

I passed her the cup of tea and it rattled on the saucer in her shaking hand.

'I can't believe it,' she said, 'I've never been discriminatory to anyone. I've spent my whole life campaigning for people's rights against discrimination.'

'I still don't understand,' I said gently.

She pulled herself together.

'Blodeuwedd came to see me. "You have to sign this," she told me. So I asked her what it was. (You know how surly and uncommunicative she is; she wouldn't have got the job if she hadn't been Penhaearn's niece and he hadn't insisted. I've tried to help her, train her. I've been like a mother to her. Done most of her work for her.)'

I took her empty cup. I still didn't understand.

'She handed me this document. And told me I had to sign it.'

'What was it?'

'That's exactly what I asked her. Her report on Antur Deg's work over the last six months and her plans for the next six months.'

'So what was wrong with that?'

'I had just started to sign it when I read it and realised it was all wrong. These were new plans that hadn't been approved by the committee. So I crossed out my signature and tried to explain why. So then she started to shout at me. She told me I had to sign it. And I refused. Obviously.'

'Was that it?' It seemed a lot of trouble over signing some form.

'No it wasn't. She went straight round to Penhaearn and complained about me. He signed the papers then wrote me a letter telling me he was taking over forthwith and I should absent myself until further notice. He had no right at all to do that. I was elected.'

She sobbed.

I shook my head.

'That's what Penhaearn's like,' I said. 'But I'm sure we can sort it out.'

'It's too late now. I've resigned.'

She sobbed again.

I didn't know what to say. There was no one else in the town who could do what Boudiccea had done.

'I feel drained, Gwalia. Completely drained. I've worked so hard to make things better. None of it for myself. I've tried to learn Welsh. Worked days and nights. I sometimes think I'm the only person that wants to make this town a better place. Not even my husband really supports me. Caught between the Welsh and the English.'

'Shall I talk to him?'

'It's too late, Gwalia. Really it is.'

She dabbed her eyes.

'I feel so cross. I did practically everything. All voluntarily. And this is the thanks I get. I asked not a penny for any of it. And there she is, getting a good salary, for my work! And her uncle Penhaearn raking in thousands in County Councillor's allowances, doing nothing for the town except to raise objections and frustrate every plan I try to come up with. While the town goes to wrack and to ruin around him. I don't think you have any idea, Gwalia, have you?'

I had only the vaguest notion of what she meant. We all knew what Penhaearn was like.

'You're sure you do really want to resign? I'm sure it's not too late to change your mind.'

Perhaps we'd been too trusting. 'I'm sorry,' I said. 'Maybe after a break you'll come back to it. We'll miss you if you don't.'

'But the town doesn't really want power, does it?'

'I think we do,' I said brightly.

'Penhaearn has no idea how much damage he is doing by pushing me out,' she sighed. 'I've done all I can for this town Gwalia, really I have.'

I still thought she was talking about water and electricity which the women of the town certainly wanted. I remember wondering if perhaps we had been a bit naive in just assuming that it would all turn out for the best, and thinking that without Boudiccea there would be no one to make it happen.

And then she said: 'He and the English will have to battle it out for themselves, now, won't they? And my guess is, he'll lose.'

That got me thinking.

And do you remember what you told me, Jon, when I told you this?

'Ah,' you said. 'The myths of Beddgelert and Blodeuwedd.'

Anti Gwenlais was full of it.

Unfortunately, Mam wasn't there so I had to listen to her clecs alone.

'She had it coming. That Boudiccea woman. Full of it she was. Pushing her weight around – well, you know what the English are like! I'm not surprised she's had her comedown.'

'Poor Lawns,' she went on. 'I don't know how he copes with her. Such a handful. Such a liability. Still, that's what you deserve if you get your wife from the small ads. I don't know what possessed him. As if we don't have enough good single women in Llanchwaraetegdanygelyn.'

Within a week, Penhaearn had appointed himself chairman of Antur Deg and Gwenlais as his deputy.

The trip to Liverpool caused an instant scandal.

'Did you see Hiraethog? In his best suit and with his Mayoral Chain around his neck, half strangling him?' Anti Gwenlais bustled in, bursting to tell us.

'No Anti, as it happens, I was busy at Y Ddwy Ddraig, minding my own business.'

'Well I went. As a representative of the Council. It's my job to keep an eye on Hiraethog, and I'm Deputy Chair of Antur Deg now, so I could hardly refuse, could I?'

'I suppose not, Anti.'

'I couldn't believe my eyes when those boys, Huw Môr and Dedai, arrived to fetch us in that big white car.'

'I think they call it a stretch limo, Anti Gwenlais.'

'Stretch! It was enormous. Why anyone would be wanting to draw so much attention to themselves, I can't imagine. Anyway, at midday on the dot, it was. I know the whole story,' she twted.

'And Penhaearn isn't best pleased. I can tell you that much. Fancy Hiraethog taking it on himself to even think of doing such a thing on his own. Going to Liverpool for an important business deal for the brothers regarding the factory.'

She paused to savour the effect that she imagined this sensational news would have on me.

'Good job you were there, then, Anti,' I said, but the irony was lost on her.

Actually, I had already heard three other versions of the story. Scandal travels very fast in Llanchwaraetegdanygelyn. And every tongue that carries clecs will turn the tale.

'Well! Bold as brass. And in a huge white car like that with smoked glass windows and a hatch in the top.'

'Sun roof, Anti Gwenlais.'

'You are wrong there, Gwalia, it was a hatch. I saw it with my own eyes, the whole thing of it. Huw Môr and Dedai in the front. Wearing suits and dark glasses. Even though it wasn't sunny. And that girl Trêsi in the back of that . . . what did you call it?'

'Stretch limo.'

'That's it. It stretched my belief, Gwalia, I can tell you. Attracted quite a little crowd it did. After all, it isn't every day you see a man from Llanchwaraetegdanygelyn in a car like that. Did you see it?'

'No Anti Gwenlais. I was busy supervising the building work at Y Ddwy Ddraig.'

'You should have seen the inside! White leather seats. All polished wood, with gold handles. But you can't stand up in them you know. Not that it was real gold of course.

'And that girl. Spread out across the leather in the skimpiest red dress you ever did see. And the skimpiest knickers to match. Well! She might as well have not been wearing anything at all. Hiraethog couldn't take his eyes off her.

'And a cocktail cabinet! Stuffed with drink it was. And a bottle of champagne already open, and three glasses poured. I was offered one, but I declined, of course. Like your Mam – and all our family going back to the Diwygiad – I've always been teetotal, and never succumbed.'

I winced only slightly at this (a sign of your good

influence, Jon) but I don't think she had meant to remind me of my own trauma and the part alcohol played in it.

'And imagine this in a car, Gwalia – two televisions. One showing girls with next to nothing on, dancing most provocatively to thumpy music. And another with some kind of film called *Grand Auto Theft* with soldiers on it firing guns. Just between the two of us, I think she might be a little simple.'

'Probably a game console, Anti Gwenlais. Did it have control units? Wires?'

'I don't know what it had, Gwalia. But I didn't notice a Bible.'

She scrutinised me carefully then, for signs that I too was an errant soul. Then, finding none, she carried on.

'Anyway, off we went. Huw Môr and Dedai in the front, in their dark glasses. Hiraethog, me and that girl in her skimpy red dress, in the back. And did you see Hiraethog and Trêsi hanging out of the hatch, glasses of champagne in their hands?'

She paused for me to twt, but I am not my mother and I am far too young to twt.

'Was there any mention of where you were going?' I asked.

'Certainly not. That was confidential, the brothers said. I made a mental note of everything, though, for your Yncl Penhaearn.'

'You know where it was you went to, then?'

'Oh yes, I know exactly. It was somewhere in Liverpool, but we didn't know that beforehand.

'I think that Trêsi wanted to get us drunk. You know how she speaks: "Ere, you want a top up or somefing, Hero? I gotta whole bottle 'ere."'

'That's brilliant, Anti Gwenlais. You do an excellent cockney accent.'

'Thank you, cariad. I used to be very good at drama in my younger days. Anyway, he said "Dim diolch." But I could see he liked her calling him Hero.

'"Go on," she told him. "We got everyfing 'ere – whisky,

gin, vodka, Welsh beer." So he had to give in then, didn't he, poor man. "Dim ond tipyn bach, 'te. Diolch." He told her.

'"Isn't this all a little dros ben llestri?" I asked them. "Oh no, mayors in cities all have big, official cars," she said. "Think of it as a reward for all your hard work for the town." Then we arrived.

'First class restaurant it was, Liverpool football players go there you know,' Huw Môr said. We were introduced to Mr Li Po and his brothers. They're the family who supply the factory in Llanchwaraetegdanygelyn, you know.'

'Weren't you a bit shy, Anti. In all that company?'

'Well, I wasn't, Gwalia. But Hiraethog was. He looked very scared. "I wish I was back home in Llanchwaraetegdanygelyn," he told me. "Or better still Dan Gelyn." But they gave him lots of wine and he became quite talkative then.

'Then this Chinese woman – Tzu – came and sat next to him. Trêsi was ogling a party of men on the next table. "Recognise them, Hero?" she said. "That's the Anfield Junior team, that is. Aint they handsome?"

'Hiraethog's mouth was full, he could only nod. And then he started to choke a little, so Tzu patted him on the back. She thought that was very funny. She was nice. I don't think Hiraethog had had Chinese food before. Neither of us could use the chopsticks. But Tzu showed him how. She was very patient with him. Her hands looked so dainty cupped around his clumsy calloused things. I just took a knife and fork.

'"You good with tools, Hero," she told him. "Big strong Hero." We all laughed at that. So she let him discard the chopsticks then and use a serving spoon. He was starving, poor man.'

'It was a good meal, then, Anti Gwenlais?'

'Oh yes. But I kept a mental note of everything. So many different flavours; a little rich for my taste, though, to be honest. God knows what we were eating. It might have been rats, cats and sprats for all I know. You couldn't tell what it was.

'Anyway Trêsi was very busy with the Chinese businessmen. Pouting and flirting. And Hiraethog was left to talk to Tzu. I think he found it easier than talking to the businessmen. I expect he was nervous in case he said something he shouldn't.'

'So what was the big important thing that you had to discuss for the town?'

'I don't really know, Gwalia. I expect that was what the brothers and the businessmen were talking about. I only heard what Tzu and Hiraethog said. She was very polite and attentive. She kept his glass well-filled.

'"I expect you are having to chair lots of meetings, Mr Hero," she said.

'"Oh yes, we had a meeting only last week."

'I think he was flattered by someone asking his opinion about something other than hedges and JCBs. She asked about Antur Deg, and about that project, you know, the one that Jon of yours prepared.

'Hiraethog was very good, fair play to him. He answered all her questions. He told me afterwards, he was practising for when he would probably have to say it all again to the businessmen.

'She asked a lot about Antur Deg. "Oh yes," he explained, "That's our community development group. With an officer. Full time."

'"And you like the sweet and sour, Hero?"

'"Oh Yes, the sweet and sour is very nice."

'"And you are very excitingly bringing electricity to Umbo?"

'"Yes. We are very excitingly bringing electricity to Llanchwaraetegdanygelyn. Yes. Umbo as you call it."

'But that wasn't true, Anti Gwenlais. Penhaearn blocked the plans. Didn't you tell them that?'

'I was there strictly as an observer, Gwalia, I quite disapproved of Hiraethog discussing all our business with some strange woman. I was ashamed of him. His face and shirt were covered in sticky red sauce. He's a pig of an eater, I don't know how poor Dwynwen tolerates him. Tzu had to show him how to use the finger bowl. She leaned very close to him.

'"Are you sure the project would be passed by the planning committee? And is it right that your brother-in-law, Mr Jones, is chairman of the planning committee?" Hiraethog was a bit stuck then, but Dedai was cocking an ear and heard so he leaned over and said. "It's just a formality, isn't it Hero," and Hiraethog had his mouth full and just nodded. "That's right. Just a formality now," Huw Môr said.

'But she wanted to hear it from Hiraethog, the man in the Mayoral Chain. So she asked him: "Is that right?"'

'He looked at me and looked at the brothers. "Yes," he said. "That's right." And Mrs Tzu shook him by the hand and then shook the brothers by the hand. And everyone was nodding and smiling.

'And then suddenly it was over.'

'What do you mean – over?'

'Over. The Chinese all got up and left.

'And we were all left sitting there – Hiraethog's oafish face, fat fingers and shirt all covered in the sticky red gore from the spare ribs – all on our own, if you please.'

She twted. And sighed.

And lent forward for the denouement.

'It was only driving back, that it dawned on us. This Mrs Tzu had been the boss.'

I knew the rest of the story, Jon. I had seen Penhaearn and Dwynwen, their faces like thunderclouds, standing outside Y Ddwy Ddraig, and had gone out to see what was going on. It was strange to see her without a microphone or film crew.

The delegation was arriving back at the Maes in the stretch limo. Huw Môr and Dedai in the front, the others in the back: Anti Gwenlais sitting very straight straight-faced, staring straight ahead, Hiraethog and Trêsi looking rather drunk and dishevelled.

Huw Môr and Dedai leapt out first.

'You got our press release, then,' Huw Môr said to Dwynwen. 'Triumphal return and all that.' He looked around. 'Where's the camera crew?'

'There is no film crew,' Dwynwen said. 'We've come to talk to him.'

She jabbed her finger at her husband.

'Who – Hero?' asked Trêsi, still clutching a bottle of Champagne and linking her arm through his.

'He is no Hero of mine. I can assure you of that.'

Hiraethog, red and messy, blinked at her, still smiling benignly.

Dwynwen put her face very close to his.

'What,' she shouted in Welsh. 'Do you have to say for yourself, Mr Mayor?'

'Ere, I hope you don't fink I bin up to nuffink with Hero nor nuffink,' Trêsi said.

Dwynwen pushed her aside.

'Look at you, Hiraethog. Look at the state of you.'

A small crowd was gathering by now. Word had spread to the Supermart. They pressed around the car, cocking their ears shamelessly. I saw the door of Caffi Cyfoes open and another group emerging.

'Have you been with the Chinese, Hiraethog?' Penhaearn demanded.

'I have,' said Hiraethog, proudly. 'I've been helping the town.'

'No,' said Penhaearn. 'You are a corrupt and stupid man. You have sold this town out to the Chinese. That is what you have done.'

'Now just a minute . . .' Huw Môr said, and took a step forward.

Penhaearn held up his hand.

There were perhaps two dozen onlookers now, with more

arriving every moment. There were women running across the Maes. Women who hadn't run for years.

Penhaearn stood his ground, drinking in the intoxication of an audience. His moment was coming. There would be many more like this. A descendant of the ancient princes of Gwynedd, he could see the mess of his stepbrother-in-law standing before him. A futile man, a man he no longer needed.

When he had the silence of the crowd, Penhaearn raised his hand and turned to Hiraethog.

'You are a complete disgrace,' he thundered in oratorical mode. 'Look at you.'

Hiraethog did as he was told. Looked down at himself and, for the first time, noticed the spare rib stains and fried rice droppings on his shirt and suit, and the oyster sauce coagulated on the Mayoral Chain. He brushed at them ineffectually with his awkward, calloused fingers.

'I don't think you will be needing that any more, do you?' said Penhaearn with the calm of a prince who is about to become King.

Hiraethog miserably shook his head and looked around for support. He looked at Dwynwen. He looked at the crowd. All eyes avoided his.

He looked back imploringly at his wife and opened his mouth to speak.

'Don't you look to me for support,' she scolded. 'You have brought this on yourself. You will be sleeping in another bed tonight.'

''Ere, you're not still thinking...' Only Trêsi saw the injustice and spoke up for him. Penhaearn's hand went up again and silenced her.

But only for a moment. She dropped the champagne bottle and turned to Hiraethog.

'Don't you let 'em do this to you, Hero. It ain't fair.'

She turned to Huw Môr and Dedai.

Huw Môr shrugged.

'You may hand your chain of office to me now,' said Penhaearn. He stretched his palm out, and kept it there while Hiraethog fumbled with the clasp, took off the chain and laid it over Penhaearn's hand.

Then he turned and walked away in the direction of the Council shed where he kept his Jac Codi Baw and his yellow jacket, shoulders slumped.

'I think you're all horrible,' said Trêsi. And she would probably have gone after him but Dedai stopped her.

'Let them make idiots of themselves,' he said.

I spoke to you on the phone that night. I told you all about it. Local gossip. But sensational. The Chinese had bought the factory.

You sounded worried.

'Let me check up on this,' you said. 'I have a funny feeling about this.'

You wouldn't say more.

The following lunchtime you rang me again.

'As I suspected,' you told me. 'It wasn't Hiraethog's fault. The Chinese already own more than half the business. After Hiraethog's chat with Mrs Tzu, they had agreed to go on supporting the factory in Llanchwaraetegdanygelyn, despite the outcome of the public meeting. And despite its losses.'

'What do you mean?' I asked.

'We had a call from Mrs Tzu yesterday. She wanted a copy of my report.'

'Why didn't you tell me?'

'I didn't know before. I phoned her back this morning and got the whole story.'

'But Anti Gwenlais said the brothers assured them the project to bring in mains electricity would be going ahead. And that is a lie, isn't it?'

'That's your Anti Gwenlais's version.'

'Ahhh.'

'The town may not appreciate it, but without Hiraethog's

intervention the factory would have closed straight away. Inadvertently, he may have bought some time. With no jobs, your town will be finished. And how long do you think it would be before all the houses go up for sale. And all the shops close?'

The enormity of what you were saying swept over me.

'It will close the town?'

'Exactly. You'd better just hope that Mrs Tzu doesn't change her mind.'

'Yes,' said Gwenlais, talking loudly enough to attract a small crowd outside the Supermart. 'Hiraethog's left Dwynwen, he's living at Jean and Billi-Jo's for spiritual guidance.'

She was getting very good audiences since her trip to Liverpool.

'She has more ears than an oracle,' said Dai Call.

'She labours tirelessly for us all,' said Elwyn. 'In her way.'

'I fear her good intentions propel her only to hell,' said Irfon, putting his fingertips together in prayer.

'Poor oaf,' Gwenlais told her audience. 'He needs more than spiritual guidance, I can tell you.'

'I feel sorry for him,' someone said.

'He has only himself to blame,' pronounced Anti Gwenlais.

News of Hiraethog's demise as Mayor reached the Chinese quickly. Mrs Tzu herself came to Llanchwaraetegdanygelyn but Hiraethog was too upset or embarrassed to see her.

After less than five minutes talking to Penhaearn Tegid Foel, she left.

It was announced that they would close the factory the following day.

The town went numb.

Penhaearn knew now, quite nicely, that he had made a mistake in taking the Mayoral Chain from Hiraethog's neck. But men who believe that they are guided by the providence of long dead souls do not attach much significance to such small setbacks.

He stopped me in the street the following day.

'You must join me in my struggle,' he told me. 'Help me strengthen our community and ensure that our Welsh way of life is not made vulnerable again.'

'Has Mrs Leakin really resigned?' I asked.

'That ridiculous woman. We have learned our lesson now in allowing her type to come into this town thinking they can impose their English will upon us.'

He looked like a man possessed.

'We must be strong. It is the time for us to be firm. We are the last stronghold of our ancient way of life. The only town left in Wales where everything is still done through the medium of Welsh. Every other town and village has weakened and been seduced by compromise. We must fight on.'

Other people had started to listen now.

'Not quite everything . . .' I started to say.

'Yes – everything,' he thundered. 'We have been weak. We have been foolish and far too understanding in our liberalism.'

Someone in the crowd shouted their agreement: 'We cannot let Llanchwaraetegdanygelyn go the way of every other town in Wales.'

People were nodding and murmuring.

'We are not going to be taken over by the English. We will protect our values and our language. We have been too soft for too long. Now we will be strong.'

He raised himself to his full height.

'As long as this town is mine, I will not let it slip from our fingers into the clutches of the English. Let alone the Chinese. This is where we hold the line,' he said. 'Our moment has come. Now the tide will turn.'

He received a round of applause for that.

At the very next Council Meeting, Penhaearn donned the Mayoral Chain himself. Penhaearn Tegid Foel. County Councillor of the Migneint. Mayor of Llanchwaraeteg-danygelyn, Chairman of Antur Deg. Heir to the Crown of Llywelyn.

Now he had rid himself of Boudiccea and Hiraethog, he was ruler of his world.

Thank goodness I had already arranged to go to London. The work at Y Ddwy Ddraig was nearly finished, with only the bar and reception area still to do. Dad would keep an eye on things while I was gone. And Dewi was there to help. I don't know what I would have done without him.

AH, YES, the myths of Beddgelert and Blodeuwedd – not bad metaphors for the woes of human nature that kick in during microeconomic recession: the blame starts, people jump ship, and then – sometimes – all hell breaks loose. Llanchwaraeteg-danygelyn was now well into that decline.

Speaking to Mrs Tzu only confirmed what I already knew: unless mains services arrived, the factory would be forced to close. It had suited her for a while to have a foothold in Britain, supporting the brothers, but production in China would be cheaper. A factory without mains services or a vibrant labour force was not viable.

As I had tried to warn you, Gwalia, your town had been teetering on the brink of recession for many years. If it wasn't obvious from the closed shops and the dated window displays with stock that never shifted, it was obvious in the people: like many other rural towns, yours was a community with an aging population, a hinterland of struggling hill-farmers and only one factory. The failed initiative that I was involved in might well have been its last chance.

Llanchwaraetegdanygelyn was a town to leave. Smart people had known that for years, which was why there were so few of them left.

How could I tell you that? You were so excited by the redevelopment of Y Ddwy Ddraig, Gwalia, and your own recovery, and you felt so optimistic about everything that no one who loved you would have wanted to spoil that. Besides, I know how hard people always find it to imagine that their communities are doomed. I see it all over Europe: old market towns like yours, former coal-mining towns – anywhere where the reason for their existence is no longer valid.

I'd already made my decision: I had to get you and Awena out of there. The prospect of you spending your whole life there, gradually turning into your mother, or Aunty Gwenlais, was too horrific to contemplate.

I'd booked your appointment with the plastic surgeon: a consultation, followed by a simple day-case operation two days later, provided you agreed. Then you would be at home with me for three weeks while the swelling and bruising went down.

I would spoil you rotten. I would keep you so busy you wouldn't have time to worry about it. And then, when you were better, I would take you away for the most romantic holiday of your life – of anybody's life. Double beds all the way. We would be a proper couple then. And you would want to live with me forever and marry me.

I talked it over with Nisha and Andrew.

'Well, if that's what you want, then that's the way to do it. Show her the big wide world, blow her mind,' Andrew said.

'I wish someone would do that for me,' Nisha looked meaningfully at Andrew but he wasn't noticing.

'Where hasn't she been,' he asked. 'Paris, Venice, Athens?'

'She's barely been out of her narrow valley.'

'There you are then. You could propose to her on top of the Eiffel Tower.'

'I can't wait to meet her,' Nisha said.

By the time you arrived in London, I had booked the holiday and organised your entire stay. You were going to be so happy at all my spoils and surprises, you wouldn't even have time to think about yourself.

Your train was half an hour late. I was so beside myself with excitement I walked down the platform to meet you a few precious moments sooner, then stood on tiptoe trying to spot you among the rush and jostle, worrying I had missed you.

Then there you were, smaller than you should have been, standing in front of me laughing, tossing your hair and shrugging your shoulders, charming me with that crease in the corner of your mouth when you smiled. Such joy!

I swept you up in my arms, lifting your feet from the ground, owning you, my mouth searching out yours, finding the soft skin of your face. The taste and smell and wonder of you filled my being, and left my heart singing.

Never mind the curse of Llanchwaraetegdanygelyn, I was going to awaken you with my princely kisses and rescue you from your lonely fate before your castle was overgrown by brambles and weeds. I would whisk you away to the most romantic place I could think of, make perfect love to you, and then we would marry and live happily ever after.

Ah, the power of fairy stories!

YOU HAD no idea, Jon, how scary it was for me, coming to London, leaving Awena and my family behind. They all cried, especially Awena. Even Dad was worried for me, what with all those bombings and knifings and gun crimes always in the news. And God knows what Mam and Anti Gwenlais imagined might happen to me staying with a black family, though they were careful not to say anything directly about *that*.

I think I was more terrified of being in London than having the operation. I felt like a frightened rabbit, wide-eyed and nervous of everything – all that noise, so many strangers. It was as if I knew something bad was going to happen.

Do you remember in the station, how I screamed at that train of baggage trolleys, driven by those two heavily-bearded Sikhs with turbans, because I thought they were terrorists? And how the police reacted? Raising their guns. And looking around. Their fingers ominously on their triggers. You were used to seeing policemen with automatic guns and flak jackets and truncheons and everything but they terrified me.

'It's all right,' you said. 'There's been another bomb scare. We're on high terrorist alert again. It was on the news.'

'I don't like news.' I said. And I meant it. 'It's always horrible.'

If I wasn't scared enough about the operation, and meeting your parents, you were overwhelming. You behaved like a different person in London, as if you owned me, talking non-stop about *our* itinerary, how we were going to do *this* and *that*. And it was all arranged. I hardly had time to think.

You took me straight to Harley Street by taxi, your arm around me all the way. You'd organised everything.

'Have you brought your passport as I told you?' you asked.

'Yes.' I had assumed it was something to do with the operation.

You wanted to come in with me to see the consultant, but I wouldn't let you. I was worried I might want to change my mind and wouldn't be able to with you squeezing my hand and controlling me. It surprised me to find that the consultant was Turkish, I don't know what I expected. 'It'll be not much different from going to the dentist's,' he tried to reassure me. And the nurse, who looked Chinese, smiled sweetly.

Nervously, I signed the papers to be operated on in two days, feeling almost helpless, wishing my Dad was there. What on earth I was doing? Now everything was out of my control.

'No one's going to make you do anything you don't want to do,' you grinned as we taxied off, your arm back around me. You were so attentive, asking about Y Ddwy Ddraig, and about Awena. So eager for me to meet your parents, so proud of me.

I reminded myself I had promised to phone at six; having no phone at home, we'd arranged for Mam and Dad and Gethin to all traipse across to Y Ddwy Ddraig with Awena.

I couldn't believe the place where your parents lived. I thought only film stars and millionaires lived in penthouses, but, of course, there is one on practically every building in London.

'I'm afraid it's a bit minimalist,' you warned me in the lift. 'Perhaps slightly more than a bit.'

The walls, tables – everything – were white, including the leather sofas. I felt as if I made the place untidy just by being there. Do you remember how I tried to brush away the footprints my trainers left in the carpet pile? I felt so shabby.

And that forty-mile view from the patio across London! In Wales you have to climb mountains to get views like that. Even the television was hidden away. It somehow appeared from the wall when you pressed a button. No S4C though.

And I could not believe your arrangement with the Italian restaurant downstairs.

'You mean you just phone up and they bring it up for you? Whatever you ask?'

'Phone *down* actually. You can order anything you like,' your Dad smiled proudly, delighted to have someone new to impress. (I could see where you got your charm from.) 'Me and Giocomo have an understanding.'

And just to prove it, he phoned down for tea and cakes straight away.

'Anything from a cup of tea to lobster thermidor – seven in the morning to one in the morning – order whatever you like. You make yourself at home here, Gwalia. And don't forget to ring them to collect the dirty dishes.'

Apparently your Dad owned the building.

'And a maid comes in for two hours each morning,' your mother told me, showing me my room. 'So don't bother to make your bed. I never even cook a slice of toast, or wash a dish or clear a plate. I'm free to be a multi-tasking wife and mother and business woman – truly liberated.'

The neatness and cleanness was almost shocking. Everything, even the clothes you wore, looked utterly brand new. I knew nothing of designer labels then, but I knew your Mum's clothes were not from the kinds of shop my family went to.

'We want you to feel totally at home here,' your Dad emphasised. 'Anything you want, just pick up the phone, dial 7 and order anything you like. Anytime.'

'I can't do something like that,' I whispered to you. 'I'm not used to behaving rich.'

'We're not rich,' you all laughed. 'You should see the private estates outside London with their helicopter pads.' I must have looked sceptical.

'I can show you the scatter graphs of income distribution if you like,' you told me. 'We're nowhere near the top, I assure you.'

'But I bet I'm near the bottom, though.'

You didn't answer that. I know you have poor people in London, and people who live on the streets, but what I saw on that visit was the wealth, expensive flats and penthouses and big cars, wherever I looked. It hadn't occurred to me before how poor we were in Wales.

Then I remembered about phoning Y Ddwy Ddraig.

Too late! Dewi said, they'd just left.

'Ydy popeth yn iawn?' he asked.

'Dw i'n iawn,' I told him, feeling cross with myself for missing them but glad to be talking my own language. 'Mae'r llawdriniaeth drennydd. It's very weird. I'm in a penthouse with a forty-mile view of London.'

'Have you got your own room?' He had sensed my mood and wanted to cheer me up.

'Oes.'

'Aren't you worried about the operation?'

Yes, I was. I was terrified.

'Ydw. Dw i yn. Gobeithio bod gen i enough courage to go through with it,' I told him. 'I have to for Jon's sake. He's been so kind and generous and lovely.'

Dewi snorted at that. 'You'll be fine,' he told me. 'And even if you decide not to go through with it, that's fine, too. I'll love you just the same.'

It felt good to be talking to Dewi. He knew me, understood me.

We talked for a while and when I finally hung up, I felt a long way from home.

'Everything OK? you asked back in the perfect lounge. 'Did you talk to everyone?'

'Yes,' I said, then realised I had lied. And felt guilty. Why had I lied?

You smiled. 'Did I mention that I've taken three weeks off, to be with you the whole time? The operation will only take a couple of hours. The rest of your time here is recuperation and holiday. I am going to give you a time you'll never forget.'

The next day you insisted on taking me to your office, near the Houses of Parliament. I'd never been in a place like it. Full of important-looking people, and everyone so clever. You showed me the Hub with its bank of video screens and explained why it looked like a circus ring. That was when I first met Nisha, at the control panel.

She looked devastating in a red and green sari with a gold edge and smiled and kissed me on the cheek and smoothly complimented me on how pretty I was. And there was me, flustered and tongue-tied in my trainers, frayed jeans and an old white blouse.

Andrew came over and shook my hand and said something to you using some word like epidemiology, which I didn't understand, and I was thinking 'What am I doing here with all these important and clever people when I've hardly passed an exam in my life?'

'I understand you have a daughter,' Nisha smiled. 'What's her name? Have you got a picture of her?'

I did, of course.

There was a long discussion about where to go that evening: a concert, or the theatre, or an art gallery?

'Where would you like to go, Gwalia, while you're in London? Any shows you want to see? Any theatre or ballets or anything?' And they all turned to look at me. But I shook my head. I hadn't even thought about it.

'There must me something.'

My mind was a blank. And in that moment it dawned on me just how stupid and ignorant and uncultured I was. I knew a little about art and poetry in Wales, but I didn't even know what was on here.

'Besides all of you, I feel like a joskin,' I blurted. And then blushed as I realised I'd used a Welsh word. 'Sorry – peasant.'

Nisha laughed.

'You should see the Indian village my family comes from. They are all joskins there. They tried to marry me to one but I ran away and lived with Andrew instead. And even he is a bit of a joskin sometimes.'

We all laughed then.

In the end we went out to a tiny little pub, the Grenadier Inn, in Barrack Mews, up a hidden lane in Knightsbridge. 'Our secret pub,' you called it. 'I bet you wouldn't find it again in a month of Sundays.'

I felt at home there, with the quaint modesty of it, the sentry-box outside and the people. They seemed unpretentious.

'Mae hon yn dafarn neis,' I said to you.

'Ron i'n siŵr faset ti'n think that,' you said and kissed me.

I wasn't allowed to drink because of the operation the following day so I was going to have orange juice. But Andrew told me I should have a special non-alcoholic cocktail.

'We're here to spoil you,' Nisha said.

And, after that, she kept me giggling all evening. I loved her Gujarati accent, but Andrew's Jewish humour seemed very strange.

This time I remembered to ring home so I borrowed your mobile phone and spoke to everyone. They all wished me luck. And Awena said something very sweet: 'Give your nose a kiss from me.'

My spirits lifted at that.

'She's so lovely,' I heard Nisha say to you as I came back.

'Two girls from small villages, you see,' said Andrew. 'Bound to hit it off.'

They raised a toast to you and me, Jon.

And we gave each other a kiss.

Lying on the bed after the operation, you told me I looked beautiful and I burst into tears. I was so relieved it was over. And I had survived. You had been so kind, bringing me to the clinic, staying with me, holding my hand, calming me.

Once the grogginess wore off I felt fine. I wanted to see myself in a mirror but you all said I should wait. And I needed to ring home to tell everyone they could stop worrying. So I rang Dewi.

Then you took me home and put me to bed and I slept.

When I woke next morning, my face felt huge and throbbing. I furtively crept to the mirror and lifted the gauze. The face that looked back at me was disappointingly familiar but so swollen I couldn't tell if my nose looked more or less squashed than before. I looked terrible.

You brought in tea and passion fruit tartlets.

'So? What shall we do today?'

'I don't want to go out. Not until I look better.' It hurt to talk.

From the disappointment on your face, you were more wounded than I was.

I felt so guilty then, so obligated to you. After all you'd done for Y Ddwy Ddraig, paying for my operation, and now spoiling me in ways that I didn't deserve.

I couldn't imagine what you saw in me. We were from different worlds, different races. I felt as if I was deceiving you. I could never begin to cope with the kind of life you lived. I had Awena and you would never come to live in Wales. How could we ever be together? Yet you were so clever and handsome and wonderful. And I was so lucky but undeserving.

I put my arms around you and hugged you. Very carefully, you manoeuvred your face to kiss my mouth so gently we hardly touched. You couldn't possibly have fancied me, the way I looked. You were probably just trying to reassure me, show me that the operation had been a success. I felt such a fraud. I don't know why I said that stupid thing about you just wanting sex.

For the next two days I refused to go out. The second day you were so bored you went to the office and I phoned Dewi again. We talked for a long time. He kept asking questions. 'What did you do today?' 'Where have you been?' 'You still haven't slept with him, have you?' And, finally: 'Gwalia. Don't forget you're going to marry me.'

After the swelling had gone down and my face had gone all the colours of a winter sunset, you tried to kiss me again. It had taken more than a week. I had got to know the Italian waiters from downstairs quite well.

'Jon, 'nghariad i, paid. Please, no,' I pleaded when you tried to caress me. I thought about that a lot: how useless I was to you. How frustrating it must be to have a girlfriend like me.

I imagined you at night lying in your bed alone. Bronwen once said boys think about sex every six minutes. I wondered if you thought about me every six minutes. I doubted it, you'd been such a gentleman.

Now that the bruising had faded, I let you take me to the Tower of London, I knew I would not feel under-dressed or awkward in a place like that. Also, I was curious.

'This was where the head of Llywelyn was brought,' I told you, 'after being paraded through Cheapside. Left to whiten on a pole for fifteen years.'

'Oh yes, Llywelyn,' you said, 'last Prince of Wales – not counting modern ones, of course.'

'The last *real* Prince of Wales. The man who would have been our king. Would have founded a dynasty and made us our own true nation. Betrayed and slain in 1282. By the English.'

'1282? And you're still worrying about that?'

'Yes,' I said, suddenly angry with you.

'Can't you enjoy anything without it being about Wales?'

'Of course I can.'

'No you can't. You refused to go to the Houses of Parliament because it wasn't *your* government. Or to Buckingham Palace because it wasn't *your* Queen. Don't you think you need to move on? And get a life?'

It was our first disagreement.

'I can't wait till Dewi sees me,' I said, looking at my new nose in the mirror the following morning. 'He bet me they'd never be able to fix it.'

You shifted uneasily at the mention of the boy you thought was your rival. So I kissed you properly and felt my desire for you stir as your hands strayed up my tee shirt onto the bare skin of my back.

We fell on the bed and I let myself go, feeling your pent-up love and desire. Your hands cupped my breasts. It was just *too* tantalising. I pulled away. Sex still terrified me. The very idea of being vulnerable to being pushed down, held down, invited

– even gently – to do things that I had been forced to do. How could I ever associate them now with love? Repairing my nose had done nothing for my fears. Men were still the same.

I checked myself. I needed to think of something different.

'Tell me about the rest of your family, Jon. You must have other relations. When do I meet them?'

You shrugged. 'I have a grandfather.'

'Am I going to meet him?'

You pulled a face but I insisted. So you took me to a flat above a greengrocer's shop in North End Road, Fulham, the shop he had rented when he first arrived in Britain way back in the Sixties, and had bought ten years later. We took to each other immediately. I suppose his way of life was something I could recognise. I liked his chaos and his homeliness better than the penthouse. And he wasn't wearing designer clothes.

So I heard your family story, Jon, how your great-great-great-grandmother (was it three greats or four?) working on the sugar plantations, just one generation since being snatched from an African village. And being so fine and beautiful, the sugar cane boss could not keep his eyes or hands off her (so you had white blood in you, too). And the story down to your grandfather coming to Britain as a young man on *The Windrush*.

'Do you know where in Africa the family originally came from?' I asked

He shook his head.

You butted in impatiently. 'It's easy enough to find out,' you said. 'It just needs a genetic test. There's a database of genetic profiles of African villages.'

'Why don't you do it? Find out where you came from?'

'What difference does where we came from make to anything? We all come from amoeba originally. So what? It's only the future that matters.'

'I would want to know, if it was me.'

Before we left, your grandfather gave me a box. I think he thought we were going to get married. I started to explain it wasn't like that, but then I stopped myself. It didn't matter if he went on thinking that.

'Jon, your whole family story is here,' he told you.

I had a look in that box later. There were family letters handed down through the generations, a family tree and birth certificates. There was even a sort of certificate granting someone who I think must be your great-great-grandmother, her freedom from slavery in the sugar plantation.'

'I think you should read it, it's very moving,' I said.

You looked at me.

'Tomorrow we need to go out shopping to buy you some new outfits.'

That hit a raw nerve! I was so ashamed of my joskin clothes, it was part of the reason I didn't want to go anywhere smart. I burst into tears.

'I'm sorry.' You looked taken aback, and puzzled.

'What for?'

'That I look so shabby compared with your colleagues and friends. And in your fabulous home. That I am such a poor, simple girl from . . .'

'You don't at all.' You were alarmed that you'd upset me.

'I can't go shopping, Jon. How can I afford to buy new clothes?'

'You don't have to. I'll buy them.' You were standing in front of me, holding my face in your hands, wiping away the tears with your thumbs.

'You would do that for me? You can't. I can't let you.'

'Of course I can. Part of your surprise.'

I sniffled back the tears. Something inside me was making my decisions for me.

'I can't let you do that, Jon. It's not right.'

'Why not?' You were incredulous.

' I'm sorry, Jon. I think you want me to be something I'm not.'

'No, Gwalia, no. I love you as you are.'

'No, Jon. You don't. I'm a simple Welsh girl from a different world. Too stupid and unsophisticated for your world of theatres and concerts and art galleries. You can't buy me clothes and educate me and turn me into something I'm not.'

'No, that's not true! I'm not trying to.'

'But you are. You know you are. We both know you are. I'm sorry, Jon.'

I kissed you. I felt so sorry.

It was the most thoughtful kiss I have ever had in my life. About how we both cared for each other. About wishing the world was different.

I loved you very much in that kiss, my heart breaking for you and for myself, for the cruelty of life that it offered so much and then made it impossible.

We looked at each other, holding hands, lumps in our throats. It was very sad.

'It's been nearly three weeks. I should go home tomorrow.'

'You don't have to. You can't. You must stay another week. I have a huge surprise planned.'

I was shaking my head.

'OK, I'll tell you. A holiday. We're flying to Italy. Florence, Sorrento, Capri. At least come away with me. Ten days you'll never forget. I promise you.'

'No, Jon. You go on your own. Oh, Jon. I'm so sorry.'

'Please. I want you to be with me. Here. For always. Llanchwaraetegdanygelyn is doomed. I can offer you a whole new life.'

'You're wrong, Jon,' I said and your face fell. 'Llanchwaraetegdanygelyn will be fine. But even if you're right, it's my home. It's where Awena is.'

'She could move here with you and me. We could get a flat here, send her to a good school. A weekend place in Wales . . .'

'If she was brought up here, it would mean she wasn't Welsh.'

'There's a Welsh school in London, I've checked it out. I have money . . .'

I was torn, Jon, I won't pretend I wasn't. Not by your offer, but by your conviction, your passion.

I knew that I loved you, Jon, I really did, but I also knew then that, as I was, I disappointed you. That I could only ever disappoint you. I could never be the woman you needed, or thought I was. I wasn't good enough for you. Not in the way that I was more than good enough for Dewi.

If I'm honest, I was in awe of you. You scared me. I joked once that you had appeared to me like a god. But, actually, you were.

My boyfriend was a god!

How was that meant to make someone like me feel? Someone from a people which has to struggle every day to chop their wood to heat their water and cook their food, someone from a village without mains electricity or water?

The following day I announced that I was going home. You must have thought I was so ungrateful.

'But you can't.'

'Why not? Of course I can. I've got a return ticket. Dad'll pick me up from the station, or I'll get the bus.'

I wanted very much to fall in love with you, Jon. You did so much for me. You were wonderful and kind and thoughtful and handsome. But my family and country turned out to be so much more important to me than I expected.

You insisted on driving me home.

I didn't talk much. Neither did you. I was thinking, worrying Awena might have forgotten me, might have stopped calling me Mam. And about Mam and Dad. And what they would think of my new nose.

In that polite silence between us, I felt like your prisoner and I longed to be home and to escape from your custody. It was not your fault, it was mine and the guilt weighed down on me. You had tried your best for me, you always had. I had always been ungrateful, never given you anything. Now, surely, I would not see you again.

It was dark when we arrived. Coming down the hill, we

could see the lights below and smell the wood smoke from the fires. I was so excited – and a little apprehensive. Awena was already in bed.

'I don't think you should wake her,' Mam said, a little disapproving, before we'd even taken our coats off.

The house seemed different coming to it from London. Smaller, darker. Much more cluttered. I felt ashamed of its dirtiness, that grime that comes from open fires and old things and houses with draughts and dark corners, spiders and mice.

'Be' dach chi'n feddwl Mam? Be dach chi'n feddwl Dad?'

'Am be, bwt?'

'My nose, of course.'

Mam made me turn my face to the Tilley lamp and gave it a few pumps to brighten it.

'It looks much the same to me,' said Mam. 'But, then again, I never noticed it before.'

'It looks wonderful,' Dad said. 'Bendigedig.'

And Mam poured the inevitable paned.

'You're prettier than ever,' Dad said. 'But still my little girl.'

'Thanks, Dad.' I kissed him on the forehead and he hugged me.

And I felt home again.

I had to go to see Awena, then. I tiptoed in, but she was wide awake.

'Helo, Mami. Wyt ti'n dal i 'ngharu i?'

'Wrth gwrs. Wyt ti'n dal i 'ngharu i?'

I hugged her then and held her. And asked her what she thought of my new nose.

''Mbo,' she said. And shrugged. And fell back to sleep in my arms.

An hour or so later, alone again in my old room, with you in the guest bedroom, I found myself picking up my diary.

My name is Gwalia. I am an Island.

THE DRIVE TO WALES had felt very sad. We should have been flying off to Italy, to Sorrento and the Amalfi coast and the famous Isle of Capri and launching our new life together. Instead I was driving you back to your obscure, depressed town.

Instead of a five star hotel, I found myself sleeping under the eaves in your parents' cold spare room, smelling the damp and listening to the timbers creaking and an owl hooting outside, turning over and over in my mind the things you had said.

Even if everything you said was right, it didn't alter the way I felt. Wasn't everyone always saying that love is never easy? Wasn't the only important thing how you felt about each other? I knew it wasn't your love that was the problem, only your attitude. You had no reason to feel inferior, Gwalia. No problem was insurmountable. But I had failed to persuade you of that.

The following morning, before leaving, I went to see how the Two Dragons was coming along. And maybe practise my Welsh a bit, though that seemed now to be a waste of time. You'd been curiously reluctant to talk to me in Welsh in London.

The hotel was looking good and I felt I deserved more credit from you than I was getting. At least I'd been able to do something to help the town, even if Boudiccea's famous initiative had failed.

What greeted me on the Maes was shocking.

A dozen For Sale signs had appeared. And the whole atmosphere of the town had changed. People seemed somehow subdued, talking in little clusters.

Your Taid – Dai Call – Elwyn and Irfon were in their usual places. I went over to talk to them.

'We should have listened to you and Boudiccea,' Elwyn told me.

'They've sacked the entire staff at the factory.'

'All of them.'

'There'll be no good come of it,' Irfon said. 'It's the devil's work.'

'From stupidity to poverty is three short steps,' said Dai Call. 'Arrogance. Recklessness. And Despair.'

'Be sy wedi digwydd?' I asked.

'The brothers sold their factory to the Chinese. And now the Chinese have shut it,' Elwyn reported. 'Because there isn't any power for electricity, you see.'

'Only the power of God can save Llanchwaraeteg-danygelyn now.'

I hurried back to tell you, Gwalia, and found you standing at the kitchen table over a pile of post addressed to the Clerk of the Council. You were talking to your Dad in Welsh.

'The factory's been closed,' I said.

'It's a fright,' your mother said. 'Everyone is talking about moving away.'

'Why didn't you tell me, Mam?'

'We didn't want to bother you, not in London.'

'I would have come back.'

'That was my fault, I'm afraid,' your father said. 'I wanted you to have time to enjoy yourself. So you could come back a new person. I don't suppose there was anything you could do that someone else could not have done.'

It hadn't occurred to anyone to ask for my help, I noted.

I was tempted to say 'If you'd followed my plan . . .' but the failure had been mine, not the town's. I should have handled it better.

It seemed such a dreadful shame. The town, you and I. Everything.

'There are already a dozen houses up for sale,' I said.

'People don't see any point in hanging on,' your father said. 'It seems awful when we are only just completing the work on Y Ddwy Ddraig.'

I wondered if he realised what that might mean for your family. The bank loan for the work on Y Ddwy Ddraig was based on stability. I hoped they would not recall the loan. With so many people moving out, the most hopeful scenario was probably for retired people to buy up the houses and reinvigorate this town. But, almost certainly, they'd be English-speaking and that would be sad for the last hundred percent Welsh-speaking town in Wales.

You looked at me and handed me a letter you had just opened.

It was from Donald Flood and Guy Ingress announcing they had formed a consortium, and would be making an offer to buy the two main terraces either side of the Maes.

'We are the only ones that can save this town,' they wrote. 'We intend to create fifty new jobs immediately and up to a hundred later. In order to achieve this we need to rapidly develop our campsites to create a holiday village with much extended facilities. We have access to substantial sums of venture capital.'

They had already set a date for a public meeting to promote their idea. The town had been left no choice.

Another envelope in the pile contained a note from Penhaearn summoning you to a meeting at his house.

I started to say something, but you were looking at me, I think reproachfully. I had this feeling that you thought it was somehow all my fault. Or perhaps you were just thinking how bad your timing had been. What could I say?

Shocking as the news in Llanchwaraetegdanygelyn was, it was no longer my concern.

I would go back to London and back to work. The media had broken a new story which had caught my ear on the radio on the way down: according to Home Office figures, obtained under the Freedom of Information Act, there were half a million illegal immigrants in the UK. The Opposition were going to town on it.

On the afternoon news show, Freddy Morgan had sounded as if he was struggling to come up with arguments to counter this racism. I knew I could help. Who would be jetting off to Capri when they could be making the world a better place?

But I did read the stuff in the box that my grandfather handed you, Gwalia. Eventually.

And I did go in search of my roots, first to Trinidad, and then to The Gambia in Africa. I walked the old wooden jetty – rebuilt, of course – where they were surely led across in chains, starved and beaten, to be packed into death ships bound for America, to be put to work to grow the sugar cane and load the ships to bring that sweet, sweet profit-maker back to England. And then the great ships would set sail again down to Gambia to load up more slaves. And the cycle would begin again with more deaths and more sugar.

I also went to a village like the one my family probably came from. Perhaps the one.

Sure, I could have had a blood test and found out if they were my distant cousins half a dozen times removed – but what has any of that to do with any of us now?

I'm living in the land of the slave owners. My standard of living, even today, is based on that exploitation and suffering. And I'm lucky, very lucky. I know that. I'm also a capitalist. But not one who wants to let people beg on the streets or let towns and businesses die. This is the world I was born into. I refuse to feel overly guilty about it: I can't go back and change history.

The best that anyone can do is work to make the world better. And tomorrow better still.

'NOW,' SAID PENHAEARN. 'What are we going to do about the infernal English?' And he looked at me, as if I was supposed to provide the answer.

'Why do we have to get rid of them?' I asked, a little naively, but mindful of all I had learned from you, Jon.

Penhaearn picked up a sheaf of papers and threw them across to me.

Planning applications from Donald Flood to extend his campsite to five hundred caravans. And another application by Guy and Wendy Ingress for an adventure centre for children in local authority care. The large conurbations were crying out for them, they said.

Blodeuwedd had the answer. She seemed liberated now. Behind her newly-discovered, smiley disposition lurked the heart of an undertaker, and under her spiky red hair, the mind of a true Tegid Foel.

'You must call a special meeting of the Council. And refuse all applications,' she said. 'We must let it be known that no one should attend the meeting. And let them know before the meeting that none of their plans will work.'

Donald Flood and Guy Ingress held their meeting in the newly re-opened Y Ddwy Ddraig. However, as it had been advertised only in English, no one apart from the English came.

I was there, though, serving beer and bags of crisps.

And spying.

Dewi was watching, too. Sniggering to himself as Donald Flood brandished the letter from Penhaearn typed in Welsh by me on Town Council notepaper.

'This is an absolute disgrace,' he thundered. And the gathering of twenty English incomers shook their heads and muttered disapproval.

'This letter was handed to me only twenty minutes ago, in Welsh, with no translation.'

'What does it say? What does it say?'

'We don't know what it says. I asked Blodeuwedd for a translation but she told me that the Council does not send any official correspondence in English. She advised me to get a translator and consider it carefully.'

It was then that someone spotted me.

'Ask Gwalia. She's Clerk of the Council, she wrote the letter. She'll translate.'

And so I was forced to stand in front of the meeting and translate the letter for them. Somehow it felt disloyal to Penhaearn and my town to be doing that, Jon. Can you understand that?

'It says: The Town Council of Llanchwaraetegdanygelyn in the County of the Migneint, is opposed both in principle and in the specific instance to any acquisition of the town or development of the kind you have outlined in your application.'

'Disgraceful,' Guy Ingress, shouted.

'How do you justify that, then?' someone else shouted.

'I am not authorised to speak on behalf of the Council. I only take the minutes of meetings and handle correspondence,' I said, a little shakily.

'Well, the meaning is clear enough,' said Guy Ingress. 'They're against us whatever we do.

'That's how you got the grants and planning permission for this place, isn't it? Nepotism! Sheer nepotism. It's anti-English. It's racism. Yes – racism, that's what it is.'

There were shouts of 'Hear! Hear!'

'I hope you realise, young lady,' Donald Flood said, jabbing his finger at me, 'just how catastrophically short-sighted this decision of your precious Council is. Your town is dying. We are the only people interested in creating new jobs here. Who else do you think is going to help you?'

I couldn't answer that.

I stood there, dumbly in front of them, feeling their resentment and anger, but feeling too hurt and angry to respond appropriately.

I forced myself to look him in the eye. And looked at the others.

'I'm sorry,' I said. 'I wish that I could help. I wish that I could help my town.' And I walked to the side.

'I think,' said Donald Flood, after a little more discussion, 'that our only option is to go away and think about it.'

The next letter from Donald Flood and Guy Ingress came two days later headed 'Freedom of Information Act', and began:

> Dear Clerk to the Council,
> Can you please supply me with a list of all councillors and when they were elected, and by what majority, together with copies of their nomination papers showing who nominated them.
> Yours sincerely,
> The Torrent Consortium
> (Donald Flood, Guy Ingress.)

'Oh, I think we should just ignore this,' Penhaearn said when I showed it to him. 'It's not in Welsh. He should be writing to us in Welsh.'

'Do you want me to write and tell him that.'

'Write and tell him that the information is available but that he would not understand it because it is in the medium of Welsh.'

'Should I reply in English or Welsh?'

'Welsh,' he barked. 'Llanchwaraetegdanygelyn Town Council does not use English!'

Their next letter was stronger:

> Dear Clerk to the Council,
> I must inform you that you have failed to provide me with the information I requested within the statutory twenty-one days. I shall therefore be referring the matter to the appropriate authorities.

I also wish to make a formal complaint against the Council on the grounds of racism. In failing to write to me in English, or to provide information in the aforesaid language, you have discriminated against me as an English person.

Yours sincerely,
The Torrent Consortium
(Donald Flood, Guy Ingress.)

I was starting to worry about what would happen to all the money we had invested in the hotel, and how on earth we were going to manage the payments on all our loans.

I doubted Dad would be able to cope.

I was worried that Penhaearn had been acting illegally, and that I was part of this conspiracy.

I put my fears down in writing and sent them off to Penhaearn. It felt like an act of betrayal but I copied the letter to every member of the Council.

Penhaearn came to the house.

'I think you are overstating your concerns, Gwalia,' he told me. 'We are only doing the best we can. We are not cheating anyone, or taking money from anyone. We are doing only what we must to protect our Welsh language and heritage.'

'But they will go to the Local Authority Ombudsman. And the Press. And the police. We could be prosecuted. Jon Bull told me.'

'Oh him. Take no notice of that boy. I've buried better men than all of them. Dwynwen is the only reporter round here. She will do what we tell her to do,' he said. 'And I am the current chairman of the Police Authority.'

'But we are legally obliged to give them the information they want within twenty-one days. We have received clear instructions about that.'

'No need to panic, Gwalia. A lot can happen in twenty-one days.'

He rubbed his hands together. I think he was enjoying himself.

Another letter arrived the following day.

It was headed

Freedom of Information Act.

Dear Clerk of the Council,

Can you please send us copies of your policy under the Race Relations (Amendment) Act 2000, together with the relevant minutes of your Council relating to any discussion you may have had relating to the disenfranchising of non-Welsh speakers.

If you have, in fact, had no such discussion, you are obliged to disclose this.

We also request copies of any minutes, including rough notes made at the time, in relation to Human Rights.

We also request a copy of your job description as Clerk to the Council, and your standing instruction together with your instructions by the council authorising you to refuse to supply information through the medium of English.

Yours sincerely,
The Torrent Consortium
(Donald Flood, Guy Ingress.)

I should have realised the moment I saw Dafydd Y Gwrthsafiad that this would be an official Gwrthsafiad operation. Probably I did realise, Jon, I just didn't want to believe it. I don't entirely understand what makes me do things, so often in spite of myself and my best intentions.

I was in denial. I didn't want to imagine it would go as far as it did, but I think I knew quite nicely in my heart of hearts. I wanted to strike a blow for Cymru, and a blow for myself, before the last totally Welsh-speaking town was overrun by English.

Without that night, it might have turned out very differently between you and me, Jon, don't you think? But I don't know if I regret that totally.

Why else would we have been going up to Mr Flood's caravan site, if not to make serious mischief?

I had told myself we were just going to take down Mr Flood's English notices, put some leaflets round the caravans promoting the Welsh language and daub a few slogans, as we usually did. But I must have realised it was more serious than that. Only a fool would not have realised! It was obvious from how tense we all were.

We met at the van.

'Don't forget now, Dewi, you promised me.'

'No, Gwalia, honestly, now, paid â phoeni, there'll be no painting slogans. We won't be daubing whitewash on the caravans, will we Rhys?'

Rhys, solemnly shook his head. I needed to believe them.

Dafydd Y Gwrthsafiad came over.

'Right, lads, put your berets on and get in line.'

'I'm only coming if you promise me,' I said.

'No talking,' Dafydd Y Gwrthsafiad said.

'For God's sake, Gwalia,' Dewi hissed. 'What's the matter with you?'

So I dismissed the anxieties nagging at the back of my mind and put my beret on. This was only for a laugh. For Wales. Worrying too much was one of the after-effects of my trauma. Always about the wrong things. I had long ago stopped trusting my instinct about which fears were groundless and which were not, and had an even greater fear of being thought paranoid.

'Right, embark,' Dafydd Y Gwrthsafiad commanded.

As we bundled in, I thought I smelled paint in the back of the van and looked around. Three big tins. White. Red. Green.

'I knew it. I knew it, Dewi. You promised.'

But the van was already moving off.

'Come on, Gwalia, you want to stop these English bastards buying up the town for holiday homes. Of course you do.'

'It's a question of economic terrorism, working at a psychological level,' Dafydd Y Gwrthsafiad explained. 'This is sophisticated strategy. Strike them in their fears, where they are most vulnerable.'

'Exactly,' Dewi said. 'We want cheap houses for young couples, we do. Affordable houses. For people like you and me. And for the rebirth of the town. This could be the best thing that's happened to Llanchwaraetegdanygelyn.'

'Yes, Dewi. Fine. But there's a difference between protest and vandalism. We have to pursue a democratic route for Wales now.'

'That sounds like that black English boyfriend of yours telling you that, Gwalia. He's done nothing for us, here, has he? Only for Y Ddwy Ddraig. You'll come to your senses, you'll see, you will,' Dewi told me. 'Now you've dumped him.'

'Stop talking now,' Dafydd Y Gwrthsafiad commanded. 'This sloppy talk is undermining morale.'

'We have to discuss it,' I protested.

'No, Gwalia, not tonight. The time for discussion is over. We did all that when you were in London. Our task tonight is to force the English bastards to think twice about buying up everything we own and turfing us out. That's what the Israelis did in Palestine. And look at the mess there is there. We don't want that happening here.'

'Dafydd, that's a stupid argument . . .'

'Silence. Don't be insubordinate to your commanding officer. Dewi, can you keep her under control? You're my corporal. If necessary, discipline her.'

Dewi took my hand and held it.

I tried to calm myself. Looking for rational argument in my confused thoughts. I had your voice in my head, Jon. Your kind of arguments – 'Even assuming the English were put off buying, then what? Where would people work? What would they do for money?'

Dewi knew me too well not to have sensed my doubts.

'We'll force the factory to re-open, we will,' he whispered. 'We've thought it all out.'

It made no sense.

Nothing did.

Not anymore.

We were nearly up at the caravan site now. I was starting to feel that same desperate panic I had felt when I was being cross-examined by everyone after the rape, the panic that could freeze me numb when things were happening to me that I couldn't control.

'Dewi!' I whispered. 'It's illegal. What if the police catch us? You know Dad wants me to take over the hotel licence. We've just re-opened Y Ddwy Ddraig. We've just got the renovations done. What if we get arrested? I'll lose all that. I'm not going to do it, Dewi. I want you to take me home.'

Dewi pulled my head into his shoulder and hugged me to his heart. It seemed useless to fight. It was somehow comforting to surrender. Just for the moment.

The Gwrthsafiad troop wagon slowed and Dafydd Y Gwrthsafiad killed the headlights. We turned onto the caravan site and jolted across the rough ground past a line of caravans. And came to a halt.

'You always used to do the road signs and the protests, you did? What's wrong with you now. Anyway, you may as well help. We'll be away quicker if you do.'

I shook my head and sat like a sulky kid.

'We should to do things by democratic means,' I muttered, almost to myself.

'Where did you get that idea, then? You always used to be in favour of direct action, until you got your black English boyfriend. Anyway we all voted on it, didn't we.'

That was when I noticed Dafydd pulling out the metal jerry can.

Petrol!

'No! You can't set fire to the caravans – it's . . . it's illegal. It's not right.'

I jumped out of the van and ran after him. I tried to grab him and stop him but he shrugged me off and passed the jerry can to Rhys. So I went after Rhys, trying to grab the can off him.

'Dewi! Keep this girl of yours under control.'

'I'm not Dewi's girl,' I screamed.

But Dewi came and grabbed hold of me, anyway.

'It's not right,' I was screaming. 'This is people's property you're destroying. It's not like protesting and graffiti.'

'Hisht! Be quiet! We'll all be caught.'

Dewi held me, pinning my arms with his around me.

'It's not right invading someone else's country either. You know that, Gwalia,' he said quietly, his mouth in my hair. 'But there's no law to protect us from that.'

'We should be democratic,' I repeated, stupidly.

'Don't be naïve, Gwalia,' Dafydd Y Gwrthsafiad said. 'How can we hope for democracy with so many English – and English quislings – here in Wales?'

'I'm going to stop you,' I said, trying to wriggle free.

'How?'

All kinds of thoughts were going through my head.

I wonder now if Dewi did all this deliberately to implicate me. To split me up from you, Jon? To unite him and me? Oh, I know, you don't believe he's bright enough to think it through like that, but people can do complicated things from instinct.

Dewi held me and Dafydd Y Gwrthsafiad went off into the near darkness to supervise Rhys as he went round the caravans, splashing petrol on the sides of them.

'Don't light it,' I shouted. 'I'll report you.'

I shouted loudly in the hope that somebody might hear.

'OK,' Dafydd Y Gwrthsafiad said. 'You win, Gwalia, let's just get back in the van, then.'

'You're going to stop, then?'

'That's right, Gwalia, we're stopping.'

I looked around their faces, I was very confused.

They seemed to be exchanging looks. I think I saw Rhys shrug and Dewi wink at him. Rhys came back, threw the last of the empty cans in the back and got in the passenger seat. Dewi jumped up in.

'We'll leave it here, then, shall we?' Dewi said, slamming his door.

'You're leaving it, then?' I stood there, confused.

'That's it,' Dafydd Y Gwrthsafiad said. 'You've convinced us. Jump in.'

I was puzzled. Doubtful. I didn't believe this but had no choice now. I climbed in the back next to Dewi.

They were all grinning at me and saying encouraging things.

'Don't worry, Gwalia, everything's fine.'

'Come on, Gwalia.'

'It's fine, Gwalia.'

The sick feeling in my stomach and their heavy breathing told me it wasn't over.

Dafydd Y Gwrthsafiad crunched the gears and we started off across the rough ground with a series of jolts.

Then Rhys wound down the window and took out a box of matches and started lighting spills

I understood now.

Dewi held me as we zigzagged through the caravans while Rhys tossed out the lighted spills.

I was shouting.

'Let me out. I hate you. Let me out.'

Many of the spills were going out, but some caught. And then the yellow flame leapt up with a whoosh.

I was trying to open the van door but the handle was stiff and awkward and the van kept lurching as Dafydd threw it around the caravans, skidding in the wet ground.

I remember crying and shouting and Dewi screaming at me to sit down and shut up. I didn't want to be part of this.

Through the glass, I felt the heat of the fires on my face.

Then I did get the door open. And I half fell, half jumped out, sprawling in the mud as Dafydd hit the brakes and skewed the van around to a halt.

I tried to get up but my leg hurt.

I heard Dewi shout, 'Oh shit!'

And heard Rhys say, 'I told you not to bring her.'

And Dafydd Y Gwrthsafiad said, 'I think we should just leave her.'

'No!' said Dewi, getting out, leaving the door open.

I was lying there in the mud, crying and shaking, the caravans flaming all around us. Frozen with panic, not thinking any more.

Dewi knelt down and bent over me. The look on his face told me how much he loved me, not for himself but for me.

'Gwalia! Gwalia! Are you all right.' This was the concern of a knight who would die for me.

I nodded, numbed and horrified. But at the same time I felt somehow content, sure now about something.

He lifted me up and pushed me back into the passenger seat, then climbed in after me while Rhys slid across into the driver's seat.

'Hurry up!' Rhys shouted. 'Quickly! We need to be out of here. Now!'

And then I was laughing hysterically, and crying at the same time, as Dewi massaged my knee and I tried to hug him.

I remember us lurching across the field, and out onto the road.

The whole stupid escapade couldn't have taken more than a few minutes, yet it seemed forever.

Then we were away.

Me, laughing, weeping, shaking – all at the same time – my knee still hurting. Dewi holding me to his shoulder, stroking my head, rubbing my knee, whispering to me, calming me. Me clutching him as if he was a new discovery.

We drove back to town, the fires blazing behind us. Through the rear window, I glimpsed the orange glow in the sky, Rhys laughing and shouting, high on adrenalin, Dewi silent with me in his arms at last.

I shut my eyes tight, thinking of nothing, making my mind go blank.

I felt him kiss my hair. Then my forehead. Then my cheek. And I started kissing his hand.

Rhys dropped us at the back of Y Ddwy Ddraig and drove away. Dewi helped me out of the van his arm around me. Holding me. Cuddling me. And took me, hobbling, into the office behind reception.

'I'm sorry,' I said, pathetically, through my sobs. 'I've let you down. I've been a wimp, haven't I?'

'It's OK,' he told me. 'You're safe now, you are. Everything is going to be all right.'

He rubbed my twisted knee until he could see that I felt better and calmer and then he kissed me.

And my mouth opened to his.

I let him take me upstairs to room 10. I knew what was going to happen. I wanted it to. Part of me was grateful to him, part apologetic for trying to stop them. And part of me loved him, I suppose. Had always loved him. But there was another part of me that said that my time for giving myself to a man was overdue long since.

And believe me when I tell you, Jon, I also wanted to see how it would be. A sort of trial run if you like, to make sure I could do it right for you.

The next day the town was full of reporters. Radio. Television. Newspapers. And police. All of them seemed to set up headquarters at Y Ddwy Ddraig.

Dewi was interviewed by detectives from Caernarfon. Then it was my turn. The one who interviewed me turned out to be Myrfyn, who I had been at school with, who always let us off when we took down signs. He was stern enough, probably for the benefit of his colleague. Dewi and I both said nothing. We were lovers now.

They went away and left us alone. They didn't ask me if I knew who'd set fire to the caravans, only if I had seen anything suspicious, what the relationship was like between the Welsh and English. I didn't even have to lie.

It was hectic in the hotel. Our town was big news now. Welsh terrorism, Welsh business moving to the Far East. English immigration. English moans. And Y Ddwy Ddraig was the place to be. People even got dressed up in their market-day best just to pop in for coffee or lunch or tea.

Mr Flood's remarks were considered particularly newsworthy: 'We moved here to escape the racist attacks in Birmingham with Asian youths setting fire to our cars. And now my caravans have been torched by the self-styled Welsh Resistance.'

He had a way with words.

Dewi seemed almost contented.

I was worrying about Awena. About my parents. And what was going to happen to the town. Worrying about everything.

Would we be arrested for the caravans? Would my parents find out it was me? I'd had sex with Dewi. How could I stop him telegraphing his triumph to the world, behaving as if he owned me. And who would he tell? He'd probably boasted to Rhys already. It wasn't as simple as that for me.

I felt as I imagined someone on death row might feel on the morning of execution. It was surely only a matter of time before my whole world came crashing down around my ears.

But nothing did come crashing down.

Everything just went on.

Dewi had changed, though. He'd become thoughtful, and attentive and proprietorial. And, actually, I liked that.

Everyone was still talking about the fires at the caravans.

Mam and Dad assumed that Dewi was part of it. Probably a lot of people did, but they would not have said a word to the police. They weren't so sure about me.

Mam approved of the arson.

'Perhaps this will teach the English a lesson,' she said. 'If you want my opinion, they have no right marching in here, and buying up our houses and land and causing our whole town to be up for sale.'

She asked no questions.

Dad was more circumspect.

'What do you think of the attack on Mr Flood's caravans?' he asked me gently, one evening while we were washing up together.

'The town is in a very bad state,' I said.

'And has setting fire to the caravans improved the situation?' I was sure he knew everything.

I shook my head. I looked into my father's eyes and he looked deep into mine.

'I don't know. What do you think, Dad?'

'I think it's lowered the prices of the houses, but it wasn't local people buying, was it?'

'We have to do something, Dad. We have to liberate Wales from English oppression. They don't care about us. Until we can decide our own fate it will always be like this.'

'But which would you make the priority, Gwalia? To make Wales prosperous or to make Wales free?'

That question stayed with me. It haunts me still.

I went with Dewi every night that week. But every time I did, I imagined you, Jon. I told myself it was a way of getting rid of that big obstacle in my head, and of making sure it would be good for you if that time ever came.

In my mind, it was a way of being faithful to the both of you.

How we can turn things in our heads!

How was it you put it, once? It is easier to fight for freedom than to plan prosperity.

I had found my freedom. But I'd betrayed you, Jon, hadn't I?

I'd betrayed us.

Donald Flood had might and right and justice on his side now. Or so he believed. He seemed to be in town almost all the time, striding around, looking at houses, negotiating deals, demanding meetings with Penhaearn and officials, proclaiming that he would have justice against the Council, against the Welsh Resistance, and against all the nationalists who had been so stupid and obstructive.

As Clerk to the Council I received several visits. There was one in particular.

'I bet you know who set fire to my caravans,' he told me, pointing his finger at my face.

Dewi grabbed his arm and pushed it away.

'Peidwch â siarad hefo 'nghariad i fel 'na,' he said.

'You must be very stupid if you think I understand that pagan nonsense,' Flood laughed. 'You're probably one of those who did it. You're always at those meetings and protests, aren't you?'

'Cer i grafu, Sais diawl,' Dewi sneered.

'Yes, you are, aren't you. The two of you. I bet you are.'

'Profwch y peth, 'te,' Dewi laughed.

The following morning, there was new graffiti on the wall of the supermarket.

This time it was in English.

Get Rid of Welsh Fascism.

Don't Let The Welsh Minority Dictate To You.

Dwynwen was out straight away with her microphone and cameras, interviewing Penhaearn in front of it.

'It is an absolute disgrace,' he told Welsh radio and television audiences in both Welsh and English. 'They have vandalised our walls with their racist slogans.

'These English people come here and destroy our language and our way of life and they are not even content to leave us with a little bit of our own culture and heritage. This shows better than anything I can say what things have come to here.'

Dwynwen had no choice but to interview Donald Flood, too. Her bosses down in Cardiff insisted on it, in the interests of balanced reporting. He appeared in a Union Jack tie, which attracted more attention, and caused more offence, than his words.

'I don't know who did this and I don't condone it for a

moment,' he said with a twinkle in his eye. 'But I can understand why the English have been provoked to go to such extremes.

'We are being discriminated against and disenfranchised. We are being denied our democratic right to know what is going on, and to have our say, in this region of this country – our country, the United Kingdom of Great Britain.

'It is high time the local Council stopped its anti-democratic and illegal nonsense of conducting its business only in Welsh. It is very irritating that last time we saw graffiti here in Welsh, Councillor Penhaearn blamed the people who provoked it and this time he blames the people who wrote it. He always seems to condemn the English and never the Welsh.

'The farce of this town has gone on long enough. I am a citizen of this country and I am being denied my democratic rights on my own home soil.

'I'm going to sort this mess out now, once and for all. I have written to the Local Authority Ombudsman for Wales. Now we shall see what happens.'

After that, Penhaearn had no choice but to agree to meet the consortium. He commanded me to be there. I attended out of duty, feeling wretched.

'I hope you have all the information I requested. For your sake,' he said threateningly.

'I have,' I told him. 'You can rest assured I have discharged my legal duty.'

Personally, I would not have chosen the Antur Deg Office, up in the attic, above the Council Chamber. But for some mad reason, Penhaearn did.

It was difficult for Yncl Penhaearn to look authoritative perched on a rickety wooden chair behind the officer's desk. Perhaps he thought if he kept the meeting informal, the outcome would be informal too, and wouldn't count. For myself, I made sure I had one of the good chairs.

Donald Flood and Guy Ingress arrived on the dot with

grim looks on their faces. They barely acknowledged me, exchanged curt formalities with Penhaearn, looked suspiciously at the rickety bentwood chairs, and sat down gingerly.

It felt to me as if life as I had known it was coming to an end and this dismal meeting was the opening bars of the final movement. I handed him my sheets of paper.

'I will refuse to speak English and they will have to go away,' he told me in Welsh, without the slightest embarrassment at talking in front of them.

'I don't think we can really do that, Yncl Penhaearn,' I replied in Welsh, smiling at our English visitors to reassure them. 'I think we might find ourselves in very grave difficulty, if we do.'

He stared down at the desk.

'If you like, I will translate for you,' I offered, hoping to mediate a little and perhaps to mollify the Englishmen.

'Are you suggesting that I am not a good speaker of English?' Penhaearn thundered.

'No, no,' I said, a little too quickly. 'Not at all.'

How could I tell him that his manner seemed much more stilted and pompous in his second tongue? Or that his English sounded fifty years out of date to English ears? Or that none of that was really to the point at all.

'You realise,' Donald Flood began, 'that this is your last chance before we go to the authorities and expose your nepotism and corruption.'

Mr Flood leaned forward and his chair morphed with him, slopping over to forty-five degrees. He looked quizzically at me. I smiled. His was the better chair.

You are always so fussy, you English, I was thinking. You have even perfected the art of criticising and complaining silently. In Llanchwaraetegdanygelyn such things as sloppy chairs were normal. We didn't complain.

'That is a very unfortunate attitude that you are adopting,' Penhaearn was saying.

'I'll be perfectly straight with you, Mr Jones. You people have been against us from the start. I've had my caravans burned, my planning permissions turned down, my letters ignored.'

'I think you are exaggerating a little there, no doubt in consideration of your own self-interest.'

Donald Flood's face went redder.

'No, Mr Jones, I'm not. We know your game. And the game is up. You've brought this town to its knees and you still won't admit it! You've blocked our proposals to bring mains electricity and water here, and you even resort to arson to oppose progress.'

'I think you should stop there, Mr Flood. That is not at all accurate, you know.'

'No, I'll have my say.' He banged his fist on the desk, making Penhaearn recoil. 'You've stopped all English people from getting on the Council – or even knowing what's going on – and now, when the town is disintegrating all around us, you are still resisting any attempt to sort things out. We are residents here, Mr Jones, landowners, businessmen. We have rights!'

Penhaearn asked me, in Welsh, if I thought Mr Flood was going to be violent.

I replied: ''Mbo.'

Penhaearn set his face and told the English firmly: 'With respect, I don't think you have been living in this town sufficiently long to appreciate the rights of local people, let alone start trying to assert your own.'

Donald Flood stiffened at that. Guy Ingress was twitching to say something. His chair was rather wobbly, too.

'Are you saying rights depend on how long we have been here?' he shouted.

'We have our own ways of doing things here, Mr Ingress.' Penhaearn's voice was shaking.

'How much do you get for being a County Councillor? Fifteen thousand pounds a year, is it? And how long have you been a councillor? Twenty years? I make that three hundred thousand pounds – nearly a third of a million – of taxpayers' money you have had.

'Do you really think you are doing a good enough job for the town to justify that? Look around you at the state of it!'

Penhaearn looked a little stung by this. He was sitting rather oddly, with both elbows on the table, as if he was holding all his weight on them.

He took a deep breath.

'I am doing my best, Mr Flood. That is all that anyone can do, I think you will have to agree.'

Donald Flood banged the table, making Yncl Penhaearn wobble.

'You have such an ineffectual, stupid way of doing things – achieving nothing, blocking progress, sabotaging any plans to improve the town's economy. Look at you. How can you be proud of what you are doing here?'

Donald Flood stood up at this point, leaving his rickety chair leaning at sixty degrees. He turned round and looked at it and stayed standing.

'There is one more thing you can do for your town,' he said to Penhaearn, glancing at me.

Penhaearn, leaning heavily on his elbows, affected nonchalance and looked away.

'You can resign. And you can let us take over.'

Penhaearn sneered at this.

'I don't think you would be very acceptable as candidates for leadership of this community, Mr Flood.'

'And why is that, Mr Jones?' demanded Guy Ingress, getting to his feet to stand next to Donald Flood. 'Is it because we don't speak Welsh, by any chance? Because we weren't born here?'

'You have had your chance,' Donald Flood thundered. 'If you won't go quietly, we will do it the hard way.'

Penhaearn looked from one to the other of them in what I thought was complete disdain. Then I realised that his chair had effectively broken under him and he was now only pretending to be sitting on it.

'You don't know anything about this place. It's not your country. You know nothing of our traditions here.'

'We know plenty, Mr Jones. Whatever you may think, this *is* our country just as much as yours. Wales is part of Great Britain, isn't it? I believe the majority of your fellow countrymen voted against your independence in Nineteen Seventy-Nine, didn't they? Isn't that right?'

Again poor Yncl Penhaearn was silent. The pretence of being seated behind the desk of the Mayor's office was taking all his concentration. I wondered how long he could keep up this pretence. And why.

'And even in Nineteen Ninety-Seven, only a very slender majority voted in favour even of an Assembly – an organisation with little more authority than an English county council. And I've discovered that most local people here are against it anyway. Because they think it's a gravy train for you and your blasted old boys' network.'

Penhaearn gave a sharp intake of breath. I thought he was going to fall. We all were waiting for him to speak, but he stayed silent. All his energy was now being concentrated on maintaining the illusion of being seated.

'No doubt you will tell me, Mr Jones, that the Welsh language is alive and well and spoken by twenty-one-point-five per cent of the population and that you therefore have the right to speak your mother tongue in your own country?'

Penhaearn grunted. He was very red in the face.

'Well, I hope you realise that the number of English people in Umbo is not zero, as you like to pretend, it is also exactly twenty-one point five per cent. There are no longer a hundred per cent Welsh speakers here. The English are moving in. And we, too, are living in our own country, wanting to speak through *our* mother tongue and exercise *our* democratic rights through that mother tongue.'

Penhaearn now looked very precarious and uncomfortable.

'I hope you are taking me seriously, Mr Jones,' Donald Flood said. 'I do not particularly want to see you go to prison. I realise that would not endear me to your relatives – which is probably most of the population,' he exchanged a smirk with Guy Ingress. He was starting to grow cocky now. Cockiness, I think, is another, most dislikeable, English trait.

'I will give you some time to think about all this, Mr Jones. Now, do you have the information I requested or do I have to make another official complaint against you under the Freedom of Information Act?'

Penhaearn looked beseechingly at me.

I opened the file.

'This is a list of all the nomination papers for all the members of the council. They're all in Welsh, of course. I have added some handwritten notes in English which should make it clear. But I shall be happy to translate anything you don't understand.'

Guy Ingress, who was closest to me, reached forward. I handed him the election results for the last five years, together with the details he had demanded – who had proposed and seconded each councillor, what their declared interests were. Not one had been elected by voters and all had been proposed and seconded by Penhaearn and Hiraethog.

'They would be in bloody Welsh, wouldn't they?' he said. 'Still it looks easy enough to work out.'

He opened the file and held up a sheet of paper and read it, then he handed it to Donald Flood and pointed at it.

'You see,' Donald Flood said. 'My point exactly. Twenty-three members of the Council. All elected unopposed. In other words – no elections, they're effectively appointed. And all proposed and nominated by the same two people. Guess who!'

He looked at Guy to make sure he had registered the significance of this.

'You shouldn't be handing me documents in Welsh,' he said to me. 'Wales is part of the United Kingdom. The official language of the United Kingdom is English. We're UK citizens. We're UK citizens living in our own country yet we're being excluded from taking part in our own local government – or even from knowing what's going on – because it's being conducted in a minority language. How many English people are there on the Council?'

'None,' I said.

'And to think that you sidelined poor Boudiccea and her Antur Deg!' Guy Ingress put in.

'Well that's a breach of the Race Relations Amendment Act, then isn't it?' said Mr Flood. 'For Christ's sake! Welsh isn't even the official language in Wales. Four-fifths of the people *here* don't even speak it. Yet we're being asked to put up with all this crap in the name of protecting some useless gibberish. We'll see about all this.'

They left clutching the file triumphantly

'You'll be hearing more about this, Mr Jones.'

Penhaearn stood up very painfully and stiffly and the chair collapsed to the floor in pieces around him.

A few weeks later, the Ombudsman sent his officer for a stern talk with Penhaearn and me.

No, it wasn't lawful for the Council to conduct its meetings only in Welsh and exclude non Welsh-speaking citizens, Penhaearn learned. And, no, it wasn't lawful to discriminate against the English or in favour of the Welsh.

In future, meetings and minutes would have to be bilingual, with equal opportunities for all.

This was another devastating blow for Penhaearn. But still he was unshakeable in his self-belief.

'The world is going dwlali,' he told everyone. 'Madness is sweeping our country. We are being colonised by English madness. But we will not be shaken in our firm resolve to restore to Wales her heritage, her freedom and her destiny.'

'I think it's Penhaearn who has gone do-lally,' my Taid Dai Call pronounced.

And Elwyn sang a little nursery rhyme, about someone falling off a horse. 'Gee ceffyl bach, yn cario ni'n dau, dros y mynydd i hela cnau; dŵr yn yr afon a'r cerrig yn slic, cwympo ni'n dau, wel dyna i chi dric.'

'It will be a fine trick if Penhaearn can get back on his hobby horse and ride to his promised land, now,' said Irfon.

Mam and Gwenlais were distraught.

This was a matter beyond twting.

'They've breeched the dam. You cannot put your nose outside the door without seeing them, busying themselves with being seen going about everybody else's business.'

'I've heard they intend to stand as councillors at the next election. Attend every meeting and ensure their English needs are catered for.'

They sipped their tea in silence.

Since the renovation of Y Ddwy Ddraig, our three philosophers, Taid, Elwyn and Irfon, no longer needed to perch on Jac's bench outside Caffi Cyfoes solving the problems of the world which now centred on Donald Flood and Guy Ingress and all the problems of our poor, bankrupt town.

Unlike most others, Taid Dai Call and his disciples remained optimistic.

'I don't think they will succeed in their colonial endeavours,' Taid pronounced.

'They don't deserve to, even if they do have justice on their side,' said Elwyn. 'And that's because it is only inferior, self-serving English justice, not the true justice of Hywel Dda.'

'It will all be the same a hundred years from now,' said Irfon. 'Except in heaven and hell.'

They had their own table now in the warm, with a clean white tablecloth every day, in our refurbished bay window overlooking the Maes. They'd been a *tamaid* reluctant to leave the bench. I think they felt a touch disloyal, but I tempted them in by putting up a picture I'd found and framed of them with Jac. And, frankly, they had the best seats in the house, but I was happier to see them out of the rain and wind. They even smartened up a little.

Now, they could see and hear everything, there were mugfuls of problems for them to solve.

'It's a terrible sight,' said Taid. 'Llanchwaraetegdanygelyn as we have known it will never be the same again.'

'It's a tragedy,' said Elwyn. 'Something I never thought to see in my lifetime.'

'This is the devil's work, the wages of sin and a godless people,' Irfon pronounced.

'Cheer up!' I said, replenishing their mugs.

'True. True. Being miserable never helps,' said Elwyn.

'No, but miserable people live longer than happy ones,' said Taid Dai Call.

'And go straight to heaven,' said Irfon.

They were looking at the dozens of For Sale signs which had sprouted all around the Maes as the panic of being trapped in Llanchwaraetegdanygelyn without work or income spread. Many people worried that if they couldn't sell their house in the first rush, they never would. There wasn't a shop or house on the far side of the Maes without a board outside. Only three had sold stickers on them. On the Town Hall side, across the cobbles, one whole terrace was up for sale as a job lot.

There were many strangers in town, estate agents, surveyors, planning officers and floods of English people, presumably sniffing out investment bargains, or places for retirement. There were builders, too, coming to frown and scratch their heads and scribble their estimates on backs of envelopes. Y Ddwy Ddraig was the natural place for people to come to discuss their work over lunch or tea or coffee. Some nights we were fully booked. Always we had people staying now.

Next to the Supermart, an English estate agent from Chester had set up a temporary office in an empty shop. Another, from Caernarfon, had a large van parked by Jac's bench which was taking customers at the side door and manufacturing For Sale signs at the back.

My Anti Gwenlais, arrived each morning with her regular huddle of gossips at exactly two minutes past eleven, for coffee and fancies, though she rarely paid. Peddling rumours had made her the wraig ddoeth leol – the local oracle – and she had put on half a stone in cream cakes, Danish pastries and sweet coffee.

'Have you seen that man who's just moved in to Mrs Roberts's old house, with a young Thai wife and two daughters?'

Her companions leaned forward, tongues salivating, ready to twt.

'They're not really his daughters, you know. He's selling them on that internet thing for five thousand pounds a time, I've heard.'

The twting chorus began.

'And the brothers who owned the factory have moved away and left that poor little Trêsi all alone. Last I heard, she was living in the office building. The whole factory deserted.'

'And I've heard that the English Consortium have filed thirteen proposals for planning permission.'

The refrain began again on cue.

I had a small team of waitresses and cooks but little time to enjoy our new prosperity. As Clerk to Cyngor Tref Llanchwaraetegdanygelyn, I had a queue of people, daily, coming to see me. And each post brought a bundle of new letters from people who seemed to think that I could help them. In those days I relied a great deal on Dewi. He was a good manager and looked quite dapper in the new uniform I had instituted, based, I must admit, Jon, on the little outfits the waiters at your father's penthouse had to wear, and which – yes! – at the time, I had been so scathing about.

Dewi had even learned to be friendly with our customers. Unfortunately, he found it a little hard to extend this charm to the English, especially the men, so I worked out a compromise. He could talk to customers only in Welsh, provided he smiled a lot and repeated whatever it was he was saying, patiently and charmingly, until they understood.

Spurred on by the appreciation he got for being charming and looking dapper, he had become quite presentable – and something of an attraction.

Busy as we were for now, everyone was worried enough about what would happen.

Dad wore a constant frown, and was less resilient to Mam's twting tongue.

'You're not doing anything to sort out our problems,' she scolded him. 'Gwalia's spending all her time working at the hotel and for the Town Council, you're spending all your time worrying about your wretched school. As if they would dare to close that down. You should be worrying about me, and the family. That's what I think.'

Dad was very worried indeed about the school. With so many parents leaving to find work elsewhere, classes were shrinking by the week. There were now only nine pupils left. Clearly far too few for three full-time teachers, a secretary and a caretaker. But Mam would not believe the school could be under threat.

'They wouldn't dare to think that such an institution could be ripped from the heart of the community. You talk as if our County Councillors are monsters. Shame on you!'

Then Dad came home one day with terrible news.

'I had a meeting with the County Education Officer today. He says we should close the school at the end of term and relocate the remaining children to Llantuhwnt.'

'But they all speak English there, and God knows what else!'

'This is the last school on the Migneint. There were six, you know, when I started teaching. This is happening all over rural Wales. Schools closing. We're none of us a special case. The process has just been more rapid here, that's all. But many other towns have had their schools close.'

'What about Awena?' Mam asked in alarm and looked at me.

'She'll have to go by bus every day,' Dad said hopelessly.

Mam shook her head and twted.

'I won't hear of it. It'll be an end to being able to walk to school. An end to school concerts, dramas and carol services in our town.'

'If the school closes, we will lose the best hall for meetings and concerts in the town,' I said.

'And all of this, after we have borrowed thousands to match the grants to renovate Y Ddwy Ddraig,' Mam shook her head. 'Where will we find sufficient customers to pay the interest? We will go broke, now, won't we? You have brought us to the verge of bankruptcy.'

Dad tried to calm her but she shook him away.

'Go and see to your precious school. I'm going to see Penhaearn first thing tomorrow.'

It was useless trying to explain to her that Yncl Penhaearn and his intransigence to any changes or improvements might be the cause of it.

She slept in the spare room that night.

The following evening she had an announcement.

'Penhaearn is in a terrible state,' she reported. 'He is taking all of the responsibilities for the town upon his own shoulders. But he has a plan.'

She humphed and leaned back in her chair to see what we had to say about that.

Dad and I looked at each other.

'What plan?' I asked.

'Never you mind,' Mam said. 'All you need to know is that Penhaearn has a plan.'

Within two days the word cynllun – plan – was on everybody's lips. Especially my Anti Gwenlais's.

'Mae gan Penhaearn gynllun.'

And this time their chorus was one of Ooos and Ahs.

'Well, the town does need a plan, I should think,' said Taid, when the ripple of the rumour reached the bay window.

'Every town must have a plan,' said Elwyn, 'Especially a town that looks so dreadful since its factory closed.'

'As ye sow, so shall ye reap,' said Irfon.

'We should have listened to Boudiccea,' said Elwyn.

'Like a kingfisher at dawn,' said Irfon.

'A fine woman, indeed,' said Taid. 'We should have seized our moment.'

'But we were blinded by her beauty,' said Irfon. 'To tell the truth, I wasn't sure myself if she was from heaven or hell.'

They thought about that for several minutes and then accepted another mug of tea.

'The important question is,' said Taid. And they all leaned forward. 'What is the plan?'

They nodded silently in unison at this. It was not for nothing that Taid was called Dai Call, Dai the Wise. They looked at me. But Penhaearn hadn't confided in me.

It was a day or two later that the details of the plan leaked out.

It came in a ripple of excitement at Gwenlais's table where there were two new faces in her group, Billi-Jo and Jean.

Bronwen sidled up to me excitedly.

'Maen nhw'n trafod y cynllun,' she told me.

I went across to clear the dishes from their table at once. It is important for the head of a business to keep in touch with all her customers on a personal level.

'Come on then, Anti Gwenlais, what's the plan?'

Around the room, a silence had fallen. Everyone was cocking an ear in our direction.

'We are going tonight to Cilmeri,' my Anti Gwenlais announced. 'To summon the ghost of Llywelyn. Jean and Billi-Jo will be bringing their dowsing rods, isn't that right?'

'It's at the intersection of two ley lines,' said Billi-Jo, a little nervously.

'And tonight is the anniversary of Llywelyn's murder,' said Jean.

'This will be Penhaearn's coroni ysbrydol – his spiritual

coronation. Without doubt, this is the most important ghost hunt of our lives.'

If Penhaearn would have preferred a smaller group for his séance, he shouldn't have told Gwenlais.

Nor should she have announced it over morning coffee in Y Ddwy Ddraig.

There were so many of us, we had to use the school bus. Gwenlais called it a siarabang, which is probably not a Welsh word at all. All the members of the Town Council were there. Taid, Elwyn and Irfon had the back seat, and borrowed the picture of their old, deceased friend Jac from the wall near their table with them, just in case he might decide to make an appearance, too.

Garmon, who was dressed in what looked like his father's old Army uniform, with khaki jacket and trousers, blancoed gaiters and belt, and brass buttons, took the role of conductor and sat in front with the driver, leading the singing. Penhaearn was escorted aboard by Billi-Jo and Jean on one side and Anti Gwenlais on the other. They waved everyone away who tried to speak to him. They and Mam and the other ghost hunters had commandeered the front four rows of the bus. And sat in silence. It was very spooky.

Strangely, Dewi had been much more relaxed about me recently, now that he thought I was his. So he sat with his mates and I was able to sit with mine. Truth to tell, Jon, Dewi and I never really had that much to say to each other alone.

Penhaearn sat in his best mourning coat, black silk tie and trilby.

The rest of us chatted quite excitedly.

We set off up the hill and off across the Migneint to join the A470.

Then my Anti Gwenlais went to the front of the bus and took the microphone from Garmon on the strict understanding that he could have it back when she'd finished.

'Tonight, is a very important occasion,' she announced.

'Today is November the eleventh. It is exactly seven hundred and eighteen years to the day after Llywelyn's death. Attempting to make contact with the ghost of Llywelyn is what we shall be doing. Nothing less. And we need every one of you to assist us. A sign is what you should be looking for, a clue. Something to tell us that now our time has come, that our waiting is over. Tonight, the Spirit of Wales is verily to be reborn.'

We all looked at each other, unsure whether to believe it or not, and tittered.

'The spirit of Llywelyn will come alive tonight and be reborn in Penhaearn Tegid Foel. We shall resurrect the Free Welsh Army and drive the English out of Llanchwaraeteg-danygelyn.'

There was a little light applause at this.

I felt quite glad that Dad and Awena and Gethin had stayed home.

'As we all know,' Gwenlais was saying, 'Penhaearn is custodian of the spirit of Wales – his father told him that, many times. Tonight we shall see the proof.'

There were murmurings around the bus at this.

'And not only that, we shall see action. Mark my words, Penhaearn will be the saviour of Wales.'

There was a little more applause.

I could see Dewi making comments to his friends and growing more and more restless.

'First he will save Llanchwaraetegdanygelyn. Then he will save Wales, uniting the Welsh nation for the first time in over seven hundred years. Would you like to come to address your followers, Penhaearn?' Gwenlais asked.

We all peered round to see his answer.

He shook his head.

So we had to go on listening to my Anti Gwenlais instead.

Dewi leapt up, went forward to the front of the bus, and seized the microphone.

'Tonight,' he told us, 'We are going to rise up and awake

our nation, after all these centuries of slumbering. Why else have we kept our precious language and ancient culture alive? We shall awake our nation. What shall we do?'

'Wake up our nation,' Rhys's lone voice echoed.

He tried again.

'What shall we do?'

'Wake up our nation.' A few more this time.

At the fourth attempt even Taid Dai Call and his little gang were joining in, though more from devilment than conviction.

'We'll raise the Ghost of Llywelyn. What will we do?'

'Raise the Ghost of Llywelyn.'

'Sais! Sais! Sais!!'

'Out! Out! Out!!!'

'English! English! English!!!'

'Out! Out!! Out!!!'

Corrupted by your intellectual rigour, Jon, I wanted to ask what rising up would involve exactly. Would we all have to dress up in armour and ride on white horses waving swords and lances? Would I be Gwenhwyfar to Dewi's Lawnslot?

Wisely, I think, I kept these thoughts to myself. These diversions passed the time. Dewi's antics amused me more than persuaded me as we zigzagged round the mountains on the A470 all the way down Wales to Llanelwedd. The voice was familiar, the message a liturgy: the dream of an independent Wales. The lure of having our own place in the world. Of being a nation. A nation state from eight hundred years ago. (See how you subverted me, Jon!)

Penhaearn stayed solemn and silent, preparing for leadership. Who knows what he was thinking.

Cilmeri itself, when we got there, could have done with being a lot more spooky. A small commuter village with modern bungalows, it was very suburban, and very English.

We parked in a lay-by, and there, through a gate in something like a small park, was a mound with a standing stone in the middle of it. There were plaques in Welsh and English. And a wreath. It was raining.

Mam looked as though she was about to speak to me. But went and stood with Gwenlais. Those of us with hoods, pulled them up. A couple of the councillors who had had the forethought to take umbrellas now had to share them with those who hadn't.

I stood awkwardly with Dewi and his friends, feeling as if I should be somewhere else taking minutes or orders for lunch or something. We all watched while Dai Ôd set up his equipment on top of the mound. Dewi was keen to join in and help, but Dai Ôd dissuaded him. Then attention switched to Jean and Billi-Jo who had started walking around the mound, reciting their mantras and doing something with their dowsing rods.

'They're testing the ley lines,' Hiraethog informed us. 'It's a very ancient art. They use it for finding water you know. In the desert.'

'I think I know where there's water,' Taid said helpfully. 'It seems to be coming from up there.'

He pointed towards the sky.

'The Lord provides,' said Irfon.

The ghost hunters conferred and shook their heads.

'What is it that they are doing?' Dewi asked.

'Looking for disturbances in the ectosphere,' Hiraethog told us, suddenly surprisingly knowledgeable about such things, the rain bouncing gleefully off his bald head.

'What's the ectosphere, then, Hiraethog?' Dewi asked.

'I'm afraid they didn't tell me that,' he said. 'Or if they did, I must have forgotten.'

'Tell me again what happened here,' Dewi asked me.

'You must know the history, Dewi.'

'Well. Sort of. I know it, I do. But tell me so I know it again.'

'This is where Llywelyn, the last Prince of Wales, and soon to be King, was killed by a British soldier. And Wales was cheated of our greatest hope of independence. Some say he was tricked away from his main army, some say the soldier had no idea who he was.'

I could sense some of the other councillors cocking their ears.

'You all know the story, don't you?' I asked

They shrugged.

'Can we hear it again?'

'Most historians agree that Llywelyn was away from his main army, with a small force, going for a meeting, camping for the night,' I said, my history popping up from somewhere. There are some advantages to having a headmaster for a father, you see.

My Anti Gwenlais came over.

'I've been sent to ask you all to hold hands and form a circle. Jean and Billi-Jo say you're interfering with the ambience, you see. But you can help us focus it if we all combine our spiritual energy.'

'Gwalia's been helping us get into the spirit, retelling the story, she has,' said Dewi. He smiled at me.

We did as we had been told and all held hands, watching in silence as they lit their candles, walked around the mound and recited incantations, first in one direction and then another.

'They're turning to all points of the compass,' Hiraethog informed us. 'Some nights it doesn't work, you know. It doesn't mean it's all nonsense though. It just means it's not working. On this occasion.'

'We understand,' said Taid, and winked at Elwyn and Irfon.

'I don't think there was much point in coming tonight,' Elwyn said.

'Perhaps after seven hundred years Prince Llywelyn has given up the ghost,' said Irfon.

'Seven hundred years in Purgatory would be enough for most men.'

'I don't think I would return from the dead for this rabble,' Taid remarked.

We were starting to feel very cold now.

Gwenlais came across again and asked us to sing 'Hen Wlad Fy Nhadau'.

We sang it very well. We always do. It didn't work, though.

Penhaearn and his team went into a huddle and then set off across the field down to the stream.

'What are they doing, Gwalia? What are they doing?' Dewi pestered.

'I think they must be going down to the spring,' Hiraethog offered. 'It's supposed to be important for some reason.'

'It's where the head of Llywelyn is said to have been washed after his beheading, before being taken to London and put on a pike staff at the Tower of London,' I informed him.

Dewi went off after them.

The rest of us went back to the bus to get warm.

A few minutes later Dewi returned and took the microphone to make an important announcement.

'All it is is a stone trough like a concrete coal bunker with a wooden cover which hinges back,' he told us.

'Did you see anything,' Hiraethog asked. 'Have Jean and Billi-Jo succeeded?'

'It was very spooky,' Dewi said. And we all shifted forward in our seats to hear better.

'As Penhaearn lifted the cover, something flew out and landed on his chest. Dai Ôd's equipment went off the scale.'

We all gasped.

'Gotcha there,' said Dewi. 'It was a frog.'

The ghost hunters climbed back on the bus in silence. Penhaearn looked as though he wished he was invisible.

Nor did they say much all the way home. Dewi sat next to me. Then Mam came over.

'Never mind,' she said. 'We've got the hotel, Y Ddwy Ddraig. We've got the family. And there's Gethin and Awena to think about now.'

'I know, Mam. It'll be fine.'

We knew there'd be no more mad ghost hunts.

That was the moment Dewi chose to hug me into his shoulder and propose yet again.

'Will you marry me, Gwalia, Please.'

I pulled away and looked at him.

He repeated it.

'Wyt ti isio 'mhrodi i?'

I smiled.

And nodded.

And we kissed gently. I felt Dewi's relief and happiness sweep over him in little shakes. I could at least make his dream true for him. Perhaps. And that gave me a sense of joy and rightness, even if no one could ever make my dreams true.

I snuggled back into his shoulder. Awena would have a father, a good man who worked hard and fought for what he believed in and had always supported Awena and me. In a way, I felt a kind of peace.

Something good at least had come out of the trip.

How can I explain to you, Jon? For the first time in a very long time, I felt cherished, at ease with myself. And independent of you, the powerful man who would have swept me up and dominated me and swamped me with his life. Someone true and good had loved me in his more modest, more appropriate way. And I had surrendered to that. It felt right, Jon. Really it did. One less battle to be fought.

I wouldn't be an island any more.

It was a few miles on, near Rhaeadr Gwy, that Gwenlais broke the silence with a statement so completely at odds with my train of thought, I felt my flesh creep.

'I think,' she announced over the microphone, 'we should ask Gwalia to ask her young man – you know the black one from Westminster who helped her renovate Y Ddwy Ddraig – if he could return to help us.'

'Yes,' somebody shouted. 'Yes.'

'He could get grants to buy all the houses that are for sale and rent them to local Welsh speakers.'

'He could get money to re-open the factory.'

'He could help the town the way he helped Y Ddwy Ddraig.'

'He could bring a new factory here.'

I felt my body stiffen with rising panic. I had made my decision. Wasn't the world supposed to change when you made decisions?

'Could you, Gwalia?'

'Please, Gwalia, ask him.'

'If we don't do something, the town will die. Or all the houses will be sold off for second homes.'

'Either way, we'll become a ghost town.'

I stood up and looked at the smiling, imploring faces, pressing in on me. I wanted to scream. Or hide. Or run away.

'Come on, Gwalia. That's a good idea.'

Dewi held my hand tightly. I squeezed it and looked at him questioningly.

He could see my panic.

He squeezed back gently, but strong and sure.

And smiled.

'It's OK, it is,' he said. 'There's nothing to stop you asking him.'

'Come on, Gwalia, you've seen the state of things!'

'It's young people I feel sorry for. There's no way they can afford to buy them and start families here.'

'Yes, ask Jon Bull.'

It was as if Dewi's strength helped me hold my panic and drive it away to that place where all my fears had now been driven. I could think clearly about it now.

There could be no harm in asking you, Jon, I thought. You could only say no.

'Iawn,' I said. – All right.

NEITHER OF US had actually said that it was over, though it obviously was. When I got your invitation, I had the idea in my mind that, perhaps, you wanted to rekindle our flame.

I realised that was wrong when I arrived to find you and Dewi waiting for me. And saw that Dewi was holding your hand. I also spotted the engagement ring. But I did see something in your eyes. A concern, a pleading, an apology. I could feel you willing me to just say yes. Just for now, at least.

Besides, I had come a long way.

Dewi led me up to the same room I had had the first time I came to Llanchwaraetegdanygelyn and dumped my bags down. The room was *en-suite* now, with fitted carpets and smart new window frames. The architects had done a good job. The hotel had an air of being businesslike and successful. There was much to be said for incentive grants.

'Gobeithio y gwnewch chi fwynhau eich arhosiad gyda ni,' he said very formally, and left.

You appeared in the doorway a few minutes later, lurking awkwardly.

'I meant to write to tell you, Jon,' you said. 'Dewi and I have got engaged.'

'Congratulations.'

'We're the same kind of people, Dewi and me. It wouldn't have worked with you and me, Jon. We're from different worlds.'

'You've slept with him, haven't you?'

Your eyes widened and then you looked down.

'It's OK Gwalia. I'm pleased for you. I hope you're happy.'

The words were like some script I'd memorised. I knew that in one sense they were entirely appropriate, in another they felt utterly fake.

My love for you was curdling in my bowels.

'Thank you for coming to help us, Jon,' you said very weakly in Welsh, coming towards me. 'The town is really in a terrible state, you know.'

You touched my arm. And tried to kiss my cheek.

I flinched and you pulled away.

'I know,' I lied. 'That's why I'm here.'

That old goat Penhaearn greeted me sullenly; he seemed a subtly different chap from the man I'd tried to deal with just a year before. And perhaps I was different, too. That curdling feeling in my bowels hadn't gone. I wondered if he knew that you had cuckolded me. There was less arrogance in both of us.

Of course he knew. Men sense these things in each other. Just as I sensed things in him. That he no longer eagerly rubbed his hands together. That the haughty stare and strident handshake were gone. He seemed more sheepish now than goatish. But I felt different too.

'Bore da, Mr Jones. Dach chi'n iawn?' I asked, numbly, but proud enough to acknowledge him in his own language. Even after all the humiliation he had caused me with Freddy Morgan and the Leyburn Institute – and that you were now causing me, Gwalia – I had this deep conviction that I must rise above my own petty feelings. My life was based on logic and idealism, and if it wasn't then I was nothing.

'Dwi wedi clywed eich bod chi'n cael problemau,' I said.

'We are seeming to need your skills,' he conceded, sourly. 'There is a crisis in my town. Though it pains me to admit it, Mr Bull, it was a sad, sad day when our factory closed.'

'I will do whatever I can to help,' I said. I felt more confident talking business. I knew this town. I had written its strategy. 'I think I have the authority of her Majesty's Government to say that.'

Perhaps it was the word Majesty that sparked his anger. Perhaps I meant it to.

'Government authority. It was your English Government that failed us, it was. Do they not realise how their economic policies have been an absolute disaster for industries in Wales? Driving manufacturing overseas. Doing nothing to protect our jobs.'

Something in me snapped.

'I suppose it's useless trying to explain the realities of modern global economics to you?'

He looked at me quite blankly.

'Still stuck in the thirteenth century perhaps. Protectionism? Stop foreigners stealing our jobs? Or selling their wares in our country? How are we going to enforce it, Mr Penhaearn Jones? Have you got your medieval sword and shield and armour, have you?'

'I don't think they should be able to take our jobs and sell their cheap, shoddy goods. It puts Welsh manufacturers out of business.'

I laughed in his face, Gwalia.

'Ha! A mercantilist's model for economics, based on gold, trade tariffs and import restrictions. I wouldn't expect you to understand contemporary macroeconomics but I would expect a County Councillor to have at least some inkling of what monetarism was all about.'

Something strange happened then.

Penhaearn somehow crumpled before my eyes. I thought for a moment he was going to cry.

'I don't think you will ever truly understand how it is for us here, Mr Bull.'

'I am trying,' I said, my frustration with him now tinged with sympathy and guilt at my own anger. I wanted to know about him. To understand why. But then I remembered there probably wasn't anyone I could discuss it with anymore.

'You see, Mr Bull. We have a very strong sense of community here. We Welsh-speaking communities are the soul of Wales – Enaid Cymru, we call it – and you can have no conception just how heartbreaking it is for us to see our community broken up in this way.'

I had gone too far. I wanted to influence and persuade him, not destroy him. I searched for words to reassure him.

'I am here to help,' I said, more gently. 'That's why I'm here.'

As he turned away, I saw the mourner's mask fall from his face, as he collapsed further into disillusion.

'I doubt that there is anything you can do, Mr Bull. Look at the For Sale signs. There is a positive stampede to leave. Many of the men have already had to move to work away. Only the elderly will be left. Your English policies have ruined us. And it is happening all over Wales. With factories closing down and jobs disappearing overseas.'

This was awful. What could I say to him? As a professional, I needed him to be strong, not wrong and broken. (It's no triumph winning an argument on global capitalism with a man who's having a nervous breakdown.) But, as a man, I couldn't bring myself to comfort him.

'What is happening in Llanchwaraetegdanygelyn is happening everywhere,' I said, trying to moderate my tone. 'Work is migrating around the world, to the places where labour is cheapest. Workers here have priced themselves out of the world market.'

Laughable as Penhaearn's feudal protectionist ideas were, it crossed my mind how it might be to come back six centuries in the future and find out how many policies and theories that I have built my mindset on were wrong – as they inevitably would be.

He rallied and his eyes met mine. Although they were the eyes of a defeated man, there was now an honesty in them, an honesty that challenged me.

'What, in one word, is your answer to our woes,' he demanded.

'Un gair?' I said. 'Strategaeth.'

'Strategy,' he scoffed. 'Always strategy. You see, Mr Bull, to me that is an empty word. A box with nothing in it. You English come here with your presents beautifully wrapped in lovely boxes, but they are empty. So we need an immediate strategy for halting the exodus? How perceptive of you! If you are half the man that Gwalia claims you are, you will do better than that!'

The mention of your name, Gwalia, stung me.

'So what kind of strategy would you like?' I asked acidly.

'We need money, Mr Bull. Even as we speak, Messrs Flood and Ingress are floating a company on the stock exchange to buy up all these houses and turn Llanchwaraetegdanygelyn into a holiday village. We need your grants: to buy up all the houses. And rent them out to local families. I've done my research Mr Bull, it will cost less than the average new roundabout scheme on a city motorway.'

I took a deep breath. This was my last chance. I couldn't go on telling him he was wrong.

'Who is going to live in these houses?'

'Young people.'

'Where are they going to work?'

'In the factory.'

'The factory is closed.'

'You are going to open it again.'

'It won't work, Penhaearn. It's not economically viable. And you won't attract new business without mains power, water and proper sewerage. Without employment you don't have a strategy.'

He was silent. Then shook his head. I thought again that he was going to cry.

'Listen, Councillor,' I said. 'If you can deliver the support and enthusiasm of the townspeople, I think I can set up a holding strategy.'

'More strategy!'

I shook my head. Even now he would not listen.

'I very much doubt you can help us, then, Mr Bull.'

'I think I can, Councillor Penhaearn. But you have to let me do it in a viable way.'

'You can have no idea how we have suffered here. Seven hundred years ago, they cruelly slaughtered our last great Prince, Llywelyn, tricked him, they did. Caught him without his army. And took his head to London where they left it rotting on a pike in the Tower of London for fifteen years.

And then they defeated Glyndŵr, our last hope beyond a last hope.'

Now I did feel sorry for him – for being so pathetic.

'I think we need to address ourselves to modern times,' I told him, using the excellent Welsh word 'cyfeirio' for 'address', with its connotations of *direction*.

'Ah yes, Mr Bull. Modern Times. Modern times is when they flooded my home town, you know, Capel Y Gelyn. For English water. Our soul – Enaid Cymru – lies drowned under twenty fathoms of our own Welsh water. That is what your English people did to me and my people. But you, of course, are too preoccupied with your stupid boxes of empty strategy to see that.

'You have no conception how my people have suffered over the centuries. And it still continues into your so-called modern times. All over Wales, the English are engulfing our towns and swamping us with their chain stores, multiplex cinemas and shopping malls. Every town the same. Redeveloped from your same cheap-skate strategies. And all in English. Drowning Wales, its language and its culture. It is no improvement!'

It was probably the word *stupid* that provoked me. That was the moment the frustration I felt with him, and the anger I felt at your engagement to Dewi, Gwalia – at your betrayal – broke to the surface.

'Yes, Mr Penhaearn Tegid Foel, I probably do seem very stupid to you. But don't you tell me I have no conception of your suffering. Look at my skin, Mr Jones. While your people were being lifted out of the Dark Ages by the greatest Empire the world had ever seen, my people were being bought and sold from Africa.'

He recoiled away from me, but I leaned toward him.

'And don't imagine we in England have no conception of your experience. Our towns are seeing wave after wave of immigrants, not just from the Commonwealth but from Poland, from Lithuania, East Germany and Africa. This is how it's always been. You Celts yourselves were once a wave of immigrants.

'You complain about the way the English trample on your culture. You had a Bible in Welsh. My people were ripped away from their land and language and culture. But you probably think we were only savages. Unknown numbers died, Councillor Penhaearn Tegid Foel. A barely documented holocaust that packed us into ships and sold us through the ports of Merseyside and Bristol – both estuaries with one coast Welsh, you notice – and took those who survived the beatings and disease and starvation in the dark holds of wooden ships halfway across the world.

'And then, on the other side of the world, Mr Jones, we were put to work as slaves. Our women were raped. Our men were beaten and killed. Many of us were worked to death. Many died of disease. Often of venereal disease caused by their rape by white people. And are you telling me none of them were Welsh?'

I could see my spit and words hitting him in the face. I couldn't stop. Until that moment, I had no idea that I had this anger in me. This cultural anger.

'And we are only part of the horror in the world, Mr Jones. While you have been worrying about being subjugated by a relatively benign colonial monster – as monsters go – all over the world there have been genocides, holocausts, nuclear bombs, starvation, children as young as seven being given Kalashnikovs and uniforms and told to go out and kill, young men and women being turned into suicide bombers, not to mention all your run-of-the-mill wars, tortures, sex-trading, drug-running, cruelty – the world's everyday kaleidoscope of atrocities.'

Each word was bludgeoning him. I searched for the *coup de grace*.

'You have no conception, Mr Jones. So don't you ever dare lecture me again on what I know and what I don't know.'

That wasn't it.

'I have learned your language. I have loved your people. I have sung your songs, feeling the sad tunes in my heart and knowing what the words meant. Please don't cheapen your culture by attacking other people's. You think you are some kind of prince here. I see no kingly deeds.'

We were both exhausted.

'I really have come here to help you, you know. You see yourself as oppressed, but the truth is in your heart, you think like a white colonialist. You see me as a man descended from slaves. And, no doubt, in your subconscious, you have all the misconceptions of the vile English slave traders – that blacks are more like animals, and certainly inferior. Not worth as much as you. All the things they told themselves so they could sleep at nights with full bellies in big houses and comfortable beds, while my people died in their hundreds of thousands, if not millions, bought and sold.'

He shook his head. But he didn't speak.

I still had anger to expend.

'Am I a savage, Mr Jones? A stupid primitive man, closer to the apes than white men? Not as intelligent, perhaps? Do you think that?

'Well, think of this Mr Penhaearn Tegid Foel. Despite the suffering of my people, much worse and far more recent than the suffering of yours, I am here to help you. Not the other way around.'

He looked up at me. A different look in his face.

'I understand your problem, Mr Jones. You are condemned to being a victim forever. All the people of Capel Y Gelyn are. Perhaps all Welsh nationalists are. You see, Penhaearn, once the Welsh Nationalists had picked up the flooding of Capel Y Gelyn as their rallying point, victims is all you could ever be. For the rest of your lives.'

He opened his mouth to say something.

I spoke first.

'Being descended from slaves – that was my people's birthright. Being victims is yours. Always seeing yourselves as victims. Well, I reject my birthright. I reject the prejudices of inherited bigotry. I want my generation – and each new generation – to start afresh. I am my own man, Penhaearn. My own man. Can the Welshman be his own man, too?'

That curdled feeling in my bowels had gone.

Whatever I felt for you – and it was a great deal – would not be changed by your weakness, Gwalia. I had loved you, the girl who brought bluebells to my room and opened the door of Wales to me. In my heart, I always would love that girl, even if she had now turned into someone else.

I knew what my priorities were.

I went back to Y Ddwy Ddraig, where Bronwen was on reception, and went up to my room with the firm intention of working. But, when I got there, I just stood looking out of the window, across the Maes. I didn't know where you or Dewi were but it was as if my heart was scanning the landscape for you. I could hear the bank of generators running at the back of the hotel. I felt disinclined to get my laptop out.

The *en-suite* had its disadvantages. No chance now of being caught by you on my way back from the shower in only a towel, Gwalia. No reason for you to dally at my threshold.

Later, I sent down for a bar meal but I didn't recognise the girl who brought it. Why would I want to see you anyway? Finally, I got down to work and drafted my task in outline.

My bag was full of background reading, but I was thinking of you, Gwalia.

I made a lot of notes and turned them into tables and bullet points, hoping that some solution might magically leap out at me. Halt the exodus. Create an economic imperative for people to stay. Protect the Welsh language. Maintain the cultural integrity of the town. An impossible challenge.

Something inside me wanted to prove something to you. Prove something to myself. That I was a better man than either of us thought. Better than the evidence showed.

I went to bed and turned the light off, but I couldn't sleep.

As I dozed, all kinds of thoughts jostled in my head: the things I had said to Penhaearn, the things I should have said; the things I had said to you, and should have said. A year ago, you had stood there in that doorway, you'd felt differently then.

Half asleep I turned the big questions over in my head.

What was wrong with me?

Why couldn't my life go according to strategy?

I thought that I was dreaming when I heard the door click and you slipped across the room into my bed.

No shyness.

No restraint.

And we made love, didn't we!

You felt it, too. I know you did.

But when I woke up in the morning, you were gone.

MY HEART WAS BLEEDING for my country, Jon.

My name is Gwalia. My name is strong.

If my words look solid on the page, the hand that wrote them trembled.

And its spirit wavered.

There is a side of me which is disgusting. As it was in Cardiff, that awful night.

I am a lustful woman, Jon. A real Mata Hari. And I lust for you. And sometimes that has nothing to do with love.

I told myself I wanted to give something back to you. I felt you had a right to it; I owed it to you after all the things you'd done for me. But if I am honest, it was really for me. I truly loved you for the things you had done for me. And for coming back, and for all the things you were going to do for my town.

I never explained to you how much I agonised about not sleeping with you in London. Something stopped me. Awena, your parents. Me. It just seemed wrong. Even now, my soul melts with shame just to think of it. It was a very narrow choice. I cried so much at the thought of losing you, my extraordinary man.

But in the end I had to think of Awena. My daughter.

Let me call her Cymru.

I had decided I had to be her mother. And make a family with Dewi. It was my own life, what matter if I spoiled it? It was already ruined, imperfect, already too late for me. I could at least make sure Awena's life was free.

Why should I not have come to your bed in the night?

Why should I not have indulged myself that once, now that you had cured the problem of my nose and Dewi had made of me a proper woman? It melted me down to look at you, to be with you, and to touch you: the naked stranger at my waterfall, the hero who came to save me. But it still felt right to be Dewi's. He was going to be my husband. I was going to be a wife and mother and you were going to help us save the town.

Dydy o ddim o bwys pwy sydd ar fai!

What could we have given each other at that time, Jon?

To you, I am a child of Umbo, full of all the contradictory ideas that I inherited! I am a citizen of Llanchwaraeteg-danygelyn, not the world.

I SOMEHOW KNEW I wasn't supposed to allude to that fantastic night again.

'Sut mae'r prosiect yn mynd?' you asked me as I walked into the dining room the following morning.

'I think I've made a start,' I said. Your face looked radiant.

'Great,' you said. 'That's good news for the town, I'm sure.'

Dewi was watching us, glancing between us. I helped myself to cereal from the buffet and sat down. The dining room had been transformed, and there were half a dozen people already eating.

'We must do for Llanchwaraetegdanygelyn what we have done for Y Ddwy Ddraig,' I said.

You smiled and I saw that little crease at the corner of your mouth and wanted to kiss it.

'I know you will, Jon. I know you will.'

You turned and strode away, your skirt kicking up behind a little too provocatively.

I felt a kind of thrill run through me.

Despite a whole evening's work, I still had nothing of any value.

It was then that I heard Dewi talking in Welsh to a couple who looked like retired teachers from England. He was miming his actions to fit the words.

'Be fasech chi'n licio?' he indicated the menu.

'Eggs and bacon,' said the man, putting down his *Daily Telegraph* crossword.

'Wyau wedi ffrio, a bacwn,' said Dewi, pointing to the words on the menu.

'Wee-aye,' said the woman. 'Wedi ffrio. Does "ffrio" mean fried?'

'Ydy,' Dewi told her, nodding and smiling. 'Da iawn. Mae gennoch chi wraig glyfar iawn,' he told the man.

The man was laughing.

'What's he saying?'

'I think he's saying you have a very clever wife,' she said.

'Da iawn,' said Dewi, miming clapping.

And the pair laughed.

'Let me try,' the man said. 'Wyau wedi ffrio a bacwn. And toast.'

'Tôst,' said Dewi.

'Tôst,' said the man, nodding.

Dewi went off to fetch the order and the couple chortled and congratulated each other.

'I didn't realise so many people spoke Welsh,' she said. 'Isn't it fun.'

'It's great,' he said. 'It's just like being abroad. I know, we'll see if we can buy a phrase book.'

'You might get one in the Post Office,' I suggested. 'The Swyddfa'r Post.'

'Swyddfa'r Post.' They repeated this.

And we all laughed.

It was worrying that my spirits seemed so high.

Is it possible for a political scientist to be happy without a strategy?

The male equivalent of a mistress. (There isn't even a proper word for it.) How does a man get into the position of being the other man, the bit on the side?

It wasn't quite how I saw myself, at the time, being your secret lover while you flaunted your engagement to my rival, but that was how it was, wasn't it, Gwalia? Some men might be proud of such a conquest, I have to confess I wasn't. Conquest? Isn't that the language of imperialism? This was the new world!

But I would have liked your wonderful softness and kisses for myself, exclusively.

And now, to make matters worse, I was also your impotent puppet in the business of the town as well. I had no idea how I'd ended up in this sad role, or why I was putting up with it.

Or how I was going to get out of it.

'Twristiaeth,' I said, slowly in Welsh, having to look it up in a dictionary on a pocket computer. 'Unfortunately, tourism seems to be the only solution.'

'No,' said Dewi in English, fascinated by my nifty finger work. 'No way.'

The stained-glass window was reflected in the polished oak of the big round table in the Town Hall. But we had cast aside the Mayor's Chair. There was no chairman now. I was determined that the emphasis had to be on democracy, and that the meeting should be in Welsh and for the Welsh, provided my electronic translator could keep up with finding words for things like 'cashflow' and 'industrial output'. We'd talk to the English later. There would be no point if I didn't get the agreement of the Welsh.

Iwan, from the Welsh Assembly, was sitting beside me. I had felt mightily relieved to see his friendly face.

A dozen or so others sat looking at me expectantly, nearly all of them unfamiliar, although I had been introduced to everybody, the names weren't staying in my head. They all seemed to be called Jones or Roberts or Davies. I was looking somewhere for a chink of light.

'Mae'n ddrwg gen i, Dewi,' I said carefully, looking around. 'Dw i'n deall fod gen ti amheuon.' I wanted to say that I understood Dewi's doubts. I also understood why he might hate me. If he didn't suspect already that you were coming to my room at night, Gwalia, surely he would discover it soon.

Dewi nodded, and said something to you, Gwalia, that I didn't understand.

Hiraethog wasn't there, nor Penhaearn; not even Boudiccea had come. The story was that she had left Lawns and moved back to London, as much a victim of Penhaearn's hubris as Hiraethog, their good intentions cut short like those of Gelert, the mythical dog.

'I think we should listen to what Mr Bull has to say,' Iwan said, a bit too sharply.

'No way,' Dewi repeated. 'We are not having this town

overrun with English bastards. First they come here for the day, then for a holiday, don't they not? They decide they like it so much they move in.'

'Tell us why you are recommending tourism, Mr Bull,' your Dad asked gently in Welsh.

My vocabulary was probably still not good enough, but as long as I stuck to simple constructions, I could get by. It was understanding what other people said that caused the problems, especially when they spoke too quickly for me. And it took only one word I didn't recognise, or couldn't guess, or guessed mistakenly, to send me tumbling into incomprehension. As long as I was doing the talking, it was easier for me, though perhaps not for everyone else.

'Tourism is the ... er ... fastest growing sector in the Welsh economy. Wales is muchly under-developed in its possible tourists. In truth, you only have to look at the Yorkshire Dales or the Lake District and see that in reality.'

I looked around the dozen faces, and saw only puzzlement. Maybe it had not been such a good idea to set up an informal group this time, and perhaps I should have strangled you when you insisted on including Dewi.

'I'm afraid I have never been to these places that you mention,' your father said.

It was clear that the success of Y Ddwy Ddraig had raised his status in the town. And yours, Gwalia. After the Supermart, your hotel was now the town's biggest business.

'Nor do we want to,' Dewi half rose in his chair.

If I was going to achieve anything here this time, I needed the agreement of everyone in the room, at the very least, before I began to think about the rest of the town.

I was aware that every sentence I spoke was taking a risk. If I alienated Dewi – or anyone else – it was probably over. This was my second chance. I was lucky to get it. There would be no third. And it had to be in Welsh.

'Let Jon speak, Dewi.'

You patted Dewi on the arm. He glanced at you and

relaxed. The perfect couple! You so proprietorial, him so obedient. I must admit it crossed my mind that if I could drive a wedge between you I would love to do it. But I must resist that urge.

'Dewi is OK to be cautious,' I said brightly. If I could persuade him, I would win.

'It is possible tourism will seriously change your character and personality. As someone who has myself struggled to be learning Welsh – and does it only less perfectly than you are hearing – I am sensitively to that and hopefully that I have taken your language and culture into my . . . er . . . accountancy. Unfortunately, in terms of economic resourcefulness, you are in a very weak positions. No industry remaining, no main services imported never and being too far located from centres of employment to be a very real town for . . .' I resorted to the English word . . . 'commuting'.

'Could we attract other factories here?' somebody asked.

I shook my head and looked at Iwan.

'Do you want to explain?'

'Jon's right. Factories all over Wales are closing. Firms are moving production to China and the Far East for cheaper labour.'

'It's not just Wales,' I said. 'It's right across Europe.'

'Offices then,' someone else said. 'We could get the Assembly to relocate some offices here. They have a policy of moving offices to North Wales.'

Iwan shook his head. 'You haven't got enough skilled people here.'

'Look,' I said in my poor Welsh. 'I know it's frustrating of you. But you can't be changing the way world economy is being working. No business will be moving here without a guaranteed workforce existing. All your clever eighteen-year-old children leave themselves to go to university and don't come back. They go where the jobs and good money are. All skilled people leave.'

'They should bring the workforce here, then, they should,' Dewi said, banging his fist on the table. 'That would solve the problem, wouldn't it?'

Iwan shook his head.

'The workforce wouldn't do it, Dewi. Uproot their children? Move from Cardiff or Llantuhwnt and come to a tiny, isolated community with no electricity and running water? Where would they plug in their plasma TVs and cappuccino-makers? No one's going to move a city-loving workforce from glamorous Cardiff to a town beyond, that's how they see you – you're beyond sheep country, here, boy. The only people who might come would be East European immigrants.'

'Think about it, Dewi. You'd be moving in non-Welsh-speakers wholesale.'

Dewi jumped to his feet. 'So you're telling us there's no solution then?'

Half of me wanted to walk out and leave them to it. They didn't deserve a solution. And then I looked at you, Gwalia. I couldn't look at you without remembering your body. The taste and smell of you. Whatever my logical mind told me, even a fragment of you made all the pain worthwhile.

'Don't panic, boy,' Iwan cautioned. But he was talking to Dewi, not me.

I rallied.

'No, Dewi, I'm not telling you that. We wouldn't be here if we were to be thinking that.'

I looked at your face, Gwalia. You looked very sad. You'd hardly said a word. You caught my eye. Was that guilt I saw there? Or regret? Or were you thinking only about the town?

'So that brings us back to tourism,' you said, hopelessly, by way of prompting me.

Your father looked around the table.

'I think, if that is our only realistic option, then we should at least discuss it,' he said. 'It strikes me that attracting anybody here will be difficult enough.'

We all looked at Dewi. He was sitting down now, staring at the table.

'Tourism is our only option, Dewi,' you told him. 'I think we should at least listen.'

433

'No!' He banged the table.

'Are you prepared to let the town die, then?' Iwan asked.

His question hung in the air.

'If the language and culture die, Llanchwaraetegdanygelyn dies,' Dewi said through clenched teeth. 'It's the only reason we're here. If Welsh dies, it would be right for the town to die with it, so it would.'

People shuffled uncomfortably in their seats.

Your Dad sucked his breath in but said nothing.

We all sat in silence, thinking about that. If only Dewi would accept tourism, the problem stood a small chance of being solvable, though even then it wouldn't be easy. As it was, I could see no hope at all. The chances of attracting any manufacturer or offices without mains power or services were zero. Tourism was the only option.

I should have given up then.

Except that something in me wouldn't quite let go. I'd like to think it was professionalism, but I think it was more instinctive than that.

'Look,' I said. 'I understand your objections to tourism, Dewi. And I understand you're the spokesman here for what a lot of people in the town must feel. But . . . If I could come up with a tourism solution which protected the Welsh language and culture – or even helped to strengthen it – would you be prepared to consider that?'

'There's no way you're going to do that, there isn't.'

'Maybe not, but if by some miracle I could . . .'

'I'm sorry, Jon,' your father said. 'Better men than you have spent their lives trying to find a solution to this one, I'm afraid.'

He looked at Iwan.

'It's certainly a tough one,' he conceded.

Dewi laughed. 'You haven't got a hope. You'd need a miracle.'

'Gwalia?' I looked at you. 'Do you believe in miracles?'

You looked defiantly at Dewi.

'Yes. I think I do, Jon. I believe in you.'

'So if I could come up with such a plan, to protect Welsh and promote tourism, you would consider it?'

'Yes,' you said. 'If you could perform that miracle. I would believe in it.'

'Dewi?'

'Yeah, I suppose.'

'Everyone?'

Everyone shrugged or nodded.

I looked directly at Iwan, now.

'So, if I could produce a strategy that had the support of the town, the Assembly would support it?'

'Of course we would, boyo! The last thing we want is for the town to die. But you'll have to move very quickly. We've got access to some emergency funding, but only until the end of this financial year. That's only six weeks. If you can't agree the strategy before then, it'll be reallocated, you know that. I'm sorry, it's not in my hands.'

'Right then. Give me a week.'

As I got up, I saw Dewi try to kiss you.

You saw me looking and shrugged him away crossly.

I went back to London, burning with disappointment, betrayal and confusion.

I was not the kind of person I thought I was. Not the person I wanted to be. I thought that I was logical. And that flawless logic was enough to make a man strong. Yet here I was, a victim of emotion, unable to assert myself to anyone. Not to you, not to the town, not even to myself.

So weak that now I had agreed – no, promised, against what should have been my better judgement – to try to achieve the impossible.

What was wrong with me that I always seemed to set myself up for failure when I was with you?

What was wrong with me, that even with all my knowledge and apparent intellect, I couldn't seem to make anything work for me?

Back in London, I should have felt better. Three hundred miles from Llanchwaraetegdanygelyn should have been far enough to view it objectively. But I tortured myself during those five hours home, trying to work out what I should say to Andrew and Nisha when they asked me how you were. What should I tell them? Should I tell them about Dewi, and about you sneaking secretly into my room? And I arrived home no further forward.

And then I thought of something.

Do you remember, Gwalia, taking me to the coast between Borth and Tywyn in Cardigan Bay, and showing me the stumps of ancient trees still standing in the sand where they once grew in soil before the bay was flooded? These are the ghosts of a more ancient Wales.

And telling me the legend that there was once a kingdom here, the land of Cantre'r Gwaelod – The Bottom Hundred – with sixteen towns. I'm sure you learned the story from your aunty Gwenlais, it has her ring about it. Indeed, you told me that some gullible people claim that on stormy nights the bells of Cantre'r Gwaelod can still be heard.

By all accounts, this long-drowned kingdom was once rich and prosperous but it had two weaknesses – its prince and its reliance on ancient sea defences. According to myth, Prince Seithennin was a drunkard and a fool and the court was drunken and licentious. His brother Teithrin warned him that the dykes were about to collapse. But Seithennin would not listen.

'They're keeping the water out, aren't they,' Seithennin argued and called for more drink.

Teithrin tried again and again to persuade his brother. But Seithennin would not listen.

'Our forefathers built those embankments. They've stood for generations and they'll stand for a lot more generations to come. If we try to mend them, we'll probably only make them worse. Stop worrying. Drink up.'

Inevitably, as is the way with morality tales, the big storm came, and flooded all the land.

Teithrin escaped with his loyal friend Prince Elphin and his brother's daughter, Angharad, but the rich kingdom of Cantre'r Gwaelod was drowned forever, leaving only the myth – and (if you are foolish enough to believe in such things) the sound of the bells on stormy nights.

What you, Gwalia, may not have known, is that historians recognise many stories of flooding around the world, just at the dawn of civilization, coinciding with the end of the Ice Age and earlier global warming. So the flooding was inevitable.

But the primitive folk who peddle primitive myths prefer to blame the foolishness of kings. The conspiracy of fate to punish the frivolous.

How then to lure your people away from their primitive myths?

Andrew and Nisha were brilliant. Even though I had firmly resolved to tell them nothing about my changed romantic status, my new role as your bit on the side, when it came to it, I blurted it all out at the first opportunity.

'Poor you,' Nisha said.

And I just stared at her.

'Poor both of you,' said Andrew. 'Sounds to me as if her bond with her home life and culture is just too strong. Don't knock yourself up about it. That's life.'

'What you did is what you felt you had to do at that moment,' Nisha said. 'Don't try too hard to analyse it or to judge yourself. In that moment it was right. Neither of you can be harmed by that unless you allow yourselves to be.'

Heartened by their wisdom, I set to my task of writing the impossible strategy: a tourism plan which would protect the town from visitors.

'That's good,' said Andrew, glad to be distracted from his desk to the Hub for a few minutes. 'That's really good. Beguile tourists, protect the language, promote the culture.'

'The logic of my strategy is impeccable, I assure you.'

'I think it's brilliant,' said Nisha. 'And it protects a language.' She clapped her hands. 'How do you say that in Welsh?'

'Amddiffyn yr iaith. You don't think it's a bit pathetic to be doing this after Gwalia dumped me for a local boy, then?'

'Perhaps when she sees your genius she will realise her mistake, and change her mind.'

She gave my hand a squeeze.

'I don't think so,' I said. 'Perhaps, for those of us who are trying to live for the future, it is a lonely road.'

'Well this is pioneering stuff, Jon. This is the future.'

'Crisis management and improvisation is what it really is. Cut out the impossible and what's left must become viable strategy.'

'Don't be so self-critical,' Andrew said. 'It's a good strategy.'

'Do you think Angela Lain and Freddy Morgan will go for it? All I need is for them to agree for me to have six months' funding to work on it,' I asked.

'I think they'll love it,' said Nisha. 'I think you should go and talk to Angela now. She's got no one with her this morning.'

But Angela was not as effusive as Nisha or Andrew.

'Realistically, Jon, there is no need to intervene. The Torrent Consortium will buy up the town and make it viable again. Job done.'

'If you went there, Angela, and saw how depressed and disheartened everyone was, you wouldn't say that. This is the last purely Welsh-speaking community in Wales. It's important for that reason alone.'

'So? You know how it is, Jon. Something's lost and something's gained. Language is constantly evolving anyway. We can't freeze everything in time. Anyway, they shot themselves in the foot when they rejected your initial plan. I have no sympathy. And Freddy will say the same. You know he will.'

'Please, Angela. Imagine if it was a species that was going to become extinct. Think what it says about us, if we just walk away. This is a deprived rural community. Of course they are defensive and aggressive. Those are the standard psychological symptoms of any disheartened and demotivated community – you know that. You can't judge them by that. They have a victim culture.'

'We gave them their opportunity, they didn't take it. You gave them another opportunity and they rejected it again. Now you want us to make the same mistake a third time?'

'I want us to do what's right, Angela. The people of Llanchwaraetegdanygelyn weren't to know their factory was going to close and the economy was going to shrink to nothing overnight. This is a bankrupt town; even if the consortium implements its strategy, the people who are bankrupt now will still be bankrupt. I need time to work on this, Angela. Please.'

'Even if I agree. What then?'

'Maybe we could get Freddy to recommend that the Welsh Assembly fund it.'

'*We* could? You mean *I* could.'

'Ok. Yeah. You could persuade Freddy. Please.'

'Why not let the Assembly run the project then?'

'No. It needs us. It needs me. This will be good for the Leyburn Institute if it works, Angela. I promise. A new string to our bow. A real success. I know it's always easier for you to say 'No' than 'Yes', because 'No' is always a self-fulfilling prophecy. This time, I'm asking you: please take the risk. Say yes.'

'I don't think you should be talking to me like this, Jon. I've made my decision. No. It's final. Leave it to the Torrent Consortium.'

'Fine then. I don't care. You can stuff your job. I resign. There. Happy?'

'If that's how you feel, Jon. It's your decision.'

I was shaking when I emerged from Angela's office. I'm not sure if it was with anger or disappointment. I had been reduced to the temperament of a five-year-old. I'd just resigned from the greatest job I'd ever had.

And all this because of a girl – because of you, Gwalia.

I walked straight across the office back to my desk and started emptying my drawers. My face must have looked as if it had just been punched. I was aware only of a kind of ringing in my ears and my own thoughts.

I'd put everything into that project, and even though I say so myself, my briefing paper was brilliant. I'd thrown myself into your language and culture, Gwalia, and, without noticing, the thread by which my own interest hung had been getting thinner and thinner. Now that thread had snapped.

Andrew and Nisha were beside me.

'What's going on?

'What are you doing?'

I couldn't seem to speak. The thoughts in my head were just too loud.

I think they heard them.

They sat me down and Nisha got me a coffee.

'You've had a shock, Jon. It's everything catching up with you.'

I shook my head. I wasn't going to cry, but I wasn't going to be angry either. It crossed my mind to kick my desk over and smash everything. As if anyone would care!

'What happened, Jon?'

'Yes, what did she say?'

I looked up in to Nisha's caring, worried face. And then across to Andrew's.

They both cared.

'I've resigned,' I told them.

'Jon!' Nisha opened her hands in disbelief.

'Tell us what happened,' Andrew said.

'She rejected it. She says it makes more economic sense to just let the Torrent Consortium take over. I've had enough. I'm leaving.'

'But Jon, that's so unfair. You've put everything into this.'

'I know.'

I couldn't speak then, I had a lump in my throat and I was afraid of crying. So I resumed my packing, tossing things into my already overfull executive case.

'Jon, let me go and talk to Angela. You need time to consider this. I'm sure you don't mean it.'

'Oh, I mean it,' I said.

I picked up my new strategy document headed *Enaid Cymru* and tossed it in the bin.

'I was an idiot to think than anyone would understand,' I said. 'Either here or there. It's all crap. All of it.'

Andrew pulled my strategy out of the bin.

'Don't do anything, Jon. Not until I've talked to Angela. Stay with him, Nisha.'

He went striding off in the direction of Angela's office.

'We understand, Jon. Andrew and I understand.'

I shook my head.

'You are bound to be feeling rejected. It's perfectly natural. You have been rejected by the girl you are loving, you have been learning her Welsh and her identity and taking it into yourself. And you have been rejected by the town. You've given so much to this project.'

'What are you telling me – that I shouldn't have got personally involved? That understanding the mechanisms for why people feel things somehow makes the feelings go away?'

'I'm saying that those hurtings will heal. It will be feeling much better tomorrow. And the next day. And the next.'

'But they need me, Nisha. They need my help. I'm the only person in the world who understands them and believes in them. They don't even understand themselves.'

'I know, Jon.'

'The town is almost medieval. Hurricane lamps, wood-burning stoves. Women washing in their back yards using poss-sticks and tubs. They haven't even got proper light in the Council Chamber. And now they haven't got jobs either. Their whole town and way of life is up for sale and they don't understand why, Nisha. They are such a proud people. Their history is everything to them. They don't understand how desperate their situation is.'

Andrew came back.

'Angela wants to see you.'

'Sit down,' Angela told me sternly.

I did exactly as I was told.

'If I back this plan of yours, you have to promise me one thing.'

I opened my mouth to speak but she held up her hand.

'You will never behave like a spoiled brat again.'

I nodded.

'You will never get personally involved again.'

'But . . .'

'No buts.'

'OK,' I conceded.

'Andrew's taken me through this document.' She picked up *Enaid Cymru* from the desk and flicked through it. 'It's a good strategy, Jon.'

I felt my heart wanting to lift, but I didn't dare allow it to.

She had made the decision I wanted.

'Come with me to see Freddy in his office now. Tell him what you told me. And don't let me down, Jon. Don't let me down.

'And don't you ever try to blackmail me again.'

Then she softened.

'What childish behaviour, Jon! You are so lucky I have young children. Ten years ago I don't think I would have tolerated it.'

A quarter of an hour later I came back to Nisha at the Hub, grinning like an idiot. Ignoring the Chinese group that Andrew was addressing with the help of an interpreter.

'What's happened?' Nisha asked.

Andrew paused in mid-sentence. 'You've got the funding, haven't you?' And his translator duly translated it.

'I've got twelve months' development funding with an option on the main strategy.'

Andrew punched the air. 'Yes. I told you!'

And the translator translated

'Thank you,' I said. And shook his hand. And Nisha came down from her desk and hugged me.

'He's got the funding,' Andrew told his audience.

The Chinese started clapping.

Then Andrew hugged me.

And for no apparent reason, we all started to laugh.

Now I could allow my heart to be glad.

I threw the strategy document high into the air. And the pages separated out and fluttered down on us like very poor, over-sized bunting.

ENAID CYMRU – the soul of Wales. What an inspiration. And what a transformation you brought to Llanchwaraeteg-danygelyn, Jon. To Wales. To me.

'Where in Wales can you go to experience Welsh language and culture?' you asked at that meeting a week later.

'Anywhere. Everywhere,' Dewi replied.

'No. I mean *really* experience it?'

Dewi shrugged and looked at me.

'Dw'mbo.'

'Yr Eisteddfod Genedlaethol?' my Dad suggested.

'A tented village that goes up for ten days once a year,' you said. 'Where else?'

Dewi shrugged again.

'Dw'mbo.'

'Say it again,' you said.

'Dwi ddim yn gwybod!'

'No – say it like you did before.'

I knew what you meant. I looked at Dad. He was smiling, but Dewi still hadn't got it.

'Dw'mbo.' Dewi said in a puzzled tone. ''W'mbo.'

We were all were laughing now.

''W'mbo.'

'Umbo!'

Then he got it!

'Oh – Umbo!'

'Umbo!'

And we were laughing and slapping each other's backs.

You had done it. You had come up with a tourism idea which not only protected the language and culture but promoted it. A festival town to celebrate Welsh. Our music, our poetry, our history and our values.

But you were typically modest.

'It's not an entirely original idea,' you told us. 'Places such as Hay-on-Wye, Oberammergau, Aldeburgh – there are towns all over the world that use festivals to draw people in. Or use their history or literary associations – Stratford, Haworth. All

I'm saying is that you can use your town to celebrate who you are – but celebrate with other people – invite people in to celebrate with you. No one else in Wales is doing it. You'll be the first. All those people who go to the Eisteddfods every year are potential visitors. And, if you plan it well, you can use it to promote the language to the English, too.'

'OK,' we said, when we had calmed down. 'Where do we start.'

And you smiled at that.

'We start, as always,' you said, 'with a strategy. A plan. Always – you have to make a plan.'

FOR THOSE FEW MONTHS, Gwalia, I seemed to be writing plans that worked. Maybe I was being more realistic, through better research, or perhaps it was because we were all working together.

You had blossomed, your business course and overseeing of the hotel redevelopment had given you great confidence and that brought out that ability and charm you always had in private. Now they were evident to the world.

The only part of my plan that wasn't working was the one for my heart. And perhaps that is something that is beyond even the most perfect research, brilliant planning and impeccable strategy.

I was invited to your wedding to Dewi and stood at the back, half wanting you to see my broken heart, half wanting to hide it. You told me you had decided we could not sleep together once you and Dewi were properly together. That would be best for both of us, you told me. I needed to move on, you said. And I could see the wisdom in that.

I sent you a ridiculous bouquet and a ludicrously expensive wedding present. For a while I thought that I would lose the will to live. After all that I had done for you and for your town. Why, you were practically my Eliza Doolittle, my Galatea.

But we don't perish, do we? We carry on.

Except that once our dreams have been shown to be false, we can never totally trust them again. Never feel invincible. Mine had told me you were the one true love of my life.

As it turned out, you weren't. Or, if you were, then I was not the one true love for you.

I busied myself in Cardiff and Aberystwyth and spent as little time in Llanchwaraetegdanygelyn as possible.

There were initial doubts, of course: would Llanchwarae-tegdanygelyn be a black hole sucking in public money forever? Some papers wrongly reported that we were trying to create a reservation, a museum village where people would come to gawp and women would wear traditional Welsh hats and shawls and children have Welsh NOT boards around their necks. That drew a little criticism, but also created publicity and interest.

Once we had put these misapprehensions right and dispelled the initial doubts, there was a real enthusiasm for the project. And as that enthusiasm grew, so the doubts subsided.

It was a relatively low-cost project in capital terms. Much of the infrastructure was already there, and no one really had to do anything differently.

You went, Gwalia, from strength to strength. First you were appointed development officer, with Blodeuwedd as your assistant, and then you were made director. The name – Enaid Cymru – was catching on. It seemed to strike a chord in Welsh speakers – the idea of a place where they could go on holiday, at any time of year, and use their Welsh, informally, without any sense of being bossed about or organised. With a constant festival of music, drama, poetry, comedians and celebrities – Welsh artists, sportsmen and women, singers, novelists and actors – and all through the medium of Welsh; that caught the imagination of a lot of people. And no one, Gwalia, seemed to be able to explain it better than you.

The big surprise, though, was the number of English people who seemed to be interested. And the numbers of Welsh people who wanted to learn, or relearn, Welsh.

We knew from the outset that it would need the hard work and dedication of dozens of people. Most of all, it needed the support of the entire town. We needed to achieve for Llanchwaraetegdanygelyn the same kind of atmosphere that the inhabitants had achieved in places such as Oberammergau, Pamplona, Bayreuth and at every Welsh Eisteddfod. And we needed the year-round success that the Guggenheim had brought to Bilbao, or the Sage Centre, Baltic Art Gallery and Angel of the North had brought to the North-East.

But, over the next few months, when you and Dewi went

flying off to these places on your research trips, much as I wanted you to be happy, and desperate as I was to see the scheme succeed, there was a little part of me that thought that you could have done rather better if you had chosen me.

WE MORTGAGED OUR LIVES to your idea of Enaid
Cymru, Jon. All of us. For those frantic months the whole
town gambled everything on you being right. There was no
other option. Even Dewi and Penhaearn had to admit *that*.
(Although, it must be said, Dafydd Y Gwrthsafiad, our brave
leader against the fierce enemy caravans, never did!)

I had never been so happy. I loved it so much, going round
talking to developers, deciding how everything should look,
planning the arrangements down to the smallest detail. What
woman wouldn't be in her element spending that kind of money
on her home town – and Llanchwaraetegdanygelyn was my home.
I was in charge of painting and redecorating her, furnishing her
and buying her an entire new wardrobe and makeover.

The visitors started coming in dribs and drabs as soon as the
first publicity appeared, well before the official opening. I found
I enjoyed that too. It wasn't hard to enthuse the journalists,
photographers and TV presenters about the plan. It was
wonderful, it really was, that we were going to save this ancient
town, the last great totally Welsh-speaking town in Wales.

And not only did the visitors come to look and satisfy
their curiosity, they also came to help. Young Welsh speakers
came volunteering to help with labouring and painting,
students in the holidays, and our Welsh academics –
historians, linguists, poets and art teachers – all came freely to
make suggestions and offer advice. It might not always have
been useful, I have to say, but it was always welcome.

I couldn't believe how much the English media took an
interest, *The Guardian*, *The Times* and *Telegraph* – and then
radio and television. I think they felt that it was time to put all
their anti-Welsh sentiments behind them. We even had to
produce a glossary of Welsh phrases for them. To be honest, I
was surprised how much they were determined to respect our
wish that only Welsh should be spoken in the town.

Many of the journalists wanted to enter into the spirit of it
and talk Welsh, or asked me to act as interpreter.

We did children's TV programmes on Welsh games for

BBC Children's Television across Britain, a radio programme on Welsh poetry, and several other programmes were pre-recorded especially for the launch.

There was interest, too, from Brittany and Eire and from Scots Gaelic speakers – and Cornwall and the Isle of Man sent messages in the Celtic languages, all close cousins of Welsh.

Journalists seemed so pleased to be able to write and make programmes about Welsh as the oldest living language in Britain – what was it you called it, Jon, that they got so excited about? – indigenous ethnic diversity. And the closer we got to the launch, the more they came.

There seemed to be photographers everywhere, all demanding to take pictures of Welsh being spoken – though how exactly you photograph a language, I still don't know.

For the first time in my life, we had English-speaking visitors who understood our need to go on using our ancient language and why we craved Welsh-speaking shops and businesses and entertainment, not just for ourselves but for our nation, which had clung for so long to this symbol of our identity.

And many people volunteered to provide it themselves. A group of artists and musicians came and camped on the Maes. And they attracted writers and poets who enthused about the atmosphere and excitement and encouraged more to come.

People rented out rooms, Y Ddwy Ddraig was almost always full, and the shops were doing very good business. People snapped up the empty ones quickly.

It wasn't me that made it happen, Jon, it just sort-of fell into place. With the people came a little money and, with that, a growing confidence.

It was just as well we had your plan – or we would never have been able to cope.

Everyone now knows the story of how, using culture, and the people who know about culture, we managed to enthuse everyone for our language, our music, our poetry – and, most importantly, for the talent and stature of the people in our generation who continue to mould those things and make us Welsh folk who we are.

YES, GWALIA, I remember it well.

The launch of Enaid Cymru came the following May at Gŵyl Delyn Gelyn. Daffodils, the flower of St David's Day, had come and gone. The bluebells were at their peak. You and Dewi had been married six months. And I was wondering how long it would be before this dull incompleteness you had left me with subsided and went away.

I worked hard to keep my attitude towards you professional, Gwalia. But I accept I wasn't totally successful. I found it hard to deny the intimacy we had taken for granted. Standing next to you, less than a touch or a word away, was particularly hard. Yet I never crossed that barrier we had created. I felt in some way that I was denying myself that joy for your sake, and that you would know that and respect me for it.

Sometimes, working together, when you betrayed no sign of appreciating my great sacrifice, I marvelled at your strength of character. Sometimes I felt angry. And then I felt my anger surface in a kind of truculence. Or I would betray my feelings in polite concern which always carried the implication that you were not as happy or as thriving as you would have been if you had decided to be with me instead of Dewi. I couldn't help myself. And I hated the mock-disinterested tone it produced in my voice.

'You look exhausted, Gwalia. You should let other people do more.'

'I'm fine, Jon' you laughed. 'You're worse than my Dad.'

And – yes – you were fine. And, oh, how I so hated that you were.

The truth was you were loving your new role.

And everybody loved you.

It was a good choice to use Gŵyl Delyn Gelyn as the launch event – a natural fair, with all those tents and stalls and festival events. I remember the fleet of buses shuttling visitors up and down the hill.

'Enaid Cymru is about us being ourselves,' you told the

media, 'not pretending to be what we are not. Gŵyl Delyn Gelyn will be as it always has been. There could be no better way to launch Enaid Cymru.'

'Mae'n edrych yn ffantastig,' people said.

'Mae'n hyfryd iawn.'

There were television and radio crews and journalists from everywhere.

Given the amount of media attention it was inevitable that a large contingent of politicians and bureaucrats would insist on coming, too. (The hospitality marquee and wine and nibbles were sponsored by the Leyburn Institute, as I remember.)

Iwan shepherded the Cardiff contingent and I was with Angela Lain and Freddy Morgan. But one great joy was that Nisha and Andrew agreed to come, too. Nisha was impressed at how many people said hello to me and that I was able to talk to them in Welsh, though – typical Nisha – she insisted I teach her to say 'Sut dach chi?' And 'Diolch yn fawr' and 'Os gwelwch yn dda' the moment she arrived.

'Can you really speak Welsh fluently?' Andrew asked me. 'Do you think in Welsh?'

'Most of the time, I do. You can't think of what you want to say in English and then translate, there isn't time.'

But Nisha, in her orange sari, and sparkling with gold and rubies, understood.

'You have to understand in the language you're speaking, don't you, Jon?'

'I see,' Andrew said. 'I see.'

And we both laughed at his puzzlement, and lectured him on how you can't understand yourself until you see yourself from the context of another culture, and especially another language.

'I know a bit of Hebrew,' he protested. And looked puzzled when we shook our heads.

'No good,' Nisha told him. 'It has to be an extra one. Outside your comfortable identity.'

'Then I've got you,' he said, 'taking her hand and giving it a squeeze.'

And, yes, he did have Nisha.

You looked radiant, Gwalia. Not only were you a good director, you had the talent of an impressario too. Your beauty and radiance translated into brilliant press pictures, interviews and TV coverage. I'm sure my oh-so-clever project would have failed if the director had been anyone else.

You had reinstated Hiraethog as Mayor of the Fair – Maer Yr Ŵyl – and had him touring the Maes, wearing his Mayoral Chain, in an old Morris thousand convertible, with Jean at the wheel and Billi-Jo beside him, waving to the crowds.

Dewi was with you, of course, but you were very busy with all your TV interviews and press conferences, and with meeting and greeting visiting VIPs. The smile never left your eyes.

The next phase of your plan, you told them, was to erect wind turbines on a hillside up the valley. There would be a hydro-electric system on the river and solar panels on one south-facing hill – it took the scientists a very long time to convince the committee that solar panels would work in Wales, you joked.

'It will work,' you assured them. 'And the cost of electricity will come down from fifty pence a unit, as it has been with private generators, to fifteen. More than the mains cost currently, but still a huge saving – and it will be environmentally self-sustaining and carbon-neutral. In the next eighteen months, every house in the town will be connected.'

You were the perfect ambassador for Enaid Cymru.

I noticed many familiar faces in the audience. Penhaearn, of course, Anti Gwenlais, Dai Call and his two friends.

Dafydd Y Gwrthsafiad, I noticed, was wearing his Gwrthsafiad T-shirt and Rhys was beside him, dressed the same.

The opening concert was held on one of the flatter fields overlooking the town – a natural amphitheatre, as it transpired. Seating had been brought in for the VIPs (others had to sit on the grass or bring picnic chairs), and there was a stage and lights and a sound system, all powered by generators.

I think it was Awena who had insisted that you perform.

It was a dutiful audience that patiently listened to all the formal speeches. Wales's First Minister from the Assembly congratulated Llanchwaraetegdanygelyn on its spectacular entry into the twenty-first century, and then the Secretary of State for Wales added his blessing. You could have been forgiven for thinking, from their reading of the scripts that Iwan and I had drafted, that they both had intimate knowledge of the project. And, of course, the Chairman of the County Council had to have his say.

There were television cameras everywhere and a feeling of great optimism and enthusiasm. The newspapers were calling this the Rebirth Of Wales As A Nation. They made much of the story of the secret valley which had kept itself hidden for centuries, tricked the English map-makers and preserved Welsh heritage and culture in so pure a form. There was talk of Llywelyn's and Glyndŵr's soldiers hiding in these hills until the time was right. And of this being the village of their descendants. They had obviously been talking to your Anti Gwenlais.

And there were several interviews with those who had been forcibly moved from Cwm Y Gelyn to make way for the reservoir, though, strangely, even the sugnwyr lemwn seemed to have a sense of optimism about them, as if at last, they were going to have the opportunity to put their bitterness behind them, and move on.

There would be something else to talk about now; they could stop being merely victims and political symbols and start to be activists in the cultural rejuvenation of their land.

It was starting to get dark by the time the real show began. And it wasn't warm. In fact it was quite windy and there was rain in the air. We were impatient for the show to begin. This was to be a showcase of Welsh culture to end all showcases, said the programme. (Every strategy must have its mission statement.)

I felt proud to be a part of it, my chance at last to share all the enthusiasms I felt for Llanchwaraetegdanygelyn with Andrew and Nisha. I suppose I had acquired a little part of Welsh identity for myself through learning the language, and by translating and enthusing for my friends, I was proclaiming it.

And, yes, I felt proud for you too, Gwalia, for the brave little town which lay spread out below us and, of course, for Wales.

As the show began, with a performance by your father's choir, we all sensed an exuberance and excitement in the performances that made our hearts lift and put lumps in our throats. All of us felt it, even Professor Lane and Freddy (with their headphones on). Welsh musicians, choirs, poets and singers – I doubt they had ever realised how different and how rich Welsh culture is.

'Language, I kept saying, is not an end in itself. It's the gateway to a whole new world.'

And Nisha spread her gold-glinting hands.

'You see. What have I been telling you all this time. Now you are ready to come to India.'

The star of the show for me was the girl who went on just before the interval as the light began to fade.

Yes, that was you, Gwalia, that vulnerable girl I'd first seen sweeping the floor in the shabby reception hall at Y Ddwy Ddraig.

The two large video screens beside the stage caught you perfectly. You walked modestly on stage and took your seat beside the enormous harp, your familiar face, with your now-perfect nose – which I never cared a jot about – was shining. The camera panned around you, and you looked so courageous and triumphant as the background moved from the lights and orchestra on the stage behind you to show you against the darkening sky, its pearly clouds scudding by, your hair billowing out in the slightly icy wind, your face strong and set against whatever storms might come.

You played the piece which had brought tears to my eyes long ago at Gŵyl Delyn Gelyn, the melody that had won you the National Eisteddfod medal the summer before your trauma. And then you sang that haunting song, in the minor key – 'Hiraeth am y lleisiau'.

As you sang, you seemed to gather strength. The beauty of your voice and the profound sadness of your singing brought such a lump to my throat I thought it would choke me. I could never possess you, but you could still so break my heart. How ironic! It was no use trying to convince myself it didn't matter. Of course it did. But I could always love you for what we had been and for the way I saw you on stage that evening.

After you had finished, there was silence. Then little Awena, sitting in the front row with Dewi, stood up on her own and started clapping. For a second, she was the only one. Then the whole audience rose to their feet. I glanced around.

I wasn't the only one weeping.

You stood in the centre of the stage looking exhausted. But there was a little smile playing on your lips.

Then Awena ran forward and jumped into your arms.

At the end of the concert, as we were just about to leave, there was a scuffle. Dafydd Y Gwrthsafiad had pushed his way roughly to the stage with Rhys behind him, and was waving the flag of Glyndŵr above our heads.

He seized the microphone and commanded everyone to sit down.

'Steddwch!'

Some obeyed. Some didn't. In front of me in the audience, I spotted Hiraethog with Billi-Jo and Jean. He was shaking his head.

My heart was racing. I was trapped in the throng, and I looked around to catch somebody's eye to stop him.

'This,' Dafydd Y Gwrthsafiad began in Welsh, 'is a proud moment for the rebirth of Wales and the Welsh language. Six hundred years we have been waiting for this. Now we must take up arms and join together and take direct Gwrthsafiad action against our English oppressors.'

Rhys, standing to attention at his side, shouted, 'Cymru am byth', and raised his right arm in salute.

The audience was shuffling uneasily. Sir Freddy was staring at me as if it was all my fault. So many people had sat down now, there was no real option but to do the same.

'Six hundred years and more we have suffered under the English yoke.'

I could see that Freddy and Angela were getting all this on their headphones. The translator was still translating.

You were nowhere to be seen, Gwalia.

'The spirit of Llywelyn and Glyndŵr lives on. We must rise up now . . .'

Some of the English starting booing. Some of the Welsh were shushing them.

The last thing that we wanted now, with all the television cameras and senior politicians, was a riot like the one at my public meeting.

I pushed my way back through the crowd to the sound box, sitting in the centre of the audience like an oversized Punch and Judy booth. Dewi was sitting at the control panel, a look of mischievous glee on his face. Other people stood around him, blocking my way. They looked threateningly at me.

Dafydd Y Gwrthsafiad's voice was still booming out over the speakers. I couldn't tell if the cameras were still filming, but the crowd was standing there listening, their exits blocked by other people curious to see what would happen.

I looked around and saw the main cables running to the control desk, traced the cable back to the mobile generators and saw you standing by the mains switch.

You threw it. The sound went dead and there was a smattering of applause.

You winked, I smiled. Then you disappeared.

A little later, I found you, Gwalia, surrounded by admirers and looking very beautiful.

You caught sight of me. And came across.

You pecked me on the cheek.

And whispered: 'Thank you.'

DEAR JON,

These five years as director of Enaid Cymru have been very mixed up and emotional for me.

Now I have learned to think like Wales.

What an idea this was of yours! And I hear that you have now moved on to Brussels to work out strategies for Europe.

The radio and television people in London seem to like me. As long as I play my harp and sing, they let me go on chat shows talking about the new Welsh politics – and even a little of my language. If it changes hearts and minds, I'm all for that.

Thanks to you, Jon, Enaid Cymru really has turned out to be a remarkable movement. You may have read about it. It has spread through all of Wales. So many towns and villages are proud enough of their Welsh identity to want that recognition and proclaim it at the entrances to their town: *Enaid Cymru: You are now entering a Welsh-speaking area.*

And the English seem to like it too. It helps them to know they're entering an Enaid Cymru area. More and more they are picking up their phrase cards in shops and bars and restaurants and trying out their Welsh.

Better still, as you predicted, it means our people can speak in Welsh without the fear of being accused of being rude. And more and more incomers are learning Welsh through classes.

You won't believe this, Jon, but I am hoping to come to Brussels. So we might meet up. The language and culture committee have been to Wales to see the phenomenon for themselves. The Bretons and the Basques want to create similar projects. And the French are interested, too. It isn't only the minority languages you English-speakers put in fear!

So . . . Wales has been invited to Brussels to help organise a seminar on minority languages next year sometime. Naturally I thought of you and wondered if you would be our keypoint speaker. (You see, Jon, I know all the jargon now!)

I love being Director of Enaid Cymru, though it can sometimes feel a little lonely. Fortunately, it's all grown so quickly, and been so very hectic, I haven't had much time to think.

I've been all over Wales and up to Scotland – there are sixty thousand Gaelic speakers in the Scottish Islands, you know – and down to Cornwall. There are groups of Cornish speakers there, you know – and even a group of Manx speakers in the Isle of Man. And Gaelic speakers in Ireland are already using their version of the Enaid Cymru idea.

I've had to learn to say 'Hello' and 'Thank you' in all of those languages!

Enaid Cymru works so naturally, telling people they are in a Welsh-speaking area and encouraging them just to say 'Hello' and 'Thank you' in Cymraeg. Rewarding people with smiles and pleasantness is so much better than punishing them with graffiti, threats and burning, I find!

Wouldn't you say so, Jon?

You'd hardly recognise Llanchwaraetegdanygelyn now. We have electricity, especially when the wind blows, and a water system! There are plans for our own hydro-electric project to pump water up to a reservoir when it's very windy and then use the hydro-electric turbines when it's not. If it goes ahead, we shall be selling electricity back to the English!

The old factory has been rebuilt. Two shows in Welsh a day – with four in the summer – drama, poetry, musicals, and the visitors pour in. They come from all over Wales to see how it is done. And the English seem to be fascinated, too. Taid Dai Call says the factory is doing the same job it has always done, except that now it is stamping 'Welsh' on people. And Irfon says that everyone will go to heaven.

Welsh is suddenly very trendy.

But you probably want to know the gossip. I still get most of mine from my Anti Gwenlais.

Dewi is now manager of Y Ddwy Ddraig, and engaged to Bronwen. (Did I tell you he and I had got divorced? We finally fell out over putting up English signs to Llanchwaraeteg-danygelyn and I realised I could never be the person I was capable of being with all his ingrained, racist ideas.)

And much to Mam and Anti Gwenlais's dismay, Hiraethog

is living happily ever after with Billi-Jo and Jean. They still spend hours twting in the kitchen speculating on what the sleeping arrangements are in *that* house.

Dad's school has expanded dramatically with the children of Welsh artists and writers who have moved here – this is quite an artists' and writers' colony now – and there are creative courses for Welsh learners as well as walking holidays and outdoor pursuits, anything, really to get people using their Welsh and not just sitting in a classroom.

Boudiccea's story was a little sad.

She and Lawns did part. They never recovered from the rift between her and her brother-in-law, Penhaearn.

She came to see me before she left to go back to England. In the end, much as she loved the Migneint, she couldn't cope with her sense of failure.

My Anti Gwenlais says that Lawns should never have married an English woman; despite her heroic efforts to learn the language, she was never going to lose her English mentality.

Caffi Cyfoes has smartened up, and even the old court building has opened as a Welsh wine bar, selling hedgerow wines, Welsh whisky and elderflower champagne.

Penhaearn is now Registrar for Births, Marriages and Deaths, and doing a very lively trade in Welsh marriages, as well as funerals. You'd be amazed how many Americans want to say 'ydw' instead of 'I do'. And even more amazed how many want to be come back to Wales to have their ashes scattered dros y ddaear Gymreig – across the Welsh earth.

You remember Trêsi? You liked her, didn't you? She's a star. She has a real flair for corporate hospitality. And she's finally learned Welsh. Between you and me, I think she picked up more at school than she liked to admit. So we run a lot of business courses through the medium of Welsh for companies wanting bilingual accreditation.

The Torrent Consortium moved out. The last I heard Donald Flood and Guy Ingress were building a condominium in Spain. I don't suppose they'll be bothering to learn Spanish.

Oh yes. And Norman deLuge. He's printed a dictionary of gay phrases in Welsh. His cotej industry, he says.

I wonder what you are doing now, Jon. Are you married? I imagine you working in some big office building in Brussels, wrestling with the ebb and flow of people migrating across the boundaries of Europe.

Our next big challenge is to have the name of Wales officially changed to Cymru. It's high time England and the rest of the world started calling us by our proper name.

Let me know if you would be interested in giving that talk when and if we come to Brussels.

Love,

Gwalia.

Hello, Gwalia,

Good to hear from you.

I'm afraid I've rather let my Welsh lapse since I used to come to Wales, so thank you for writing in English. I've got a passable smattering of French and German and Italian now – and this from the boy who failed his languages at school! It was learning Welsh that taught me how to do that. So I am very grateful to you.

I wish I had started on languages earlier. There are so many it would be useful to know. But, of course, you never speak a learned language like your own. And one is always in danger of making terrible mistakes, missing nuances. I find it is always safer to have a translator for work.

Your letter, Gwalia, had been sent to my parents' flat and Mum forwarded it on to me in Brussels. Yes, I'd be very happy to give your keynote speech, but I am often away. You'll have to let me know when it is.

I'm still striving to make the world a better place, but nowadays less sure how to achieve it.

Hardly a year goes by without some ethnic friction somewhere in the Community. We have come to understand the causes well. Sometimes we can even predict where the problems will come. But it will take generations for that wisdom to percolate down to the minorities themselves. Their problems are urgent, their priorities unintellectual, their attitudes entirely understandable. I don't think I had realised how wide the gulf is between understanding social problems and solving them. Only with better education can we succeed.

The people here have a different perspective. The younger ones talk about the end of the market economy, of how the notion of one-world democratic capitalism has turned out to be as much of a blind alley as communism.

The older ones console us with talk about the great progress we have made in Europe, not only in eliminating warfare amongst the old empire builders, but also among many nation states.

Perhaps they both are right.

We are certainly more alert than ever to conflicts, and we have managed to democratise the former Eastern bloc countries who have joined, as well as Greece and Spain. These are great triumphs but we must never think that holocausts and ethnic cleansing can't still happen. The hatreds of the oppressed can explode at any time. These are the places where I go, helping people who are better diplomats than I. But I take the sweet lesson of Llanchwaraetegdanygelyn – and its phenomenal success – with me wherever I go. It is famous in many surprising places.

So it was wonderful to hear from you. It's been a long time. I thought you had forgotten me. I think about you often enough, though, and I confess that sometimes in my lonely hotel rooms, I do look up the progress of Enaid Cymru on the internet and pictures of your valley and the mountains and try to remember the names of flowers in Welsh.

No I'm not married. You and Maria share sole honours in my heart. I found a picture of Maria once, on an archaeologists' website. She has children now, has put on weight, and seemed to have lost that glow that I once thought I saw.

Love, Jon.

Dear Jon,

It was so good to hear from you. And thank you for sending your e-mail address. I can e-mail you whenever I like now. Your work sounds terrifyingly important. I suppose there are many men like you out there trying to make the world a better place for all of us, your efforts unsung, your failures blazoned.

Yes, Enaid Cymru has been a phenomenal success. Llanchwaraetegdanygelyn thrives. We have even had the name officially changed from Umbo. It will take years to appear correctly on the maps but annually published road maps like the AA are doing it from this year. And that's only one – quite minor – success.

We have lots of people moving here now, many of them young and some English. And they want to learn Welsh. We offer a very fast ten-week course – and, yes – it uses your plan of ten words a day (though a bit more structured and professional)! And about sixty percent of people succeed in learning the basics in that time. You were quite right in what you told me once: most newspapers use vocabularies of about six hundred words. Of course, some people take a little longer, but, mostly, they love it.

Did I tell you we have artists and writers settling here, now? Quite a community. So Llanchwaraetegdanygelyn really has become an important creative centre for Wales – for those who want to live and work through the medium of Welsh; and of course that brings students, media people, photographers and the curious.

This is a wonderful place to be full of like-minded people, people with a broad-minded view of the world. You've no idea the difference it makes to the quality of life. We even have a few more of the Welsh-language poets starting to look outside Wales. So now we have conversations about alternative comedy, postmodernism and – yes! – *athroniaeth*.

And it's not just Llanchwaraetegdanygelyn that is thriving. As you predicted, we have been the catalyst for a *renaissance* of interest in Welsh. Even Mam and Dad are happy again.

Each month more towns and villages across Wales seem to be signing up to be members of Enaid Cymru and making their communities ones where Welsh is spoken first and where English speakers and speakers of other languages are given all that extra consideration and attention that you suggested. I don't think we Welsh realised how much being nice to people can achieve. So much better than being always defensive.

Now, instead of taking signs down, I am helping put them up – to Llanchwaraetegdanygelyn, Land of Fair Play under the Enemy.

And, do you remember how the big corporations were always complaining about the cost of providing bilingual material when only one percent of people ever filled in forms in Welsh? Well, last year ten percent of forms were completed in Welsh and we reckon we can double that in the next five years. Isn't that brilliant? – and all by being nice!

Even the most obnoxious English are starting to like us, and that is a real shock to our psyche, I can tell you! Television presenters being nice about Cymru, Cymraeg and Cymry!

Sorry if this sounds like a corporate presentation – quoting your ideas back to you – but that's how I spend my time now, in a state of great excitement and enthusiasm. The people in the media in Cardiff call me Mrs Smiley now.

Finally, some sad news.

Mrs Leakin – do you remember her, Boudiccea? – has died. Apparently, in her will, she asked for some kind of memorial service in Llanchwaraetegdanygelyn to mark her passing. And she would like all the people she knew to come.

It is rather sad, given how hard she worked for the town. Without her work, and bringing you in, we wouldn't be where we are today.

I'll let you know when the memorial service is. If you want to come, you can have the best suite at Y Ddwy Ddraig. Compliments of the house.

I would love to see you again, you always were ... fy nghariad mawr,

Gwalia.

Gwalia,

Of course I remember Boudiccea and I feel very touched to have been invited to the funeral. I'd like to come but I don't think I should.

Incidentally, I was speaking to our cultural commissioner last week and I mentioned Enaid Cymru. She asked if Wales had thought of applying for Special Status for Cymraeg as a minority language, as Ireland has for Gaelic.

When I explained how the words translated, she asked lots of questions and got quite excited. She was horrified at the idea of the Welsh being 'foreigners' in their own land and asked why Wales didn't change its name to officially Cymru? It's a worldwide trend these days for former colonies to adopt their names in their own language. So why not Cymru? She loved the idea of Y Cymry – the compatriots.

If you wrote to me officially, here in Brussels, with endorsement from the Welsh Assembly, I could make sure the application got to the right people and help set the wheels in motion.

Best wishes,

Love,

Jon.

Jon,

What a wonderful idea. You've always been so good to me, Jon Bull.

They've decided now that Boudiccea's funeral will be more of a memorial event. It's in two weeks.

What do you mean you don't think you *should* come? Of course you should, you are a hero in this town. There are daily flights from Brussels. It's just a couple of hours. I could pick you up wherever – Liverpool, Manchester or Birmingham –

you say, I'll come myself. And take you back the same day if necessary. I would love to see you, though the prospect is a little scary.

I think I mentioned that Dewi and I were divorced. I live on my own now, with Awena.

Love,

Gwalia.

Gwalia,

Yes. I was sorry to hear that you and Dewi had parted. That's how it is these days, though, isn't it.

A memorial event sounds slightly more fun than a funeral but I still think it would be better for me not to come.

Jon

Oh come on, Jon,

There's still time to change your mind. It's going to be this weekend, drennydd – remember? – the day after tomorrow, and a big occasion. It will be such a shame if you can't be here.

Boudiccea wanted her body to be floated out across Llyn Y Gelyn on a raft at dusk and then burned in Celtic style with flaming arrows arcing out to ignite her. (Dad says she must have got mixed up with the Vikings, and that the Celts just buried people) but obviously the authorities wouldn't quite permit that. So Penhaearn, chwarae teg iddo fo, did come up with a compromise.

There will be a torch-lit service in the grotto, by the waterfall where I first saw you. Then we take her ashes in procession, along the riverbank to the lake. Twm Slwtsh and his pals have built a raft from logs with six blazing torches so she will almost get what she wanted.

Please e-mail me back and say you'll come. I'll even book the flight for you!

I'd like you to deliver the teyrnged.

Don't let me down, I'll give you a big kiss.

Gwalia.

467

Dear, Sweet Gwalia,

I'm sorry. I have thought long and hard about it and I just don't think it's a good idea. Our romance was in the past. We have both moved on.

It is truly wonderful to know that you and Enaid Cymru are so successful and I will be delighted to see and help you when you come to Brussels, but who you are now is not the Gwalia I fell in love with. And I don't think I am the Jon you fell in love with either.

Besides, I don't think I could handle coming back to Llanchwaraetegdanygelyn.

I probably shouldn't be e-mailing you like this, the internet can be an insidious friend, especially when it is late, and I have had a few drinks.

Best wishes,

Jon

Dear Jon,

I'm sorry you missed Boudiccea's memorial service. It was quite a send-off and got a lot of media coverage. There's talk of making the ceremony an annual event. I was very disappointed that you didn't come.

I have to confess, I cried when I read your e-mail. You sound so sad. I hope you are not drinking from loneliness.

You're right about memories. I always imagine you as you were that day I first saw you: your white smile and soft voice.

I realise that in my heart everything I have done here, I have, in some strange way, done for you. When things were difficult, I imagined your reassuring hugs and the kind of advice and encouragement you would give. And when things went well, I imagined your joy and praise. All through the memorial service, I was imagining what you would think of the town now. And how there is such an optimism amongst the people. Even Anti Gwenlais has stopped complaining. (And she has given up smoking!)

If you saw it, you'd be so proud of what we – what you – have achieved.

Love,

Gwalia

Dear Jon,

You never replied to my last e-mail. It's been a long time. And I have missed hearing from you.

I've been working down at the Assembly on a new project to promote Enaid Cymru in America. Lots of Welsh people emigrated to America, many in the twentieth century, so we're organising a tour through New York, across Pennsylvania and then down to Patagonia to promote Welsh culture and encourage people to visit their roots.

Once we have done that, I can think about Brussels.

I know what you said about love, but don't you think it would be fun to meet up and see if we still have feelings for each other?

What if we still do!

Love,

Gwalia

Dear Gwalia,

I'm sorry I haven't written. I thought it best to let things go, but perhaps it wasn't.

I've been thinking rather too much about you and Awena. And about Llanchwaraetegdanygelyn. Actually, I rather regret now not coming to the memorial event.

You remember that old lady in Caffi Cyfoes that day I saw you kissing Dewi? Marged I think she was called. We were going to go to see her, but never did. Is she still alive?

Andrew and Nisha have split up. They are sharing the care of the twins between them, but it was a painful break-up. At least we never married, we saved ourselves all that.

Even for people who are as much in love as they were, there is so little hope. As you know for yourself, marriage

469

statistics are appalling, especially in the UK. It just doesn't work anymore. But living alone can be worse – damned either way.

How could Jon Bull and Gwalia have survived – even if we had decided we loved each other really and truly – what hope would there have been?

I think we should both congratulate ourselves on our lucky escape.

All the best,

Jon.

Dear Jon,

Yes, Marged is still there.

Your e-mail prompted me to go and visit her. We had afternoon tea with china cups and saucers, real leaf tea, and her own home-made Welsh cakes, warmed on the hob. And she still looks immaculate at ninety-two. And she remembers you!

I told her about our correspondence, And showed her our e-mails. I hope that was all right with you. Well, I could hardly talk about it to Mam or Anti Gwenlais, could I?

Marged put some ideas into my head. One idea really.

It is either totally mad or very clever.

As she pointed out, we are both of us a little lonely – perhaps for each other, she said. And that's why neither of us have someone special to talk to any more.

She told me that love is a dance. An age-old dance of love and hate. And the answer to dancing is never to let go unless you know you are going to return to your partner's hold.

So I asked her: 'How do you know who is your partner?'

And she smiled a very contented, happy smile. 'You just know,' she said. 'You just know.'

So how do we convince ourselves, Jon?

How do we find out if we should meet up again? And what should become of us?

My suggestion is this: why don't we go back over our

relationship and e-mail each other with what we can remember about how we felt.

Perhaps if we should have been together – you know, fate, if anyone can believe in that – then it might become obvious – even to us.

I know it's loopy, but dim ots.

Tell you what, I'll start. I have my old diary here.

My name is Gwalia. I am an Island. Head of Brân, soul of Llywelyn.

If you agree, then I can start tonight.

Love,

Gwalia.

OK, Gwalia.

You start.

Jon

THE END
and
THE BEGINNING

6 **Llyn Y Gelyn** – In the 1960s the Tryweryn valley, near Bala, was dammed, and the village of Capel Celyn flooded to create a reservoir for Liverpool. The protests that resulted from what was seen as an outrage against Welsh people, gave huge impetus to Welsh nationalism. **Celyn** is a Welsh word meaning holly. **Gelyn** means enemy. Llyn Y Gelyn means lake of the enemy.

9 **Etifeddiaeth** – Gerallt Lloyd Owen is one of the foremost Welsh poets. This heartrending poem agonises over the guilt and shame of the Welsh nation at letting its precious language and inheritance slip through it fingers, generation by generation.

11 **Brân** – the mythical last Celtic ruler of Britain, whose head continued to inspire a small group of men for eighty years after it was cut from his body. The head was finally buried on the site of the Tower of London.

11 **Llywelyn** – Last prince of Wales defeated by Edward I in 1282.

11 **Gwalia** – an ancient name for Wales, used in poetry.

11 **Cymru** – Wales.

11 **Cymry** – the Welsh.

11 **Wales** – from the Old English *Wealas*, originally meaning foreigners.

11 **Anti** – Welsh form of Aunty.

12 **golchi dillad** – washing the clothes.

12 **Yncl** – Welsh form of Uncle.

14 **Paned arall?** – Another cup of tea?

14 **Os gwelwch yn dda** – Yes please.

15 **Saeson** – English people.

18 **Hwntws** – North Welsh name for South Walians.

18 **Gogledd** – North.

18 **Tylwyth teg** –the Welsh fairies.

19 **Mabinogion** – a collection of ancient Welsh legends and myths.

19 **Llanchwaraetegdanygelyn** – fictional town, on the Migneint where this novel is set, literally translated as, Land-of-fair-play-under-the-enemy.

21 **Y Ddwy Ddraig** – the hotel where Gwalia works, The Two Dragons.

21 **Rheolwraig** – manageress.

23 **Gwrthsafiad** – the Welsh Resistance (fictional).

35 **Bore da, Gwalia, sut wyt ti bore 'ma?** – Good morning, Gwalia, how are you this morning?

35 **Dach chi eisiau paned?** – Would you like a cuppa?

35 **Y fferyllfa** – the pharmacy.

35 **Y Maes** – the village green.

37 **Taid** – grandfather.

41 **Be sy'n bod, Mam?** – What's the matter, Mam?

43 **Digwyddiad** – event.

49 **Godrapia** – a moderately mild curse.

51 **San Steffan** – Westminster, Parliament.

52 **Dros dro** – for the moment, temporarily.

52 **Sugnwyr lemwn** – lemon suckers

54 **Cymraeg** – the Welsh language.

56 **Diwrnod Santes Dwynwen** – St Dwynwen's Day, the Welsh equivalent of St Valentine's, January 25th.

56 **Cynghanedd** – literally *harmony*, a poetic form using patterned alliteration and rhyme.

56 **Englyn** – a traditional form of short poem in cynghanedd.

59 **Gelyn** – enemy, but also the name of a fictional man-made lake, Llyn Y Gelyn, flooded to provide water for the English.

60 **Ysbrydoli** – enliven, motivate.

62 **Sut dach chi?** – How are you?

62 **Iawn, diolch** – Fine, thanks.

63 **Paned arall, Dai Call?** – Another cuppa? (the nickname *Call* = wise).

68 **Migneint** – the bogland area between Blaenau Ffestiniog, Penmachno and Bala, here, a fictional county encompassing the fictional lake, Llyn Gelyn.

71 **Wmbo** – slang for 'I don't know'.

71 **Umbo** – the English name for the fictional Llanchwaraeteg-danygelyn, so-named because the inhabitants couldn't understand the original map-makers when they asked the name of the place and answered 'Wmbo' or ''m'bo'.

72 **Bore da, Gwenlais. Sut dach chi?** – Good morning, Gwenlais, how are you?

72 **Iawn, diolch.** – Fine, thanks.

75 **Yr Hen Gotej** – The Old Cottage.

75 **Dynion** – Men.

75 **Merched** – Women.

75 **Ti'n edrych yn . . .** – You're looking . . .

76 **WEDI CAU** – Closed.

76 **YN ÔL MEWN DWY AWR** – Back in two hours.

77 **Yn union!** – Exactly!

79 **Antur Deg** – Fair Initiative, name of development agency.

81 **Drefnus** – (nickname) 'Organised'.

82 **Druan bach** – Poor thing!

87 **O'r Nefoedd** – Good heavens!

90 **Fy mamiaith** – my mother tongue.

90 **Tŷ Popty** – (nickname) The Bakehouse.

90 **Gwallt Coch** – (nickname) Red Hair, or 'Ginger'.

90 **Heddlu** – Police.

91 **Mae'n ddrwg gen i. Euog ydw i. Rhaid i mi siarad Cymraeg. Dw i'n gwybod.** – I'm sorry. I'm guilty. I must speak Welsh. I know.

92 **Wrth gwrs eu bod nhw** – Of course they are.

94 **Pwnc llosg** – burning issue.

96 **Nain's** – grandmother's

96 **Cawl** – soup.

101 **Ar lan y môr** – At the sea's edge (a well-known, nostalgic song).

102 **Ych-a-fi!** – Yuk!

102 **Bach** – little one (term of endearment).

102 **Paned** – cup of tea.

103 **Hissht!** – Shush!

105 **Is-gymalau adferfol amodol yn y Gymraeg** – conditional adverbial sub-clauses.

105 **Noswaith dda** – Good evening.

105 **Pwy sy eisiau te? A phwy sydd eisiau coffi?** – Who wants tea? And who wants coffee?

105 **Wfftio** – (nickname) to flout.

113 **Cofiwch Y Gelyn** – Remember the enemy.

114 **Joskin** – slang word for peasant.

117 **Llundain** – London.

122 **Ga i'ch helpu chi?** – Can I help you?

123 **Ffedog** – pinafore.

123 **Dw i'n credu** – I believe.

130 **Neuadd y Dre** – Town Hall.

132 **Peidiwch â bod yn wirion!** – Don't be silly!

135 **Y dyn o Westminster dach chi, dw i'n siŵr** – You're the man from Westminster, I'm sure.

135 **Cynghorydd Sir Y Migneint ydw i** – I'm the Migneint County Councillor.

135 **Faswn i'n hoffi'ch cyflwyno chi i'r Maer** – I'd like to introduce you to the Mayor

136 **Ydy o'n Sais neu o Affrica** – Is he English or African?

136 **Jac Codi Baw** – JCB.

137 **O, na, na, na. Byddwch ddistaw!** No, no, no. Be quiet!

155 **meddwl meddal** – soft thought (something a fluent Welsh speaker wouldn't say).

157 **Ti oedd yn ymddangos o 'mlaen i fi fel rhyw fath o dduw y bore 'ma** – You appeared before me this morning like some kind of god.

162 **To bach** – literally 'little roof', the circumflex accent on certain letters, like ŵ.

165 **Mae hi'n ddiwrnod braf heddiw** – It's a fine day today.

165 **Rhaid i mi ddefnyddio'r tŷ bach** – I need to use the toilet.

166 **Esgusodwch ni, Mr Bull** – Excuse us, Mr Bull.

166 **Mae o isio mynd i'r tŷ bach** – He wants to go to the toilet.

167 **twpsyn** – idiot.

167 **Ydy. Mae o.** – Yes. He is.

168 **Ein ffynnon** – our spring.

170 **Brodyr y Ddraig** – Brothers of the Dragon, a fictional faction of young nationalists.

170 **Cymraeg yn unig** – Welsh (language) only.

172 **Cr'adur bach** – literally, poor creature.

173 **Clecs** – gossip.

173 **Be am be am be am . . . Be am be am be am . . . Be am – ein Cymraeg.** – What about . . . what about . . . what about – our Welsh.

173 **Dw i ddim yn gallu siarad efo ti yn Saesneg** – I can't talk to you in English.

173 **Mae hi'n braf** – It's fine.

179 **Gŵyl** – feast, holiday.

181 **Dan ni angen trydan** – We need electricity.

181 **Dw i yma!** – I'm here!

184 **Cariad** – love.

184 **Gwên fer** – literally, a short smile.

184 **Bore da, ddynion** – Good morning, men.

190 **Drws y Coed** – Door of the wood.

193 **Clychau'r gog** – bluebells, literally: the bells of the cuckoo.

194 **Botwm crys** – Stitchwort, literally: shirt button.

194 **Suran y coed** – wood sorrel.

194 **Ti'n anobeithiol** – You're hopeless.

197 **Ti'n weird** – You're weird.

199 **Da iawn** – Well done.

199 **Diolch yn fawr** – Thank you very much.

199 **Gwylliaid Cochion** – literally: wild red men, a legendary tribe reported to have lived in a remote valley near Dinas Mawddwy, sometimes said to have been survivors of Glyndŵr's army.

204 **Paned** – cuppa.

205 **Aderyn** – bird.

208 **Iechyd da** – 'Good health', the traditional Welsh toast.

208 **Da iawn. Da iawn** – Well done. Well done.

208 **Ewch ymlaen** – Come along.

211 **Fy mam a 'nhad** – my mother and father.

214 **Clwb** – club.

214 **Pori Rotri** – rotational grazing (agricultural term).

215 **Ffedog** – apron.

216 **Nain's** – grandma's.

217 **Nos Fercher** – Wednesday night.

221 **Ynte?** – isn't it?

226 **Ynganu** – pronounce.

230 **Cadwch Gymru yn Gymraeg** – keep Wales Welsh.

230 **DIM SAESNEG** – No English (language).

230 **Ffasgwyr Saesneg Allan** – English Fascists Out.

230 **Dal dy Dir** – Hold your ground.

230 **Cofiwch Lyn Y Gelyn** – Remember Llyn Y Gelyn (literally: lake of the enemy).

234 **Ynte?** – isn't it?

239 **Ga i'ch helpu chi?** – Can I help you?

239 **Ga i goffi please, os gwelwch yn dda?** – Can I have a coffee please, please?

239 **Helpwch eich hun i laeth a siwgr. Pum deg ceiniog, os gwelwch yn dda.** – Help yourself to milk and sugar. Fifty pence, please.

240 **Shw' mae?** – variation of 'How are you?'

240 **Sut dach chi, Marged? Dach chi'n iawn?** – How are you, Marged? Are you well?

241 **Da iawn, diolch, Gwalia. Sut wyt ti, cariad?** – Very well, thank you, Gwalia. How are you, love?

241 **Iawn, diolch** – Well, thank you.

241 **Rhaid iti gadw gafel ar y dyn 'ma, un da ydy o** – You need to look after this man here, he's a good 'un.

241 **Peidwch â phoeni** – Don't worry.

241 **Dw i'n bwriadu gwneud hynny** – I intend to do that.

241 **Fy musnes i ydy hynny** – that's my business.

243 **Wrth gwrs** – of course.

244 **Lesbiaid** – lesbians.

249 **Esgusodwch fi** – excuse me.

249 **Dw i'n dy garu di** – I love you.

252 **Cusan!** – Kiss!

252 **bois y crachach** – upper-class boys.

258 **Mae o'n afiach!** – It's awful!

262 **Sut dach chi?** – How are you?

262 **Iawn, diolch. A chithau?** – Fine, thanks. And you?

264 **Cefn gwlad** – the countryside.

264 **Asgwrn cefn y wlad** – The backbone of our country.

265 **PAID, DEWI. PLIS!** – Don't, Dewi, please!

265 **Cer! Dewi. Cer!** – Go! Dewi. Go!

267 **Noswaith dda, bawb, i chi i gyd. Diolch am ddod heno.** – Good evening, everyone. Thank you for coming tonight.

268 **Gwrandwch!** – listen!

274 **Helo, Gwalia, sut wyt ti?** – Hello, Gwalia, how are you?

274 **Wrth gwrs!** – Of course!

281 **Dyma Mrs Morris gyda'r paneidiau te a'r bisgedi** – Here's Mrs Morris with tea and biscuits.

281 **Amser toriad** – break time.

281 **Mae'n ddrwg gen i** – I'm sorry.

282 **Hiraeth** – homesickness.

283 **Ar lan y môr, mae rhosys cochion** – along the seashore there are the red roses.

291 **Croeso** – You're welcome.

294 **Gwarchod** – look after.

299 **Sgen ti waith cartref?** – Have you any homework?

303 **Ardderchog!** – Excellent!

305 **Yn wir!** – Truly!

307 **Dw i yma . . . i ymarfer fy Cymraeg** – I'm here to practise my Welsh.

307 **Wyt ti wedi bod yn dysgu Cymraeg?** – Have you been learning Welsh?

308 **Ti'n ffantastig!** – You're fantastic!

308 **Mae dy acen di yn fendigedig** – Your accent is excellent.

309 **Mae'r *gath* yn eistedd ar y mat** – The *cat* is sitting on the mat.

309 ***Eistedd* y gath ar y mat** – The cat *sits* on the mat.

314 **Dach chi'n iawn?** – Are you OK?

314 **Dwi 'di clywed ti'n siarad Cymraeg 'wan** – I hear you speak Welsh now.

314 **Ydw** – I do.

314 **Ti'n iawn, cariad?** – Are you OK, love?

314 **Wyt ti'n deall Cymraeg?** – Do you understand Welsh?

314 **Ydw. Dipyn bach.** – Yes, a little bit.

315 **Cofiwch Lyn Y Gelyn** – Remember the lake of the enemy.

316 **Drychwch ar glychau'r gog** – Look at the bluebells.

316 **Drycha!** . . . **Hebog.** – Look! A hawk.

316 **Wyt ti'n chwysu?** – Are you sweating?

318 **Ti'n ôl reit** – You're all right.

318 **Nofiwch cyn rhewi** – Swim before you freeze.

318 **Rasio ti i'r canol** – Race you to the middle.

319 **Rasio ti ar draws!** – Race you across!

319 **Joskin ydy'r ola!** – Last one's a peasant!

321 **Hastwch! Dewch!** Hurry up!

321 **Brys** – Quickly.

321 **Un, dau, tri . . . whî!** – One, two, three . . . wheee!

321 **Eto** – Again.

321 **O, mae'n hyfryd** – Oh, it's fine.

321 **Gŵyl Delyn Y Gelyn** – The Festival of the Enemy's Harp.

321 **Drycha ar y gwenoliaid du** – Look at the swifts.

322 **Paid â dweud** – Don't tell me.

322 **Beth ydy?** – What are?

322 **Wrth gwrs, cariad** – Of course, love.

323 **Ga i hufen iâ?** – Can I have an ice cream?

323 **Mae 'na rai yn deud** – There are some who say.

323 **Wrth gwrs mae o'n gwybod** – Of course he knows.

324 **Perfformiad** – Performance.

324 **Merched y Wawr** – literally, Women of the Dawn, Welsh equivalent of the Women's Institute.

324 **Paid â syllu!** – Don't stare!

324 **Noson Lawen** – traditional evening of variety entertainment.

325 **Eisteddfod(au)** – Welsh cultural festival of competitions, where the supreme prize for poetry is often a chair.

326 **Roedd hwnne'n wych, Mami** – That was excellent, Mummy.

330 **Ffafrio perthnasau** – favouring relatives.

330 **Uwchlaw awdurdod** – without authority.

335 **Mae'n anhygoel. Pentre mawr o gan mil o bobl i gyd yn siarad Cymraeg. Siopau, arddangosfeydd, popeth yn Gymraeg** – It's incredible. A large town of a hundred thousand people all speaking Welsh. Shops, exhibitions, everything in Welsh.

335 **A stiwdio teledu gyda chyflwynwraig bert iawn** – A television studio with a pretty presenter.

337 **Tair miliwn** – three million.

337 **With jwst a chwarter miliwn Cymraeg speakers** – with just a quarter of a million Welsh speakers.

337 **Anhygoel** – incredible.

337 **Bobl** – people.

337 **Dim syniad o gwbl** – No idea at all.

337 **Y Pethe** – The Arts (literally: the things).

338 **Iawn, 'te** – Fine, then.

345 **Diolch yn fawr, Gwalia. Ti'n glên iawn i mi.** – Thank you, Gwalia. You're very kind to me.

349 **Diwygiad** – The 1904-05 Religious Revival.

351 **Dim ond tipyn bach, 'te. Diolch.** – Just a little, please.

351 **Dros ben llestri** – over the top.

366 **Ydy popeth yn iawn?** – Is everything OK?

366 **Dw i'n iawn** – I'm fine.

366 **Mae'r llawdriniaeth drennydd** – The surgery is the day after tomorrow.

366 **Oes** – yes.

366 **Ydw. Dw i yn. Gobeithio, mae gen i . . .** – Yes. I am. I hope I have . . .

368 **Mae hon yn dafarn neis** – This is a nice pub.

368 **Ron i'n siŵr faset ti think that** – I was sure you would think that.

369 **Jon, 'nghariad i, paid** – Jon, my love, don't.

385 **Paid â phoeni** – don't worry.

394 **Peidwch â siarad hefo 'nghariad i fel 'na** – Don't talk to my girl like that.

394 **Cer i grafu, Sais diawl** – Go scratch yourself, English devil.

394 **Profwch y peth, 'te** – prove it, then.

401 **Dwlali** – doolally, mad.

402 **Gee ceffyl bach, yn cario ni'n dau,**
   dros y mynydd i hela cnau;
   dŵr yn yr afon a'r cerrig yn slic,
   cwympo ni'n dau, wel dyna i chi dric. – Traditional Welsh nursery rhyme, sung bouncing a child on the knee, about going on horseback hunting nuts and falling off in a stream.

402 **Hywel Dda** – the reputed codifier of the first Welsh laws *c.* 850-950.

402 **Tamaid** – a little bit.

404 **Wraig ddoeth leol** – the local wise woman.

404 **Cyngor Tref Llanchwaraetegdanygelyn** – Llanchwaraeteg-danygelyn Town Council.

406 **Cynllun** – plan.

406 **Mae gan Penhaearn gynllun** – Penhaearn has a plan.

407 **Maen nhw'n trafod y cynllun** – They're discussing the plan.

407 **Penhaearn's coroni ysbrydol** – Penhaearn's spiritual coronation.

408 **Siarabang** – charabanc (an old-fashioned name for motor coach).

413 **Hen Wlad Fy Nhadau** – Welsh National Anthem.

414 **Wyt ti isio 'mhrodi i?** – Will you marry me?

416 **Gobeithio y gwnewch chi fwynhau eich arhosiad gyda ni** – I hope you will enjoy your stay with us.

417 **Bore da, Mr Jones. Dach chi'n iawn?** – Good morning, Mr Jones. Are you OK?

417 **Dwi wedi clywed eich bod chi'n cael problemau** – I've heard you have problems.

418 **Enaid Cymru** – The Soul of Wales.

419 **'Un gair?' I said. 'Strategaeth.** – 'One word,' I said. 'Strategy.'

421 **Cyfeirio** – refer to.

426 **Dydy o ddim o bwys pwy sydd ar fai!** – It doesn't matter who is to blame!

428 **Sut mae'r prosiect yn mynd?** – How's the project going?

428 **Be fasech chi'n licio?** – What would you like?

428 **Wyau wedi ffrio, a bacwn** – Fried eggs and bacon.

428 **Da iawn. Mae gennoch chi wraig glyfar iawn** – Well done, you have a very clever wife.

429 **Tôst** – toast.

429 **Swyddfa'r Post** – the Post Office.

430 **Mae'n ddrwg gen i, Dewi** – I'm sorry, Dewi.

430 **Dw i'n deall fod gen ti amheuon** – I understand you have your doubts.

438 **Amddiffyn yr iaith** – Defend the language.

444 **Dw'mbo**––I don't know.

444 **Yr Eisteddfod Genedlaethol?** – The National Eisteddfod?

444 **Dwi ddim yn gwybod!** – I don't know!

452 **Mae'n edrych yn ffantastig** – It looks fantastic.

452 **Mae'n hyfryd iawn** – It's very fine.

456 **Steddwch!** – Sit!

464 **Athroniaeth** – philosophy.